PENGUIN BOOKS

The Gulf Between

Geraldine Bedell is an author and journalist. She lives in London with her husband and four children. *The Handmade House* was published by Penguin in 2005.

The Gulf Between Us

GERALDINE BEDELL

PENGUIN BOOKS

PENGUIN BOOKS

Published by the Penguin Group
Penguin Books Ltd, 80 Strand, London WC2R ORL, England
Penguin Group (USA) Inc., 375 Hudson Street, New York, New York 10014, USA
Penguin Group (Canada), 90 Eglinton Avenue East, Suite 700, Toronto,
Ontario, Canada M4P 2Y3 (a division of Pearson Penguin Canada Inc.)
Penguin Ireland, 25 St Stephen's Green, Dublin 2, Ireland (a division of Penguin Books Ltd)
Penguin Group (Australia), 250 Camberwell Road, Camberwell, Victoria 3124, Australia
(a division of Pearson Australia Group Pty Ltd)
Penguin Books India Pvt Ltd, 11 Community Centre,
Panchsheel Park, New Delhi – 110 017, India
Penguin Group (NZ), 67 Apollo Drive, Rosedale, North Shore 0632, New Zealand
(a division of Pearson New Zealand Ltd)
Penguin Books (South Africa) (Pty) Ltd, 24 Sturdee Avenue,
Rosebank, Johannesburg 2196, South Africa

Penguin Books Ltd, Registered Offices: 80 Strand, London WC2R ORL, England

www.penguin.com

First published 2009
1

Set in 11/13 pt Monotype Dante
Typeset by Rowland Phototypesetting Ltd, Bury St Edmunds, Suffolk
Printed in Great Britain by Clays Ltd, St Ives plc

PAPERBACK
ISBN: 978-0-141-03860-5

TRADE PAPERBACK
ISBN: 978-0-141-03861-2

www.greenpenguin.co.uk

Penguin Books is committed to a sustainable future
for our business, our readers and our planet.
The book in your hands is made from paper
certified by the Forest Stewardship Council.

'The Italians call it a *coltello*, the French a *couteau*, the Germans a *Messer*, but the English call it a knife and when all is said and done, that is what it is.'

Englishman on the Grand Tour

Acknowledgements

While I was writing *The Gulf Between Us*, my husband was working on a book arguing that creativity is an essentially collaborative process. A novel might seem to be the exception, but, in this case, that would not be true. In particular, I am extremely grateful to my agent Georgia Garrett and publisher Juliet Annan for their joint and several insights, thoughtfulness and good sense.

Many thanks are also due to the various people who gave me help, literary and other, in the course of writing: Elaine Bedell, Clive Brill, Alex Clark, Jonty Crosse, Henrietta Davies, Naomi Leon, Hen Norton, Freddie Norton, Meg Rosoff, Nader Shaheen and especially J—, for his diligent checking of the Arabic and things Arab. Any remaining mistakes with the number of 'a's in the transliteration are mine.

Without my eldest son, Freddie, this book would never have been written. I am very grateful to him for his inspiration, as well as for being so tactful with his view that the ending was awful when he didn't have the complete manuscript.

Most of all, I want to thank my husband, Charlie Leadbeater, for putting up with my spending so much time in Hawar. Without him, nothing would be possible.

One

I was thinking about happiness. (I was meant to be thinking about menus but my mind had wandered.) Specifically, I was thinking about how no one knows what to believe in any more, let alone where to look for it. How there are so many different routes on offer, especially in a place like this where people come from all over, bringing their contradictory ideas with them. The particular route I had – I won't say chosen; been encouraged to believe in – was that happiness would result from another person's coming along and spotting me, identifying something uniquely perfect, if admittedly not very visible, about me. And that would be that. Sorted. This happens all the time in books, and then they end because there's nothing more to say. There's never any suggestion of having been spotted by the wrong person, or of having accidentally let something else go. Never anything about the person dying and leaving you on your own with three children.

It was staggering that I'd gone along with this as long as I had. At least my children had been exposed to soap operas and reality television and the internet and weren't girls, so they hadn't been encouraged to think that if they sat and waited in a spirit of passive good-naturedness someone would turn up and solve all their problems. Which only made it more mysterious that Will was getting married, now, when he was so young and there seemed to be no pressing reason for it.

I'd just come back to this point about Will and the wedding when Katherine said something that made me stop thinking about happiness, that made me scrape my coffee cup noisily into my saucer.

'I saw Adnan last night,' she began, 'and he said James

Hartley's got the Al A'ali House from the beginning of October.' She looked around complacently over the top of her clipboard.

'But surely he'll stay in one of those suites on the beach they built for the GCC summit?' I replied stupidly, given she'd just said he wouldn't.

'So he'll be there for the reception?' Matt asked, looking up. Until now he'd spent the brunch reading the film listings in the *Hawar Daily News*, even though there are only two cinemas in Hawar.

'I know,' Katherine said, 'but they're being understanding and I think we can too. It's not every day . . .'

'We'll have to invite him to join us,' Matt said, 'at least for a drink. We can't be in his garden and ignore him. It'd be rude. Maybe he'll bring some producers and casting directors and people? Maybe I'll be spotted.'

'You don't need spotting,' I muttered irritably.

'Bloody film!' Peter Franklin probably would have been reading the *Hawar Daily News* himself if he hadn't been the bride's father and required to look interested. 'I'm sick of it already and they're not even here yet. You'd think nothing else had ever happened in Hawar.'

'Well . . .' Matt said.

'I don't know if you've missed it, Matthew, but we're about to have a war.'

'He's been saying we're about to have a war for at least eight months,' Katherine told Matt cheerfully: she was too pleased about James Hartley to be put off by the imminent explosion in the region of chemical and biological agents; 'ever since Bush started going on about his axis of evil. Which if I remember rightly was in January. And here we are in September, and it still hasn't happened!'

Peter raised his eyes to the roof of my veranda, meaning to convey that if his wife thought we'd got away without a war then she was stupid.

Matt shrugged. I don't suppose he really thought there was

any chance of avoiding the war, but he might have believed it wouldn't touch us in our tiny, strategically insignificant emirate. In 1991, he'd been eight: all he could remember about Desert Storm was journalists flying in and hanging around the hotels, making their way into the bars, lounging by the pools, doing pieces to camera against the sunset. It had all seemed rather glamorous, as if for a moment we were at the centre of a world that usually ignored us. And it is true that the epicentre, if that's the right word, of the American invasion of Iraq was going to be about 400 miles away, assuming things went to plan, which with wars is always a bit of an open question.

I considered backing Peter up – pointing out that we didn't know how many weapons of mass destruction Saddam Hussein had or how far they could travel or what mass exactly they could be expected to destroy. But we were organizing a wedding and it hardly seemed the moment. Besides, I was still thinking about James Hartley.

'Anyway, he won't be remotely like whatsisname, you know,' Peter warned his wife.

'Don't pretend you don't know! Porchester.'

'Why I'd be familiar with the name of a time-travelling professor of genetics who doesn't actually exist . . .'

Katherine ignored him. 'Anyway, he might be. Like Porchester. We haven't met him yet.'

'Er . . . Mum has,' Matt said.

'Annie? *You've* met James Hartley?' Katherine stared at me in a way that was, under the circumstances, bordering on rude.

'It was a long time ago.'

'When? How?'

'We lived in the same street.'

'They went out,' Matt said, without looking up from his paper.

'No!'

It is true that James Hartley is a film star whose name is known to remote tribes without telephones and I'm a mother of

3

three who's quite good at making lists, but why the incredulity? He had to come from somewhere. And I'm not *so* hideous.

'Well, you kept *that* very quiet!' Katherine said offishly, as if I'd lied to everyone, which I hadn't – although I hadn't made a big thing about it either. I knew that once the word got out I wouldn't be able to go into Al Jazira to buy a lemon without people asking me about it and whether I'd be seeing him when he was here and why didn't I throw a party for him?

'We'll definitely have to invite him, if you know him,' Katherine said.

'Knew him … It was a long time ago. And perhaps Maddi and Will won't want a stranger at their wedding?' I looked at them sitting side by side on the sunlounger in khaki shorts and white T-shirts, like twins dressed by their mother. Their knees were thrust up in an awkward posture that made them seem eager, as if they were somehow on call for the future, his dark head and her blonde one glossier than everyone else's.

Sam chose this moment to push open the sliding glass door, still in his pyjama bottoms, but no top, so you could see every nubbly ridge of his skinny, sixteen-year-old ribs.

'Morning, Sam!' Katherine said brightly. Perhaps breeziness first thing in the morning is allowed if you have daughters. Not that it was first thing in the morning for anyone except Sam.

Sam muttered something, which might have been 'Yo, coz,' took a croissant from the table and slid to the floor with his back against the door. I silently handed him a plate.

'James Hartley's staying at the Al A'ali house, and he's arriving in time for the reception!' Matt said loudly, as if addressing a person of limited faculties.

His younger brother blinked, which was quite a lot of response from him.

'I still don't really understand how the Sheraton could have done this,' I said. 'It's not as if it hasn't been booked for months.'

'Well, Adnan did sort of mention it a while back,' Katherine admitted, 'but I didn't think anything would come of it.'

So she'd known. She hadn't bothered to alert me. Presumably, though, Maddi and Will wouldn't want to be upstaged by a film star at their own wedding? . . . That was what I was hoping, anyway, until Maddi said how exciting she thought it would be to have James Hartley at the reception. Evidently, Katherine's news hadn't come as much of a surprise to her – which must have meant that Will had also known. I should have been better prepared for his keeping things from me: he may have been my child, my first-born, but he often seemed alarmingly alien – a large-limbed, stubble-faced, rangy creature powered by purposes of his own. What was he doing, with his top grades, his three musical instruments and cricket blue, his Oxford degree and job offer from an investment bank, at the age of twenty-three, before he'd even started work, before – surely – he had any idea who he really was – getting married? Why the rush? And why – although this may of course have been related – had he started going to church on Sundays, despite no previous record of spiritual questing or interest in the numinous?

I certainly wouldn't have predicted a couple of years ago that he and Maddi would have wanted all this – the Friday brunch with the parents, the succession of menus and lists, the hassle about where to sit my brother. And if I couldn't have anticipated something as fundamental as their wanting to get married and in the most traditional way possible, how could I predict what feelings they'd have about inviting James Hartley? Perhaps, like Maddi's mother, they imagined he'd be like his most famous role, and that Hawar was about to entertain a laconic, sexy genetics professor with his own quantum teleporter.

'I expect if he's taken the house knowing there's a wedding reception he'll have made plans to be filming, or something,' I said vaguely, writing 'tabbouleh' next to the word tabbouleh on the menu provided by the Sheraton.

'You must be curious to see him, after all this time?' Katherine said.

Obviously, I was curious to see him. *Obviously* I'd thought about whether we'd meet and when and how that would be and if he'd be as interested to see me as I was to see him. I was intrigued to know how much of the person I used to like and still thought of fondly would have been dermabraded and perma-tanned off, turned into an artificial construct, a high-grossing film star. I was fascinated to see whether with all that teleporting he'd managed to keep his personality intact, so that I could still recognize him. Obviously I don't mean physically. Everyone would recognize him physically.

But I also thought that if we invited him and he didn't come – and really, why would you bother with an expat wedding in a small Gulf state if you were him? – then people would be disappointed and think the event had been a failure. And if he did come, it would be almost worse: breezing in with his aura of celebrity, of being cleaner, shinier than everyone else, upstaging everything because that was what he did, that was his job, and no one being able to concentrate on what really mattered, which was Will and Maddi.

'We can't have a wedding in his garden and not invite him down for a drink,' Matt said again.

Why couldn't we? It wasn't his garden; it belonged to a hotel. And we'd booked it first. Just because Adnan had made a mistake with his system, I didn't see why we had to start inviting random hotel guests to our party.

I didn't say so, because it would have revealed how nervous I was about meeting him. The fact was that when it happened I wanted to be able to concentrate, to make sure he didn't get the wrong impression, didn't imagine that I'd made mistakes, married for the wrong reasons (like, say, to get away from home, or out of insecurity, or thinking I was getting something I wasn't). I didn't want him to think I'd come to Hawar with-out properly thinking about it, or that I'd got stuck, staying on basically for my children who now didn't really need me any more or that it had taken the death of my husband in a car crash for me to stop feeling disappointed, to get a sense of what I wanted from life, or that, by the time I had, it was too late, so that I was now marooned in a backwater, without either a career or a man.

While this was one possible interpretation of what had happened to me, there was another one, which was equally plausible: that Hawar was no more of a backwater than anywhere else, was in fact full of people of different nationalities and views (about happiness for a start, as I had been thinking only recently) and was consequently as fascinating and demanding as anywhere else.

I looked around at my children – Will handsome beside Maddi, Matt carelessly sprawled, Sam gnawing his third croissant in an endearingly feral way, hair flopped over his face – and I thought that even though I might not have had the first idea what I was trying to achieve most of the time – somehow, I had done *this*. Helped to, anyway. It wasn't failure, nothing like it. They were nearly men, and they had the ability to feel adult emotions, love and all it led to. They had their own points of view. It didn't matter that this was a very ordinary thing to have done, that people had been having children and bringing them up for ever. It was still incredible, and while James Hartley might have had a private jet, he hadn't done it.

That was the side of me I'd have preferred him to see, but I could appreciate that it could take some setting up.

I kept on telling the boys that Adnan's alleged mix-up did not oblige us to invite James Hartley to the wedding reception, and, at times, I almost persuaded myself it was true. But not quite, so after a couple of days I delivered a note addressed to James to the offices Gulf Films had set up in the Diplomatic Area. A glamorous young Hawari woman took it from me and I imagined her passing it on to a phalanx of fierce assistants employed solely to guard James Hartley's privacy.

The last time James and I had communicated, he'd said he never wanted to speak to me again. You had to assume he'd probably got over that now, but it was still difficult to get the tone right. I explained about the double booking and hoped that he'd join us for a drink, along with any of his colleagues and friends who were with him. (For all I knew, there could be a girlfriend, even a small harem. He'd been photographed with enough women over the years; it was hard to imagine he'd managed to fit them in serially.) I wondered whether he'd actually see this careful composition. He was dyslexic and probably paid for people to read things to him now.

I drove home afterwards along the Corniche, peeling along the edge of the emirate, the sea to my right heavy with the weight of salt, gleaming dully through the thick air like an opaque mirror; then on up the Jidda Road, through palm groves and smallholdings to Al Janabiyya compound. I was thinking as I drove how odd it was that James Hartley had never married any of those beautiful women. Presumably he hadn't needed the security, once he got successful. The plethora of people available to sleep with him must have been enough.

As I turned into the compound, I saw Andrew's Jeep parked by our wicket fence. He lived in central Qalhat, along with most of the posh expats in Hawar – people like Peter and Katherine Franklin, who regarded compound living as a bit suburban and preferred more authentic and often inconvenient older houses in proper streets in town, as long as they were equipped with new air conditioning and perhaps also had a pool in the back garden. The chaplaincy did not have a pool and Andrew couldn't afford to join any of the sports clubs or hotels so he liked to come out to us and play on the tennis court and swim in the decent-sized and prettily landscaped pool we shared with the nineteen other households on Al Janabiyya compound.

The pair of them were sitting on our veranda, dressed in shorts and tennis shirts, rackets propped up against their chairs – Andrew, as usual, looking too big for the space around him, even if that was outdoors. The way his leg was draped over the arm of the garden chair reminded me of those slinky toys the boys used to have when they were little: if he tipped slightly to one side, his whole body might come behind, rolling over on itself.

They got up and ambled over to the carport to help me unload the shopping.

'OK if Andrew stays for supper?' Will asked.

Andrew's hands, as he picked up several bags, seemed oddly outsized, for a vicar: more suited to scaffolding, or rugby, or piano.

'Sure.' I was pleased by Will's friendship with Andrew, if perplexed by the amount of churchgoing that went with it. Until now, my eldest son hadn't been a great one for hanging out. It wasn't that he hadn't *had* friends, exactly, more that they seemed to be a by-product of more purposeful activities: the cricket team, the school string quartet, further maths groups. His relationships usually seemed to involve an awful lot of work, usually practising something or other – bowling, or the works of Haydn – but with Andrew he seemed happy merely to sit and talk, or even stare into space. They seemed to be at ease with each other, although I found Andrew rather formal and proper. Will (who could probably come across as a bit formal and proper himself) told me this was all wrong and I hadn't understood him at all.

Even Will's relationship with Maddi seemed to be rather hard work these days. As we went indoors, he told me the pair of them had spent the day trying to sort out flights for her South African cousins, who'd originally said they weren't coming to the wedding but then decided they were, although only if they could get aisle seats on a particular flight out of Cape Town.

'Don't they have travel agents in South Africa?' Matt asked, from the sofa, where he was curled up with his best friend Jodie and a girl from the year below at school called Maya, watching a re-run of *Sex and the City*. 'Thank God you're home,' he added to me, making a point of taking the Lord's name in vain since Andrew was around. 'I'm starving.'

'When you talked about your gap year, there was a lot of stuff about earning money and challenging experiences. I don't remember the part about watching fictional women in Manolo Blahniks discuss their orgasms,' Will said. He hadn't had a gap year. He can also be a bit of a pain.

'I didn't want to overwhelm you with the possibilities,' Matt said, yawning. 'And I *have* been earning money. I've had a hard day at the office.' He had a job with a local publishing house, working on a publication he said you had to describe as a high-net-worth-lifestyle title. 'I'm only in Hawar because of you and your wedding. Otherwise I'd be trekking through Borneo or somewhere by now, insh'allah.'

Jodie raised her head from his shoulder and looked at him sceptically. She was working at the Presbyterian Mission Hospital before going off to Columbia University to study to be a doctor and she thought Matt's days writing captions about unaffordable consumer items were a risible way for him to be spending his time. Generally speaking, she treated him as if he were her slightly hapless younger brother. Matt seemed to like this.

'How's your dad?' I asked her, meaning 'Does he know when the war's going to start?' Jodie's father was a senior officer at the American military base.

'It's no good, mum,' Matt disentangled himself from the girls and cushions and got to his feet, 'he's not going to let Jodie know when he's invading because she'll only tell.'

'He's fine, thank you,' Jodie answered. 'Busy. And no, he hasn't given me a date for the invasion, mainly because he doesn't have one, but I think you'll be able to get Will and Maddi's wedding over and done with.'

'And the film made, I guess?' Maya said. 'I mean, someone must have said it's safe to bring James Hartley here?'

'I have to make my mother a cup of tea,' Matt informed the girls, 'before she starts going on about how at our age she'd been working for three years.'

'And in a proper job,' I pointed out, 'not just to earn money to go to Costa Rica. But it's fine. You carry on with what you're doing.'

He followed me into the kitchen anyway. 'Actually, I had a very draining day,' he said as he put on the kettle. 'How many interesting things are there, frankly, to say about boats?' He held out a mug inquiringly to Andrew, who was unloading the shopping on to the counter, then leant back and looked at him as if he found him very puzzling. 'Are you, like, you know, meant to convert people?'

'If you want to be converted, I can give it a try,' Andrew said good-naturedly.

'You've done him, haven't you?' Matt nodded at Will. 'How did you manage that, then?'

'Trade secret.'

'Well, don't come near me.'

'Oh, I can do it from a distance.'

'Probably only when people are weird in the first place.' He ducked to avoid the orange Will threw at him.

'Boys . . .' I said warningly. 'And Matt, you're not being help-ful. If you can't make me a cup of tea without provoking food throwing, you'd be better off watching television.'

Matt changed the subject. 'Granddad rang again just before you got home.'

'Oh, no, what is it this time?' My father, who lives in south London, thinks it's extravagant to phone the north of England, but this was the third time he'd called Hawar in a week.

'Just the usual – when are the Americans going to invade Iraq, and is it likely to be before the wedding?'

'I hope you told him no?'

'Plus, he can't quite bring himself to say so, because he knows it's wrong, but I think he's also wondering how he's going to avoid people who look Muslim.'

'Yes, well.' I stuck the labneh, milk and butter in the fridge. 'Is Sam around?'

'No, he's out with Faisal.'

Sam was always out with Faisal these days, although there isn't really anywhere to go in Hawar, at least at six o'clock on a Wednesday evening. The Pearl Mall? The Corniche? Everywhere you might have thought of loitering around in a moody adolescent way was full of Hawari families. Sam was reticent about what they got up to, but he was reticent about everything.

Their main interest, as far as I could work out, was setting up web fanzines for indie bands that had no fans. Sam and Faisal communicated with people like themselves in Stockholm or Munich or Carlisle, but only as long as the numbers involved remained tiny: as soon as any band they'd adopted started to acquire a serious following, they had to drop them. While it seemed rather pointless trying to publicize groups you didn't want anyone else to know about, it also appeared unlikely to lead them into any serious trouble.

Will and Andrew had booked the compound tennis court for six o'clock; Matt went back to the girls and the orgasms. I took a glass of water out on to the back porch and sat down as the muezzin started calling in Ghafir, the nearest village: the dusk call that begins in the violet light and ends in darkness and seems to be full of longing. I leant my head back on the wall and felt the night collect around me. All the plants in the garden that looked tired during the day, the life leached out of them by the heat, seemed to start breathing again in the dusk, to acquire solidity, density, weight: the oleanders, the palms that looked like banana trees but that were actually palms, the fluttery bougainvillea. It's the best time of day: the yearning call from the mosque, the dusk that comes as a relief, enveloping the garden, making it suddenly substantial, lush.

Then Cheryl pushed through from next door.

'Ohmigod, Annie, is it true?' She stood with her hands on her hips, her legs slightly apart as if tensed for activity, wearing a pink check Lycra vest and matching three-quarter exercise pants. I blinked at her silhouette, a vision against the vegetation; 'about you and James Hartley? – I mean, I know you look great and I've told you before, all the men I know say you're sexy, but . . .'

'It was a long time ago.'

One of the boys once told me that all the cells in the human body die off every seven years, which meant that James Hartley had been, roughly speaking, three different people since I'd known him. (Annoyingly, they seemed to have been getting better-looking, which is not what usually happens.)

'Are you going to get him out here to Al Janabiyya? You should have a party.'

'I imagine they'll be very busy.'

Cheryl came up the porch and sat down. 'What's he like, anyway?'

I hadn't seen him since he was nineteen. Everyone kept asking me what he was like, but I'd known him for three years when he was an apprentice plumber in Thornton Heath, which is a very different thing from being a film star in Hollywood . . . I didn't see how I could possibly have anything useful to say. He'd always wanted to be an actor. And I hadn't taken it seriously, because I hadn't thought it was a thing plumbers from Thornton Heath did. This wouldn't have been interesting to Cheryl, but it was what I thought when I remembered James Hartley – that I'd been stupid back then: half-formed, clueless about most things. I hadn't allowed myself to think big. I'd believed there were certain things to which I shouldn't presume. Most things, in fact. This wasn't a particular failing of mine: most people I knew were the same. It wasn't even conscious. We had imbibed it, swallowing it as naturally as if it had been part of the fish-fingers or baked beans or salad cream we had for tea. It had turned out that James had been much more exceptional than any of us realized, not so much for having deep blue eyes and an impressive bone structure as for, somehow, from somewhere, having managed to pick up a sense of entitlement. And that did make him different.

*

Over dinner, Andrew told us about a visit he'd made to the Dariz Palace earlier in the day. It seemed that even the emir was excited about James Hartley's arrival, despite the fact he should really have had other things on his mind, such as running the country and persuading the Americans not to invade Iraq. While Andrew was describing the various parties Shaikh Hassan was intending to throw in James's honour, I found myself wondering if he (Andrew, not the emir) had found whatever he'd been looking for when he came to Hawar. It seemed an odd place for the Church to have sent him, when the Anglican needs of the emirate would so obviously have been better served by someone older and less ambitious, with a wife who was prepared to join the gardening club and organize cake sales. Andrew's parishioners wanted the Church to carry them back spiritually and emotionally to Bournemouth or Bridlington or wherever they'd grown up – places where there was obviously a God, and he was fairly British.

It may be that the Church was like the Foreign Office, which tended to send us either dynamic youthful ambassadors, or older, tired Arabists getting their one head of mission before retirement. Andrew reminded me of the younger diplomats: he had the same kind of restlessness. He'd tried to bridge religious divides by forming alliances with various mosques, as well as with Father Joseph at the Sacred Heart. Unfortunately, this wasn't what his parishioners mainly wanted from religion. People in Hawar pushed past one another in the souk, worked together, even lived together, if you overlooked the fact that the white expats who dominated Andrew's congregation tended to have spacious villas on compounds, while their Filipina or Sri Lankan house maids, who mainly worshipped at the Sacred Heart, occupied breeze-block servants' quarters in their back gardens. But this was generally felt to be enough proximity. Religion was one of the many ways of honeycombing Hawari society, of making coexistence possible. It was like compounds for expatriates, or the women's quarters in Arab households: a way of dividing people, allowing them to get away from one another, remember who they were. In the confusion of people, in the babble of Arabic and Malayalam, Sinhalese and Filipino, Urdu and dozens of other languages, religion was a way of asserting a separate, more secure identity.

After dinner, when Will was driving Andrew back to the chaplaincy, Matt said, 'Have you noticed how Andrew always acts like someone's trying to catch him out?'

'That'll be you, then.'

'Me?' He pretended to be shocked. 'Really, though, what d'you think they talk about? I mean, tennis may be fascinating' – Matt loathed tennis: he said it was too hot and he couldn't bear the responsibility – 'but it can't keep them going all the time.'

'I don't know. They're clever. Maybe their minds run on a different track. Sort of more elevated.'

'What, like a monorail at a theme park?'

'I don't know. Maybe. Anyway, he's good for Will and you shouldn't be hostile.' Matt, who'd only left the International School in the summer, still had friends living in Hawar – Jodie, for example, to whom he was very close, and Maya, who might, I thought, be his girlfriend, or at least be heading in that direction. Will had left the International School more than three years earlier and his friends were scattered across the world, studying or working. The only young men here of his age were the equity dealers and commodity brokers whose idea of a good time was to get smashed in Trader Vic's on Thursday nights and shag the HawarAir crew. And that wasn't his thing.

Will had been ten when his dad died, and I'd worried ever since that the loss had ruptured his confidence. He had, I suspected, too little of that blithe sense you should have in your childhood, your teens and early twenties – a belief that life basically works out OK. Obviously, it doesn't, always, but that seemed a hard lesson to have had to learn at ten. I worried that his life had been shadowed, making him different from other boys. In which case, it had probably been a mistake to keep him here in the Gulf, which was so unreal, an affluent bubble in a cloudless sky, confected in a few decades from desert subsistence into cities, hotels and high rises. Hawar could hardly have been more insecure. Apart from its painful environmental fragility (built on petroleum revenues, dependent on air conditioning) it was also politically precarious. Nothing about it made any real sense – its modern cities rearing up out of pitiless desert, its archaic hereditary dictatorships – so how could you expect it to give you a secure sense of identity? How could you base your sense of yourself on somewhere so shiny and unresolved, built on a kind of lottery win and so much at odds with its surroundings? Will was an Englishman in the desert and a stranger in England. He might be getting married to get something clear about himself.

Two

'There were a lot of Arabs on that flight,' my father said, pushing his trolley into arrivals at Hawar International Airport. He blinked and looked around the hall, absorbing the fact that there were even more of them here – all over the place, adjusting white or red-checked ghutras, folding back one side with an air of judicious activity or fiddling absently with worry beads. 'I mean, I don't know why they checked *my* shoes.'

'The shoe bomber was white,' Matt pointed out. 'He had a British passport. Anyway, they're not supposed to discriminate.'

'I hardly look like a terrorist, though,' dad said plaintively.

I thought it was typical of my brother and his wife to have let him come through immigration and customs into this packed arrivals hall on his own, to be buffeted by the press of unfamiliar people – Arabs, Keralites waiting for the Cochin flight, proudly self-contained men in spotless white thobes and Armani sandals, hungry-looking labourers in dusty brown shifts watching anxiously for cousins, brothers, kin. My father's knuckles were closed tightly over the handles of his trolley, as if he thought someone might try to take it. He had the pale, hollowed-out, lost look of someone just tipped off a long flight.

'This has changed,' he said, making conversation, not wanting me to see how rattled he was. 'It used to be brown.'

It was the old 1960s building he remembered, its walls swathed in brown formica. He hadn't been back for twelve years: it was too hot, he'd protested, whenever I'd suggested it, and the humidity was exhausting for someone his age. He hadn't been sure either about the way you were thrown together with people you wouldn't necessarily spend time with at home.

That one time he had come, he'd been to dinner with some

posh people who kept on referring to the locals as towelheads, which even he knew wasn't right – he knew you couldn't do that these days – and he thought they might have been joking but he couldn't tell. Matt had said afterwards they were being ironic, 'or at least semi-ironic', but what did that mean? That they knew you weren't supposed to say 'towelheads' but they were going to anyway? Because they could? Because the rules somehow didn't apply to them? Because he was there and he might be shocked? Or because they thought he might secretly sympathize? It was all too much of a minefield and he couldn't overcome the sense that they were poking fun at him. He was blowed if he wanted to get into it.

I took his arm and steered him gently through the mêlée of men with foreign purposes and women in abayas, the shiny black cloth over their heads and clothes drawing attention to the flash of eyes, softness of skin, the shape of lips as they drifted past, wrapped up in mysterious lives. Matt stayed by the barrier, waiting for Chris, Karen and Andrea.

We had a statement airport now, with glass-walled walkways and moving ramps and waiting areas upholstered in blue and gold, the colours of the national flag. In place of the old rattling boxes wheezing out of the walls, there was silent air condition-ing, purring softly, barely there. A steel superstructure flung gleaming arms above, arcing across the hot sky; below, the shops glittered with borderless merchandise, repulsively enticing: designer bags, scotch whisky, flash watches, globally marketed perfumes.

Karen was through customs now and beside me, complaining: 'I told her not to wear that skirt. I *told* her people would stare.'

Her fifteen-year-old daughter Andrea was wearing a denim mini skirt that exposed most of her thighs, which were not in any case unobtrusive. My dad was always saying worriedly, 'She's a very well-developed young lady, Andrea.' She kissed me and Matt, then stared at him, chewing gum speculatively and sexily.

'Don't do that, Andrea!' Karen said sharply. 'It looks horrible.'

'Other boys not here?' Chris asked, managing to imply that we hadn't made enough effort.

'Will had to be at Maddi's, and Sam's legs are so long now he takes up most of the car.'

Actually, Sam hadn't got back in time.

'It's *not* suitable, though, is it, this skirt?' Karen persisted, pulling at her daughter's clothing. 'For Arabia?'

'It's OK. We're going straight to the hotel. It's only in the souk that you have to be really sensitive. And during Ramadan, but that's not till next month.'

'I don't think she's *got* any sensitive clothes. Christ, it's hot!'

We crossed the car park. The temperature had dropped in the last couple of weeks – the breeze no longer hit you like spurts of steam – but it had been a long, insufferable summer and the air was thick with humidity. If you weren't used to it, it was like walking into a sponge. There was always a moment when you thought you might not be able to breathe.

'Sensitive?' Chris repeated, 'is that what you call it? So, what, you just adopt their point of view, no questions asked? . . . I'd've thought you'd be all against it, making women cover up. If they want to cut off your hand for stealing, is that OK too? Do we have to be sensitive about that?'

'They don't cut off anyone's hands,' I said irritably. Why didn't I have a normal brother, who'd be nice? Why did I get one who was so boringly obnoxious? 'Shorts are fine on the compound,' I explained to Karen, 'and round the hotel pool, but probably not to the supermarket, at least not Al Jazira, the one in town – out where we live it's mainly expats who use the supermarket, so it doesn't matter so much . . .' The rules, I realized, although never codified, were actually quite complicated. Andrea's skirt wasn't really suitable – it was making an issue of her sexuality in a place where everyone would already be tiresomely aware of it – but I didn't want to be the one to point it out. Not right now, anyway, when she'd only just arrived.

I put my arm around her, wondering what it would have been like to have a girl, to have to negotiate all those worries about where to put herself, and the morally compromising subtext of skirts.

Matt and Chris loaded the bags into the Jeep and I took the family in the Toyota. We drove out of the airport, across the causeway over the shallows and on to the Corniche, the red tail lights of four lanes of traffic fizzing in the damp heat.

'I don't remember any of this,' dad said worriedly.

'The whole area would have been under water last time you came,' Matt said; 'right up to that shopping mall over there.'

The city of Qalhat was the opposite of the lost city of Atlantis: it had been pulled out of the sea – the land reclaimed, the buildings thrown up – with an insistence on the power of people over nature.

We drew up behind Matt in the Jeep at the bottom of the hotel drive, where a couple of Hawari Defence Force soldiers had sauntered out from their post and were looking in a cursory way at the luggage. They wore guns slung over their shoulders like style accessories. They asked me to open the boot, then waved us on.

'Is that because of the terrorists?' Karen asked.

'Not really. Not Al Qaeda, anyway. The prime minister owns this hotel and there are quite a few people who'd happily blow it up.'

'And you've put us here?' Chris said.

'There haven't ever actually been any bombs. There was one small uprising in the village of Umm Wafra in – I think – 1987. But that only involved sticks and stones.'

'What are they worried about, then?'

'The Al Majid, the ruling family, are sunni, and so are most rich Hawaris. The shi'ite population isn't that big, but the shi'a feel they haven't done as well out of the last few decades ...' But I'd pulled up in front of the hotel now, and Chris had already climbed out of the car. He didn't want to know about the high

20

birth rate, the youth unemployment, the unrealistic expectations of young people, the disappointment that could turn to disaffection.

By the time I'd parked and joined them in the lobby, they were already checked in.

'You shouldn't have,' dad muttered: 'it's so luxurious . . .' He looked around the atrium, taking in the lavishly upholstered sunken lounge, the rotating gold statue in the fountain, the stained-glass windows, the indoor foliage, the glass lifts sliding up and down marble walls.

'You've got to do your best to enjoy it,' I told him. I knew what he was like: he'd spend the whole time worrying that he didn't deserve it.

'What're you doing tonight, then?' Chris asked Matthew as we glided up in one of the glass lifts.

'Nothing,' Matt admitted.

'In London you said there was always stuff going on. You should show Andrea what life's like for young people in Hawar.'

'There's a barbecue at the Franklins' tomorrow,' I said, 'there'll be loads of young people there.'

I noticed that my father had been led down the corridor by the bellboy and went to find him. He was a few doors down, being shown how to operate the multimedia system from the bath. He wasn't actually taking in any of the instructions; he was fumbling in his pockets for a tip. All his effort was concentrated on trying to get the money out discreetly, on working out the dirham exchange rate and how he was going to hand over the notes in a natural way, as if he did this all the time.

Perhaps it was only the effect of the flight, but he seemed to have shrunk. He'd only ever been averagely tall – the boys had got their height from Dave – but now his skeleton seemed to have retreated, shifted inwards, leaving his flesh at a loss.

I knew I hadn't been able to rely on him for years – probably since my mum died, certainly since Dave had been killed. He couldn't bear the thought of his daughter being on her own with three children, and it had left him helpless. But I'd assumed up till now that he could more or less look after himself.

Matt came in from the other room, shaking his head. 'What is it with Uncle Chris?'

I smiled broadly at dad, who was following the bellboy out of the bathroom, being shown how to operate the curtains from the bed. 'You know what he's like,' I whispered back.

'No . . .'

'I expect he finds the Arab world a bit intimidating.'

'Why? He's only got to sit on a beach and go to a wedding. Are you saying he's racist, so we've got to make allowances . . .?'

'Of course not. Only that we should try to be hospitable. They're family and they've never been here before.'

'Exactly. They never bothered to come. Even when dad died.'

Karen put her head round the door. 'Annie looking after you, Ted? When you're ready, we thought we might go down and try this international buffet thing in the coffee shop. Andrea's just doing her make-up.'

'I hope she means taking it off,' Matt whispered, 'because if she put on any more, she'd fall over.'

'Matt!'

'Well, she's got huge. Don't look at me like that – actually, she's not unattractive – but you can't deny she's put on a few kilos. And it's not sexist or sizeist or whatever you're going to say. It's true.'

I started to protest, but Karen put her head back round the door. 'Oh, by the way, Annie, I found a website, and it's not true that you don't need to take malaria tablets.'

The following morning, a reply arrived from James Hartley, or rather, from someone who signed herself 'Fiona Eckhart, assistant to Mr Hartley' – thanking me for the invitation, passing on James's best wishes, and saying he very much hoped to join us at the wedding but wasn't sure about his arrival time in Hawar. Fiona Eckhart, assistant to Mr Hartley, asked me to forward my phone number in case he needed to contact me.

He appeared to be keeping his options open. I thought it was a very irritating kind of RSVP, but Katherine and Maddi were thrilled.

'It sounds like he really wants to come!' Maddi said.

'He must want to see you again!' Katherine added.

'He asked for your phone number!'

'It would have been more polite to give an answer one way or the other,' I pointed out. But they were convinced that James Hartley's non-committal response meant he was desperate to rekindle his friendship with me. I hadn't got time to argue, because I had to go to the Sheraton to collect the family for a tour of what would have been Hawar's tourist attractions, if we'd had any tourists.

'Such a shame Matt couldn't come,' Karen noted when I met them in the hotel lobby. 'It's lovely how he chats away. Unlike *some* teenagers I could mention.' She looked over to where Andrea was sitting moodily beside the fountain with the giant rotating gold-plated falcon.

'Sam, for instance,' I said, not wanting to join her in criticizing Andrea, whose slight air of awkwardness, of not knowing how to be herself, reminded me uncomfortably of myself at her age, and presumably wasn't helped by the constant carping from her parents. 'He doesn't even do whole words.'

Matt had always appealed to adults. Other parents at school had compared him favourably to their own children, remarking on how easy he was, how refreshingly prepared to speak to people over the age of twenty. Although I would have liked to believe this was the result of my exemplary parenting, it hadn't worked with Sam so I had to accept that it was due to Matt's essentially sweet nature. He pretended to be cynical and sarcastic, but everyone could see through that – his smile was always vulnerably threatening to erupt, his eyes were a blink away from laughter – and he was always gratifyingly happy to wander round the supermarket gossiping with me, or to sit on the veranda in the evening discussing some films he'd seen or lesson he'd had. He didn't seem to mind me finding out about his life.

I herded the family into the car and drove up the Jidda Road, through date groves thick with honeyed fruit. Herbs and vegetables grew in beds beside the road, in green beds hatched with irrigation canals that flung back the bright blue of the sky. We stopped at Bani Jamra, the weavers' village, and bought bread from a conical outdoor oven.

'Nice,' Karen commented, 'though I expect it goes a bit rubbery when it gets cold.'

From there we went on to Beit Mukhanis, the potters' village, where we drank little glasses of sweetened tea in a potter's breeze-block workshop as sand sifted over the road. Everyone agreed the tea was delicious, although Karen wondered aloud to dad where they did their washing up. Perhaps she thought because they looked foreign and did pottery, they had no education and didn't speak English.

As we headed back to the city, I talked to them about Qalhat's rapid growth – from a sleepy fishing port ruled over by tribal sheikhs only around seventy years ago to the shiny capital of today – and tried to give them a sense of what life would have been like in earlier times.

'The pearl divers were mostly slaves,' I explained, 'and they had to go down ten times a shift, four shifts a day, for four months – so by the end of a season, they'd have done a forty-hour week without air.' I knew I was lecturing them, but I wanted them to understand. 'Even then, the entire region only picked up enough pearls in any season for two first-class necklaces.'

We passed roundabouts garish with petunias, oleanders and statues of coffee pots, and drove towards the souk, where I parked the car and the family picked their way along the dusty streets. Karen said what a good thing it was that the old houses and windtowers were being turned into restaurants and day spas. Andrea trailed along at the back, disconsolate and bored, and I wished then that Matt *had* come, because he loved the carved wooden doors and dilapidated overhanging balconies, and his enthusiasm might have been infectious.

I tried to be infectious myself, but I could sense that my animated tourist guide spiel wasn't really impressing them. They had their own ideas about my life here, rooted in a substrate of prejudices – about Arabs, the Middle East, people who flightily moved abroad, a long way from their families and then it served them right if their husbands were killed in car accidents, because everyone knew Arabs were terrible drivers. By the time I'd finished the tour, I was convinced that they'd never understand what it was that I loved about these last, fragile fragments of Hawari life, before the steel and glass and concrete. Not only would they have failed to appreciate the warmth of Hawari hospitality or grasped that it owed everything to the memory of having nothing, but they wouldn't care.

'So this is the compound,' I said brightly, as we turned in through the gate.

'There's a guard,' Chris observed, 'is that to keep you in, or other people out?'

'I'm not sure how good he'd be at either.'

All the compounds had guards. Ours were often asleep. Not that there was any noticeable threat. For most of the time I'd lived in Hawar, the emirate had been a police state. There were no burglaries, because there were informers in all the villages and the penalties for petty crime were severe. Not as severe as the penalties for the crimes that really worried the authorities and required the presence of informers in the first place, but enough to make petty crime a terrible career choice.

Three years ago, though, the emir had sacked his hated head of security, a red-faced Englishman with acne scars, who'd started his career bloodily suppressing the Mau Mau rebellion in Kenya. A year later, we got (or rather they got; expats couldn't vote) a parliament. The elected members, who had to organize through mosques, since they weren't allowed to form political parties – which was a bit of an own-goal in these Islamist times – were also forbidden to question the prime minister, Shaikh Jasim bin Talal Al Majid, who was appointed by the emir, Shaikh Hassan bin Talal Al Majid, who happened to be his brother.

Modest as they were, these changes did mean that the atmosphere was now much less repressive. A degree of political dissent was tolerated and there was some room for the modern form of self-expression that comes through theft, although property was still more respected than in most places in the world. As I pointed out to the family, I left the front door open and the car unlocked. All the same, the history of discrimination against the shi'ite population had left a resentment that could easily erupt at some point, should something happen to trigger it – and if so, it would probably be in a place like Ghafir, the village half a kilometre up the unmade road past our compound, where scruffy goats picked in the rubble, children played in the dust, and bits of tattered green material, rather than the blue and gold Hawari flag, stirred in the hot wind from the empty quarter.

I pointed out the swimming pool, which Chris said was 'a bit small' (though this has never seemed the case to us) and the tennis court, to which they could find nothing to say because the compound is old, the gardens are mature, and though the houses are a bit tatty, it does mean the tennis court is one of the loveliest in the emirate, surrounded by oleander and tangelo trees, palms and hibiscus.

'I suppose they're all repressed,' Chris said, when I enthused about the low levels of crime in an effort to impress them just a little bit. 'We know where that leads.' He paused for effect.

'Huh?'

'Those bombers were all sexually frustrated. It's well known.'

'Is it?'

'I've read articles.'

How did Chris get from low crime rates to the supposed sexual frustration of the 9/11 bombers? It was like one of those games in which you have to link, say, Britney Spears to Mahatma

Gandhi in three moves. September 11th had ploughed a hole in our understanding of ourselves, I sometimes thought, which people – and I don't want to seem sexist about this, but it seemed to be mainly men – seemed to want to fill up with all their personal neuroses.

'Actually, things are a lot less repressed than they were,' I said. 'Al Jazeera's made a big difference.'

'That TV station? It's just propaganda, though, isn't it? Tapes of Osama bin Laden.'

'No, the talk shows, I mean. Sam says it's amazing, what gets discussed. How much disagreement there is.'

Even listening without being able to understand the meaning, you could tell there was a geyser of debate bubbling away under the solidified mud of the conservative regimes all across the Middle East. In Hawar, though, it had to be said that the main manifestation of the slight easing of the previous stifling consensus was that these days you could hardly go into the souk or get in a taxi without hearing cassette tapes of sermons by Mohammed Alireza, a charismatic young shi'ite cleric, popularly known as the electronic mullah. Only five years ago, Alireza had been serving the early part of what was meant to be a fifteen-year prison sentence for sedition. Now he was out of prison and preaching at his own mosque and anywhere else with access to a tape machine. He was thirty years old, slim and handsome, a former Communist, said to be a politician at least as much as a religious figure, but he'd refused to stand for election to parliament on the grounds that it wasn't going to have any power. He preferred to post his thoughts on the internet and make audio tapes. He had to be careful – anything too political and even now he could find himself back in jail – but the beauty of Islamist politics is that it doesn't have to sound too political, at least not on the surface.

Alireza didn't talk about how much of the country's oil money had gone into private banks in Switzerland, particularly those held by the prime minister, Shaikh Jasim. He didn't ask why Hawaris had been bought off with welfare payments and job creation schemes – the guards on the compound gates or non-jobs in the bloated ministries – or point out that this was, like bribing children with sweets, ultimately self-defeating. He didn't ask why there wasn't more investment in industries that might stand a chance when the oil ran out or the world started to take global warming seriously. He confined himself to such topics as the need to be a better Muslim, the likely American invasion of Iraq, or this new (or at least rediscovered from the sixth century or thereabouts) idea that foreigners in the holy lands of Arabia were an insult to the faith. But those other things were why people listened. And with repeated hearings, his followers might in time come to believe that they were part of some sort of inspiringly cosmic struggle.

Once inside the house, Karen went into professional estate agent mode, eyeing up fixtures and fittings. I tried to see it through her eyes: low-slung, flat-roofed, with sliding glass doors protected by flyscreens opening on to a long front veranda. An L-shaped, open-plan living space: sitting room, dining room, hall; a big kitchen at the back; four bedrooms off to the side. It was a house plonked down in the desert in defiance of the weather, a building that would have been at home on the out-skirts of any number of cities in America, an outpost of the empire of suburbia.

She peered over my shoulder as I reached for the milk. 'D'you always keep your flour in the fridge?'

'It's because of the weevils. If the flour gets hot, they hatch out and infest.'

'Ugh!'

'I think they're there, potentially, in all flour,' I said defensively.

'They're not, though, are they? You never hear of weevils in England.'

'D'you know there's a man in your garden?' Andrea asked, frowning out of the kitchen window.

'That's Babu. He's the gardener.'

Andrea made a face. It is true that Babu is not terribly attractive, but he's very poor, and not helped by spending all day in the dirt.

'You have a *gardener?*' Chris said, as if this were typical of my recklessness.

'Only for two hours once a fortnight. He doesn't do much, as you can probably see.'

I keep him on mainly because I can't think who would employ him if I didn't. He grows a lot of marigolds, which I hate, and every year I ask if we could possibly have something different and he nods vigorously and says 'Yes, madam,' and comes back a month later with the same old smelly orange weeds, which he then arranges in a straight row on either side of the path. I used to ask for tomatoes (thinking if at least I got those I'd be prepared to put up with the marigolds) and he'd nod and say yes but they never appeared. I planted them myself a couple of times, but they died. I won't go so far as to say they were sabotaged, but it was mysterious.

I knew I ought to do something about this situation – all Babu does is water the grass with what we call sweet water (i.e. not salty) from the springs that account for the greenery in this little corner of the emirate, and this is hardly very complicated – but I don't speak Urdu and he doesn't speak English, at least not the words 'no' and 'marigolds'.

'I expect you have to be firm with them,' Chris remarked, throwing himself into an armchair and picking up a copy of the *Hawar Daily News*, 'these people.'

Maria, who had just come in, showed no sign of having heard this remark, in which case she has better manners than my brother, because he'd almost certainly realized she was there when he made it. She shook everyone's hands limply, as though it was for them to take the initiative with the shaking, and said, 'Welcome, madam, welcome, sir.'

I should say here that I've been trying to avoid being called madam for as long as I've known Maria. When I first took her on, a week before Will was born, I said to her firmly, 'Please, don't call me madam. Call me Annie.'

She answered gravely: 'Yes, madam.'

Possibly it was some kind of test, which I failed. She could see what kind of easily exhausted person she was dealing with. In retrospect, I can see that she was marking out her territory, making sure she was on familiar ground, because there were things that you could do with a madam that you might not be able to do with an Annie – things like the potato tax, for example, whereby ten per cent of any vegetable purchase disappears soon after arriving in the house. I know there are certain women in Hawar – like Antonia Horwood, who's always saying she only employs girls straight from Sri Lanka whom she's trained herself – who would be appalled that I have never, in twenty-three years, confronted Maria about the wandering veg. Sometimes I fear that Maria herself doesn't realize I'm being generous about the potato tax and assumes I haven't spotted it. But my guess would be that she doesn't want to know that I know: she wants to outwit me, even only in a small way and now and then. She wants, at some level, to be in charge.

This is a cause of sadness to me, because Maria and I have quite a lot in common and perhaps, in different circumstances, we might have been friends. We're both women on our own in a foreign country (though Maria, whose husband is still in Colombo, usually drunk, has the distinct advantage over me of a handsome Pakistani lover in the Hawari Defence Force). But there's too big a difference in our circumstances, too much that embarrasses me, because there's no reason to do with intelligence or aptitude why Maria should be a maid and I shouldn't. So I pay her extremely well, and don't say anything about the potato tax.

I carried the tray of tea into the sitting room, feeling disappointed. I'd hoped Chris and Karen might find something appealing about Hawar, might bring themselves to say something different from the glib, dismissive things they'd been saying for the past twenty-five years. I'd invested all this time here, trying to make our lives work, and I resented their presumption that that was a mistake. I know that in some ways Hawar is charmless, that expats are drawn here mainly to make money and don't bother to learn Arabic (I'm not excluding myself here; it's a language in which you can make a dozen different words out of the same three letters, so you'd have to be some kind of genius to master it) and then they complain about not being able to get to know the locals. I know there are lots of things wrong with life here and that many people view their stay as a kind of unfortunate interlude from civilization. Their posting, they call it, as if there were no choice and the decision to spend three years or so seeing something of the world and getting richer were foisted upon them, an act of sacrifice for the public good. Which is not a very attractive attitude, and doesn't make for a very attractive place: a lot of misfits and money-obsessives, flung together on this barren peninsula on the edge of a shallow sea, thinking about how quickly they can amass enough to get away again. But I go on thinking – perhaps I have to go on thinking – that if you can get past the arrogance of some of the Americans and Europeans, then it's as interesting as anywhere. More interesting, even, because in a couple of generations Hawar has gone from being a simple tribal society to a multicultural melting pot. There is Islamic civilization here, and pre-Islamic, come to that, if you know where to look for it – but Gulf culture has been semi-dormant for centuries, battered by the climate, suppressed by other people's empires, exhausted by neglect and poverty. And now it's no longer poor and has pushed itself into the modern world while trying to hang on to its identity, Islamic, tribal, hospitable, proud. How could that not be interesting?

The Franklins' pool gleamed in the darkness, an unearthly blue puddled yellow and red with the reflections of flares hissing in the hibiscus. The fairy lights Katherine had threaded through the bougainvillea blinked like stars among the papery flowers spilling over the terrace and the side wall.

The house dated back to the 1930s – which made it very old for Hawar – and was originally built for some British protectorate-era official. It was situated on a quiet, dusty street behind the Gulf Hotel in central Qalhat, and had leaded art deco windows and a large walled back garden, big enough for a pool and an area of planting beyond. The kitchen and dining room opened out on to a deep terrace covered with bougainvillea like a prickly magenta waterfall.

'Twenty-three is young to be getting married, nowadays, isn't it?' Karen observed airily, when we parked the car down the street, which was already lined with cars, and made our way towards the house.

'Sure, but they know what they're doing,' I said uneasily.

'They like doing it properly, anyway, don't they?' dad said. 'With their wedding list at that General Trading shop and everything?'

'Have you talked to him about it?' Karen asked. 'I mean, it's obviously not as if she's pregnant or anything, because they've been planning it for months.'

'Of course she's not. And no, I haven't. I couldn't possibly.'

If I were to ask Will why he was getting married, it would come out sounding like I was asking why he was marrying Maddi, which wouldn't have been what I meant at all. I loved Maddi: I'd watched her learn to swim underwater at the age of two and start school at the British Primary School with Will at four and fly off to boarding school in England at eleven. And though Will had stayed in Hawar and gone to the International School, they'd always been able to pick up in the holidays from where they'd left off at the start of the previous term. They were the only two children from their infants' class whose parents still lived in Hawar and, when they'd coincidentally applied for the same college at Oxford, there seemed to be something almost fated about it.

But I didn't love Maddi just because she'd been around a long time. I loved her because she was truthful and unobtrusive and generous. And she and Will were both clever enough to understand the risks involved in marrying so young, so I had to assume they'd thought it through and had no doubts. Will didn't talk about his feelings much, but he was intelligent, and so was Maddi, and they must have decided they couldn't live without each other. I may have had my doubts about romance – or about how much emphasis had been put on it in my case – but Will and Maddi had lots of other things going on in their lives. They weren't relying on it to save them.

Besides, I still wanted to believe that romance could work, for them if not for me. It was too deeply ingrained in my way of seeing the world for me to slough it off. I knew that what I'd once assumed – that I didn't have to cultivate much character, just wait passively, looking nice, because love would come along and reveal me as someone of great depth, would make me *matter* – was rubbish. I'd have realized that sooner if I'd ever said it out loud, but I didn't, because it was implicit in everything I thought and did and too deep-seated for me even to spot that the foundations of my life were cracked.

So I married too young, when my sense of myself was still fuzzy. If I'd been the person I am now I think I'd have seen Dave more clearly. But that was then, and it was different for Will and Maddi, I thought: if you already had a sense of yourself, if you were competent and could cope with what was thrown at you, love might affirm the best things about you, make you feel more yourself. Bring out the best in you. I hoped that was what they felt, that they made each other believe in the future.

The Franklins' garden was packed, and quite a lot of the guests were unfamiliar, which was unusual for Hawar, where there's a tendency to see the same people at every party. Maddi's cousins had flown in from South Africa, along with a sizeable contingent of Franklin relatives from Britain and around twenty friends of Will and Maddi's from university, plus quite a lot of people who used to live here and had moved away but had come back for the wedding. I spotted the Woods, who now lived in Singapore, talking to the Helgesens, who'd flown in from Dubai, and Mark, Will's best man, who was staying on Al Janabiyya compound with my friends the Grants, talking to Maddi's grandmother, who had once been a famous opera singer and was still beautiful ... the garden was noisy with knots of jollity and the atmosphere was exuberant. You don't get many big family weddings in Hawar expat society. Love stories here more often involve the middle-aged and are tainted with boredom and betrayal, embittered exes and quarrels about money.

I picked my way round the pool, leading Chris, Karen and dad towards Peter, who was helping out the staff with the barbecue at the back. He preferred being busy: Katherine was host enough for both of them, adept and charming, and he'd once confessed to me, when slightly drunk, that on occasions like this he felt slightly superfluous. He kissed me – 'whoops, two is it?' – while half concentrating on turning steaks and asking the others whether they'd managed to see anything of Hawar. Andrea looked him up and down and veered off to talk to Matt on the other side of the garden.

'Oh, all those bits of old cloth and basket,' he said knowingly, when Karen described what we'd been doing. 'Very interesting.'

'What is interesting,' Chris said, 'is the price of booze. Annie took us to that Nip Inn place this afternoon. Crazy prices, for a country where they don't want you to drink.'

'They don't mind us drinking,' Maddi said, joining us half way through this and kissing everyone, 'as long as we don't look drunk. And they make a fortune out of Saudis coming for the alcohol.'

'Why do they black out the windows then?'

'I guess so people don't have to look in if they don't want.'

'What, so they don't mind the shops being there as long as they can't see in?'

Maddi shrugged. 'Perhaps it's a way of being tolerant. Sort of having it both ways.'

'Bit bloody hypocritical, if you ask me. Either you have a religion or you don't. It's not meant to be a bloody pick'n'mix counter, is it? "I'll have the Quran but without the public executions."' Maddi started to say that public executions are nothing to do with Islam, but Chris bulldozed on. 'You should be against it, anyway, you women. Just be grateful *we* don't kill you if you have sex with the wrong person.'

Maddi gave up. 'I think you have the wrong idea of Hawar,' she smiled.

'Oh yeah? You saying it's not stuck in the past, the Persian Gulf, then?'

'Arabian Gulf,' I said automatically, 'we usually say Arabian.'

'Whatever,' Chris said dismissively. 'Gulf of Whatever. Even their calendar's stuck on fourteen twenty something.'

'1423,' said Maddi.

' – and, to be fair, Britain probably wasn't very civilized in the middle ages.'

'How was the rehearsal?' I asked Maddi, changing the subject.

'Well, I hope Andrew's done a wedding before because he seems to think the service mainly consists of bad jokes. I'm sure there wasn't so much about frogs in blenders at the last one I went to.'

After this I introduced Chris and Karen to the Helgesens and my dad to Maddi's grandmother and left them for a bit. Andrea seemed to be getting on well with Matt, Sam and Faisal, although when I spotted her half an hour later, the younger boys had gone and she seemed to be pinioning Matt into a corner mainly by means of her breasts.

'She insisted on wearing that vest!' Karen grumbled, coming up behind me. 'It's very revealing. And as for those sequins . . .'

She's got so much flesh, it's hardly necessary to expose it like that. It's not as if we don't all know it's there.'

'She's fine.'

'I wish she'd dress a bit more like the Franklin girls.' Karen looked across at Millie, who was wearing an elegant green linen dress that emphasized her coltishness. Katherine had been a model before she married and Maddi and Millie had inherited her long legs and Slavic cheekbones.

'Girls go in for that preppy look here. It's different for Andrea: she lives in London.'

'Not everyone in London dresses like a cheap prostitute.'

'Nor does Andrea.' I thought privately that if Karen stopped making such a big deal of it, Andrea's need a) to have a lot of flesh, and b) to expose as much of it as possible, might well subside. But now didn't seem the right moment to say, so I suggested we went to get some food instead. I got my dad a plate while I was about it.

'Oh, thanks, but nothing for me,' he protested when I took it over to him. 'Leave it for the young people.'

I promised him he wouldn't be depriving anyone of food and he took the plate and ate the steak, the salad and the baked potato, and then the chocolate mousse I also brought. While I was about it, I took Chris a steak and the largest potato left in the bowl, because I was worried by the way he kept haranguing people about Islam. I'd have to remember to warn him not to do that on Saturday because roughly a quarter of the wedding guests would be Muslim.

I thought ruefully that I might have tried too hard to persuade my father and brother and his family that life in Hawar was easy and comfortable, might have been too successful. Chris seemed to have gone in a day from thinking I was living in a dangerous nest of terrorists and white slave traders to thinking it was OK to be pissed in public and insult Islam. He clearly had no idea that our life here was also fragile, that we stayed on in Hawar on sufferance, and that while life may be comfortable, that comfort came with conditions, the first of which was to take care of not offending. All expatriates had to be sponsored by a Hawari, and sponsorship could be withdrawn. The whole basis of my life was provisional, dependent on the legal backing of a man I didn't like and found it quite hard not to be rude to.

In practice, of course, sponsorship was rarely withdrawn from Americans, Europeans or other rich expats, unlike Sri Lankan house maids who made accusations of abuse or Indian construction workers who dared to demand better working conditions. But the knowledge that it could be had a restraining effect: we were careful at the very least not to be drunk in public, or to insult the ruling family. Self-censorship can be at least as powerful as the more obvious and open variety.

By ten o'clock, Chris had drunk at least three times as much as anyone else at the party and I went in search of Karen to suggest it might be time to make a move. When he was in this state, he reminded me of when I'd had to fetch him from parties as a teenager. I used to wait for him in the street because he was too young to walk home by himself (too young to be at the parties, really, but my dad was all over the place after my mum died) and I could still recall the nervous anxiety that used to run through me at the prospect that he'd come out drunk, throw up in the gutter, shout in the street, go off in a different direction. That I wouldn't be able to stop him and get him home, because he was twice my size. I seemed to have spent most of my late teens worrying about how adrift he was. And despite the financial success and the house and business and everything, I couldn't get over a sense that he wasn't much less vulnerable now.

'I just didn't expect an Arab country to be like this,' Karen was explaining when I found her. She was sitting at a table at the back of the garden with Peter, Millie, Sam and Will.

'Auntie Karen thought Hawar was full of terrorists,' Sam explained.

'Well, all we see on the news is Osama bin Laden.'

'But auntie, he hasn't lived in the Gulf for years . . .'

'The thing about this part of the world,' Peter said, gesturing for me to sit beside him, 'is that people are very courteous, and part of that is to be respectful of people's differences.' He poured wine into a spare glass and pushed it towards me, smiling. Once, years ago, he put his hand on my knee at a dinner party. I had politely taken it off again and the incident hadn't been mentioned since, but there was a frisson between us sometimes on evenings like this. I was grateful to him for never having tried again and for having been scrupulously polite ever since. Possibly he was grateful to me for not taking him up on his offer. I had never heard of him as being a man who had affairs and it was probably a momentary aberration, about which he now felt a little foolish.

'I don't think I could live here myself, though,' Karen added, 'it's got no history.'

'Oh, but apparently Hawar was the Garden of Eden,' Millie said. 'You can't get any more historic than that.'

'According to Hollywood,' Peter said.

As far as we knew – which means as far as the *Hawar Daily News* knew – the film James Hartley was coming to the Gulf to make concerned some secret uncovered by archaeologists about the Garden of Eden. James was playing a CIA operative who goes undercover to protect the secret and the oil-rich Gulf state that's suddenly been identified as the cradle of civilization. Surprisingly enough, there really is a theory that Hawar was the site of the Garden of Eden, which they make quite a lot of at the National Museum. It seems to be based on a single line from the *Epic of Gilgamesh* and I don't think it has many adherents. Most scholars seem to think that, as far as it existed, the Garden of Eden was in Iraq.

'Still,' Peter added, 'if James Hartley's prepared to come here, we'll overlook any inconvenient historical truth.'

'James Hartley's coming?' Karen echoed. 'To see you, Annie?'

'Yes, sure,' I laughed. 'No, to make a film.'

'But he knows you're here? Does Ted know?'

Peter sighed. 'Katherine went over to the Al A'ali House today and the staff didn't think they were coming for a few days. So it looks as though we might be able to get the wedding over before the hysteria starts.'

'Oh my God! They're coming that soon? – I never knew him: I'm younger, obviously – but Chris has told me all about it . . .'

'No, right, well, it's time to go,' I said, standing up.

'He was furious when they split up.'

I said, 'People are always furious when they split up. Often even when they've initiated it.'

'But he didn't.'

'It was complicated.'

'He asked her to marry him, you know.'

'Only after it was all over. He was pissed off with me. He was just trying to get some reaction out of me when I wouldn't come to the phone.'

Millie's eyes widened. 'Annie! Really? How could you not *say*?'

'He didn't mean it.'

'Is it a thing people do without meaning it?'

'In this case, yes. He'd have reconsidered soon enough if I'd said yes.'

The party was thinning out, to my relief. I extricated myself from the group at the table, mainly by ignoring Millie's excited questions about how exactly James Hartley had proposed to me and what exactly I'd said and whether we'd ever spoken since ('on the phone', 'don't be silly' and 'no' were the answers). I rounded up Chris, dad and Andrea, and drove the family back along the Corniche to the hotel, waited in the car outside until they'd disappeared through the revolving doors, then headed home. Will had promised to bring Matt and Sam back from the Franklins' in the Jeep, and I hoped the party had continued to break up after I left, because although it wouldn't occur to the boys, this was the last-but-one night of this part of our lives, and I wanted us all to get home and make the most of it. I wanted to relish (secretly: they'd have been appalled if I'd told them) my sons with their apparently insatiable needs for tea and toast and their enthusiasm for taking on the world as they lolloped towards adulthood. They were growing away from me, I knew – they'd had their own ideas, preoccupations and privacies for a long time now – but they were still capable of being shaky and fearful, almost childlike, and I knew that home (and let's face it, that meant me, because who else had there been?) still gave them much of their security and sense of themselves. I had achieved something here, without even realizing that I was doing it, and I wanted to relish it for one more night, the four of us together, not even noticing we were happy.

Three

The church was packed. The Franklins knew everyone who was anyone in Hawar and, with three boys, I knew everyone else. There were Hawaris in expensive silk suits or thobes and gold-edged mishlahs, women in exquisite saris and shalwar kameez in chiffon, silk and beaded satin; designer outfits – Chanel, Valentino, Versace – from the upscale shops in the Pearl Mall and custom-made clothes from the tailors in the souk. Hawar is never knowingly underdressed, and gold glittered around women's necks and expensive watches on men's wrists; diamonds sparkled as though fairy dust had been sprinkled over the congregation.

Matt, who was an usher, led me to my place in the second pew, directly behind Will and his best man Mark. Maria, already in position a little further along, looked up, mouthed 'Hello, madam!' and returned to what seemed to be fervent prayer. I turned and smiled at dad, Chris, Karen and Andrea in the pew behind. My sister-in-law and my niece were whispering furiously at one another. Will swung around, smiled briefly at me, and then turned back to the front.

'D'you think he's OK?' I'd asked Matt and Sam earlier, when he'd gone off for a swim after breakfast.

Sam didn't look up. He was drawing a cartoon of Mohammed Alireza on an ad in the *Hawar Daily News*. 'He's always been weird.'

'That's not true . . .'

'Mum, you don't have to have maximum emotion about it,' Matt said. 'You won't make any difference.'

'He looks so anxious . . .'

'That's just how he is.'

41

Was it? They were all so different, my boys, and though I liked to think they were close at a deep and inarticulate level, mostly they found it easier to ignore each other. Matt was too emotionally unplugged to have much connection with Will's focused ambition, and Sam was too busy being evasive.

Now Mark was attempting to make conversation with Will by asking him questions about the church. Will rudely wasn't answering so I leant forward and explained that the stained-glass window over the altar had come from a house in Persia. I'm not sure how close he and Will were, really; I had a feeling he was more Maddi's friend. 'It was imported when the church was built,' I added, 'in the seventies.'

'And the locals didn't mind having a Christian church here?'

'No, there's a Catholic one as well. Which is much bigger – has a congregation of several thousand.'

Maria's one stipulation when she'd taken the job with me (I say this as if I was the one in control of the situation, which I wasn't) had been five hours off on a Sunday for church. The Sacred Heart was where she went to meet cousins, old neighbours from Colombo, friends. It was where she'd originally learnt that Dawn, the house maid I'd already employed and whose references I'd diligently checked, wouldn't be returning from her month's holiday in Sri Lanka to take up the job. It was where, in effect, it had been decided that I would employ Maria Rozairo instead. She always went off on a Sunday wearing a lot of make-up.

'There used to be C of E services in the British embassy originally,' I added, 'but when the expat population started expanding in the 1950s, they had to move on to the tennis courts.'

Will let us talk among ourselves. He clearly didn't want to join in a discussion about how much that would have been a test of faith in July. I wished he might have been less tense, might have seemed to be relishing his wedding more visibly, but I told myself his anxiety was excusable: this was the day that Katherine and Maddi and he had spent the last year planning, finally here, all its perfectible moments needing to be knitted seamlessly together.

Andrew billowed into the church and I found myself wondering if he was wearing shorts under his surplice. He wore shorts an awful lot, for a vicar, not that I suppose there's anything against it in the rulebooks. He wafted about lighting candles and shifting things in a slightly look-at-me manner, but then he caught Will's eye for a moment and I was struck by the unpleasant thought that he felt Will needed encouraging.

I resisted the temptation to lean forward and hug my eldest son. I put a hand on his shoulder instead and he half nodded in acknowledgement. It shouldn't have surprised me that he was tense: he'd spent his entire adolescence trying to get life under control, as if he thought it might slither away from him if he didn't pin it down. Even when he hadn't been studying or at cricket nets or doing clarinet practice, he'd been making lists of batting averages by county and the top ten players for Manchester United or the best rugby clubs in the world.

He could have been a county cricket player himself, if he'd had a county. That was what Katherine thought, anyway – 'Such a pity he didn't go to school in England,' she'd said a few months ago, watching him open the bowling against the Bahrain Cricket Club. I couldn't have afforded to send him to school in England, even if I'd wanted to, but it seemed to me that he could hardly have done better than he had at the International School or, come to that, under the local Indian cricket coaches. He'd made the best of our slightly awkward circumstances – of being part of a household headed by a mother in a place where that was barely acceptable, of having less money than any of his friends. Now, though, for some reason, a memory came to me of driving him home from a cricket match when he was about fourteen. He'd turned to me abruptly and asked if I'd ever had the feeling I was on an aeroplane but it was the wrong flight to the wrong destination, and I was surrounded by people who were appalling.

43

I'd said yes, without really thinking, because I imagined he was talking about living in Hawar. Afterwards, though, I wondered if he'd been trying to tell me something else. But the moment had passed and, though I tried, I hadn't been able to re-open the conversation.

Matt and Sam, handsome in their new suits from Soft Hands Tailors, joined me in the pew. Yvonne Carlisle, music teacher at the International School, launched gamely into Clarke's Trumpet Voluntary and Maddi came swishing elegantly down the aisle on Peter's arm, shooting me a swift, almost shy look as she passed.

At the chancel steps, Andrew looked at Will and Maddi gravely, then half smiled, as if he understood why they were there, what they meant by it. Then, 'God our Father,' he began, 'you have taught us through your Son that love is fulfilling of the law.'

The smallest bridesmaid, the daughter of the Franklins' house maid Magdalena, shifted from foot to foot beside me, pointing her slippered toes in front of her, admiring her skirt.

Andrew's voice was rich and he found resonance in the familiar rhythms, but I lost track. Even as I tried, as Matt said, to have maximum emotion about it, the whole thing seemed to flash past in seconds, sand through my fingers. I remembered afterwards that the sermon was more like a best man's speech than a sermon and that people laughed, but I couldn't recall the detail of it. I stared at Maddi, her high-necked silk jersey dress backless under her veil, hoping that beneath their poise and restraint, she and Will felt teeming passion, that they were so shaken by love that the world looked different.

The Al A'ali house was one of the oldest in the emirate, built in the early twentieth-century colonial style, with large square rooms cooled by ceiling fans, teak pillars and joists, galleried verandas and wide shallow steps that led down on to the lawn. It was named after its previous owners, one of the leading merchant families in the emirate (the gas company, the aluminium smelting plant, the Gulf's biggest retail furniture business) although the house was originally built for the British Resident and had later been occupied by the British Council. The Al A'alis had bought it in the 1960s and lived in it for twenty years before incorporating it into the Sheraton as a kind of villa-annexe with a private cook and butler. When they sold the hotel to the prime minister, Shaikh Jasim, in the early 1990s, the house had gone with it.

You could see why it would have appealed to James Hartley, or to the people who organized things for him; why it would have seemed a more atmospheric place to stay than the modern villas on the beach where I'd initially assumed they'd put him, even though they'd been built to accommodate heads of state from the Gulf Cooperation Council.

Fortunately, though, he didn't seem to have arrived – there was no sign of any of the film people in the house – and I could concentrate on the wedding.

After dinner, I wandered out on to the lawn, thinking about Dave and how absent he was, even though Will had referred to him gracefully in his speech and various people had said to me during the day that they expected he was looking down on us. It wasn't a hope I shared: the idea that he might have acquired some power to see through dimensions – even if he was too dead to do anything about it – was alarming. He did in fact stick around for a couple of nights after the car crash: I'd heard him in the house, blundering about and knocking into the furniture, but Dr Al Rayyan said that this was quite normal, one of the tricks that grief plays on the bereaved, and that I might also spot him in the street. I never did, though, and bashing into chairs seemed a much more typical manifestation.

I hadn't wanted then to think he might be able to see us, and I still didn't – because if he could, would there be anything to stop him seeing everything, right through into the heart of me?

Most of the guests were outside, talking, strolling in the light of flares around the edges of the garden and lamps hanging from the trees. Over on the veranda, Will and Maddi's friends were lolling on Persian carpets sharing a shisha. The scent of apple tobacco hung in the air.

Maddi's grandmother, the former opera singer, marched up with my father in her wake. 'I've taken Ted on,' she announced loudly; she was a bit deaf; 'otherwise he'd happily spend the whole evening by himself in a corner.'

My dad made some feeble noise of protest.

'. . . which is ridiculous when there are all these interesting people to talk to! People in such lovely costumes, from all over the place. We were just speaking to a lovely lady from India who's a Parsee. Do you know about Parsees?'

'A bit . . .'

'Very *old* religion. Ancient! She was telling us. D'you know about the bodies on the mountaintops?' Before I could answer, she went on: 'Tricky, I imagine, if you don't live near a mountain.'

'Or any vultures,' dad said, making an effort.

'Quite. Very difficult, to have a religion today.' She gestured grandly, operatically, across the lawn. 'All these different nationalities, beliefs – must be hard for everyone to live together. There's got to be some give and take: God, Allah, Ahura . . .'

'Mazda,' dad supplied, 'like the car.'

'Precisely! You say the name of your God and people think of a car. That can't be easy for the Parsees! Come on, Ted, let's go and meet some others!' And she led him off, but he didn't mind, because she'd barge up to anyone and introduce herself and then him, her dear friend Ted, even though they'd only just met, and it *was* more interesting than spending the evening in the corner.

Over by the shrubbery, Cheryl was talking to Karen about fitness.

'You're so right that it's never too early – otherwise you find you're forty with a whole lot of flab and cellulite and you don't know *where* to begin. You'd never credit how some people let themselves go ... I went back to Singapore last year and met a couple of old friends who'd really ... well, it's the sun, partly – but it was horrible. I mean, it made me feel slightly sick ... Anyway, Annie, darling, we were just saying how amazing you look. That Salman of yours at Soft Hands has done a really good job. Pale colours are so good on you, what with you not having very strong colouring yourself. Have you ever had your colours done? I know this brilliant woman – but you probably don't need it, you've got good instincts. You always look attractive, even when you're obviously not making any effort. You'd never guess you had those grown-up boys. And wasn't Will's speech lovely? I only hope Kyle's that nice about me when he grows up ... But you're like me. Lucky with your genes. I always think I'm younger than my biological age, and you're the same ...'

'Chris asked Matthew to dance with Andrea,' Karen complained to me, 'and now she's saying she doesn't want to! Honestly, I don't know what it is with her ...'

'Maybe we should just leave them to sort it out for themselves?' I said vaguely, smiling back encouragingly at Dr Al Rayyan, who was waving across the grass.

'You know Chris, though: if he thinks something needs saying, he'll say it,' Karen answered complacently, 'specially once he's got a few drinks inside him.'

I was wondering whether it was a good idea to point out that this was a completely crap quality when Anwar joined us, saying, 'How are you lovely ladies?' – which somehow suggested that he didn't think we were lovely at all.

Anwar is our sponsor at the British Primary School, where I am the school secretary. He is the majority owner; it's a requirement of Hawari law that a Hawari national should own at least 51 per cent of any business. Our head teacher, Sue Forrester, owns the rest. Anwar comes in from time to time and hangs around, but there isn't much for him to do, certainly not if we can help it. He also has some sort of junior deputy under secretary job at the Ministry of Education, where I suspect they don't give him many actual tasks either.

'Ah, it is a wonderful thing to have boys!' he sighed to me now, which is what he always says. I introduced Karen and he asked her if she had boys as well.

'No, just the one girl.'

'Aha! A mistake!' he cried, which is Anwar's idea of a joke, although it's getting harder to tell because lately he's been saying more and more outrageous things. I don't know if his intolerance, or enthusiasm for expressing it, is anything to do with the growing influence of Mohammed Alireza, but he's taken to telling me how disgusting dogs are and also that it says this in the Quran or the hadiths; he doesn't distinguish. He claims he's wary of shaking hands with British people for fear they've been indulging their sentimentally filthy habit of touching them. More recently, he's moved on to the role of women, which does not seem to include anything of very high status, and I've begun dreading his visits to school in case he says something really appalling and I have to respond rudely.

'Of course,' Anwar added, 'if William were a Muslim, he would be able to do this all over again.'

'In our country, England,' Karen said, possibly thinking he was flirting, 'men don't need to marry more than one woman.'

'No, you have the divorce.'

'I was just telling Matthew he can't come back from his gap year engaged,' I tried to change the subject, 'because I can't possibly do this again for another ten years.'

Chris swayed up, a bottle of champagne clutched in his fist. Where, how, had he got a whole bottle? It wasn't a swigging from the bottle event.

'This is Anwar,' Karen announced, 'who thinks it's a good idea to have four wives.'

'What about the nagging, though?' Chris asked, frowning, and adding irrelevantly, 'Jihad: that's a Muslim thing.'

'Jihad,' Anwar said sententiously, 'means the struggle against tyranny, or *zulm*. From the root *jhd,* meaning strain, struggle, endeavour. The first, greater jihad is the spiritual struggle within yourself, the second, the struggle against oppression.'

Yousef Al Rayyan joined us in time to hear the end of this. '*Ijtihad*, the tradition of independent reasoning, questioning and debate, comes from the same root,' he observed. 'This can be confusing.'

Karen said: 'In Christianity, we believe in loving thy neighbour.'

'And so do we,' agreed Yousef. 'In the Quran we have the words *wa ja'alnaakum shu'uuban wa qabaa'ilan li-ta'aarifuu* – "And I have created people and tribes so that they could get to know each other."' No one appeared to have an answer to this, so he went on: 'It's funny, until after 9/11 I never thought of myself as a Muslim. I was, of course, but it never seemed that important. It was in the background, a part of my identity but, to be honest, I hardly gave it any thought at all. But since 9/11, I find that a Muslim is what I am.'

Anwar frowned. There was no way being a Muslim could or should be in the background.

'How d'you mean?' Karen asked.

'Well, at the most obvious level, I haven't been to America this year. I used to go every summer; I expected my daughter to study there. But the stories of what happens at immigration are too unpleasant. You also hear about Muslim students being ostracized in the classroom.'

'Is that true, though?'

'I don't know, Annie. Many people believe these stories. I am not sure, myself, that I do believe them, but I believe enough in the possibility that I don't want to take the risk.'

'You can't blame the Yanks,' Chris said, 'not after what happened.'

'I do not blame them. I admire America. My son did his postgraduate study at Stanford. My point is that I feel estranged from the America-loving part of myself. What has happened has made me something called a Muslim, who is somehow in opposition to America, whether that's what I want to be or not.'

Anwar was blinking rapidly, wanting to ask why you wouldn't want to be a Muslim, but afraid he might get an answer. Even to get this far with his thoughts was making him angry.

But Chris had lost interest. He leant towards me and said: 'They think they're it, don't they?'

'Sorry?'

'Your kids. Just because they can play tennis and waterski, it's like they don't come from Croydon at all.'

'I don't know what you mean ...' They were born in Hawar. They didn't come from Croydon. They'd hardly ever been to Croydon.

'Yes you do. Going round the way they do ...'

'Chris, I'm not listening to this. I don't know why you want to ruin it for me, but you won't.'

I marched off, blinking away tears that seemed to have been welling up since childhood, wondering why he was always so unpleasant, what I'd done to make him permanently irritable with me? And why, despite the fact that he hardly ever spoke kindly to me, I still felt sorry for him. I headed back to the marquee, my heels digging into the lawn where, all week, the sprinklers had been whirring and spraying, soaking the grass in preparation for our big day.

The band were on their last set and I was outside the marquee again, talking to Will and Matt, Al Helgesen and our family doctor, Yousef Al Rayyan. It was the first time I'd ever seen Yousef in a thobe; in the surgery he always wears expensive pale grey suits.

Al was describing life in Dubai. 'Sometimes you can't find your way home from the office, because the streets have changed while you're at work.'

'Is there a master-plan?' Will asked, 'or does Shaikh

Mohammed just wake up and decide to have some islands in the shape of a palm tree?'

'They say he fancied a bit more beach.'

'An Arab world capital,' Yousef twinkled, '*such* presumption.'

'Or a property bubble,' Al said sourly.

'At least Shaikh Mohammed's trying to do *something*,' Matt observed – which surprised me, because he's never been very interested in politics.

'We are improving a little, here in Hawar,' Yousef replied: 'I have high hopes for the crown prince.'

Yousef is a member of a liberal group called Al Muntada, which translates as The Forum. They call themselves a think tank, because they'd quite like to be a political party but they aren't allowed. They're not allowed to publish anything either, so really they're more of a talk tank. There are rumours that the emir's son, Shaikh Rashid bin Hassan Al Majid, who studied politics and international relations at Manchester University, has been to some of their meetings.

'Is it true he's a bit wild?' asked Al. 'The crown prince?'

'Does that mean interested in human rights?' Yousef asked drily.

'I heard more, you know, parties, drugs.'

'Have you met him?' Yousef asked Will, ignoring this. Shaikh Rashid would only have been a year or two older than Will.

'No, never. I think Matt might have?'

'Once,' Matt said vaguely, looking around for Jodie, 'at Shazia's stables.'

A classmate of Matt's at the International School lived at the emir's stables out at Jidda. Her mother was French and her father belonged to a distant branch of the ruling family, who'd made it a condition of his getting a good job in government that he marry a Hawari cousin who'd been picked out for him years before, no matter that he was already married to Marie-Therese and had two children. Officially, Shazia's parents were no longer together, but Marie-Therese had stayed on in Hawar to run the royal stables and it was rumoured that she and Shaikh Abdullah still spent rather a lot of time together. The family didn't mix in expatriate circles and probably not much in Hawari ones either, and Shazia was secretive about what went on at home. She rarely invited anyone to her house, but she'd made an exception for Matthew because he was such a good rider.

Al's wife Marisa came running across the grass at that moment and threw herself at her husband, clutching wildly at his sleeve, gasping: 'There's been a bomb! ... In Bali!' Al made a strangulated, throaty noise, but Marisa went on, the words tumbling out, 'No, no, it's OK, Molly's safe. She just rang. Our daughter's there,' she added to the rest of us, looking distractedly around the little group.

'Are you sure?' Al said. 'What about Clare?'

'She's fine too, but they wanted us to ring Clare's parents because they couldn't get through ... Sorry,' she said bleakly to me, 'I didn't mean to ...'

I put a hand on her arm. 'It's fine. You're sure she's OK?'

'Yes, but she was quite close ... It was on the beach. She's travelling with a friend – gap year. And, you know, you worry about them when they're away, but you don't think someone's going to blow them up ... It was just young people, having a good time ...'

Al put his arm round her. 'Come and sit down.'

'Yes, we should call the Reillys ...'

Al started to lead her away. 'They're only young,' she said helplessly. 'And that's what they do: drink on the beach in Bali ...'

They were making for the house, Marisa stumbling a little, when Chris almost barged into her. He was still clutching a bottle of champagne by the neck, although not, I fear, the same one.

He looked back at Marisa indignantly then turned to me: 'Izzit true? Someone said something about a big bomb.'

'In Bali.'

'Their daughter is there,' Yousef added, nodding back at the Helgesens. 'Luckily, she seems to be OK.'

Chris staggered slightly and half fell into Matt. Recovering himself, he announced, 'So! Eat, drink and be merry, becaush tomorrow you may be blown up by an Arab terrorist.'

'I don't think they'd be Arabs in Bali,' I said stiffly. Yousef was standing beside me.

'You saying they're not Muslims, then?' Chris glared at me, then turned back to Matt. 'S'true, mate. Should be getting your end away ... Lots of pretty girls here ... bloody lucky for them I'm not twenty years younger ...'

'Right.'

'You young people now, though, you're all up yourselves ...'

Inside his new suit, Matt tensed.

'We used to think if you couldn't fuck a girl at a wedding, you couldn't fuck one anywhere,' Chris said loudly. 'Drunk on the romance. And the booze. Thought it was ... whasser matter, Matthew? No need to look like that. Not interested?'

'No.'

'Why?' He stumbled again. 'What are you, queer or something?'

'Actually,' Matt said, 'yes.'

That was the moment that James Hartley chose to arrive. I didn't notice at first. I was too busy staring stupidly at Matthew, wondering what does he mean, *yes*? He's *gay*? Since when?

'I'm sorry,' he said to me, 'perhaps it makes sense of a few things.'

No. Why would it? It hadn't occurred to me. Nothing about him had seemed odd, or wrong. How had I missed this? When I was his mother?

My first cogent thought was he wouldn't be able to have children, which was stupid because I'd never thought about him having children before. My second was that I was going to lose

53

him to some kind of netherworld of promiscuity and leather and fetish and flouncing.

The moment was burning itself into me. I thought I'd always remember this instant of landslip, when Matt and I fell and ended up in different places. I stared at him, making sure to imprint his features on my mind before I lost him. He was gay, and the person I'd believed in, even hoped for, was fading. He was not the boy, young man, I'd taken him to be. The buzz of conversation in the late, warm evening, the scent of frangipane mixed with apple tobacco – these would always remind me of the moment I lost Matthew and got a gay person instead.

For a moment, I didn't realize that Peter Franklin was gripping my elbow and steering me towards the veranda. 'We seem to have some late arrivals.'

I looked around. A change had come over the party, but not for the obvious reason, the reason that a change had come over me – because of what was going on up by the house. Something like an electric charge was running round the garden. Someone had arrived and someone had *noticed*, and then someone else, and the noticing spread: shoulders had straightened, sightlines had shifted, glances had slid across the lawn; it was as if a little of the intensity of each conversation had leached out and gathered in a force field over James Hartley's head.

He was standing on the veranda, by the steps, wearing a pale linen suit and a dark T-shirt. He seemed to gleam in the darkness, irradiated by celebrity. A dark-skinned man stood on one side of him and a tall, effortfully thin-looking woman on the other.

Peter was pushing me towards them. I looked around distract-edly for Matt, 'I can't, not now!'

'Annie, we can't *leave* them. And no one else can do it.'

'You don't understand, something's happened . . .'

'He's only here because of you.'

Now, that *was* silly. That was almost as absurd as Matthew being gay. He was James Hartley, paid millions of dollars a film,

54

interviewed by hyperventilating journalists, cosseted by people whose entire jobs were about supplying his needs . . . I stumbled up the steps.

'Annie!' He threw his arms around me. His body was older, stronger, but something about him, perhaps a smell or something even less tangible, felt familiar. He hugged me, and went on hugging me. 'Hey!' he said delightedly, 'you haven't changed at all!'

He released me eventually and held me away from him. 'You look amazing!' he said delightedly. 'Look, I'm sorry, we only just got in and we're not even properly dressed, when you're so lovely . . .'

'No, it's fine. It's nice to see you.'

'Oh no! I changed the flight. I was hoping to get here a bit earlier, but Nezar . . . Let me introduce you: this is Nezar Al Maraj – who's Hawari – and Fiona Eckhart, my assistant.'

Fiona smiled thinly. I shook her hand and said something polite about being pleased she could join us. The Hawari didn't seem to have shaved. I assumed he must be some kind of fixer.

'*Salaam aleikum,*' I smiled politely.

'*Waleikum as salaam wa rahmatullah wa barakatu.*' This was an unnecessarily florid reply – And unto you be peace and the grace and mercy of God be upon you – which made me feel I should say something further, so I added: '*Ahlan wa salan.*' Be welcome.

I really shouldn't have abandoned Matthew.

He, however, seemed to want to go on. '*Ahlan wa sahlan biki. Shlonik?*' How is the respected one?

'*Al hamdulillah,*' I answered dismissively: God be praised. I was trying to work out how to get away from James without seeming so rude that I blew all chances of a further meeting.

'*Shlon sahatik?*' he persisted. How is your health?

It was at this point that I became fully aware that in circumstances that were by any measure cataclysmic I was exchanging formal greetings in Arabic – a language in which I can say no more than five simple things – with a fixer who hadn't even been

55

invited to the wedding. *'Al hamdulillah,'* I repeated, with as much finality as possible.

'Shlon al-umuur?'

He was asking now how was my *life?* Oh, well, if we were going to get started on that, I thought bitterly, my life was *terrible.* One of my children was gay and I hadn't noticed. James had turned up and I was ignoring him. Everyone at the wedding was staring at me and probably wondering why I was being so rude, and I was being publicly humiliated, laughed at, by a fixer who wanted to see how long I could keep this up.

I didn't say any of this. *'Al hamdulillah,'* I lied. How dare he be amused by my efforts to include him? Perhaps my accent was even more appalling than I knew, or I'd missed out some crucial reference to the all-mercifulness of God. That was Arabic for you: frankly, it was a wonder Arabs ever got anything done with all the courtesy they had to get through every time they met someone.

'Very impressive,' murmured Fiona, 'but I think, Nezar, darling, you've had your fun now.'

'Oh, I was rather enjoying it,' James said cheerfully. I coloured: shit, had they *all* been laughing at me? 'Nezar's our producer – did he just tell you that?'

'No,' I said stiffly. 'We didn't get past whether we were happy with our lives.'

'Best to get the ontology over with first,' he said.

I could have hit him. He'd guessed I thought he was some kind of gofer/odd job person. He knew I'd been patronizing him: that was why he'd been teasing me. And now he was using words I didn't even properly know the meaning of. I smiled at him distantly, acknowledging that he'd had his little joke.

'Nezar mostly lives in New York,' James added. 'And is this your husband?' He indicated Peter, who was hovering behind me, so then I had to explain who he was, and also that Dave was dead, that he'd been killed in a car crash on the Arad Road, and that I had two other children . . . I was gabbling, because

I was wondering again where Matt was and if he was OK.

How was all this happening at once? I was talking to a film star and my son was gay. There were no events of note for years, and then everything happened at once.

James was frowning. 'Annie, is everything OK?'

'Yes. No. Not really. That is . . . I'm fine. I just had some news . . .'

'I hope not bad?'

No, fine, I wanted to say. Good news, in fact. Perfectly OK. I looked around for Matthew.

But I couldn't in all honesty say it was good news, and I couldn't see Matt, and anything else seemed unimportant. Al Maraj was frowning at me. I suppose they wouldn't have been used to talking to people who looked over their shoulders, past them, casting around for someone else.

I tried to focus, because I knew I must seem rude, but all the details about our lives that I was used to repeating, about gap years and International Baccalauréats and Will's investment banking job and Maddi's in management consultancy – the stuff I used to think portrayed my family – seemed suddenly nonsensical, like a pointillist painting in which you can only see a lot of meaningless dots. The details about exams and jobs didn't cohere into anything. Matthew was gay and that obscured everything else: it was a spreading stain on the story I'd told of our lives.

'D'you want to talk about it?' James asked.

'No, not right now . . . I'm sorry . . . d'you mind? I need to find my son . . .'

'This is so like you,' he said with amusement. 'I spend twenty-five years looking for you and then when I track you down, I get less than five minutes.'

'I know. I promise next time you can have at least ten.'

'Thanks. Only have I got to wait another twenty-five years? Because I could easily be dead.'

This was better; there was a thread here of something

remembered, something we could perhaps pick up another time.

Fiona said, 'James, we've arrived terribly late and the party's clearly almost over.'

'If I could just introduce you to my wife and daughter before you leave . . .?' Peter said tentatively.

'We have got rather a lot to sort out,' Al Maraj said. 'We only intended to look in and say hello.'

James saw Peter's disappointment. 'But obviously,' he told the others, 'we can't leave without meeting the bride . . .'

'It's you they want to see,' Al Maraj said. 'I'll wait upstairs.'

James leant over. 'Go and find your son. I hope it works out.' He waved me away affectionately. 'Annie, you're hopeless.'

I looked out over the sea of heads on the lawn. Everyone seemed to have come out of the marquee into the garden, where they were pretending that they were absorbed in conversation and not staring at James Hartley.

By tomorrow, all those people would be talking about us. They'd have heard Matt was gay and they'd be gossiping. It would be big news in a place where not much happened, where sex wasn't on the surface and no one was openly homosexual – 'Matt Lester came out at his brother's wedding, can you imagine? What a time to choose! And fancy Annie not knowing . . . Of course, you could see it years ago. He's going to study drama at university. Well. Quite. Yes, always useless at sport. Not like his brothers.' So they'd be talking about us here, and they'd be talking about us in other places because Hawar is an entrepot for misfits, for nomads who mass and disperse, still gossiping about each other. – 'You know that wedding at the weekend? In Hawar? The groom's brother came out. Yes, gay. I know, appalling timing. His poor mother had no idea. Unlike everyone else, of course . . .'

I looked around for Matt, but saw only Sam, talking to Faisal and his brother Abdullah, and hurried towards them.

'Were you *hugging* James Hartley?' Faisal asked, impressed.

'He's an old friend.'

'It looked like he didn't want to let you go!'

'Have you seen Matt?'

'No, don't think so. What did he say?'

'I don't know. Nothing.'

'Why was he staring at you like that?' Sam asked.

'Like what?'

'I don't know . . . all keen.'

'We haven't seen each other for ages.'

'Are you going to see him again?'

'Maybe . . . I don't know . . . I'm way out of his league. Are you sure you haven't seen Matt?'

Abdullah thought he might possibly have caught sight of him near the shrubbery at the back of the garden.

I set off, walking purposefully and avoiding making eye contact with anyone, because they'd only want to ask me about James Hartley.

I could remember walking with Matt in the Ladies' Garden when he was no more than two or three and him telling me he was dreaming the world, which is quite a sophisticated philosophical position for a three-year-old. He always had a tremendous sense of his own power and indomitability: it was typical of him to think he might be capable of bringing the whole world into existence through the sheer exuberance of his imagination.

But you can't make up your own world. Other people do exist. You have to fit round them. It's one of the things you have to learn.

Eventually, I found him sitting on a bench hidden in the bushes, kicking up gravel like a child. If he'd been seven, I'd have told him to stop. It would ruin his shoes.

I sat down beside him on the stone bench. We were out of sight of everyone else, screened by thick-stemmed, fleshy shrubs, dark green in the stuttering torchlight.

'I'm sorry,' he mumbled.

'Don't . . .'

'Not for being gay. I ought to have found a better way of telling you. A better time.'

'I should have realized.'

'It just came out. I was so angry with Chris.'

'I know.'

'Have you seen Will?'

'No, I got dragged off to meet James Hartley.'

'Oh, how was he?'

'OK. I was a bit distracted. He had a horrible bloke with him who . . . Anyway, I really only wanted to get away, so I wasn't concentrating.'

'Oh, God, I'm sorry.'

'Don't be. It's not important.'

'Will's furious.'

'What for? Didn't he know?'

Matt shook his head. 'He thinks I shouldn't have come out at his wedding. He's right about that, as it happens.'

'Did Sam know?'

'No.' Matt wasn't interested in Sam; he was still worrying about Will: 'He thinks it's ruined everything: he said, "whenever mum thinks about it, she'll think about this."'

I frowned. 'He's not getting married for my benefit.'

'He thinks I've upstaged him and Maddi.'

'Matt, I suppose you *are* sure?'

'Yes.' He scuffed the gravel. 'Parents always say that, apparently.'

'Oh. Sorry to be so predictable. Stupid. How long have you known?'

'Since I was about eight, I think – but it was all mixed up with dad dying. I couldn't work it out in my head. But then when I hit adolescence . . . I did *try* with girls,' he added, as though I might think he hadn't made enough effort. 'The thing is – when you kiss a boy . . . it's completely different. Then you know.'

'Right. Have you – are you . . . in a relationship?'

He hesitated. 'No.'

'But you have been?'

'It's not all in my head, mum.'

'No.' I paused. There was clearly a limit to what I could ask him about sex. Or, in fact, wanted to know. 'When you say it's all mixed up with dad ...'

'I don't mean that that's made me gay.'

Dominant mothers, wasn't that what people said? How the hell was I supposed to have been anything else, when their father was dead?

The sound of clapping drifted over to us through the night air. I looked up. 'Oh, no, Will and Maddi must be leaving! We must see them off.'

I took his hand and tried to pull him to his feet. He shook his head. 'I'll stay here, if that's OK. I don't want to upset Will any more. You go on.'

'That doesn't seem right ...'

'Please.'

I tried to persuade him, but he was determined to stay where he was and I wanted to wave goodbye to Will and Maddi. So I kissed the top of his head. 'I love you.' And I did, I did, and always would, but I was afraid that he was going somewhere I couldn't follow, somewhere I wouldn't be able to understand, into a place of furtiveness and promiscuity and hysteria and disappointment. 'It's not your whole identity,' I said, hoping that was true.

'No. I think you're supposed to think of it as like being left-handed.'

I nodded, although I was actually thinking that he'd managed to keep me in the dark, all these years, and now he was receding into the darkness himself.

'I didn't choose this, mum,' he said. 'It chose me.'

Four

I lay awake all night, or that was how it felt, going over and over it. Matthew's gay. I hadn't realized. Yesterday he'd been one thing. Now he was another. Something had taken him out of reach into another place, of beardy kisses. You know when you kiss a boy and it's different. Scratchy, square-jawed, fierce. I thought of things I'd heard – of back rooms in dark bars where men assaulted each other in arcane rituals of self-disgust, men who had to take drugs just to be there, to work up the courage to participate, to cancel the pain. I saw them in my phosphorescent imaginings, the sort of men he'd be mixing with now, brutalized and self-hating men who wouldn't realize how much he was loved, how valuable he was. They'd want to corrupt him, would think he was corrupt already. That life wouldn't suit him, surely, all that bitchiness and queeniness and flouncing?

I was still awake when the muezzin called at dawn, a wail of protest on the quiet air. I turned my pillow over for the hundredth time. Would he ever find someone to love? Someone who'd love him? It's hard enough – it turns out – if you're heterosexual. And what proportion of the population is gay?

The sun was already beating against the blackout lining of the curtains when I finally dozed off, only to be woken again, apparently minutes later, by the noise of the television blaring from the sitting room. I looked at my watch on the bedside table. My head was fuzzy and my body felt more tired than when I'd gone to bed. But it was nine o'clock already and we were due to be out of the house by ten.

Sam was sitting in front of the news, half-dressed in long shorts and an old T-shirt. On the screen there were pictures of fractured masonry, steel reinforcing rods sticking pathetically into the air, a litter of rubble on a beach, bars that were an unrecognizable chaos of overturned tables, fallen ceilings and crumbled concrete. A hollow-eyed Indonesian was gesticulating; urgent commentary filled the room.

'Oh God . . .' I sank on to the sofa.

'Awful.'

I squeezed Sam's hand, which he removed.

Two hundred people believed dead, the reporter said. Many more injured. Mostly young holidaymakers. The hospitals couldn't cope and they were flying people to Australia.

The images blurred in front of me.

'You all right, mum?'

'This is terrible.'

'I know. But otherwise?'

I nodded. 'Is Matthew up?'

'Not yet . . .' He flicked the remote and the television screen went blank. 'Will was weird last night, wasn't he?'

'I didn't see him properly – afterwards, I mean. Did you really not know about Matt? Either of you?'

'I thought it was possible. When he has a headache it's like anyone else's raging migraine.'

'You didn't say.'

'No, well, it's not a big deal, is it?'

Not a big deal, as if Matt were the same person he'd been yesterday. But yesterday, he'd been a hundred things; today he was only one thing. At nineteen, at a time when his life should have been opening up to possibilities, he was reduced to this single overwhelming . . . *thing*.

And it was a thing I didn't understand. Yesterday, I'd known him.

He emerged blearily from his bedroom in a pair of shorts, pulling on a T-shirt, ambled across, picked up the remote and stared for a moment at the television pictures of sunshiny debris on a distant beach before flicking them off again and shaking his head. Then he put a hand on my shoulder and went to the kitchen. I watched him covertly, to see if he'd do anything gay.

He put two slices of bread in the toaster, peered in the teapot, and put the kettle on.

How long would I have gone on inventing relationships with girls, thinking he had a thing for Maya, that his sense of drama and love of gossip were just Matthew? I tried to think of what I should ask him about it. But the phone was ringing.

'We still on for today?' Chris asked when I returned to the sitting room and picked it up.

'Sure.'

'Matthew coming?'

'Of course.' The important thing was not to let Chris – or anyone, come to that – see how much this had affected me. Had to stick up for Matthew.

'So, what are you intending to do about dad?'

'Do?'

'He'll have to know, if Matt's going to stay with him next year. Ann – are you still there? He might not like the thought of it under his roof. And what if Matt wanted to bring a friend home?'

'Chris, we can talk about this later.'

In reality, I'd been thinking about dad half the night. If this was difficult for me, how would it be for him? He came from a time when those sort of people (that was how he'd think of them, as if they were unnameable) didn't live among you, or if they did, they had the decency to pretend to be normal.

'Why he wants to shove it in our faces anyway, I don't know,' Chris complained before ringing off.

The phone went again only moments later: it was Peter, this time, to report that Maddi and Will had called from the airport, where they were about to board their plane for the Maldives. I felt a twinge of jealousy that they'd rung the Franklins and not us, mixed with irritation at Will for not having called to commiserate with me about Matt or, rather, to reassure me that commiseration was unnecessary.

Peter appeared not to have heard about that – at least, he didn't mention it. 'I don't suppose anyone will ever forget that a man who gets paid large sums of money to pretend to be someone else once came to a wedding in Hawar,' he said, affecting boredom. 'He seemed annoyingly pleasant, too – I think he would have been happy to stay longer if his friends hadn't been so keen to get him away.'

'That Al Maraj bloke, looking down his nose.'

'James, as I suppose we can now call him, told me you hadn't changed a bit.'

'Yeah, well,' I said, 'right.'

Fifteen minutes before we were due to leave, Matt came out of his bedroom, where he'd been playing Motown very loudly, and announced that he didn't think he wanted to come.

I paused, midway through chopping mint for the potato salad, knife in the air. 'Sorry?'

'I don't think I can face another day with Uncle Chris.'

'But it's organized. Everyone's expecting you. And it would be like running away.'

'He's awful. He's homophobic. You know he is.'

'He won't say anything.'

'It depends how much he's had to drink . . .'

'He won't, though – not with granddad there . . . And, Matt, not going would be giving in, don't you think?'

'I don't see . . .'

'And how am I going to explain it?'

'You could say I'm ill.'

'But you're not. I'm not sure we should start lying.'

He shook his head at me, as if I didn't get it. I wished now that I'd never agreed to this day out. I'd wanted to give the family a good time before they left for Dubai, and the best thing about living in Hawar is getting out on the water. Since I don't own a boat – it's expensive, Dave was never interested, and, afterwards, whenever I considered it, I was convinced I'd end up running out of fuel, floating in the tanker lanes in the dark, adrift and alone with several parched children, while shipping powered up and down the Gulf around us – I had no option but to go with other people. It would have been easier, though, if on this occasion they'd been other other people.

'They won't get on,' I'd insisted to Diane, when she'd first suggested it. 'Antonia and David will hate my brother and sister-in-law and my dad will feel uncomfortable.'

'They don't hate you. Why should they hate your family?'

It was difficult to explain without insulting someone. Diane was Australian and impervious to the small snobberies that eddied remorselessly through Hawari expat society. She breezed along regardless, and if people tried to insult or patronize her it didn't work because she simply didn't notice.

'I suppose everyone will be gossiping already,' Matt said gloomily as we drove along the Corniche. 'That's why I didn't come out sooner. It'll be the most exciting thing that's happened in Hawar for about three decades.'

'You flatter yourself,' I said, swinging the Jeep through the gates of the Marina Club. Dad was standing outside the clubhouse on the shimmering tarmac, wiping his face on one of the handkerchiefs my mum used to hang on the tree for him at Christmas, now washed so many times they'd gone a murky grey colour. I felt upset that he hadn't gone inside, into the chilled air – but he would have been worried that the Marina Club was for members only, that someone would challenge him.

How was he going to get his head around Matthew? He thought life was threatening enough, what with muggers and binge drinkers and kids who carried knives and swore at their teachers. But he'd only read about those things; he didn't actually know any kids who were muggers or binge drinkers who carried knives.

There hadn't been any gay people when he was young. There couldn't have been, because there hadn't really been any when I was young. Kenneth Williams in the *Carry On* films: that was about it. Or those two on the radio, Julian and Sandy (had that, in fact, been Kenneth Williams too? Was there only one person taking all the gay parts in mid-twentieth-century entertainment?): they were on *Round The Horne*, a programme I assumed, as a child, that everyone was too full of Sunday dinner to get up and turn off, because it was impossible that anyone would actually choose to listen to it . . . And that seemed to be all there was by way of homosexuality, a camp joke I didn't get and wondered if anyone got, because those men didn't sound happy, sending themselves up, titillating a nation Brillo-ing meat slurry off its roasting pans. Had there been any space beneath the performance for those actors to feel that they weren't essentially silly and misbegotten? Any part of them that hadn't felt marginal, and seeping self-disgust?

I was going to ask dad to accept that Matthew was like that, was one of them? It was ridiculous. Anyone could see he wasn't.

I parked the Jeep and the boys jumped out and started unloading. Dad came across, miming wanting to help, and collided with Sam and a cool box. Then he tried to lift the waterskis out of Matt's arms, though since they were already perfectly balanced, he only managed to upend them. He turned his attention to the beers, which were still in the back of the Jeep.

I wanted to tell him impatiently to leave them to Sam, who is tall and wiry and fizzing with adolescent energy, but I knew he'd take it as criticism, would think I was saying he was past it, only good for standing by and watching. He didn't know how to have a role without being subservient, without making an enormous fuss about not taking without giving; he was going to make absolutely sure we noticed he'd put aside all self-interest, all pleasure, because he knew he wasn't important enough to be there other than to be useful to the rest of us.

I hated this lack of entitlement, which he'd spent his life trying to pass on to me, and which I often felt I was still struggling to overcome.

Matt and Sam tolerated his attempts to help good-naturedly. I wondered if they'd had practice at that, if their attitude to me had already become like their attitude to him, and had started to include pity.

I left them all to it and walked down the jetty towards Diane, who is the year four teacher at school: plump, freckly, enthusiastic, always behind the celebrations of people's birthdays and the nights out with the girls. Antonia was coming along the pontoon from the other direction from her own boat and called out to me: 'Hello, darling! Wonderful wedding ... Absolutely bloody hangover today, though ...' She looked across the marina to where Karen and Andrea were standing on a different jetty. 'I think your sister-in-law may be over there. She seems to be having a row with her daughter, so I thought I'd leave them to it.'

The Horwoods had the biggest ski boat of anyone we knew – David is the general manager of an Arab bank – which was no doubt partly why Diane had included them. Antonia greeted Matt and Sam without curiosity and directed them towards this vast craft. She couldn't have heard about Matt's coming out yet either.

I rounded up Chris, who was inspecting the yachts, and Karen and Andrea, who were fighting in an angry undertone about whether Andrea should be wearing heels with her shorts. Diane organized everyone, distributing us between the boats: Chris, Karen and me with her and Alain, everyone else with the Horwoods.

David and Alain started the engines, eased the boats away from the jetties and idled through the marina. I settled down at the back, not minding the engine noise as we let rip into the Gulf, grateful not to have to think, to be able to let go and be bumped mindlessly over the water, staring out at the expanse of sea as my hair whipped round my face and salt dried on my skin. I could taste the Gulf on my tongue; the hard brightness of the sky filled up my vision and rinsed my senses.

After about half an hour, Alain slowed the engines as we

negotiated the shallows and Karen moved to the back, to sit beside me.

'Chris told me about Matthew,' she said in a voice dripping with concern; 'I'm very sorry.'

'Uh-huh,' I said non-committally. There was no way I could say out loud what I felt. Not to Karen – not, I suspected, to anyone. I was alarmed by how politically incorrect my thoughts seemed to be. I wasn't going to give any opportunities to people who actually were politically incorrect.

She put her hand on my leg, fingers damp on my bare flesh. 'It's such a shame . . . but, perhaps, you know, it's just a phase . . .?'

'I don't think so.'

'Perhaps he could see someone?' she suggested. 'Counsellor, therapist, someone like that?'

She thought he was sick, needed therapy, was mentally ill.

It made sense of why he'd been reluctant to come out before now, anyway. If people were going to assume you were sick in the head, you probably wouldn't go out of your way to explain yourself to them. Matt was a perfectly happy person who had loads of friends, and who posed no danger to himself or to other people. So to be thought sufficiently psychologically disturbed as to be in need of help from mental health professionals must be quite upsetting.

Clearly, it wasn't a phase. You wouldn't expose yourself to suggestions that you get your mind fixed if you weren't absolutely sure.

'I think he might find that rather insulting,' I said quietly. 'It's not something that needs curing.'

You'd think by coming out you might seize the initiative. But the reality was that Matt seemed to have ceded it. He probably thought he was saying 'This is who I am, now live with it,' but Karen was hearing something quite different. She now saw him as some kind of inferior, damaged being about whom she and Chris were entitled to speculate as much, and as publicly, as they liked, because he was less than whole. Given other circumstances, Chris and Karen could easily have been the sort of secret police officers in totalitarian regimes who get people locked up in asylums because they don't like the look of them, or because they want their flat.

'All I mean is that there could be a reason for it,' Karen persisted. 'It could be like . . . attention-seeking.'

I imagined the two of them in their room at the Sheraton, picking over Matthew's sexuality – a whole new topic, with a satisfying range of accompanying emotions all the way from injury to self-righteousness. 'Will's always been so clever and everything,' Karen went on, 'and then getting married, and to such a beautiful girl . . .'

'I don't think . . .'

'Perhaps he does feel he's, you know, *gay* – at the moment,' Karen went on, 'and I dare say he believes he can't help it – but you do hear about people who get over it and marry and have children and lead very good lives.'

'Do you?'

'Perhaps it's like any temptation, and it can be overcome?'

I stared at her, then I stood up and said 'This is Al-Hidd. It's just a sandspit, but very nice.'

I felt exhausted already, and this was only my first conversation about it. Prejudice might well be unacceptable in some parts of the world (though not, unfortunately, here in Hawar) – but even in supposedly sophisticated places it was clearly far from non-existent. Karen lived in London, a city about as tolerant as you could find, yet she not only felt that Matthew's sexuality made him in need of curing, she was prepared to say so, out loud, and to me, his mother. She didn't think there was anything to be ashamed of in that.

Her hostility made me determined to stick up for him. Not that I hadn't been already, but now I felt militant.

'About your dad,' she said quickly, glancing up at the others, at the front: 'Chris doesn't want to be the one to break it to him.'

'He won't be.'

'When are you going to do it? Before we go to Dubai?'

'Yes, perhaps. Or when you get back.'

'What, next Sunday? We're only here for a few hours!'

'Oh, for Chrissakes, Karen, I'm going to do it, OK?'

Alain must have heard something – perhaps only my tone of voice: he looked up and raised his eyebrows. I jumped over the side of the boat and waded to the shore, getting my shorts wet.

Antonia was already on the sand, putting up an umbrella while Matt helped spread out towels. 'I should ski,' she urged him, 'before David changes his mind and wants a beer. Matt's promised to teach Andrea,' she explained to me and Karen, who was trudging up the sand behind me.

'To waterski?' Karen sounded doubtful.

'He's very good.'

'Really?'

Antonia looked oddly at Karen and turned back to me. 'Wasn't the wedding terrific? The Franklins are *such* a lovely family,' she said loudly, sensing something awkward, unspoken, in the atmosphere and deploying her usual tactic against embarrassment, which is to turn up the volume. 'I hadn't seen Millie for ages, but she's going to be beautiful, isn't she, like her mother? And Maddi, of course,' she added. 'Katherine said Millie's already been offered a bit of modelling work ... And then it was all topped off by James Hartley turning up! Amazing, really ... What was he like? Had he changed much?'

'I only spoke to him for a couple of minutes.'

'Is he as sexy as in his films?'

'I suppose, yeah, quite,' I acknowledged, not wanting to make him seem less interesting.

Antonia handed me a beer from the cool box and stood up to watch Andrea trying to get up on her skis.

'Honestly, look at her,' Karen grumbled, joining us, 'she's not going to do it like that.' Matthew was leaning out of the side of the boat, calling out instructions. 'She's like a porpoise, all bottom and middle. No, there she goes!' Andrea flopped awkwardly into the water.

'It always takes a few goes.'

'She won't diet. Then she wonders why she hasn't got a boyfriend.'

'How old is she?' Antonia asked briskly. 'Sixteen? Frankly, dear, boyfriends are *not* what you want at this age. My Flissi's sixteen and she's had several and they're all ghastly. Either they're spotty and inarticulate or they're older and you wonder what they could possibly want with your daughter . . . Ooops.' Andrea had fallen off her skis again.

'I sometimes think everything she does is to spite me,' Karen complained. 'Eating chips on the way home from school and spilling out of those awful tarty clothes she insists on wearing – it doesn't matter how self-destructive it is, if it annoys me.'

'That's how they are at this age,' Antonia said – 'all over the place, looking for ways to hurt themselves because they think it'll punish us, which of course it will. Just be grateful it's not worse. She could be anorexic, or cutting herself . . .'

You had to admire her posh bravura. Flissi had had a whole year off school, in and out of clinics, trying to get over her bulimia.

Matthew was in the water now: we watched as he rose, dripping, from the waves, slim but muscular, like a minor deity on a monoski, zipping over the wake and back, jumping and landing, and I thought it was almost painful, how much I loved him.

Diane and Alain came back from their walk to the other end of the sandspit. Sam was up on the monoski now, less flamboyantly; then Matt drove the boat so that David could have a turn. Alain started the barbecue and by the time the others came in, it was blazing.

'God, did you see me?' Andrea exclaimed, throwing herself down on a towel. Her eyes were red from the salt. 'I was *terrible*.'

'You'll get up next time,' Matt promised, taking a swig from a bottle of water and passing it to her.

Panic passed like a shadow across her scoured features. 'Um . . .' she avoided his eyes, 'd'you have another one?'

'Good heavens, Matthew's not got germs!' Antonia said disapprovingly, though she pulled an unopened bottle out of the cool box and threw it to Andrea. 'I thought young people didn't care about that sort of thing . . . Mine don't, anyway – Toby's fridge in Bristol, honestly, it's like some sort of salmonella breeding tank!'

I walked down the beach, feeling awful. I was his mother. It was my job to stand up for him, to point out that being gay doesn't make you HIV positive and anyway you're not going to become infected from a water bottle. I was supposed to defend him.

But that would have meant making an issue of it: telling people in the wrong way, sort of accidentally. Plus it would have ruined the day. No one would have been able to think about anything else. I wouldn't have been able to protect my father in front of these people, who already intimidated him . . . Was that what Matthew would have wanted, for me to make a scene?

I felt slightly sick. This had been my first mother-of-a-gay-person test and I'd failed. I could have said something but I'd said nothing. I was filled with self-loathing.

'Now, that *is* a boat,' David was saying, his feet in the water, peering out to sea through his binoculars. He handed them to me, because I happened to be nearby. I looked politely, although I'm not that interested in boats.

'Surely not other people?' Antonia said exasperatedly, offering us an olive from a plastic container. 'I really thought on Sunday we might have the place to ourselves.'

'People with boats like that probably don't have to work.'

Diane squinted into the haze. 'Oh God, it's not full of call girls?'

I handed her the glasses. I had a pretty good idea who it was, and I thought that they wouldn't land here once they realized the sandspit was already occupied. They must have a crew on that gin palace who'd be able to think of somewhere else to take them?

But the trouble was there weren't that many places like Al-Hidd off Hawar. Most of the islets had been seized by members of the ruling family and now had palaces on them, fenced round with gold-tipped wrought iron. Here, you could almost have been in the Indian Ocean, the sand was so white and fine, the lapping water so warm, the sky so endless. You'd never have known you were in the Gulf, with its busy lanes of tankers and warships, its aluminium smelting factories and desalination plants stringing the foreshore, its rearing cities and steaming tarmac.

The launch slowed about a hundred metres offshore. The crew could be seen moving around the guardrails, preparing to launch a tender.

I went back up the beach and fished a T-shirt out of my bag. While James Hartley could conceivably persuade himself I hadn't changed much when I was dressed in a dusky pink silk dress from Soft Hands Tailors in the souk and high-heeled sandals from Mansouri Footwear in the Hyatt Tower, I didn't think this illusion could be sustained if he had to look at me wearing only a bikini.

'Will they try to throw us off the island?' Karen asked.

'Why on earth would they do that?' Antonia said. 'We were here first.'

The tender was launched; four people clambered in and chugged towards us. As they approached, we could see that they were James Hartley, Fiona Eckhart and another woman, plus Nezar Al Maraj, who was steering. We hovered, not knowing whether to pretend we hadn't noticed and were having a great time by ourselves or simply to stand and stare.

'Mum, he's stalking you!' Matt said.

James jumped out first and, leaving the others to pull the boat in, he bounded up the beach.

'Annie! What an amazing coincidence! And – is it? Can it really be – Ted? I was trying and trying to find you last night. Where were you?'

He hugged my dad, leaving him pink and breathless. 'And Chris?' he said, slapping him on the back, 'you look great, mate.'

I introduced everyone else. Nezar Al Maraj was wearing a pale blue linen shirt and khaki shorts, both obviously expensive; he had, I could now see, deep-set eyes that looked as though they were probably capable of assessing any situation. In the light of a brilliant cloudless day, he seemed like someone who was generally in charge of things. I blushed, then felt a rush of dislike. He had made me look a fool. Nobody noticed, though, except perhaps Al Maraj himself, because they were all focused on James, who was shaking hands enthusiastically, still exclaiming at finding us here. It is odd to be beautiful: people want to stand next to you, to bask in your presence. They want you to like them, and they put themselves out to accommodate you, to make your life easier and pleasanter. James had always been handsome and I suspect that things had always been like this for him, long before he became famous.

'And these are my sons,' I said at last, 'Matt and Sam.'

'She doesn't look old enough to have all these children, does she, Nezar?'

'No.'

'You really do look fantastic, Annie . . .' he said enthusiastically. 'And this is Rosie Rossiter,' he added, gesturing to the tall, gamine girl with hair scraped into a baseball cap, who'd picked her way up the beach behind him like some delicate wading bird.

'I saw you in something last year,' Diane said to her, 'weren't you that character who had the DNA of a plant?'

Rosie grinned. 'Yes, that was my first big role. Half human, half rubber plant. Now I'm James's love interest. I suppose it's promotion.'

Everyone laughed, although she was young enough to be his daughter.

Fiona shook her head at the beer Antonia was trying to press on her, although James accepted, as did Al Maraj. Probably some Hawari thing about hospitality.

'Everyone's delighted you're here,' David said ambassadori-ally, meaning in the Gulf rather than standing around on this bit of sand self-consciously as if at some semi-nude cocktail party. 'We thought the film might fall through, with all this Iraq talk.'

'Nearly did,' James said cheerfully. 'Nezar's single-handedly rescued this project three times since July.'

'Everyone here is hoping your film will say something a bit different about the Gulf,' Antonia explained: 'We do get fed up when people at home think everybody here's a terrorist.'

'You can imagine the trouble with the insurers, with all this war stuff,' James said.

Alain frowned. 'Some of us are still hoping there won't *be* a war.'

'Well, we can hope,' Al Maraj said in a way that suggested hoping was a complete waste of time.

'We're trying to persuade Ann to come home if it does start.'

'Dad, this is home!'

'It won't be like 1991, you know,' Al Maraj said severely.

I looked at him coolly. 'We know that.'

'Come down here, Annie,' James suggested, walking towards the shore. I blushed at the brazenness of his attempt to get me on my own. 'Is everything all right?' he asked with concern, as soon as we were out of earshot. 'I was a bit worried about you last night.'

'Yes, thank you. I'm sorry; I was all over the place.' I took a deep breath and looked into his eyes, which were the eyes of someone I knew, someone I'd turned to long ago, when Chris and dad were being impossible, when my mum was dead and everyone expected me to look after them, to cook and iron and worry on their behalf and talk to people on their account and *cope*. I hadn't been up to it, but James had helped, not least because he offered me escape, into something entirely different, sexiness and irresponsibility. 'It was . . . only,' I hesitated . . . but I could do this. '. . . Matt had just told me he was gay.'

'Blimey! What, at the wedding?'

'Yes, about two minutes before you arrived.'

'Oh, great timing on our part, then . . .'

'It would have been weird whenever.' I smiled. 'But I'm not usually that inarticulate.'

'You weren't. Not at all. But . . . so . . . this was . . . a surprise?'

'A shock, I think, more than a surprise. In a way, I can't believe I didn't realize.'

He looked at me carefully, then smiled. 'It's great to see you again,' he said, 'really fantastic. You know, I've never known anyone like you . . .'

'No?' I said doubtfully.

'I've missed you. And the thing is, Annie, you're as sexy as ever . . .'

'James, I'm sorry,' Fiona Eckhart interrupted, joining us, 'but we probably shouldn't keep the chef waiting much longer.'

'No. He's been flown in from Spain specially,' he explained. 'Besides, you'll be wanting your barbecue. But, look, I'd really like to see you again.'

Fiona tutted. 'Please, James, don't go making any arrangements without checking your schedule with me first.'

We walked slowly back up the beach, it seemed to me prolonging the short distance, to where Diane was flapping a recycling sack ready for James's beer can with a lot of important rustling. Al Maraj and Rosie seemed to have exhausted the conversational possibilities and were fidgeting but if James noticed how keen they were to get away, it didn't bother him. 'How is Thornton Heath?' he asked Chris genially. 'I never get back.'

'No, well, you wouldn't, would you?' Karen pointed out. Chris took the opportunity to explain that, actually, he and Karen lived in Caterham now, and they were trying to get dad to move as well but he was very stubborn, even though they'd be able to get him a really good deal, because of being in the estate agency business – at which of course they'd done very well in recent years, thanks to property prices, which were likely to continue because whatever people said, there really was no prospect of a slowdown in the foreseeable future.

'Chris,' I interrupted, 'I think they have to get back.'

James kissed all the women on both cheeks, adding a hug for me. The others all shook hands. Al Maraj looked at me in a way that seemed unnecessarily astringent, although I wasn't the one who'd set out to make people look stupid.

'I hope we haven't ruined your day,' I said, walking with James back down the beach. 'You were probably planning to swim here.'

'Oh, we can swim anywhere.' To be honest, their boat was nearly as big as the island. 'I don't suppose you're going to be at this reception at the embassy tomorrow night?'

'No, 'fraid not.'

He frowned. 'They haven't done a good job of getting together people I actually want to see. Look, will you come for dinner?'

'Sure.' There was something anxious in his improbably blue eyes. I smiled. 'Call me.'

As soon as the tender had chugged away, they all turned on me.

'What were you talking about all that time?'

'How friendly *were* you before?'

'Oh, didn't you know?' (That was Karen.)

'Well, he's obviously madly in love with you still,' Antonia declared.

'Don't be ridiculous!'

'If he'd looked at me like that . . .' Diane said, grinning and raising her eyebrows at Alain.

'Are you seeing him again?' Antonia demanded.

'I don't know. Fiona Eckhart says they're going to be very busy.'

'You'll have to bring him over to supper. I'm sure he'd like to see a bit of local life.'

'Darling,' David said, 'you are not local life.'

'We were very young,' I explained, when Diane asked me why on earth we ever split up. 'And, to judge by his casting opposite Rosie, he still is.'

'She's very pretty, isn't she?' Karen said wistfully.

'I think she looks like a head on a stick,' Matt replied. 'I bet she won't eat much of the specially flown in Michelin-starred lunch.'

'That Al Maraj doesn't say much, does he?'

'Probably just as well,' I said, 'because when he does he's quite unpleasant.'

'He and Fiona didn't like it *at all* when James was talking to you.'

'No, he glared and she got more tense than she was already,' Diane agreed. 'Obviously, *they* can see there's unfinished business . . .'

'I told you he'd want to see you again,' dad said.

'You lot!' I laughed. 'You wouldn't be this interested if he was still a plumber.'

'I don't know,' Antonia said, 'if he looked like that . . .'

'Anyway,' Diane said, 'he's not.'

We ate the steaks while the others asked a whole lot more questions about my not very interesting Friday nights in the King's Head and Saturdays at the pictures twentysomething years earlier. When we'd exhausted that – which didn't take long, to be honest – we talked about how cold Al Maraj and Fiona Eckhart were and how much more likeable James was, how unaffected, despite being so rich and famous, and also very good-looking, which always helps.

It came as no real surprise to anyone that I didn't tell dad about Matt before the family left for Dubai that evening. We stayed on Al-Hidd until nearly sunset, then cruised back to the Marina Club over water spattered crimson and orange. Andrea still hadn't managed to get up on waterskis, despite a couple more attempts. Chris had succeeded on his second try and said that waterskiing wasn't nearly as difficult as everyone wanted you to think.

By the time I'd driven the family back to the Sheraton, there wasn't time for them to do much except shower and change while we loaded their bags into the Jeep. I organized a taxi and we followed it out to the airport.

'They often say,' Karen observed at check in, watching Matt unload the luggage from the trolley, 'that with, you know, people like that, Matt, there's a fear of the opposite sex.'

'All his friends are girls,' I objected. 'Jodie, Maya, Lucy . . .' I should have realized that wasn't normal.

'I wonder if they can *tell*, just by looking at each other? Not that there can be many of them here. It's against the law, isn't it?'

'There must be the same numbers as anywhere else,' I said, hating myself for having been inveigled into this conversation, in which 'they' were once again a sort of sub-species.

I remembered Matt coming home when he was thirteen and announcing that a boy at school had told him that there's an Arabic saying: 'a girl for babies, a boy for pleasure, a melon for ecstasy'. It was the sort of rumour that did go round among westerners about the Arabs and might easily have been put about in the first place by Hawaris, to amuse themselves at our expense. But for all I knew there could well be a powerful homoerotic current running through Hawari society, in the coffee shops, mosques, the rooms from which women were banished . . .

'In Soho, you sometimes see them walking down the streets, holding hands,' Karen said with distaste, 'all over each other. It's very annoying when you come out of the theatre. At least they don't do that here. I mean, I'm not against it in private . . .'

In fact, it was perfectly acceptable for men in Qalhat to walk down the street holding hands, though you saw it less now than you used to. It was men and women who weren't allowed to touch in public, although I'd seen couples in thobes and abayas holding hands on the beach. As ever, the whole thing was more complicated than it looked.

'We should go through,' Chris said, coming up with the boarding passes.

Karen patted my arm. 'You're doing very well, considering.'

At home, Matt unloaded the waterskis and I cleared out the cool box, wondering if I had somehow made him gay, or if he'd been born gay, or if it was a combination of the two, and if so, what had triggered it, whether something in the womb, or subsequently. Not that there was much point to these thoughts: I wasn't going to come up with the answer. Later, I heard the clatter of a keyboard from his room. I put on the dishwasher and poured a glass of wine, sat down on the sofa and looked around. Apart from the fact that Will had gone, everything appeared normal: furniture, curtains, books, magazines, a pair of Sam's flip flops in the middle of the floor. I hadn't had much sleep, so that may have accounted for it, but I felt as though my world, which for so long had been uneventful and even quite boring, was suddenly subject to entirely different forces, as if I could no longer rely on gravity to hold things down. We were being shaken up and jolted around in space and there were no rules for landing, or none that we could make sense of. Matt was gay. James Hartley was in Hawar. He'd said I was sexy. It was as if the poles had flipped: anything could happen.

Five

'Darling, no, he didn't! But that's so *mean*! Your hair's *gorgeous*!'

Matthew seemed to have got gayer. Did he used to laugh in that high-pitched screechy way? Did his phone conversations require quite so many exclamation marks?

Perhaps he felt that he had permission to be camp now. Much as I loved him, and even though I could see that it might also be permission to be himself, I thought I could come to find this a bit trying.

'Morning, madam.' Maria slid into the kitchen, kicking off her sandals on the back step in a single, practised flippy movement.

I wondered if she already knew about Matthew – if, perhaps, she'd known before. She knew Dave was dead before I told her, though she'd pretended not to.

'Madam, was lovely wedding,' was all she said now, clearing away the breakfast plates. 'Maddi look very beautiful.'

She swayed across the kitchen, plump and slow and erotic – which is not, perhaps, the ideal mode for someone whose main job is housework. But she'd been great with the kids, especially when they were young, making up in lusciousness for what she lacked in speed. When she rolled down the track from Al Janabiyya compound to the main road and the bus stop, swinging her arms as if inviting the world into herself, she seemed to be in rhythm with the earth.

'And Will handsome,' she went on, 'and he made very good speech.'

Maria had two children of her own in Colombo. They were grown-up now, both graduates, but they'd been four and five when she came to work for me. They'd lived with Maria's mother, safely away from Maria's husband, who could be violent when he was drunk, which was most of the time. The revelation of the children's existence, a month after Maria started working for me, had upset me: it was no wonder she was so loving to Will when her own children were a thousand miles away, missing being held because she was holding him. I immediately said we'd pay for her to go home for a month every year, rather than the two years required by the employment laws. The following day, she'd come to me and asked for the money instead.

That was when I realized how unalike we really were. I agreed, obviously – how could you not? – although I was appalled. But I was humbled too. I simply couldn't imagine what it would be like to think like this. To need to. Maria came from a place where seeing your babies was not the most important thing. It was disturbing that two such different ways of understanding the world could exist so closely. Under her placid winsomeness, her sexy torpor, Maria was raw with life's harshness in a way that made me feel inadequate.

'Father Andrew make good address too . . .'

'I'm not sure he calls himself Father,' I said vaguely, looking around for the car keys.

'And film star come.' They were under the *Hawar Daily News*. He was everywhere: his photograph took up half the front page. 'Madam know him.'

'Yes, but not for years, since I was about Matt's age.'

'He will come here, madam?'

'I don't know. Probably not.'

'He is not married, madam.'

'Sam,' I called, 'are you coming? Only we're going to be late.'

At school, staff kept dropping by my desk for a chat, wanting to know what James Hartley had said to me at the wedding and whether he'd changed much and if I was going to see him again, interrupting my internet investigations into the legal status of homosexuality in Hawar.

As I suspected, being gay or, at least, doing anything about it, was against the law all over the Gulf. In Hawar, homosexual activity carried a maximum penalty of ten years' imprisonment, but it appeared that no one had actually been charged for more than a decade – although in 1995, a dozen Filipinos had been deported without trial for 'engaging in immoral activities', which seemed, reading between the lines, to have involved some kind of gay sex party.

In theory, homosexuality was a serious crime. You certainly wouldn't have wanted to get caught. But the authorities didn't appear to be over-zealous in their attempts to root out gay men. Or not, anyway, at the moment. It was always possible things might change: parliament was given to flexing its muscles from time to time over cultural matters, largely because it didn't have much power to do anything else. There had been a big fuss last year about the rights of government employees to wear beards and, a few months before that, some MPs had been behind the street demonstrations that eventually stopped a concert by a female Lebanese singer, on the grounds that she was supposed to be a bit raunchy. The Gulf may have been the only place in the world where young men can be persuaded to demonstrate because a woman is showing too much cleavage.

'Are you OK?' We were in the dining hall and Diane had been describing our day on Al-Hidd to Sue.

'What? Oh, yes.'

'You were miles away.'

'Probably thinking about James Hartley!' Sue said.

I wondered if I should tell them now about Matthew – after all, it was the pretending that was poisonous. That was what I'd decided: that it was a good thing that he'd come out, so that the secret wouldn't sit like pus under his skin. But I wasn't sure I was up to dealing with the fuss today – with Sue's officious concern, with all the questions when the news went round the school. It was bad enough having everyone ask me every five minutes about James Hartley, without them wanting to know about Matt as well. They'd find out soon enough. That was the sort of place it was. Plus, we were surrounded by small children. It was easy enough to find reasons to avoid saying anything. So I didn't explain, and then regretted it later, thinking that all the time I didn't say, the knowledge was suppurating.

Shopping malls are an art form in the Gulf: despite the desert outside, you can shop under Italian colonnades where roofs mimic blue skies scattered with cirrus clouds (never in reality seen in this part of the world) or wander through a fantasy of Arabia, created out of stained glass, pink concrete and crenellations, where Debenhams, Accessorize, Marks & Spencer, J. C. Penney, Virgin Megastores and assorted other international brands vie for attention behind plate-glass windows. We have fewer of these gruesomely themed edifices than most of the other Gulf states, because of having less oil and so less money for crazy development. This seems to me a good thing, although not everyone agrees. Cheryl says it's ridiculous that you have to go to Dubai for top-grade sportswear.

The Pearl Mall, through which I was walking later that day, was positively restrained, with its skiddy marble floors, spotlights, water pouring down stainless steel columns and white sculptures on the ceiling in the shape of dhow sails. The really big retailers don't bother with Hawar, so the shops in the Pearl Mall tend to be stylish rather than brash – although, unfortunately, also prohibitively expensive. I was only taking a shortcut to the French baker's in Seef Road, mainly because it was deliciously cool inside. It was also empty. The Pearl Mall is never crowded, even in the evenings, when the local families come out to shop and be seen, but this was lunchtime, and there was no one here apart from a few Hawari women idling near the shops selling Dior and Versace. I was thinking about all the signs of Matt's difference over the years, things I'd chosen to miss or overlook: his attempts to get out of football practice at primary school, the time he'd been to play with his friend Ben after school – he would have been about six – and ended up spending the afternoon with Ben's sister Amy and her My Little

Pony collection instead. 'Matthew's the only boy I've ever met who likes My Little Pony!' Amy had announced breathlessly when I arrived to pick him up. Then there had been that silk scarf he'd bought in a second-hand shop in London and worn for months when he was fourteen, which now seemed like code for something he couldn't say ... I was so deep in thought I almost missed Andrew, even though he was wearing a lime green T-shirt.

He was looking in the window of Al Fakhro Shoes. When I stopped to say hello, he said he'd been looking for a pair of Converse trainers, but his feet seemed to be too big.

'There's a better place, in the souk, where the boys go. You know where the gold souk meets the materials souk?'

'Near the old post office?'

'No, that's the other end. I could draw you a map ...' I groped in my bag for a pen and paper.

'We could have coffee,' Andrew suggested, 'if you've got time?'

'Sure ...' We walked towards the other end of the mall, shoes slapping on the marble, surrounded by cool empty space, assaulted by the artificial brightness.

In the Starbucks outlet at the far end of the mall, a young Hawari couple were whispering at a table in the back corner, half in shadow, the young woman's abaya pushed backwards across her hair. They looked up briefly, then went back to each other.

I went over to the counter to order the coffees, while Andrew politely chose a table as far from the couple as possible and flicked through the *Hawar Daily News*.

'They're going to make it illegal to buy alcohol in national dress,' he said, closing the paper as I came over.

'Will that change anything?'

'I can't see how ... Presumably Hawaris will send their house boys and the Saudis'll change into tracksuits at the border. You'd think the parliament could find something better to do.'

He nodded down at his coffee. 'I had another house-maid slavery case this morning. Father Joseph gets three a month.'

He pushed aside the newspaper; James Hartley stared out of the front page into the middle distance.

'I spoke to his producer last night at the embassy. Al Maraj,' he said, nodding at the photograph.

'Oh, I'm very sorry.'

'I thought he was a friend of yours?'

'No.'

'He said he'd met you twice.'

'Once he spoke to me entirely in Arabic. The second he hardly spoke at all, just looked grumpy. He's rather pleased with himself, if you ask me.'

'Oh,' Andrew was taken aback, 'I thought he was rather interesting. He wants to try to get some sort of local film industry started – to set up a fund with his studio and emirati investors to back local directors.'

'You obviously made more headway with him than I did.' I stirred my latte. 'Maybe he's one of those Arab men who hasn't got much time for women?'

'He's not as immediately charming as James Hartley, obviously,' Andrew said mischievously, 'but that seems unlikely: he's lived a long time in New York . . .'

'Must just be me then.'

He smiled. 'How are things – you know, with Matthew and all that?'

I looked up at him in surprise. 'You know about Matt?'

'You don't mind? My mentioning it? I thought . . . well, Will rang and told me.'

'He rang you from the Maldives?'

'No, before they left. From the airport.'

So the Franklins had merited a call from Hawar International Airport, and so had Andrew. And I hadn't.

'I think he felt a bit guilty for overreacting,' Andrew said – although, if this were true, it would have been all the more reason for Will to phone. If there was some sort of apology being offered here, I didn't want it second-hand through the vicar. 'It must have been a shock, Matthew coming out like that,' he went on and I was afraid that he was moving into professional mode, complete with a specially concerned voice.

'Mmn. But, you know,' I said breezily, 'it's fine.'

'It's not the whole of him, of course.'

Something about this struck me as not quite right. 'You don't disapprove?' I asked. I knew the Church was always arguing about gays.

'Me? Goodness! Not at all.' He picked up the sugar packet and tore tiny nicks in the top.

It occurred to me that even if Andrew didn't disapprove, Will's recent entanglement with Christianity might have given him the idea that homosexuality was a sin. While this didn't seem terribly plausible – it was 2002 and Will had a degree in history – I couldn't think of a better reason for the huffy behaviour. 'But the Church . . .?'

'Ah, well, yes,' Andrew said, as if this was a whole different matter. 'The Church is in a mess about it, frankly. It's like women priests all over again, but worse. Because of course there are more women.'

I wasn't sure I was following, entirely, but Andrew evidently had something important to say on this subject and he intended to finish. 'The Church officially now accepts that people may not be able to help being homosexual – it's not in itself a sin – but they're not supposed to do anything about it. This leads,' he tore too roughly at the top of the sugar packet and the contents spilled on the table, 'to an obsession with what people do in their bedrooms.' He swept the sugar into a pile with the side of his hand. 'So, if I had a gay couple, who were living together, come to church – which probably isn't going to happen in Hawar, but still . . . what am I supposed to do?'

'I don't know,' I said, 'ignore it?'

'Overlook it because politeness is more important than sin?'

I think this was perhaps meant to be a trick question, although as it happens I do think politeness is pretty important, and I have quite an obscure sense of sin.

'The trouble is, these prejudices are deep-rooted in our history. Half the thirty-six crimes punishable by death in Mosaic law involve sex.'

Did he talk like this to Will? Did Will talk like this to him? Matt was right, they were weird.

'Anyway,' he sighed, 'we're hoping the new archbishop will sort it out.' He tipped the last of the sugar into an ashtray and looked at me properly for the first time. 'So, how about that map?'

In the car, I pushed my abaya back under the passenger seat where it had been lying since September 11th, unused and almost forgotten, except on days like today when Sam kicked it out on his way to school. Even though I'd never felt I needed it, I still wasn't quite ready to return it to the shelf at the top of the wardrobe. There had been a different kind of restlessness in the villages in recent months: people stared at you with franker hostility, as if they thought you'd taken something from them, as if you might be on the other side. The atmosphere was more febrile than I could remember. It wasn't a clash of civilizations, like some people said, but there was an unease with each other's foreignness, more of a souk mentality than ever before: this street for spices, this one for cloth; this village for shi'ias, this one for sunnis; this area for locals, this for expats.

If the Americans invaded Iraq – and I suspected Al Maraj was right that they would – this suspiciousness would probably grow. It wouldn't be anything like 1991, when most Hawaris had viewed Saddam Hussein's invasion of Kuwait as an act of aggression against the rest of the Gulf. Any American-led invasion would be the act of aggression. Even the emir had come down off the fence sufficiently to say publicly that he hoped there would be no interference in Iraq (though there had certainly been no attempt to scale down the American base here). As for us, the American, British, probably even French individuals living here, the upshot would be that we'd be seen by the locals as some kind of neo-colonial fifth column, regardless of what we thought of the actions of our governments. I tucked the abaya back under the seat, out of scuffing and scurfing reach of Sam's trainers, thinking that if I did need it, it would be covered in whatever lived under there – fragments of apple and banana, old sweets and dusty wrappers. I wouldn't look like a Hawari woman at all.

'You've got endless messages on the machine inviting you to dinner,' Matt announced, when I got home. 'Antonia and David Horwood, the Davenports, Shaikh Isa bin Mohammed and Ali and Robin Verbeck. It must be because I've come out.'

I put the kettle on. 'Should we talk about it?'

'I'm not sure there's much to say, but OK.' He hooked his leg over the kitchen bench and looked up at me obligingly.

'Like,' I fumbled for what it was I needed to understand, 'were there other gay people at school?'

'No. Not openly.'

'You weren't bullied?'

'Not at the International School. A bit at primary. You knew I didn't fit in. I wasn't that interested in football. And I was in love with a boy called Adrian Price.'

'Who?'

'Mum! My first love and you've forgotten him already! Dark hair, pale skin.'

All the things you miss, even when you think you're concentrating. Matt had been bullied and, even though I'd worked at the school and been there all the time, I hadn't noticed.

'I didn't say anything,' he admitted. 'I'm not completely stupid. And then it happened again when I was about ten, which is when I decided that if the feelings were natural, which they obviously were, they had to be OK.'

'I wish you'd said.'

'You would have thought it wasn't possible to know. You'd

90

have said something like, "Oh, well, that's fine darling, but don't make up your mind, eh? You might feel differently in five years' time." So we'd have been in exactly the same place now.'

I didn't think so. 'How old were you when you told your friends?'

'Thirteen. I told Jodie and Chloe, first . . . Then I became quite camp at school, in the hope, I think, that people would work it out for themselves.'

'And Will didn't?'

'I was a bit beneath his notice at school. You know how wrapped up he was in all his stuff . . . Look, I know you're thinking I should've told you sooner. The trouble is, there's never a right time. Once I hadn't said at eight, it was always going to be too late.'

I hated to think of him longing for something he wasn't allowed to speak of, bewildered by shame.

'So, if there wasn't anyone at school . . .'

'Mum, this is a bit tricky . . .'

'Why?'

'There are some things I need to keep private.'

'But how do you . . . how do people . . . There aren't any gay bars here, are there?'

'There are other things. Coffee shops. Private parties.'

I stared at him, thinking that he must have lied to me about where he'd been. Private parties?

'There's a high level of tolerance among Hawaris, in fact, as long as it's discreet. If you tried to have a gay identity, your family'd probably cart you off to a psychiatrist. That's if they didn't throw you down the stairs. D'you remember that incident on the Nile last year? The Queen Boat?'

'No.'

'Mum, you must! Lots of people were arrested.'

I had absolutely no recollection of anything to do with a Queen Boat. Things that happened to gay people hadn't seemed that important last year.

'It was a party boat for gay men in Egypt,' Matt explained. 'There was a raid. A lot of people are still in prison, awaiting trial. It was all political.'

I frowned, not understanding.

'Islamists,' Matt said patiently. 'They're a threat, so governments try to look Islamic. To, like, undermine them.'

I was still trying to remember, to work out why I hadn't cared about this. It sounded terrible.

'People used to get worked up about women,' Matt said, I think echoing something Andrew had been saying earlier (though I couldn't be sure, because his conversation had seemed to be with himself as much as me), 'but only the Taliban seem to do that now. If you want to whip up outrage, even in Egypt, you have to go for gays.'

'So if a Hawari thinks he's gay, he has to pretend he's not?'

'Yes. Sex is manageable, on the whole. It's love that's the problem. But it's not really surprising when you think about it – it's like, at the magazine, there's a sense of what's appropriate to publish, that thing about avoiding *fitna*. Which can be good – no one really wants social upset – but can also lead to complete denial . . . And you know what they're like here: family means more than anything. It's inconceivable you could lead a responsible life other than by getting married and having children.'

It occurred to me that I'd let Matt down in the last few days by seeing everything about him through the prism of his sexuality. I'd been prepared to dismiss all the things I love about him, and that other people admire – like his intuitiveness and interest in other people – as a function of his being gay, as if his appealing qualities could now be explained away by his being more feminine than other boys, by a distorted brain and nervous system, endocrine upset. His charm, sense of humour, his capacity for empathy were all (in this way of looking at things) undermined and invalidated by the weirdness of his being homosexual, his attractiveness only a side-effect of something unfortunate. The logical conclusion of this way of thinking was that he would have been better off being insensitive, inarticulate, and straight.

I could begin to see now how unfair this was. He *was* thoughtful and intuitive, and it didn't matter why. Those qualities weren't his homosexuality. They were Matthew and, while it may have been the case that his emotional maturity probably owed quite a lot to his having had so much more to think about than most kids, if he hadn't had, or found, the warm, ready intelligence, he couldn't have come to terms with his difference. If he hadn't been morally courageous, he couldn't have been so determined to get through, negotiate the straight world from his peculiar starting place. It seemed to me that he had achieved something impressive here, accepting emotions the world denied existed for young boys and that his parents probably wouldn't have chosen for him, asserting himself with dignity and modesty. That was something to celebrate, not dismiss, and it was integral to who he was. I was starting to see – and this feeling was to grow as the days passed and the fact of his sexuality no longer jolted me – that the least I could do was to follow his lead and stick up for him.

Matt's homosexuality did not have to prevent people, including me, from seeing anything about him except that he was gay. It was my job to make sure that he was not obliterated by his sexuality, segregated either in actuality or in people's heads. (But also that his being gay was not ignored, because, obviously, that would be obliterating him in a different way. It was a bloody minefield. Still, at least I could see a role for myself now, which was an improvement on feeling useless because I hadn't even noticed.)

The flyscreen creaked and Cheryl appeared in the kitchen, in blue check Capri pants and an orange vest. 'Hey, guys, mind if I join you?'

'Nothing personal, Cheryl, but I was just off for a swim.' Matt slid off the bench.

'Weren't you going riding?'

'Later.'

'Did Sam say if he'd be in for supper?'

'Haven't seen him.'

The only rule, really, was that they were supposed to tell me where they were and if they wouldn't be in for meals. I didn't like not knowing what Sam was doing, especially now that I was so aware that their real life was subterranean: glugging fluids, boiling hormones. Perhaps he was gay too? Did it run in families? Most of the time I had no idea what he was thinking. It could be gay things.

Still, I thought, pouring Cheryl a cup of tea, he spent all his time with Faisal and Faisal definitely had a girlfriend. He'd had her on my sofa, in fact. I'd come home early from a meeting at school and caught them in a state of semi-naked, post-coital collapse. When I'd objected about this to Sam – we were not a brothel, how was I supposed to face Faisal next time, not to mention his parents, sitting on the sofa was now much less appealing, etc. – Sam had protested that they had nowhere else to go and it was my fault for coming home when I'd said I was going to be out.

'Have you invited James Hartley round yet?' Cheryl demanded, 'only you know what'll happen: he'll get sucked into spending all his time with the Al Majids and Hawari merchants and a few posh Brits . . .'

'I'm not sure how much time they'll have for socializing.'

'You really should have a party. We have to get a trip out to Al Janabiyya compound on to his schedule. He must want to see the countryside?'

'The what?'

'Well, you know,' she said defensively, 'vegetables grow round here. You see them by the roadside. Those leaves.'

I laughed.

'Well, it's the only place in the emirate things *do* grow naturally . . . And, frankly, what else is there to see here?'

Matt walked past in swimming shorts, trailing his towel. Cheryl followed him with her eyes all the way to the door, then, once he'd shut it behind him, murmured, 'God, he's got handsome!'

This was clearly the perfect moment to begin my new regime of being an out mother. 'He's gay.'

'No!' she turned and stared at me. 'You're joking!'

I shook my head.

'When – how . . . my God! – when did you find out?'

'A few days ago.'

'Are you *sure*?'

'Yes.'

'It's not just a phase?'

'No.'

'Oh my *God*! Poor Annie . . .! Look, I don't really want to say this, but . . . d'you think – maybe – it comes from not having a dad?'

'Who knows?' I shrugged, though I was irritated by her need to blame someone. Me, in fact. Why? To persuade herself it couldn't happen to her?

Whoever thought up the dominant mother theory of homosexuality was really very clever, because it implies that a) that it's dangerous for women to be assertive in case of getting a gay son, and b) that a gay son is a faulty product and that if he were a fridge, say, you'd return him.

'He says he was aware of it before Dave died.'

I didn't see how it could possibly be as simple a matter as absent fathers, otherwise a large proportion of boys in history – certainly whenever there had been a war – would have been gay.

Not that I'm suggesting Matt mightn't have benefited from having a man around. I might, so he might too. People probably wouldn't have been as rude to me, for a start. And I'd have had someone to talk to, ideally someone who was unfailingly on my side. If you lived with a person for years, I thought, there might be some hope of their intuiting all the muddle and particularity of your thoughts, grasping something of your multifaceted, contradictory emotional life, getting a bit closer to the authentic you. Because, quite a lot of the time, I find, people completely misunderstand what you're trying to say. Still, I'd learnt enough to know that for any of this to happen it had to be the right man. And it turned out that this really complicated things.

'I might not mention it to Tel, just yet, if you don't mind,' Cheryl said, after a moment's thought. 'Not that he's prejudiced or anything, but you know what he's like, all red-blooded New Zealand male!' Her husband Tel imported meat. 'And he'd worry about Kyle . . .'

'I don't think living next door to Matthew will have made Kyle gay. I don't think that's quite how it works.'

'No, no, course not . . . well, I never! Is he,' she lowered her voice, giggled, 'd'you know?' she whispered: 'an on top or an underneath?'

'I'm sorry?'

'Giver or taker? You *know*!'

It was Karen all over again. Cheryl felt she had permission to talk about Matthew as if he were a non-person whose sexual preferences were an acceptable subject for general speculation. She wouldn't have dreamt of asking me if I preferred having sex on top.

Over the years, I'd managed to persuade people in Hawar that my sons weren't suspect and delinquent on account of not having a father and I wasn't a nymphomaniac slyly stealing husbands because I didn't have one of my own. But now, suddenly, we seemed to be exposed in ways I couldn't control.

'I have no idea,' I said coldly. 'I haven't asked.'

Perhaps Cheryl realized she'd gone too far then, because she made moves to leave, still making sympathetic but scandalized noises. I let her go, wondering what gay people could possibly do sexually that everyone else didn't, or couldn't imagine. Surely, not that much? – so it was a mystery why gay sex was so endlessly fascinating, as if it must be more titillating and wicked than any other kind: unimaginably, thrillingly dreadful.

Sticking up for Matthew evidently wasn't going to be entirely straightforward. It had seemed easy enough to tell Cheryl – I hadn't had to screw myself up to get the words out – but as soon as she knew, Matt became for her simply one of those people who did *that*. His Matthewness was obscured by whatever ideas she had about homosexuals: misfits, freaks, moral failures, sexual perverts, whatever – and she no longer felt any need to be polite. So while it hadn't been difficult getting the words out, I could see that dealing with people's reactions could become quite wearing. (My own reactions had been a bit intemperate initially, I know, but I was his mother and entitled to be disturbed. Besides, I was getting past all that now.)

It seemed farcical that Karen thought he needed psychiatric help and Cheryl couldn't focus on anything except whether he liked penises inserted into him or preferred doing the inserting. Especially when you considered that this was Matthew – sweet, inoffensive Matthew – who, when he was a toddler, used to creep into the bed in the middle of the night between me and Dave, padding through the house into our bedroom, clambering up and slipping silently into the space between us. And then, when I woke, there he'd be: unnoticed as I slept, getting exactly what he wanted. Soft breath on my cheek, one arm hooked around my neck. If he could find the space without disturbing us, he preferred to sleep in a ball, as if he'd clambered back into the womb, relieved to have abandoned yesterday's stretching and straightening and testing his strength and to have gone back to being a tiny, protected infant. I remembered how softly his skin would lie against mine, a buttery curl of a baby, hot life coming out of his mouth: vulnerable and trusting, relying on me to make everything right. And even though now he was six foot two and powerfully built and having gay sex, quite a lot of that was still there between us.

Over the next few days I persisted with my new policy of including Matt's gayness in any conversation I could, as if it were the most normal thing in the world. By now quite a few people already knew – Antonia, for instance, who called to find out if I'd seen James Hartley again yet and if I was ready to bring him round to dinner at her house. 'By the way, darling,' she said when I explained that I hadn't seen him and didn't know anything about his plans, 'I heard about Matthew's big coming out ... what a hoot. I suppose you couldn't tell us on Al-Hidd, with your family there? – I imagine they could be tricky ...'

Not everyone was as efficiently networked as Antonia, however, and, most of the time, I didn't know if people knew or not. So when I bumped into Siobhan Armstrong, the mother of a girl who'd been in Will's class, in the jam aisle at Al Jazira and she asked how the kids were doing, what was I supposed to say? 'Well, Will got married – I expect you heard? – and he and Maddi are on honeymoon, but moving to London next week, and Sam's back at school working on his IB, and Matt's gay'?

This would definitely have been a good tactic if Siobhan already knew about Matt's sexuality and was uncertain whether to raise the topic herself. In that case, if I *hadn't* said anything, she might have thought I was in denial. So I did mention it, but in a passing kind of way, at the same time as saying he was working at Palm Publishing and going travelling next year and starting his English and drama degree at Manchester in October.

Immediately, I realized that Siobhan not only hadn't known, but would much rather not have done so – or, at least, not have been told by me, because she had no idea how to respond. It was way too much information; I could see from her sympathetic but alarmed expression that she thought I must be terribly distressed to be blurting it out like this without invitation at near-strangers in the supermarket. It wasn't the kind of thing you said in passing, to mere acquaintances; it put them in an awkward position, because they didn't know if you wanted commiseration, or praise for your insouciance. She thought it had induced a mad Tourette's-style compulsion in me.

The one person I was not remotely tempted to tell was

Anwar, who came into school on Tuesday, parking his Hummer across the entrance in the place where it said 'No Parking', then loitering in my office.

'I have been listening to a tape of Mohammed Alireza,' he announced, leaning against the filing cabinet. 'It is a pity you don't speak Arabic. You should hear it. The west wishes to destroy our values.'

'Are you sure?' I said, not really concentrating.

'For example, the Americans want to nuke Mecca.'

'Hang on a minute, Anwar, I don't think so.'

'No. It is true, it was on a website.'

'If that's true, it's just one person. Mad person.'

'And in a magazine the Americans have written that this is no time to be precious about individuals – that to stop the so-called terrorists they should invade our countries, kill our leaders and convert us to Christianity.'

'That's probably one person too. There's no control over the press in the United States. And you can write anything on the internet. People who say things like that are crazy. Everyone thinks so.'

'There are many crazies in America. They shoot each other in high schools. And they think they are the good guys!'

'Anwar, there are loads of things you love about American culture . . .'

'Alireza says if things are going wrong in the Arab world, it cannot be the fault of Islam.'

'No, well, I don't suppose it is . . .'

'So either we are not praying enough, or it is the fault of outside influences. Or both. Perhaps Islam and *kufr* will never mix under any circumstances.'

It was difficult to know where to start. Why are people always trying to make you join in with their prejudices? It would be OK if they were just bigoted in a quiet personal way. But they will insist on turning them into demands on you.

I felt irritated by Anwar until late in the afternoon, when

James rang and said – and as if he really meant it – how lovely it had been to see me on Sunday.

'You too,' I answered, and then realized that this was silly, because obviously it was lovely seeing him. The whole point of him was that he was lovely to see, which is why he had a manicurist and a masseur and a personal trainer.

Dealing with James, I could see, might require some adroitness. He was in a whole other key.

We eventually settled on dinner at the Al A'ali House on Sunday – which, what with dad, Chris, Karen and Andrea's stopover on the way back from Dubai, and Will and Maddi's on the way back from the Maldives, plus his filming schedule, was the soonest we could manage.

I had no idea what this impending dinner date amounted to or what he wanted from it. He talked to me with a kind of flirtatious intensity that seemed a bit strong if he saw me simply as an old friend and wanted to catch up. There was a kind of sexiness which – even though I only had a hazy memory of the last time I'd had sex – I was sure was directed quite deliberately at me.

There hadn't been a vast quantity of passion in my recent past. I'd had plenty of offers, but what had actually taken place had proved rather desultory: a couple of short affairs with divorced men who'd been in Hawar earning money to pay for ex-wives and keep children in private education, and whose emotional focus, it turned out, had really been elsewhere; a brief fling with a married man who'd complained phonily, tactically, about the state of his marriage, and whom I'd ended up disliking rather a lot; a one-night stand with a bloke who'd never married and I felt afterwards I could sort of see why.

I could have been much busier; could even, if I'd wanted, have been married. More than one man who failed to get my clothes off had suggested a lifetime of cohabitation instead. (How was that going to work? Men can be quite thick.) Single women over the age of thirty are in short supply in Hawar, and there was an assumption among the single men (and an alarming number of the married ones) that I must be available. I was a bit like Everest, demanding to be conquered because I was there. But the men involved had rarely seemed worth the hassle of an affair – which is not to say I didn't often feel quite wretchedly sexed-up. Sometimes I thought the reason I was targeted for quite so much flirting was that unsatisfied sexiness was sort of spilling out of me wherever I went. I continued to go around being a school secretary and mother of three as if nothing was happening, imagining the sexiness was entirely invisible. You couldn't see, hear or even smell it; but, unfortunately, you could obviously pick it up in some other way, which led to an embarrassment of propositions. On occasion – and this was more difficult to deal with – I also developed crushes on people, but they were mostly married to other people, women I knew, and I am not completely stupid. Plus, they were only crushes, directly traceable to not having been held by anyone for months on end. Desire swilled around me, looking for an object, and settled on whatever was about. Which I knew, deep down, wasn't enough. Not even, under the gossipy village circumstances in which we found ourselves, for a fling. To justify lying to the boys, potentially upsetting their lives, the possible exposure, I would have had to meet a man in whom I believed utterly. And that would have changed everything. In some ways it was easier that there was so little chance of its happening here.

The best you could say for me and sex was that I'd had just about enough to remember the order in which things usually happened. I certainly wasn't unused to attention from men, but they were most definitely not men like James Hartley. When he fixed his lighthouse-beam of sexiness on me, it was unexpected and unlooked-for and quite delightful and, right now, I couldn't actually have cared less what it amounted to. A man had arrived in Hawar who would also have been hugely attractive to women who were already having a normal amount of sex. And he was interested in me. All I could do was enjoy it while it lasted.

Six

Chris bothered to call from Dubai, even though, as he pointed out, hotels slapped a sodding great surcharge on the phone bill. He didn't bother with a preamble – no nice beaches, how are you? having a great time – just started straight in: 'You have to tell dad about Matthew. I can't keep it secret any longer. It's embarrassing. I'll be on the point of saying something about it to Karen and I'll realize he's standing there.'

'Can't you find an alternative topic of conversation?'

'It's not me who wants to talk about it. Dad's the one who keeps saying how nice Matthew is . . .'

'Well, that's true.'

'. . . And what a lovely girl Jodie is and do I think she's his girlfriend? What am I supposed to say to that? . . . Ann?'

Now they were back, with a few hours to spare before their flight on to London. Chris and Karen were lying round the pool at the Sheraton, Andrea had gone down to the beach, and I'd brought dad inside the hotel.

'Can I get you something?' I offered. 'Beer?'

Dad looked at me in alarm, thoughts of Happy Valley expats mad with boredom sliding across his face. 'It's the afternoon!'

'Yes. Sorry.' What was I thinking? Dad's need for alcohol had always been satisfied by the odd sherry at parties and a couple of snowballs at Christmas.

I indicated a low table and chairs. 'Tea, then?'

'OK,' he said, still puzzled as to what all this was about. 'Not the perfumed one, though.'

Narrow-hipped Thai, Filipina and Indian girls in long colourful tubes of skirt drifted noiselessly between the tables. I caught the attention of one of them and ordered a pot of tea.

'I wanted to talk to you ...'

'Have you heard from Will?'

'No, but they'll be back on Wednesday. It's about ...'

'Where are the boys, then?'

'I don't know.' Why was he looking round the atrium? Did he think they might be lurking in the foliage? 'They'll be here later. Actually, it's about Matthew – what I wanted to say.'

'I'll try not to fuss too much, when he comes. I understand they don't always have proper mealtimes.'

'Yes, it's not that, exactly ...'

'Oh, thank you, dear,' he interrupted, as the whippety Thai girl silently delivered tea cups.

'The thing is,' I took a deep breath, 'you should know before he comes to stay – not that it ... but, of course, you should know anyway ... So, anyway, last week, Matthew told us he was gay.'

I finished in a rush: toldushewasgay. Not is gay. As if it might just be one of those crazy things kids say.

Even under the subdued lighting, I could see too much of dad's face. The skin seemed to be stretching apart around the pores, opening up a sieve of pockmarks. That must be why grey bristle seemed to be crusting on his chin, because it was out of character for him not to shave. All the elasticity was going from his flesh, as if his body couldn't make the effort any more.

I felt terribly sorry for him. I reached over and touched his hand. 'It's a shock.'

Dad stared past me. 'It must be a mistake,' he mumbled.

'No, I don't think so.'

'But he's so normal.'

'He is.'

'Are you sure it's not a phase?'

'It might be,' I allowed, 'but it's the phase he's in.' I didn't want to sound flippant, but still – 'and has been, as far as I can make out, since he was five.'

'What happened to him? Did someone do this?' He curled

his hands into fists on his knees, so that the veins on the backs protruded raggedly. 'Who?'

'No one.'

'Who's got to him? Is that what they do here? Is it some Arab?'

'Dad!'

'Well, who, then?'

'It's not like that . . .'

'Is it because Dave died?'

'I don't think so.' Why didn't people just come out and say: 'You did this, you mad selfish lone parent, staying here, keeping him from his family, instead of settling down with someone else'?

'He says he felt it when Dave was alive.'

'How *can* he? Even think of it?'

'It's not a choice. He can't not think of it.'

'What about Aids?'

I rubbed at my temples and forehead, pushing at the skin with my fingers. Sweat had dried on my face in the ferocious air conditioning: the fine sandy dust from outside had set like cement in my pores. 'They've had Aids education since they were eleven or twelve. Anyway, HIV isn't a gay infection: it affects far more heterosexuals than gay people.'

'In Africa!' dad said scathingly. 'Why have so many of them died of it, then? Because of what they do!'

'Only at the beginning, when they didn't know what was going on.' I was sure it was politically incorrect even to be having this conversation. 'Gay men talk about their HIV status now,' I said, piously repeating some internet factoid I'd managed to pick up. 'The ones who are most at risk are those who are married, or forbidden by their culture or whatever – who are behaving furtively, no questions asked. Happily, that won't be Matthew.'

I hoped this was right. Actually, I hadn't asked Matthew whether he'd taken risks in the past or might in the future. He'd only lie. And it was bad enough not having been able to say, 'Oh, how lovely, a gay son: just what I've always wanted!' without compounding the failing by suggesting that his sexuality was the equivalent of a fatal disease.

I felt guilty about this. You should, presumably, be capable of pointing out life-threatening hazards to your children whether they want to hear about them or not.

'What is it about us, that we're so unlucky?' dad complained. 'First your mother, then Dave, now this . . .'

'Matt's not dead, dad.'

'I'm supposed to have him to stay? He's still intending to come?'

'As far as I know. We haven't talked about it recently, but . . .' He had some unpaid work lined up as an ASM with a theatre company in London for six weeks in March and April, before flying off to Costa Rica. 'Obviously, if you've changed your mind . . .'

If you're such a selfish homophobe, I did not say.

He rubbed his hands together in his lap: a kind of aimless, repetitive chafing. He stared past his tea and the glass coffee table, past the carpet, into nothingness. If I'd reached across, I could easily have pushed him off his chair: there wouldn't have been any resistance. I experienced a senseless, unpleasant urge to do it.

'What about Will and Maddi's children?' he mumbled eventually.

'What?' Who?

'What will they think? How will they be told? How are we going to manage all that? It's not much of an example, is it?'

I'd been thinking about having this conversation ever since Matt came out. I'd spent quite a lot of time worrying about the emotions it might unleash and exactly what my dad might say. But even with all the planning, I hadn't factored in the possibility that we'd end up discussing the responses of people who were, as yet, hypothetical.

'Why do young people feel this need to "come out" anyway?'

'These are deep feelings. Matt doesn't want to be misunder-
stood.'

'Why do they need to make their private lives public? I don't
know – when I think what we went through, the shelters every
night, everyone thinking about dying . . .' What was he going
on about now? 'There wasn't any room for all this then. Now
they think they have a *right*. They've got to be *true to themselves*,'
– he pronounced this scathingly – 'or they're missing out on
something. As if they're entitled to happiness! As if everything
in the world is there to serve them! They talk about fulfilment,
as if that's a right. They don't know the half of it.'

Whatever he was saying here, it seemed to be only
tangentially to do with Matthew.

'I don't know, there's you drifting around without a husband . . .'

I sometimes thought he believed it was careless of me to have
let Dave die. He almost certainly believed it was selfish not to
have taken up with someone else, because it was all much of a
muchness anyway, all dwindled to dullness in the end . . . Except,
if that were the truth, why would you bother?

'What am I supposed to do if he wants to go to gay clubs?'

'Nothing. I don't suppose he'll tell you anyway.'

'So every time he goes out I've got to *imagine* him at gay
clubs?'

'If it's a problem, he doesn't have to come.'

Dad sat back. His eyes looked rheumy. 'I can't say what I feel
about it now. It's too soon. If he did come – which I'm not saying
he will – I wouldn't want it shoved in my face.'

All this shoving, as if Matthew were an item of heavy plant
instead of a boy. What constituted a shove? How discreet would
he have to be, not to force his homosexuality on his grandfather's notice? This morning he'd come down to breakfast
singing 'Diamonds Are Forever'. Now he was out, I couldn't
believe I'd ever thought he was anything other than gay. It was
impossible to avoid it – not shoved in your face, but visible on

Matt's, along with (and was this new, or another thing I'd previously failed to see?) what appeared to be tinted moisturizer.

Karen rushed up the moment I came out on to the pool terrace, pulling a linen shift over her head. She must have been watching for me.

'Have you done it?' she breathed.

'Yes.'

'Where is he? Is he OK?'

'Yes, he's coming out here in a minute.'

'Is he still having Matthew to stay next year, because I know I said before that we had room for him, but you know what Chris is like . . .'

I didn't bother to point out to Karen that an entire male *corps de ballet* with their tops off in the spare bedroom would be unlikely to persuade Matt to move in with Chris.

Karen pulled down her shift, irritated that I was trying to minimize the gravity of the situation, to make my side of the family seem less troublesome than it actually is. 'I hope you went easy on him,' she warned, as if he were her dad instead of mine; 'it's difficult for him. He's not like you people here.'

'What's that supposed to mean?'

'Lots of money and anything goes.'

In Karen's view, I'd lost my moral bearings: I lived among people who were profligate, deracinated and out of control and they had corrupted me. Hawar was a louche place where money came and went and everyone, including me, had too much to pay it proper respect. I don't know where she got this idea: I suppose it suited her and Chris to believe that I was richer than I was, to insinuate that I'd acquired comfort too easily, almost by accident, by happening to live in an oil-rich part of the world where money sloshed about recklessly.

Many people do, it's true, leave Hawar with chalets in Verbier, houses in Notting Hill, forests in Wales, yachts in Cannes, portfolios of investments. I was not unfortunately going to be one of them. I owned a small house in Devon which I rented out and where I thought I might perhaps live eventually. I was fond of it, but it didn't make me rich. The cost of living is high in Hawar, much higher than in Europe, and I wasn't particularly well paid.

Circumstances hadn't been as much against Chris and Karen as they liked to pretend, either: they'd owned a successful estate agency business through the longest housing boom in history. Chris was a good salesman, since he had a knack of believing anything he was saying, at least while he was saying it, and Karen was clever with money and made sure they didn't spend too much.

'And anything goes is so much *not* how things are here,' I added.

'All I mean is your dad's lived in Thornton Heath ever since he left Rotherhithe; he's not been on the other side of the world, mixing with all sorts. He grew up believing you had to hold tight to your values, or you'd end up in poverty and chaos. They had no bathroom, you know: no bath or inside toilet. They had to work hard to keep up appearances.'

'I know this, Karen, he's my dad . . .'

'He thinks you act like the rules don't apply to you . . .'

Did he? Perhaps. Certainly that's what Karen herself thought – that I'd been ranging round the world, free of constraints. All this mixing with people who sent their children to boarding school and had offshore investments was getting above myself. And, looking at it like that, Matt's sexuality was just retribution, only what I could expect for not having hung on tightly enough to my values (though I noticed she conveniently didn't specify which ones I'd let go).

None of it was fair. I was a school secretary who'd been married to a photocopier salesman. In Hawar, where most European expats were bankers, lawyers, general managers, IT experts or other professionals, that put us a long way down the social ranking. It wasn't as if I'd escaped into some racy classless world where background didn't matter: Hawar was probably more class-conscious than Britain. Here you were thrown up against people whether you wanted to be or not: sometimes it seemed important to keep your distance, and class distinctions were a reflexive, no-thought-required way of doing it. The people the boys called Team England – the sort who already knew someone before they arrived because they'd been together at prep school, or they used to live next door to a lovely family in Fulham who'd been in Dubai – might, like Antonia, tolerate me. They might accept I'd acquired a kind of status simply as a result of having stuck it out here for so long. They might even have warmed to me since Dave, with his drinking and his irredeemably lower-middle-class job, had gone, or after Will had gone to Oxford and then married one of the beautiful, Marlborough-educated Franklin girls. But they would never have made the mistake of thinking I was one of them.

'Here's dad,' I said wearily, seeing him come out of the hotel into the heat.

He made his way across to us, awkward in his flip flops. I moved up the sunbed so that he could have the shaded part.

'Are you going to have a last swim?'

'I don't think so.'

'I gather Ann told you?' Karen said.

'Yes, thank you Karen.'

My sister-in-law shrugged and applied suncream to her legs.

In the end, I went off for a swim, because the silence was too awful.

Three-quarters of an hour later, I was back in the hotel lobby, waiting for the others to come out of the changing rooms. Matt and Sam were with me, though Sam was scowling because he didn't think he should have been dragged away from doing something more important with Faisal, like sitting in his bedroom.

'I told granddad, by the way,' I said to Matt, 'about you being gay.'

'Oh, right. Is he speaking to me?'

'I think we can safely say he didn't see it coming, but he's fine.'

'You mean his worries about me marrying an Arab girl and converting to Islam have faded?'

'There is that. You may have to be a bit sensitive, though.'

'What's that supposed to mean?'

'Well, you know . . .'

'I'm gay and I'm fabulous, mum. It's my birthright.'

But he kissed me on the top of my head.

Dad shuffled up to us, saying 'Hello there!' without meeting anyone's eyes. Matt kissed Karen, slapped Chris on the back, said cheerily, 'Hey, granddad, how's it going?' then busied himself with the bags, which he and Sam were taking out to the airport in the Jeep.

The others came in the Toyota with me.

'Dad doesn't want to talk about it,' Chris said as we pulled out of the parking space.

I looked in the rear-view mirror. My dad was staring out of the window.

'No one wants to talk about it except you,' Andrea said. 'Matt's gay, dad, get over it.'

'Bottling things up is bad for you,' Karen said sententiously.

Andrea turned her attention to the guards at the bottom of the driveway. She waved, and they waved back. 'Hey, mum, we didn't get blown up after all!'

'You can laugh at me all you like, Andrea, but the fact is that there are a lot of people in this world – in this part of the world – who don't like anything modern and think their ideas are God's ideas. How they know that I'm not sure. But if you think that, you can do anything.'

By the time we reached the airport, the boys were parked and had unloaded the bags. We met them in the terminal, where Matt was inspecting the queues at check-in and deciding which was the shortest. We waited in line while he kept up a rattling stream of consciousness about security procedures and the pros and cons of e-ticketing and how to get a bulkhead seat and the likely in-flight entertainment and what time it would be when they got to Gatwick. My dad seemed to have receded, physically and emotionally: he was hanging back as if he wanted to dissolve into the queue, as if he'd already given himself up to being washed along gleaming corridors and moving walkways, through gates and tunnels, to being as inconspicuous as possible in front of officials inspecting papers and faces for identity fraud.

I wished that Matthew didn't have to make so much noise, or so mindlessly, even though I knew he was only doing it to cover his grandfather's embarrassment. It was better to be brash and loud than see in his granddad's eyes that he was feared. I wondered whether he'd had to do this before – if this was why gay people so often seemed shouty – and how often he'd have to again. Would it eventually cease to be a performance and become ingrained, identity fraud?

'If only you were coming with us,' Karen sighed, touching my arm. 'I don't like to think of you here, especially with the war coming and everything. All the chemical and biological weapons. And you've got to admit, it's a bit weird, spending all your adult life in a foreign country, not belonging?'

Was it weird? Would my life have been less weird if I'd lived it somewhere else? I liked the outsiderishness of Hawar, being accompanied by strangeness, by the busy whirr of the air conditioning units and the wailing mosques. I liked strolling through cold marble malls on the edge of a thick, salty sea, surrounded by men in dazzling white and women shrouded in black, liked seeing the evening sun flaring in a cloudless sky, falling lazily into the sea, and the shock of things not being as they were set up to be by childhood. Of course, none of it was exactly a novelty now, none of it jolted me out of my assumptions any more, but there was still a feeling of being more alive that came from seeing things from a different latitude.

'Still, I suppose there have been advantages,' Karen reflected.

'It would've been hard for you at home, having three children and no husband ... Even so, Ann, you do need to think ahead. Soon the boys won't need you in the same way any more, so you'll have to start putting yourself first. You don't want to become a burden.'

In the annoying way that she sometimes had, I thought as I drove home, Karen was right. The boys had filled up all my available space for as long as I could remember, but even though Sam still had two years left at school and Matt would need a home when he was at university (and possibly, knowing his predilection for clean towels, for some time after that), they needed me less and less. Will was already married; the other two would become more and more detached. The years of feeling comfortably harried and put-upon were coming to an end, along with the security of ready-made decisions: if something was good for the boys, then we did it, and if it wasn't, we said no, and it was easy. I couldn't go on thinking like that without my life diminishing, becoming a half-life, slightly pitiful.

All the same, whatever putting myself first meant, it clearly wasn't going back to Thornton Heath and working in the estate agency, which would have been Karen's solution. Not even with Karen's assurance that so much of it was on commission that it was like working for yourself.

I wasn't sure that finding yourself in the Gulf was that much weirder than finding yourself anywhere. It was the yourself bit that was tricky.

'It'd be fine, you know, if you brought someone here,' I said casually one evening as Matt was leaving, allegedly to go round to Jodie's. What I actually meant by this was 'I hope there's a relationship and you're not just having sex.'

He didn't reply, but I pressed on anyway: 'I mean, I know Will hardly ever brought Maddi back but that wasn't because I didn't approve, and obviously the same rules apply to you ...'

'Yeah, thanks,' he said vaguely. 'Gotta go, or I'll be late.'

He didn't say: 'Ha! You got me bang to rights! I'm off to a private gay party.'

Perhaps he wasn't. As far as I could see, his life was too staid and orderly to leave much room for illicit meetings with promiscuous men. He went to work during the day, and sometimes in the evenings he saw his friends. More often than not, he stayed in and watched television or emailed people from school who'd gone off to college. I wished now that I could have told dad he was gay a bit earlier in his visit, so that he could have seen how unthreatening his sexuality was, how it manifested itself mainly in a lot of dancing round the kitchen to Radio Hawar.

Will and Maddi were due back from their honeymoon early on Wednesday morning, and were planning to spend the day in Hawar to open their wedding presents and tie up loose ends, then stay overnight at the Franklins' and catch a flight to London the following morning.

I left school promptly when the final bell rang at two o'clock on Wednesday, calling Sam on the mobile as I walked out to the car. 'D'you want me to pick you up?'

'What, like now?'

'Yes.' We'd discussed this at breakfast. Was he on drugs? 'We're going to see Will and Maddi. Katherine's invited us for lunch.'

'Only I already ate.'

'Sam, I *said* . . .'

'Do I have to come? Yo, man!'

I think this last bit was probably a greeting, and not meant for me.

'Shall I give you a lift?'

'Is Matt coming?'

'Later, when he's finished work.'

'Is Will still pissed off with him?'

'I don't know . . . No, I don't suppose so.'

'Thing is, mum, Faisal and I have got stuff.'

'What stuff?'

'On the computer, *stuff*.'

'They're expecting you.'

In fact, Katherine had said, 'Bring the boys if you like.'

'They never speak to me.'

'That's because you don't speak to them.'

'Oh. Right.'

'Look, you don't have to come now, but will you put in an appearance later? You should see Will and Maddi before they go back.'

'So they're going to be there?'

'Sam, I know you're not big on talking right now, but you could at least listen . . .'

'Yeah, whatever. Keep it real!'

I had to hope he wasn't doing crack. There came a point when you couldn't stand over them – a series of points, in fact, starting from when they wanted to ride their scooters out of sight in the Ladies' Garden at the age of six. Giving them room to become themselves seemed a process fraught with danger, although when Will and Matt had gone off, I'd always felt I had a fair idea of what each of them was up to – playing competitive sport (Will) and drinking lattes with girls (Matt). I had very little sense of what Sam was doing. Still less thinking. And though I felt that Faisal was probably a good influence, his attempt to turn my house into a sort of Japanese love hotel aside, he was pretty opaque too.

Perhaps Sam was gay, I thought at the traffic lights, waiting to turn on to the Corniche. He was very artistic. Always drawing. And he hadn't brought any girls home. He was always with Faisal. And just because Faisal was heterosexual, it didn't mean Sam was.

Or they could be bisexual. There probably wasn't so much stigma attached to that for Arab men.

Or – and this made more sense because Sam wasn't very traditional – they could be post-gay, which was something I'd found on an internet site run by American teenagers for people who didn't need categories. Post-gays sometimes fancied men, sometimes (less often, I think) women. They didn't want to be pigeonholed or have to act up to stereotypes. Maybe Sam was one of them. He was very vague, generally speaking, so maybe, in his fuzzy world, gender was irrelevant.

Clearly, I was going to have to ask him. And hope he didn't just say something like 'Yo, coz!'

Will answered the door at the Franklins', looking tanned – 'which is amazing,' Maddi smiled, putting a hand on his shoulder, 'because he spent our entire honeymoon under water.'

'Annie, darling!' Katherine called out vaguely from the kitchen. 'Peter's not back yet – got delayed at some meeting – but do come through. I thought we'd eat by the pool.'

'Maddi's been telling us about spa treatments,' Millie said, raising her eyes as I went into the kitchen. 'We were just getting on to stone therapy.'

Katherine put a bowl of salad into my hands and I took it outside on to the back terrace. Maddi followed with the plates.

'Will really spent most of the time diving?' I asked as she adjusted knives and forks.

'Apparently, it's one of the best places in the world to learn.'

That wasn't quite what I meant. 'And you don't dive?'

'I can't bear it. I tried once when I was fourteen and had a panic attack . . . It's all right, honestly . . .'

'That your husband abandoned you on your honeymoon?'

'Actually, it's quite hard to abandon someone on an island you can walk across in ten minutes. We had loads of time to sit on our veranda on the water, looking at the stars and thinking Copernicus was wrong: the world obviously revolves round us.'

'I hope so.'

I remember sitting at a Greek taverna on a beach once, about eight years ago, waiting to pay the bill. The boys weren't there: they must have already gone back on to the sand. I was idly finishing a glass of wine when a couple at a nearby table asked a waiter to take their photograph as they posed by the low fence separating the restaurant from the beach. I watched them, my mind vacant, drifting, until something about them, an intensity, a complete *lack* of posing, attracted my attention and I realized that, for them, being in this cheap restaurant on this not particularly special beach was as perfect as it gets. It was as if they were luminous with belief in each other. On his way out, the man caught my eye and smiled – not at me, particularly, or not me as an individual, anyway, not pityingly or kindly – but simply at another person who'd noticed, who'd got caught up in their happiness as it rippled out, a spreading circle of delight.

I wanted to believe Maddi and Will felt like that, but sometimes I wondered. People don't always marry for reasons of luminosity, even though they should, because marriage is hellish without it. But luminosity may, I suspect, be quite rare.

As Katherine brought out the lasagne, I went back into the kitchen, where Will was making the salad dressing.

Perhaps it was the fault of the conversation with Maddi about the diving, but I started off all wrong. 'You didn't say goodbye properly,' I said to him, anxiety translating, somewhere between my brain and my mouth, into accusation.

'Sorry . . . Didn't I?' he said vaguely. 'You'd disappeared.'

'Matt didn't mean to come out at your wedding, you know.'

'Right.'

'Chris was being appalling. You saw what he was like, and Matt couldn't help himself: it just slipped out.'

'Yeah, well, he does like to upstage everyone.'

'He was mortified afterwards.'

'Perhaps he should've thought about that before he opened his mouth.'

'I don't understand,' I said helplessly. 'It shouldn't be a big deal. I mean, I don't care who Matt sleeps with as long as he's happy. And if I'm not fussed about it, I don't see why you should be. Half the people you know must be gay.'

'No . . .'

'On the way here I was thinking that Sam could easily be

gay, too – I mean, *I* don't know – and if he were, that would be absolutely fine.' He said nothing. 'So what *was* so awful about it?'

'Nothing.' He stirred the dressing vigorously. 'It's OK.'

'He'd hate it if he thought he'd spoilt the wedding for you. That wasn't his intention at all. He couldn't keep quiet any longer – and, frankly, why should he have to?'

'I've said I'm fine. *Really*.'

'Well, please tell him that. Will?'

'OK, OK . . .'

He picked up the dressing and made for the door.

'Did you really have no idea he was gay?'

'No. Yes. I had no idea.'

'Are you two coming out?' Katherine called from the garden.

How, I wondered, could I have produced one child who was so emotionally out there – for whom life was a sort of emotional rumpus room – and another who was so stiff and starchy? Will had emotions, I was sure, but he kept them out of sight. They were probably turbulent and spuming down there somewhere, at the bottom of some crevasse, but it was a mystery how you'd get to them.

When we got outside, Millie asked whether I'd seen James Hartley since the wedding, so I explained about his having turned up on Al-Hidd.

'I bet he was the one who decided to come off that gin palace,' Millie said, when I got to that part.

'Mmn, I don't think his friends would have been rushing to do it.'

'He really likes you! You could see that at the wedding.'

'He's probably fascinated by how different we are. We started in the same place and he's a multimillionaire and incredibly famous, and I'm not.'

'I think it's a bit more complicated than that,' Peter said.

'Yeah, well, perhaps he wants to get in touch with his past self.'

'Sounds more like it's you he wants to get in touch with.'

After lunch, Maddi and Will opened the wedding presents from guests who hadn't known about the list at The General Trading Company, or who'd wanted to bring something they'd chosen themselves. Being Maddi and Will, they were relentlessly charmed by everything, even their fourth gold latticework tissue-box holder.

'Lovely,' murmured Millie, 'one for every room.'

Sam turned up at about five, slouching in, lean and louche.

'What's been keeping you?' Peter asked genially.

'Stuff.'

'Oh, *stuff*.'

Perhaps he was stung by Peter's tone, because he muttered, 'I got made editor of the school newspaper.'

'The *International*?' Will said, 'but don't you have to get voted?'

'Yeah.'

'That's brilliant!' I cried. 'What, does the whole school vote?'

'Uh-huh.'

'I didn't know you were standing.'

'Oh, OK.'

Sam has always drawn cartoons for the school magazine, mostly satirical caricatures of the teachers, and they're often the best thing in it. But as editor he would presumably have to deal with words as well. There was little evidence that he had much familiarity with those.

'When d'you start?'

'Around Christmas. It's for a year.'

'So he gets the last two terms to concentrate on exams,' Will explained. His brother scowled.

'What was your pitch?' Maddi asked.

'Huh?'

'What d'you want to do with the magazine?'

'Oh, right. Like, be more in touch.'

'With anything in particular?' asked Will.

118

'Events,' Sam said pityingly.

He dived into the pool, surfaced and swam to the side. 'And Faisal's my deputy, so it'll be a laugh.'

By now, everyone was ready for a swim. Will, who always preferred to have some kind of focus, organized a game of water polo, so I didn't stay in long because it was highly competitive and I could tell he was getting annoyed with me for being useless and on his team. I sat beside the pool, flicking through Katherine's copy of *Vogue* and trying not to mind that there was an in-transit feeling to the fading day. We seemed to be marking time, waiting for Will and Maddi to leave. The period of their living with us was running out; this time, when they left, they would never come back in quite the same way. They'd no longer be coming home.

Perhaps Peter felt as mournful as I did, because once Will got out and settled himself down with a book on the financial services industry, he started up a conversation with him about a meeting he'd had earlier with Shaikh Abdullah bin Ahmed at the Ministry of Trade, who'd kept him waiting in an ante room for an hour and a half.

Sam, lying on his stomach on the next sunbed, muttered, 'Typical bloody Arab.'

'Sam!' I protested, 'you can't say that!'

'Why not? It's true.'

He doesn't say anything for months and then when he does it's racist.

'No, Sam's right: it is typical bloody Arab,' Peter acknowledged. 'The Hawaris use their customs against us. But we do it to them, too. We insist punctuality makes us more efficient, but it doesn't necessarily. Not here, anyway.'

'You still can't say racist things,' I objected. Peter seemed to be slightly missing the point. 'Just because Shaikh Abdullah runs late, you can't write off the entire population.'

'Why not, when it's true?' Sam said lazily, without lifting his head. 'Peter said. It's their culture, innit? And they do it to us to wind us up, because they can. They want to prove they're in charge.'

'That sounds very silly,' I said, 'given that your best friend really is an Arab.'

'It's like dad, though . . .'

'What is?'

'Some Saudi kills him in a hit-and-run accident . . .'

I swallowed. 'You don't actually know that.'

'OK, *someone* kills him in a hit-and-run accident, but even though the other car must have been pretty smashed up, no one finds it. Why would that be, now? Maybe because they don't bother to look?'

'Sam, that's . . .'

'You're saying that there isn't one rule for rich Arabs and another for the rest of us?'

'Yes, I am.'

I flushed. I didn't want to go into this now. I needed to clear this up with Sam, but not here, not now.

'It's *institutionalized* that they're better. The law operates in favour of them and against us.'

'We get a very good deal, Sam,' Katherine said, bringing out the teapot, followed by Magdalena with a tray of cups and saucers.

'Yeah, OK, we do. If we were poor Indian construction workers we wouldn't have any rights at all. There'd be no law at all then.'

I said wearily, 'What does Faisal say when you start talking this rubbish?'

'He agrees. And it's not rubbish, mum, and you know it.' He lifted his head and became suddenly and alarmingly articulate. 'He says it's understandable when you think about it: they're a hundred times richer than us, but their country has no standing in the world and they've got no say in how it's run. They're not even supposed to think about things, because their religion's meant to have all the answers. All they've got to fall back on is a chippy sense of their superiority.'

It was hormonal. He was just trying on attitudes. Sometimes his frustration exploded in random outbursts, emotional erections as unreliable and misdirected as (I presume) the physical ones.

'Even if you think that, you can't say it,' I told him. 'You're wrong, but even if you were right, dismissing a whole population isn't acceptable.'

'What, so we don't speak the truth any more?'

I sighed: this wasn't the time or the place to go into this. The fact was that, no, we did not necessarily speak the truth. Even though I had always emphasized the importance of honesty and been offended when I discovered Matt had concealed the fact he was gay, I'd consistently and deliberately lied to them. I'd decided it was better for the boys not to know their father had been drunk when he died on the Arad Road, or that he'd caused the accident, or that I knew perfectly well who else had been involved. It was easy to lie in Hawar, because the police had no desire to talk to the press, the authorities preferred not to acknowledge that anyone was ever drunk on the roads, and the death of an expat was a thing to be hushed up and forgotten as quickly as possible. I had colluded with the instinctive furtiveness of the place, intending to tell the truth eventually, not realizing how much a lie might fester.

Fortunately, Matt arrived at that moment, matey and back-slapping, hugging Will, talking noisily about the traffic and how good it was to see everyone, covering up any leftover awkwardness. Will was civil to him, if distant. But that was how he was, anyway: if Matt was a person who was habitually effervescent, slopping over the edges, Will was someone in an airtight container with flip-top catches, dishwasher and microwave proof.

Before there had been any chance for them to have a private

conversation, the doorbell rang again and, a few moments later, Magdalena showed Andrew into the garden. He'd been passing and seen my car outside, he explained, and he'd realized Will and Maddi must be here. Katherine bustled around making more tea while he told us his news.

'I was at the embassy for lunch,' he said, his large body collapsing haphazardly into a chair, 'and the emir's had a stroke.'

'No!'

'When?'

'Last night, apparently.'

'It hasn't been on the news . . .'

'It wouldn't be, Mil.'

'He's alive?'

'Yes, but Richard doesn't know in what state.' He meant Richard Crossley-Tennant, the British ambassador. 'He's in the Hawari Defence Force Hospital.'

'Poor man,' Katherine said, passing him a plate of Magdalena's home-made chocolate chip cookies. He took two; he doesn't cook much for himself at the chaplaincy. 'So is the prime minister in charge?'

'Yes. The crown prince is in London.'

'He'll be heading back now, though,' Peter said. The crown prince and his uncle were known to disagree about the future of Hawar. Shaikh Jasim was a conservative and viewed his nephew as dangerously radical, not least because he threatened his freedom to siphon off 10 per cent of any contract. The locals scathingly referred to the prime minister as The Elephant, on account of the fact that, in any negotiation, it felt like he was in the room.

'Wasn't the crown prince in some sort of trouble in London?' asked Katherine vaguely.

'He gave a speech,' Peter said. 'He was supposed to be on a private visit, but he spoke at some debate at the LSE. It was only a student thing.'

'What does that mean?' Matt asked, 'only a student thing?'

'Yeah, dad,' said Millie. 'You should know better.'

'The speech went a bit far,' Andrew explained. 'He hadn't cleared it with Shaikh Jasim, Richard says.'

'Perhaps because he wouldn't have approved,' suggested Will.

'Oh,' Katherine said, 'I heard it was drugs.'

'According to Richard, the Al Majid line is that the speech was a mistake because it gave the impression that there's an argument inside the ruling family about the pace of reform, which there isn't.'

'Not much there isn't,' said Millie.

'So what will happen if the emir dies?' Maddi asked.

'Or if he's alive but too sick to run the country,' Sam suggested brightly.

'I don't think Richard knows. The embassy's known this was coming, but they were hoping not to have to deal with it for a while yet.'

Millie said: 'The last thing you want is regional instability when you're trying to start a war. Specially an illegal one.'

'I think we're technically supposed to be trying to avoid the war.'

'Yeah, right.'

'Richard seems to think it doesn't matter so much which one of them comes out on top, as long as one of them does. His main worry is that if the differences in the ruling family become too obvious, some of the shi'a, or the other disaffected young people, might think there's a power vacuum and decide to riot and that then sunni–shi'a tension might spread to other parts of the Gulf . . .'

'It's ironic,' Matt said, though generally he wasn't bothered about politics, 'that the British and Americans go round claiming they want democracy in the Gulf states, but they're actually terrified of getting it.'

'Come on, Matt,' Peter said, 'if the Al Majid are overthrown and Hawar gets some kind of democracy, the Islamists will take control, and that'll almost certainly be the end for all of us. We're *all* frightened of democracy.'

'So,' I said to Sam later, when we were at home, 'are you gay?'

'Mum, what kind of a question is that?' He flicked the remote.

'Only I know it can run in families.'

'You're nuts.'

'And you haven't brought any girls home.'

'Would you've been happier if I'd done it in front of you?'

There was no need to be vulgar. 'Post-gay?'

'What the hell is that?'

'It's for people who don't want to have to live up to the stereotypes. Who think the whole obsession with sexual identity is unnecessary.'

'Where the hell d'you get this from?' He'd found *The Simpsons* now and he threw himself back in the armchair to show he was busy watching, although he's seen most episodes at least five times.

'If they fancy boys, they don't also have to be camp or join the caring professions or whatever.'

'Mum, I've got no idea what you're going on about.'

'Only it'd be fine.'

'D'you *want* another gay son? Am I disappointing you in some way?'

'No, but I don't *not* want one. I wouldn't want you to think . . .'

'Look, I don't fancy boys, OK? I prefer girls. This is the most embarrassing conversation I've ever had. Can I just watch the telly?'

'OK, OK . . .'

I went back to the kitchen.

Seven

I was driving to the Al A'ali House, thinking that quite a lot of things might be like theme park rides. You know how at the age of sixteen or seventeen you'll try anything? Vertical drops that leave your innards behind, roller coasters that wrench you round while haphazardly upending you, nausea-inducing spinners that hurl you about until you're not sure if your bones are inside or outside. At that age, you want the sensations. But you don't get many middle-aged women on roller coasters. Maybe that's because middle-aged women know that death happens – or maybe there's some complicated hormonal reaction going on, producing feelings of fragility and nausea. Maybe we just have more flesh to wobble and protest. Whatever, there comes a time when you can't see why you ever thought it was a good idea to queue for an hour in order to experience a minute and a half of queasy terror. When you realize the importance of having someone on the ground to hold the bags.

I wondered if spending time alone with James Hartley might be like that: something that once seemed thrilling but was now largely incomprehensible, which only made sense when you were seventeen.

I was wearing a new, simple navy dress, which I was hoping was deceptively demure, provocative in its refusal to be provocative. It was, I thought, an outfit that was putting up a bit of a challenge – 'OK, only take me on if you think you're *really* seductive.' Matt got it – he said I looked great, and he's gay, so he does notice – but for all I knew, the signals might be too complicated for James, who might just think I wasn't making enough effort and looked like someone's secretary, which is what I am.

The door to the Al A'ali house was opened by a tall North

Indian, with James crossing the hall not far behind him, wearing a pale blue shirt that emphasized the splashy, Hockney-in-California colour of his eyes. He'd hardly put on any weight over the years: his chest and shoulders were more solid but his waist and hips were slim and his neck hadn't fattened – unlike the necks of most middle-aged men I knew – or gone scrawny.

He hugged me for a moment – holding on slightly too long again – and led me into the drawing room, which was lit by at least fifty fat candles, guttering against the dark wood and the Persian carpets. They were Qashqais – my favourite – and, a little nervously, I started chattering away about the door-to-door carpet salesmen who try out their merchandise on your floors, rug after rug until they spot a weakness, then up and leave without any money, so you can find out how you feel about it. The annoying thing about carpets is that you almost never go off them: if you like one, you're going to like it even more a week later.

I was prattling and James didn't know anything about carpets and didn't have much to contribute to my stream of conscious-ness, so it was a relief when the handsome waiter came in with champagne.

James indicated a place on the sofa and I sat down. He sat next to me, knees closer to mine than you'd put them if you were trying not to give someone the wrong idea.

'I want to know all about you,' he said. 'Everything. Why are you here?'

'You invited me.'

'No, I mean in Hawar. Why did you stay on?'

'I hadn't planned to ...' Fourteen years ago, everyone had assumed that I'd leave, including me, because I had three children under the age of eleven and my husband was dead and it seemed unlikely I could live in an Arab country without a man. Some people (Chris and dad) couldn't understand how I could live here *with* a man, what with the heat and the Hawaris.

But then, one afternoon, about a week after Dave's accident, I was driving home along the Corniche and, for no good reason, perhaps simply because everything was off balance, I didn't turn off up the Jidda Road to the compound, but carried on driving towards Saffar, which was still a fishing village then, toppling into the salt flats at the western tip of the emirate, the houses made of gypsum, the roads rough. I parked the car at the point where the road petered out, and walked along the rubble track to the place where palm trees sprouted along the shore and the land and sea seemed to wrap into each other. An old Hawari was crossing the mudflats on a wooden cart pulled by a white donkey, a pile of conical wooden traps behind him. There was near-silence, aside from some rustling palm trees, the occasional shout of a child in the village behind, the soft squelch of wheels through muddy wet sand. I stood for a long time, losing track, watching the sun sink through the sky like a slow weight until it touched the water, seeing the horizon spit up its oranges and pinks, its yellow and mauve livid lights. I felt the heat sink out of the day and the darkness fold over.

That was the day I decided to stay. The idea wasn't completely irresponsible. Sue had offered to keep me on at school, which I knew would take care of the rent and mean that Anwar would sponsor me. So I could stay legally, and I could afford to stay. And standing there on the shore, it occurred to me that I didn't need protection – at least not the kind my dad and Chris were talking about – in Hawar, where so much that was meaningful was veiled in politeness. With everything so quiet and reflective and the sea and sky seeming to pour back their colours into each other, I realized that it would be perfectly possible to live here.

'You haven't regretted it?' James asked, when I explained some of this.

'Well, no, although you always wonder how things might have been different.'

'Yes,' he said, so meaningfully that I blushed. 'It must have been hard, though,' he added, 'being on your own.'

'I wasn't really. I had three children.' I didn't want him to feel sorry for me, or think I felt sorry for myself. He said something then about my obviously being a great mother, which was just flattery, because all he knew about my children was that one of them was gay.

Most of the time, as I confessed to him, I believed I was only getting it half-right – unlike, say, Maddi's parents, who'd known what they wanted from the outset, and had cultivated various accomplishments, musical instruments and off-piste skiing. I hadn't known that off-piste skiing even existed, and I'd brought up my children haphazardly ... But the truth is that you can only be self-deprecating and oh-I'm-rubbish-really about motherhood up to a point, because you run the risk of suggesting your kids are failed kids, useless and disappointing, whereas in reality they'd have to become murderers or heroin addicts or something for you to feel that, and probably even then you wouldn't.

'Well, I think you're incredible,' he said at last. 'And you always were determined. I knew you'd be brilliant at whatever you put your mind to.'

I raised my eyebrows, trying to look lightly amused in a sophisticated way, as though film stars were always paying me compliments. I asked about him, to give myself a moment to re-establish my composure, although, in reality, I knew what had happened, because I'd read the profiles. I knew that he'd only been in Los Angeles a few months when he'd got his first part in a low-budget movie, and that three years later the director Brett Berkovic had cast him as a drily witty time-travelling professor of genetics, a role he'd since reprised five times.

'It's mad, all that,' he concluded. 'But you're in the real world,' he added, as though that was something to admire. 'You have all these kids and people to worry about.'

'No,' I said, 'that won't work. That real world stuff. I'm not going to feel sorry for you because you're too busy to get out to your ranch in Arizona more than twice a year.'

'OK,' he said, smiling. 'So, anyway, we seem to have

established that you were prepared to go abroad with Dave, even though you wouldn't with me?'

'It was a long time ago.'

'I want to know where I went wrong. People generally find me fairly attractive.'

'You are,' I smiled. 'You know you are. You always were.'

'Well, then?'

'I suppose . . .' I glanced at him uncertainly, but he seemed genuinely to want an answer. 'I suppose I felt left out. It was your decision to go.'

'But I asked you to come . . .'

'Only at the end. I didn't feel it was about me.'

'It was always about you.'

'I thought at the time I couldn't trust you. Now . . . well, I think that perhaps it was myself I couldn't trust.'

'OK, maybe that's acceptable. That's quite gracious. I think we can live with you taking the blame for messing up our relationship.'

I remember thinking at the time that James was selfish, but what had seemed like self-obsession then now seemed more the kind of youthful drive and ambition that would allow a person to become successful. I'd grown up in a very enclosed world, where you were a bad daughter if you didn't pop in to see your parents every day. I'd been too insecure to contemplate leaving Thornton Heath; I'd lacked the imagination to envisage a larger world. I could have had a bigger life, an oxygenated life, only I'd been too frightened to take it. I had turned down experience and adventure, while James, very sensibly, had gone ahead and seized it.

The waiter arrived to say that dinner was served and we moved into the dining room, although I wasn't in the least bit hungry.

Over sashimi followed by sea bass – at which we only picked – we made general conversation, a lot of it about the film and Al Maraj's ambitions for it.

'Nezar's idea is that Arab investors won't put much money into an industry they know so little about,' James explained, doing rather a good job of pretending to be discussing matters of general interest while actually staring at me and touching my ankle with his toes. He'd kicked off his sandals under the table and his flesh against mine sent little shocks of sensation through my body as he shifted his feet. 'They need one or two films to release well, so they can see that the business can make money – and he's obviously hoping that this is going to be one of them.'

'It's asking a lot, though,' I observed, trying to ignore his toes just above my ankle, 'that the Arabs should get involved in an industry where they're so often seen as the enemy.'

'I suppose that's partly the point – to prove to Hollywood they aren't the enemy, and to show the Arabs that Hollywood can help demonstrate that to the rest of the world.'

'It's ambitious, anyway.'

'That's Nezar, though. Look what he's achieved here, making a film in a location that's about to become a war zone.'

'He seems rather stern,' I said carefully, 'as if he disapproves of a lot of things.'

'Does he? Like what?'

'Well, me, actually.'

'He's probably jealous.'

'Of what?'

'He probably thinks you're going to distract me.' He pushed away his plate. 'I hope you are.'

'Oh, and how do I go about that?'

He smiled. 'You haven't changed.'

'I'm afraid that's not true in any sense . . .'

'– You're fun, you're incredibly sexy. You're not after anything.'

'Oh, I wouldn't be so sure . . .'

He grinned. 'You see: that's what I mean. Most women are too serious. At least, around me. They think they're going to get noticed. I often feel like a kind of soapbox. Women use me to stand on, so the paparazzi can get a better view of them. I can never tell whether they're genuinely interested in me or if I'm just a career opportunity.'

'I think you can safely assume they want to be with you. People generally speaking would.'

'You'd be surprised.' He looked at me intently. 'You know, I haven't had a proper relationship – not one that's been really meaningful – since you.'

I didn't quite know how to respond.

'I meet a lot of women like Rosie.'

'You're dating Rosie?' I said in alarm. 'Isn't that illegal?'

'What?'

'Isn't she underage?'

'Oh, I see.' He grinned. 'I'm *not* dating her, though she might if I were interested – which I'm not, because I've got my mind on other things – but the point is, I wouldn't know whether she was just using me to claw her way up. She's very ambitious.' He smiled. 'Shall we stop pretending we're hungry?'

'The waiter will be gone soon,' he murmured, as he steered me into the drawing room, his hand in the small of my back.

'I have to tell you, though, that I'm jealous,' he announced in a different tone, as we sat down to wait for the staff to finish clearing up: 'I consoled myself all those years with the idea you wanted security – that you didn't want to leave home – but now I find that as soon as I was out of the way you ran off to the desert.'

I didn't want to talk about Dave. 'If I remember rightly,' I pointed out, 'you wrote me a letter saying I was dull and that it would serve me right if I married someone at the insurance company and lived in Thornton Heath for the rest of my life. What was I *expected* to do after that?'

'Did I? How appalling. I can't believe that was me. I don't write letters.'

'It was very badly misspelt.'

'Oh, right. Probably was, then.'

I had a sudden swooping sensation of familiarity as he bent his head towards me; a jolting moment of recognition, of the shape of his skull, the blur of his face as he came close. I registered shock that this was happening, that James Hartley was about to kiss me, and then he was, and then a few moments later he broke off, scooped me off the sofa and in a single movement only possible for someone who did weight training, carried me towards the stairs.

I burst out laughing. He'd done this the first time we'd ever had sex – lifted me off the sofa and carried me up the stairs of my house when my dad and Chris had gone off to visit my nan in Frinton. I'd thought then (you have to remember that this was well before the gesture was rendered ridiculous by too many schlocky movies and also that I was only seventeen) that this was the most romantic thing that had ever happened to me. I'd been scared about sex – about getting pregnant, about sexually transmitted diseases, which they implied at school were rife, about sleeping with a boy who if he wanted to have sex with you had probably slept around with slags, about *being* a slag, about getting it wrong and not knowing what to do. But I'd been excited too, and James's carrying me upstairs had misted up the lens, made it hazy with romance. My ankles may have bashed on the banister and my shoulder scraped along the woodchip wallpaper but I was a princess being carried away from a tower. Clearly I was not a slag.

'You can put me down, though, now.'

'Why?'

'I'm heavy.'

'No!' he lied. 'Not at all! Same as ever.'

Oh no, I thought: he's going to trip over the corner of one of these Persian carpets and cut his head open on some piece of Indian carved furniture and it'll wreck the shooting schedule and cost the producers a fortune, or at least their insurers . . . and maybe he'll need plastic surgery and never look as good again and his career will be finished and it'll all be my fault.

And then I thought that was typical. Here I was, being carried upstairs like Scarlett O'Hara or a princess from a tower, about to be seduced, and I was thinking about insurers.

The staircase was much wider than the one in my dad's house in Thornton Heath and this time I didn't graze any part of my body on the fixtures and fittings.

And then a door slammed downstairs.

'Oh,' said someone. 'Oh, right.'

I couldn't see a thing, but you would have to guess that the person was pretty pissed off.

James spun round. I thought he was going to drop me. Even action heroes can fall over, especially when they've been drinking champagne.

'Nezar!' he said, out of breath (he had been lying about my weight) 'bit busy, as you can see.'

'Ah-hah,' said Al Maraj, or something like that. 'Hruff. Hmp. You've got a five-thirty call.'

'Fiona said six.'

'It's five-thirty.'

'James, can you put me down?'

'No, we're going up.'

Why were we whispering? We could still be heard.

'Good evening, Mrs Lester,' Al Maraj said coldly.

'Annie,' I offered, over my shoulder. 'For God's sake, James, put me down!'

He finally did then, but awkwardly, so my foot twisted slightly as I landed and I staggered, like a drunk person.

'Good evening.'

'I suppose this was bound to happen,' he said – sneered wouldn't actually have been too strong a word, 'but, really . . .'

But really what? And why was it bound to happen? Did he think I'd thrown myself at James? Did he always shag old girlfriends?

Al Maraj turned and went back out, slamming the front door.

'What odd behaviour,' I said. 'Is he allowed to barge in, just like that?'

'He uses the house as an office. He's got a room here.'

'Why didn't you tell me?'

'He was supposed to be out. It didn't come up. It's a big enough house. I thought you knew.'

That seemed to be too many reasons, not all quite fitting together, but I didn't say so. I was wondering if there was any chance of getting back to where we'd been before.

James must have been too, because he said, 'Now, where were we?' and lifted me up again, although it was quite a lot harder from a standing position.

'We need a stunt couple,' I suggested, but he didn't smile, just took a deep breath and trudged on up the stairs.

It's a funny thing about sex that it's physically quite limited. There are only so many things you can do: a limited number of body parts to pay attention to and a finite number of positions, only some of them wholly practicable. Emotionally, on the other hand, almost anything could be going on. It's perplexing that the same physical process can leave you feeling so entirely differently. Unfortunately, given the sameness of the moves, you can't always be completely sure what emotional variant you're getting. Unless there's some transcendent moment when you look into one another's eyes and divine the intensity and scope of the other person's feelings, you can't be one hundred per cent sure their mind hasn't floated away to tomorrow's shooting schedule or whether to buy the latest Ferrari.

I suppose I hoped that by having sex with James, I'd be able to answer that question everyone kept asking me, 'What's he really like?' I'd acquire some special insight from shagging.

It didn't happen, though the shagging was good, in the sense that he was very expert (much more so than I remembered; evidently, he'd had plenty of practice). But despite our neatly timed orgasms, I can't say I really lost myself. I didn't ever forget that I was having sex with a film star, and I'm not sure he forgot I was either.

I caught myself almost feeling sorry for him. People must expect so much of such a perfect body, of a man whose sexiness was hyped around the world. That could be quite paralysing: how could he not be conscious of being James Hartley? Of the fact that just by getting into bed with you a woman had achieved most of what she was going to get out of the encounter, so that it almost didn't matter what happened subsequently? She'd still have been to bed with you. And whatever did happen would almost certainly be a disappointment, because being good-looking and a competent actor did not in fact mean that you were a sex god. How could you hope to live up to your image? But at the same time, how could you not try? You'd have to put on a performance, to concentrate on being James Hartley, suave and sexy; and in the process, you could easily forget to focus on who it was you were in bed with.

'Sorry about the morning,' he said sleepily, at last. 'Look, stay here as long as you want, OK? They do breakfast downstairs for us, and I'll get them to leave everything out for you – or you can get anything sent over from the hotel.'

A few minutes later, he was asleep. I lay looking at his outflung arm, thinking you could pick any part of him and admire it.

Perhaps if he'd asked me to go to America in a different way, he might have got a different result. Or perhaps, by the time Dave asked, ten months later, the fact that James *had* left, done something entirely different, made me realize I could too. I remember joking that I couldn't keep turning down men who wanted me to go abroad with them. And writing in my diary that this was my best chance of happiness.

I could see now that I'd been quite insecure.

It was a mystery why James was lying in bed beside me, and I had no expectations of anything much beyond the here and now. But I didn't have any regrets; I didn't feel insecure any more.

James and I weren't unequal, because, for all his ability to get women into bed, he seemed needy, as if he thought there was something he wasn't getting while he hurtled and lurched from relationship to affair, movie to movie, shedding bits of himself like skin in all the different beds he slept in. He believed I was the opposite – that I was grounded, I'd had relationships that had lasted, children to slow me down and make me take things at their pace. The certainty and durability of my emotions seemed, I think, tantalizingly different to his own fleeting, opportunistic, expedient relationships.

What seemed only a very short time later, a telephone rang in my left ear, and I stirred into consciousness of lying shoulder to naked shoulder with James Hartley, his hand lying lightly against my hip. The bedroom door opened and someone – one of his staff, I think – brought in a pot of tea and two cups on a tray and James was awake and out of bed and in the shower.

I stretched and yawned and made myself sit up and look at my watch, which said five o'clock. James came out of the bathroom wrapped in a towel, and I had to take him in bit by bit, because it was all too much at once.

He sat down on the edge of the bed. 'Thank you for a great evening.'

'It was no trouble.'

'I'd really like to see you again.'

'OK . . .' I said cautiously, 'that can probably be arranged.'

'The thing is, though,' he added awkwardly, 'I think we should keep it quiet. Just for now.'

'What d'you mean?'

'Once people start finding out, it will change.'

'I don't understand.'

'No, because you haven't been in this situation before.'

'You think?'

'Have you been out with someone like me?'

'I've been out with someone exactly like you.'

'I mean a movie star,' he said, getting dressed.

'Well, not often, no,' I accepted, though it was a bit early in the morning for him to be pulling rank.

'So you don't know what it's like.'

'I see,' I said tightly. 'What is it like?'

He came back to the bed. 'Look, Annie, I want to get to know you again. I don't want to lose this feeling.'

'No, it's a very nice feeling,' I agreed.

'But we will if other people get a piece of it. Which they will, once they start finding out. So all I'm saying is that we should keep it quiet for a bit. Keep it to ourselves.'

'Al Maraj already knows,' I pointed out. 'And the staff here. And Matt and Sam knew I was having dinner with you last night, and you can be sure they'll have noticed I didn't go home.'

'I don't mean Nezar. Or Fiona. And obviously I'm not asking you to lie to your sons. Just generally. Gossip gets out of hand so quickly, and the papers will print anything if they can get away with it. And then even you start to believe what people are saying ... Anyway, I don't mean for ever. Just till we get to know each other a bit better.'

'Oh,' I said disappointedly. 'I was about to come downstairs with you.'

'Really? We only have coffee. And then go out to the cars.'

'If you don't want me to, I won't.'

'No, I didn't mean that. Look, fine, come down if you want. But you're not even dressed ...'

'It's not as if I'll waste time choosing what to wear.'

He smiled. 'No. You'll have to find your clothes, though. They're all over the shop ... Look, I've got a couple of things to run over with Fiona, so I'll go ahead. But you come down when you're ready. And if we've already gone, I'll call you later.'

Once he'd left I went into the shower and stood under the steaming water, thinking that one of the big attractions of sleeping with a global sex symbol was telling people about it. But of course, he knew that.

I retrieved my clothes from the floor and put them on, found a hairdryer and ran my fingers through my hair, cleaned my teeth with a new toothbrush I found in the bathroom, then went downstairs into the dining room, where James was sitting in the corner reading a script, and Nezar Al Maraj and Fiona Eckhart were standing by the table. Everyone looked up when I appeared. Fiona frowned, Al Maraj looked disapproving, and James said with embarrassment, 'Oh, hi, Annie. You've met everyone?'

'Yes. Morning.'

Fiona pursed her lips. 'Nezar, what is it with this country? We still don't have permission for filming at Wadi Ghul ...'

'It's where the crown prince likes to ride, I'm told,' he said, staring at me. I stared back. 'Good morning, Mrs Lester. Coffee?'

'Annie. Yes, please.'

'But I thought he wasn't even in the country?' Fiona asked.

James was sitting in the corner armchair, frowning at a script. 'Wasn't he in trouble in London?'

Al Maraj handed me a coffee cup. 'He gave a speech,' he said. Did I imagine it, or did he shake his head at me? What, in despair?

'Would you like some breakfast?' He indicated the dining table, which was piled high with enough bread, pastries, fruit, juice and cereal for at least ten people.

I was starving, even though it was nowhere near breakfast time. I hadn't eaten much at dinner. I helped myself to a chocolate croissant and took it over to a small table in the corner.

James glanced up from his script, smiled at me encouragingly, then went back to his reading.

There were two chairs at the table and, as soon as I'd sat down, Al Maraj came over and joined me.

'James told me about your son,' he said quietly.

I frowned. 'You mean Matthew?'

'Yes.'

I looked over at James but he was still engrossed. Al Maraj leant forward. 'This is a difficult time politically,' he said quietly. 'It's doubtful whether the emir will recover from his stroke.'

'Right . . .'

'Matthew should be careful.'

'Er, well, it's sad, about the emir, but I'm not sure what it's got to do with Matt.'

'Homosexuality is illegal in Hawar.'

'I know that.' Did he think I was stupid? I was the one who lived here. 'I think he's careful.' Why was he hectoring me like this? Was he homophobic? Did he want to make me feel bad? 'No one's been arrested, have they?'

'What?'

'For years. They haven't arrested anybody.'

'That's not the point . . .'

Wasn't it? Why not?

He frowned and said, 'Hawaris aren't ready for the whole gay lifestyle . . .'

'That's a shame, given how many gay Hawaris there are. But if you mean they're not ready for Matt, you've got him wrong. He's not the campaigning sort.'

Al Maraj sighed, as if I were missing the point. 'Tell him to be careful. That's all,' he said, and looked at me hard. Why did he keep doing that? I looked back, equally hard.

Fiona said the cars were waiting. 'Goodbye, Mrs Lester.' She whisked past with her arms full of clipboard.

'Annie.'

She smiled thinly.

'Can we give you a lift anywhere?' Al Maraj asked.

'Her car's round the back,' James said. I think even he wanted to get rid of me now. But he dropped a kiss on the side of my head, somewhere near my ear, and whispered that he'd call, and then they were gone and I was left alone with a small mountain of food.

I sat down to gather myself for a moment. I could see it might take a little time to work out what this thing with James amounted to. He seemed keen enough – almost painfully so – when we were on our own, but awkward and embarrassed in company. Still, it was probably worth investing a bit of patience in trying to understand him and the exigencies of his celebrity. He had to be careful with people, clearly. He was used to not giving too much of himself away. Being famous was a bit like burlesque – you showed a bit of yourself and then had to whirl away again to hide it.

The guard shuffled out of his post to lift the barrier into the compound, smirking as if I'd proved something of satisfaction to him personally. Western women are sluts, presumably. I wanted to lean out of the car and say, 'I was with James Hartley, actually,' to see if his expression would change (it would have) but obviously I didn't.

I slid the car quietly through the compound, left it in the carport and let myself into the house, closing the front door quietly behind me.

I could hear Matt talking in his room and, for a moment, I thought he might have someone in there. I'd reiterated the point about it being OK to bring someone home and he'd said: 'Really, mum, you've been fantastic about all this, but I don't think you're ready yet for gay sex.'

What did he mean? Was gay sex particularly noisy, or intrusive in some other way I hadn't thought of because of having a limited sexual imagination?

I did remember once seeing a television programme about the trial of Oscar Wilde and there was quite a lot of fuss in that about semen and faeces mixed together on the sheets at the Savoy. So perhaps he had a point. Perhaps I would be ready for gay sex when he did his own laundry.

The trouble was that for as long as he didn't bring anyone home, I was left thinking he was having random and promiscuous sex with men he met in coffee shops and at private parties or down some back street of the souk. My investigations on the internet suggested that gay men generally speaking had a lot more casual sex. I'd come across an online diary by a gay man (I don't know who was in charge of the censorship software in Hawar, but he was incompetent) who claimed devotion to his boyfriend was consistent with his also having something called tricks – which seemed to be one-night stands – and something else called fuck buddies – who were friends he had sex with every now and then, like other people might meet for a coffee. He thought heterosexuals got themselves into a muddle about monogamy.

So perhaps Matt assumed I wouldn't understand the whole business of tricks and fuck buddies, and he was right, I wouldn't.

He didn't seem to have anyone in his room. He'd been on the phone. Now he wandered into the kitchen. 'And what time d'you call this?'

I put the kettle on. 'You're up pretty early yourself.'

'Website training.'

'Were you on the phone?'

'What? Oh, that was Jodie. Trouble with Adam again.'

Completely unconvincing. There were some things, clearly, that he wasn't going to tell me.

'So, it was a success then,' he said, getting butter and milk out of the fridge, 'with James Hartley?'

'Yes, thank you. Although Al Maraj didn't like my being there and Fiona Eckhart could barely bring herself to speak to me this morning.'

'You've rattled them.'

'They might just be rude.'

I poured two mugs of tea and handed one to him. 'Matt, we agreed – James and I – that we wouldn't say anything to anyone at the moment about seeing each other.'

He frowned. 'It's a bit late for that, isn't it? You already did.'

'I don't mean to you. To anyone outside.'

'Why not? Is there some kind of union rule? You must have

had a certain amount of Botox before you can officially date a film star?'

I laughed uneasily. It hadn't occurred to me that this might be about the way I looked. 'It's more that he's kind of public property and people feel they've got a right – you know, to take a view.'

'So you don't want me to tell anyone?'

'Please.'

He poured some orange juice. 'Pity. It's the only glamorous thing that's ever happened in our family. I could have been glamorous by association.'

He took his juice and went back to his bedroom to finish getting ready. By the time Sam had to get up, fifteen minutes later, he'd already left the house.

'You stayed out last night,' Sam said in an accusing tone, as soon as he walked into the kitchen.

'Uh-huh. Toast?'

'Is it because he's famous?'

'Is what because he's famous?'

'Is that why you stayed the night with him?'

'How can I possibly know? He is. I can't do anything about that.'

Sam sat down at the table. 'Or are you attracted by his money?'

'Don't be ridiculous, Sam! I'm not going to get any money out of it. We're not getting married. It's an affair.'

'That's disgusting.'

'No, Sam, it isn't.'

'You dumped him when he was a plumber.'

'I don't see what that's got to do with anything.'

'Well, if you can't see what it looks like, I'm not going to explain it . . . Why've you made me toast? I don't want toast.'

'You always have toast.'

'I want muesli.'

'OK.'

I removed the toast.

'You realize people will talk about you?'

'Actually, they won't, because we're not going to tell anyone.'

'Why not?'

'People will gossip.'

'What, so he's ashamed?'

'No! It's . . . fragile.'

'You just said it was a silly affair.'

'I don't remember using the word silly. All I meant was I'm not sure it has much chance and . . .'

'No, well, he could go out with anyone.'

'Well, thank you for that support.'

'What *is* he doing with you, though?'

How do you explain passion and regret, pleasure and nostalgia, a sense of something left behind and lost to a sixteen-year-old? Sam didn't want to contemplate the possibility that I might have sex that wasn't either procreative or dedicated to holding a family together.

'I don't think he's had much in the way of real, sustained relationships.'

'So he's not very good at having girlfriends? What, can't he hold on to them?'

'Sam, you're being needlessly hostile.'

'You've got to admit it's weird.'

I put the milk jug on the table and said wryly: 'That should make it easier to keep secret.'

'Yeah, well,' Sam said through a mouthful of muesli, 'I don't suppose it will last anyway.'

When Khaled brought the post later that morning at school, there was a letter from dad. He said he'd had a lovely time at the wedding and how nice it had been seeing me in the Gulf looking so well and that James Hartley had obviously thought so too. He wondered if I'd had the chance to see him again and hoped everything was all right with Matthew and he was sorry if he hadn't taken it as well as I'd hoped at first but it wasn't something people of his generation found easy, because there didn't used to be so many gay people. Now it felt as if a lot of them had suddenly come from nowhere. He didn't know if there really were more but it was hard to believe that that many people had been pretending all that time, so perhaps something really had changed because they say all the fish are turning female, which is something to do with plastic bags and hormones, so you have to wonder what's being done to us.

I don't think he was really trying to say that Matt was an early warning of environmental catastrophe. I think he was trying to apologize.

For me, everything that day passed in a bit of a blur. It was like jetlag only with something better to look back on. I worked mechanically, avoiding actual conversation with people whenever I could in the hope that no one would notice that I was drifting around in a daze.

Will called half way through the morning, except that it was early morning for him and he was on the bus, rattling into work. He wasn't very focused, either: I could hear him rustling the *FT* even while he was telling me that work was fine, the flat was fine, Maddi was fine, fine, fine, fine . . . I knew his mind was really on the day's meetings and all the other hectic City stuff he'd have to deal with once he got into the office – instant info, breathless exchanges, just-in-time trades. But I couldn't really blame him because he was talking to a brain-furred school secretary in a global backwater, and she wasn't making any effort either.

At lunchtime, Karen rang. 'Don't tell Chris I've called you,' she said in a rush, 'because he thinks it's too expensive, but I'm worried about your dad. He's called Gay Switchboard.'

'Chris?'

'No, Ted!'

'He's not planning to come out as well?'

'Annie, please! It's not funny. Chris won't talk about it . . .'

'Were they helpful, at Gay Switchboard?'

'I don't know! They gave him a number for some other organization and now he's going to a meeting.'

'That's OK, isn't it? He's not making you go with him?'

'Don't you think it's weird?'

'I don't know . . . Not if he's got questions . . .'

Actually, I couldn't imagine my dad going to a meeting of any kind, least of all one about gay people.

'I think he might be going senile.'

'I don't know, sounds the opposite of senile to me: making calls, going to meetings.'

'Oh, I should have known you'd be like this!' Karen sighed bitterly. 'It's all very well for you. You don't have to deal with him. And Chris didn't want gays in his family in the first place . . .'

'He'd be much happier if he stopped being so bigoted.'

Until Matt came out I'd hardly been aware of prejudice. I suppose I might have suffered, relatively, from being female: sometimes I suspected I'd been beguiled by romance as a means of corralling and containing my sexuality. But this was no one's fault – no one had specifically said, 'Let's keep Annie Lewis's sexuality under control by making her watch soppy films and read romantic novels.' So I hadn't noticed, because I'd grown up with it and hadn't questioned it and anyway it was a really nice idea. But now Matt's coming out had exposed me to rampant and barely-disguised prejudice, to which, incredibly, I had previously been oblivious. I felt as though I had been sensitized, and would forever more have to examine people's responses more carefully, for hidden thoughtlessness.

'Yes, well, he's how he is . . . Annie? Are you still there?'

I explained that I'd had a disturbed night and promised that I'd talk to her properly about it when she'd found out exactly what kind of meeting was involved.

James called in the middle of the afternoon, as he'd promised. He was affectionate, but clearly rushed, snatching a minute when he was off the set to speak to me. 'Look, I've only got a sec,' he apologized, 'but there's this trip to the desert being planned for Friday, on camels or something. Nezar's organizing it. Would you like to come?'

'With Nezar?'

'And a few others. Not a big group, though.'

'I'm not sure they'll want me.'

'Don't be silly, of course they will. Anyway, I've asked you now . . . Look, I'm really sorry, but I've got to go.'

'So,' I told the boys over dinner that evening, 'it's obviously good that he's asked me out again, but less good that it involves a load of other people.'

'Maybe you'll like them once you get to know them,' Matt said unconvincingly.

The main reason I didn't like them was that they obviously didn't like me, and I couldn't see that changing.

'I thought this James Hartley affair was supposed to be a big secret,' Sam said. 'So why're you going out in, like, a big group?'

'I suppose Al Maraj and Fiona Eckhart and those people don't count.'

'What, so his friends can be trusted and ours can't?'

'Not really . . . they're part of the deal. The whole James Hartley thing.'

'Oh well, I suppose even a crap date will be something to look back on afterwards.'

'Sam, why are you being so hostile?'

He shrugged. 'I'm not. Go. But do you really think anything's going to come of it?'

'I don't know.' I thought teenage boys were supposed to like irresponsible shagging. 'That's not really the point.'

Eight

I was in the fruit and veg aisle of Al Jazira when it happened. We have big, brash supermarkets in Hawar – Saveway up near the compound, or the new Carrefour hypermarket in the Al Riqqa mall with their briskly air-conditioned aisles, every imaginable pancake-mix and sixty different types of salad dressing. But I tend to stick to Al Jazira, where I'd shopped since I arrived in the emirate, which is down a side road in central Qalhat. Parking is a nightmare and the shop looks a bit scruffy, but it sells organic vegetables and can be covered on foot in under half an hour.

I was standing by the tomatoes when they moved in front of me. For a second they trembled in a bloody blur and then I realized the floor was trembling too and thought it must be me – that there was something wrong with me – and then the air seemed to rearrange itself, as something soundlessly frisked the room and everyone in it. And then I heard the noise: a rumble that started a long way off and rolled, over and over, penetrating right into us.

For a moment, nobody spoke, absorbing the aftershock. It was as if an invisible hand had found its way in and fiddled with, disarranged us.

'What d'you think that was?' asked a European woman – I thought probably Greek – who was holding a cabbage in front of her like a shield.

I wondered where Matt and Sam would be. I opened my mouth to answer the probably Greek woman but then it came again: the bounce and shudder, then the long reverberating boom unsettling the air, rattling the plate-glass windows and jiggling the metal shutters, rocking the tins on their shelves and making the dry goods whisper.

At first I thought the war must have started, or that Saddam had launched a pre-emptive strike. A part of me was waiting for the nerve gas and thinking that it was undignified to die in the fruit and veg section of a supermarket, although somehow apt, and that if I could have chosen, I would have chosen a different end. More edifying. I considered for a moment picking up a tomato and taking a bite out of it because it would be better to be doing something than passively waiting to die – though, ideally, you'd want salt if a tomato was going to be your final meal. Still, at least eating would be living – but by the time these inane thoughts had flittered through my head, I'd realized I wasn't going to fall in a blistered heap like the Kurds in Northern Iraq. The adrenalin was already seeping away, leaving a metallic-tasting dread about what it could possibly mean.

Someone who'd been by the door, or gone there after the explosions, came back with the news that there was no smoke or anything else to show where they'd occurred.

'Must've been a long way off,' someone said nervously. 'The American embassy?'

For a moment, we all looked each other defencelessly in the eye, and then we stiffened and turned away and fumbled for our mobile phones and called the people who mattered. I tried to reach Matt and Sam, but like everyone else in Al Jazira, I found it impossible to get through. The lines were all busy.

I finished shopping sketchily – staring too long at the shelves or throwing things into my basket carelessly. I couldn't remember any more what I'd come in for.

Sitting in the traffic on the Al-Liyah Highway, I tried to call the boys again and still couldn't get a line. The road out to the port was closed. It took fifteen minutes to get round the Pearl roundabout and the traffic was at a standstill up the Jidda Road. Helicopters thudded overhead and sirens complained through the nearby streets, but it was impossible to get a sense of where they were heading until one rushed up behind you, blaring importantly, and even then you only knew that they were passing, going somewhere else.

I switched on Radio Hawar, hoping for some kind of emergency bulletin, but they were playing The Eagles, so I switched it off again. Finally, half way up the Jidda Road, my phone rang and I snatched it up from the passenger seat, only to see that it wasn't either of the boys. It was a number I didn't recognize.

My fingers were slippy with nerves. 'Annie?' James said. 'Just checking you're OK.'

'Thank you. Yes, I'm fine. It's good to hear you. But how did you get a line?'

'I don't know. Nezar knows someone.'

That was typical. The film company could get a line because Al Maraj knew someone, even though they couldn't possibly need one, otherwise why would James be calling me? Meanwhile there must be thousands of frantic parents trying to reach their children.

'I haven't been able to get hold of Matt or Sam, though. D'you know what happened?'

'Suicide bombers. One tried to get on to the set, here at the port. Then there was a car bomb near our office.'

'God, are you all right?'

'I'm fine. A couple of our security guys are badly hurt. They may be dead: no one's telling us much. A load of people have been taken to hospital . . . but they're saying it was worse over at the office . . . Oh, hang on a minute, Nezar says d'you want us to try to get hold of Matt and Sam for you?'

'Could you? Oh, please, James, if you could . . .'

I gave him the numbers and laid the phone down on the passenger seat as carefully as if it were itself a bomb. It was good of him to have called me, and reassuring to hear his familiar, throaty voice.

Gulf Films' headquarters was more than a mile from the publishing company's office on the edge of the souk, but Matt often went out on assignments. The diplomatic area, despite its name, was actually Qalhat's upmarket business district, all banks and corporate headquarters, so Sam was unlikely to have been there but it wasn't impossible ... And half the people I knew worked in those tall buildings, sprouting like weeds on the thin soil of the reclaimed land.

I'd crawled up the Jidda Road and taken most of the shopping indoors when James called again. 'Spoken to them both,' he reported cheerfully. 'Matt's at work, and Sam's at someone called Faisal's? In Jidda? Does that make sense?'

'Oh, God, yes, thank you ...' I'd switched on the television as soon as I'd come in. Hawar TV was showing a documentary about Victoria Falls. There were no pictures yet on the satellite channels.

'We told them you're OK.'

'Thanks.'

(I found out later from Matt and Sam that Al Maraj had actually made the calls.)

'I don't understand,' James was saying, '– Nezar promised it wasn't like this. He said we'd be safer here than at home. He didn't say there were going to be car bombs in the AmEx building.'

I don't know why I hadn't realized, because I'd been to Gulf Films' office to drop off the wedding invitation. But it was only now, when he said it, that I remembered which building they were in.

His words sliced into the moment. There was before, when I hadn't known, and after, when I did.

'Millie!'

'Someone you know?'

'Maddi's sister. She's been working there.'

'The one who looks like a model ... ? Shit – but, look, I'm sure she'll be OK.'

'Yes.' She would. Of course.

He said they'd had to stop filming for the day and I asked if he wanted to come round.

'Oh, I'd love to,' he said with genuine regret, 'but Rosie and I have got to run through a scene and I'm not even sure if I can get out of here . . .'

'No, sure,' I said feeling suddenly foolish.

'I'll see you on Friday. I can't wait. I keep thinking about you. It's very distracting.'

I made tea, slowly and deliberately, as if I were making a point of being alive. As if just pouring the water into the teapot was an act of defiance and sitting down on the sofa was heroic. As if I'd been through something, even though I'd actually only been on the edge of something, mostly in the way of ambulances.

I worried about Millie and whether I should call the Franklins, or Will – but this would have seemed like overreacting before there was any firm news – and what if they hadn't heard yet where the bomb was? I flicked through the channels and found a report on Al Jazeera. I couldn't make much sense of the Arabic, but the pictures were clear enough. The diplomatic area, our gleaming business district with its confident commercial architecture, its glass bubbles and metal shards, now looked like 1980s Beirut: smoky rubble, drifting dust, confusion. A litter of concrete lumps, bent metal, shattered glass.

The phone rang and Will was on the line, his voice tight and struggling to stay steady. 'We think Millie's been hurt.'

'Oh, Will . . .'

'She's alive. They're taking her to the Hawari Defence Force Hospital. We don't know how bad it is. Peter and Katherine are trying to get down there. They can't get through the traffic. I thought . . .' he trailed off, in disbelief, 'I thought I'd better check you're all OK.'

'Yes. We are. I heard the explosions. Everything shook. The others are fine.' I told him what James had told me, but I didn't know what else to say. 'I'm sorry.'

'Maddi's on her way home from work. She may come out to Hawar.'

'Can I do anything?'

'Not yet. When we know, maybe.'

'Are you going home?'

'Yes. There's a call coming in. It might be her. I'll have to go. I'll let you know.'

Mainly because of the film stars, the Hawar bombs were a big news story all over the world. There were pictures of James Hartley and Rosie Rossiter on all the satellite channels and the front pages of newspapers and soon people who hadn't previously heard of Hawar could have told you where it was. On the inside pages of the papers there were potted histories of the emirate, explaining the recent introduction of limited democracy and the rise of the Islamists, and asking whether the Hawar bombers were likely to be linked to Al Qaeda or to represent a new kind of home-grown, autonomous Islamic militancy.

What seemed to have been established was that a twenty-one-year-old Hawari with home-made explosives strapped around his waist had tried to walk through security on to the film set down at the old port, killing two Pakistani security guards and injuring three Hawaris, a French woman and a Filipino. A second man, aged twenty-three, with the same kind of explosives packed into the boot of his ancient Toyota Corolla, had accelerated off the road over the rough, stony ground of the diplomatic area and into the reinforced plate-glass front of the AmEx building, killing one Sri Lankan, one Egyptian and one Indian, and injuring twenty-five other people, including Millie.

Both bombers had come from Ghafir, the village closest to Al Janabiyya. Police cars had been screeching and bumping up and down the unmade track beyond the compound gate all day.

The reporting had a hysterical air. Sam and I found ourselves watching some American politician on CNN insisting that the film stars should be brought home and attacking the producers for making them come to what he called a terrorist region.

'Oh, great,' Sam said, 'a couple of losers from Ghafir work

out how to make a bomb and the entire region is populated by terrorists.'

'Oh, look, even better: it's Mohammed Alireza.' The internet and cassette tape cleric was standing outside the mosque by the Hafeet roundabout, slim and impeccably thobed, explaining to a BBC reporter the background to sunni–shi'a tension in Hawar. 'Do they have to give him airtime? Why can't they get someone normal on? I suppose that's not what they want, sensible people. They want mad mullahs.'

'He's not mad.'

'What, apart from the whole cosmic struggle thing?'

'It's just talk, all that. He's the only serious opposition to the Al Majid.'

It seemed to me like the Al Majid were quite capable of creating their own opposition from among themselves. 'People outside the country will think everyone here talks like that. Like we're all waiting for an apocalypse.'

'Mum, you're not listening to what he's saying . . .'

'They're making him look like he matters, that's the trouble.'

A picture of Millie filled the screen. Someone had taken it at the wedding: her head was half-turned and her eyes were wide and expectant, her mouth open in the beginning of a smile. She looked so beautiful you'd have thought she couldn't be touched by trouble. She was in intensive care; her doctors were saying her condition was stable.

It took a while for Maddi to sort things out with her new employers and by the time she could get away, the planes to Hawar were full of journalists. The only seat she could get was on an overnight flight; she arrived on Wednesday morning, a day and a half after the attacks.

I offered to pick her up so her parents wouldn't have to leave the hospital, but Peter wanted to collect her. He said he needed to prepare her.

Maddi herself called me on Wednesday evening, to report that Millie was doing OK but that she couldn't talk much now because they were about to have a meeting with the doctors. She suggested I meet her the following afternoon, once school was finished, so, on Thursday, I drove south out of Qalhat for about forty minutes along a highway that sliced across the scrub, leading into the desert, going nowhere else. At the end of it, the shimmering white edifice of the hospital reared up, vast and lonely in a moonscape of salmon pink shale. It was typical, somehow, that this hospital was here with its world-class facilities and highly qualified staff, part of the twenty-first century, raring to go, while all around it camels grazed in a baking, wind-scarred desert that was working to a different time scale. It was, like so many things here, at once dynamic and utterly precarious.

There was a lot of security round the hospital – armed guards at the entrance to the car park, four wheel drives dotted round the perimeter fence – and I remembered that the emir was here too. I parked the car and went inside, shivering in the hospital's attack-mode air conditioning. Presently, Maddi came downstairs, emerging from one of the banks of lifts, her face both drawn and swollen, her eyes red. She hadn't washed her hair.

I steered her towards the coffee shop and collected a couple of cappuccinos. Then we sat down and I asked about Millie.

'She's got this thing – did I say last night? – blast lung injury. She's still in ICU because of it, but they seem to be managing it . . . when you're that close to an explosion, it can sort of collapse your lungs. You can't breathe. Her lungs are torn, is how they put it. And there's a lot of swelling . . .'

'I'm so sorry.'

'They think they can deal with that. Her face is cut, though. She got hit by some of the flying glass.'

Millie had been outside the building, coming back from lunch.

'You know,' Maddi raked her fingers through her limp hair, 'I keep hoping that at the last minute the bombers realized it was all a horrible mistake: there was no heaven and no seventy virgins and they were just deluded and small and stupidly destructive.'

I wondered whether I should tell her about the theory I'd read, that martyrs (not, of course, that the Ghafir bombers were martyrs) weren't entitled to seventy virgins in paradise after all, but raisins. White raisins, in fact. It was something to do with the idea having come from Christianity centuries before, and having been clumsily translated from Aramaic into Arabic. White raisins would have been pretty scarce in seventh century Arabia, and presumably before, at the Christian time when the idea was thought up, or maybe even pre-Christian time (the whole thing had a pagan ring, when you really thought about it). Was there any consolation for Maddi, in thinking of the suicide bombers turning up in heaven expecting girls and getting raisins instead?

Probably not, right here and now. Anyway, I don't think it was a very widely-held theory. I asked her instead if she'd managed to get any sleep.

'I dozed a bit in a chair. Dad wants me to go home tonight. He says there's no point everyone getting exhausted, and he's right. But mum thinks she mustn't close her eyes, because it's only her powers of concentration making Millie better. Anyway,' she glanced distractedly at her watch, 'I really ought to get back in a minute.'

'Sure. Whenever you want.'

'OK. Thanks for coming.' She didn't seem to register that we'd only been together for about eight minutes. Her coffee untouched, she stood up, kissed me and went back to the ward.

Anwar came into my office the next morning and said, 'Of course, there are reasons why young men want to blow themselves up.'

'Really?' I said, sarcastically enough that anyone else would have crumpled into a little heap on the carpet. Unfortunately, my scathing wit always passed him by.

'It is wrong when people want to eliminate your religion.'

'No one wants to eliminate your religion.'

'Or your identity.'

'Anwar, if you're going to tell me there's something that makes it OK to blow up Millie Franklin, please don't.'

'You should listen to Mohammed Alireza.'

'We've been here before, Anwar.' I tapped some papers together on the desk. I was obviously incredibly busy. And annoyed, because I was speaking through gritted teeth. Anyone else would have tactfully left the room.

'Why else do the Americans want to invade Iraq?' Anwar persisted, 'if it is not to destroy us?'

'Weapons of mass destruction? Oil? To prove something?' I didn't know, either, but I didn't think the main aim was to destroy Anwar's religious identity. 'You're not saying now that Saddam Hussein's some great symbol of Islam?'

Anwar had always hated Saddam Hussein. He said he was a bad Muslim.

'Mohammed Alireza explains it: we are at war and we have been since the Crusades.'

'Look, Millie Franklin's not a Crusader, OK? She was born in Hawar in 1983. She's not even a Christian – no, she's not, Anwar, not in any meaningful sense.'

'OK, the imperialism may be a matter of western products now, and western values. But it comes to the same thing.'

'I can't talk about this, it's too upsetting. Millie's in intensive care ... I can't have a discussion about ... whatever it is we're discussing.'

'It is unfortunate what happened to this young woman, but all I am saying is it would be better if you understood why it did ... You know, in your year 800, in the first century of Islam, there were fifteen cities of fifteen thousand people in the Middle East and only one in Western Europe, Rome. The west is determined to make sure that never happens again.'

'That was more than a thousand years ago!'

It was the wrong thing to say.

'Exactly. The west has been at war with us ever since. It cannot bear the thought that Islam was so great. Mohammed

156

Alireza has written on his website this week about Palestine, for example. You should read it. He puts it in English, too. He says that many United Nations resolutions have said that Israel's occupation of the West Bank and Gaza is illegal. Yes, they have said this not once, but many times. Yet 40 per cent of all American aid goes to Israel. What is that, if not an act of war against the Arab nation?'

'We're not talking about Palestine. We're talking about the Hawar bombs where no Americans were injured or killed, and even if they had been . . .'

'The British, they were the same,' Anwar interrupted. 'When they were here, they backed people like the Al Majid, who would side with them and keep the population under control, keep us poor and weak . . .'

'Anwar, I know all this,' I said, 'but it hasn't got anything to do with Millie.'

'That may be how you see it, but it is not true.'

After that, I asked him to leave. Sod him being our sponsor.

It was part of my job to be nice to him and he was so surprised to be ordered out of my office that he actually went.

After he'd gone, I tried to concentrate on the letter I was supposed to be writing to parents of the year fives. But it was hard, because I kept thinking that at some level Anwar probably felt guilty (after all, one of his countrymen had maimed Millie) and I should try to engage with his philosophical difficulties about it. Still, if he felt bad, he could've just said sorry.

Half an hour later, James called to finalize the arrangements for the next day. I said I didn't feel I should go now, with Millie in hospital.

'But I thought you weren't allowed to see her . . .'

'That's not the point.'

'And you've seen Maddi already . . .'

It was true that I hadn't been a great help when I had seen her and I wasn't expecting to do so again for several days.

'I might be needed.'

'Really?'

No. He was right. It was very unlikely that I'd be needed.

'Surely you lot aren't going still, after what's happened?'

'Seems like it. We're all pretty desperate to get out of Qalhat. It's overrun with journalists. Rosie and I did a press call yesterday but they keep asking for interviews and there are photographers everywhere. It was all very pleasantly anonymous until this happened. Please, Annie, I've been so looking forward to it . . .'

'I'd love to, of course, but it feels wrong to be having a good time in the desert when Millie's in intensive care.'

'You sitting at home and moping isn't going to help anyone.'

This was true, so, despite my various misgivings, I drove over to the Al A'ali House the following afternoon and showed my driving licence to the more than usually alert guards on the gate – proper HDF soldiers, not the usual security police – who waved me on up the drive.

Nezar Al Maraj was waiting on the forecourt and came over to open the door of the Jeep.

'I'm terribly sorry about Millie,' he said, as I jumped down.

'Yes. Thank you.'

'How is she?'

'OK. Stable now. Her face is cut, and no one seems to know how it will heal but she'll be home in a few days. I'm very sorry about your security guards.'

'I went to the funerals yesterday. One had a wife and child here, but the other family was in Karachi . . .' He shook his head. 'How are Peter and Katherine?'

I was impressed that he remembered their names. But I supposed that was how he stayed in control of things. 'Understandably distressed.'

He was about to say something else, but James and Rosie came out of the house on to the top step and we both instinctively looked up. Either of them, on their own, would have been conspicuous; together they were dazzling. Al Maraj and I lost the thread of what we were saying. They were deep in discussion about one of their scenes, and didn't notice us.

'So I should try touching you,' said Rosie, 'and you could ignore it.'

'But there's that line where I say I want things I can't have, which I'm sure is about you.'

They seemed to be arguing about which one of them fancied the other one more. I shuffled and James saw me, smiled and came down the steps; Al Maraj moved away smartly. He'd been quite friendly up till then, so perhaps it was only when I was with James that I turned into some kind of contaminant.

Rosie looked as if she was made of flexible wire, rather than the usual bone and muscle. She'd tied her hair in a ponytail and she was wearing khaki trousers that tapered at the ankle and looked frail and strong all at the same time, which was a clever look mainly achieved by being very thin.

Various other people were coming out of the house now: Brian, the assistant director; Chrissie, his girlfriend, who worked for Gulf Films; Dymphna, who was Al Maraj's assistant; Jens, her Danish architect boyfriend, who was visiting for ten days; and Fiona Eckhart. Al Maraj divided us up – I went with James, Rosie and Al Maraj – into three cars and we drove out to Umm Hisin, on the edge of the desert, where a dozen camels were waiting with their Hawari handlers.

We were assigned a camel each and, after the handlers had tied our bags on the back, they helped us on to the wooden saddles. The animals lurched to their feet.

'Nezar, is this safe?' called Brian. At least, I think it was Brian: we'd all tied gutras round our faces to keep off the sun, so although two of us would have been recognizable to a large part of the world's population, you couldn't tell which ones.

'I am *so* not convinced their skinny legs can carry us,' Rosie said.

'You don't weigh anything, darling. It won't be you who has problems,' Fiona replied, which I'm sure was exactly the response Rosie had hoped to hear. If you're not allowed to eat, you probably have to look for pleasures elsewhere. Anyway, it wouldn't be her either, so it was a mystery whom she might mean.

My camel seemed alarmingly young and spirited and set off briskly behind Al Maraj's camel, its smelly head pressed to the other animal's smelly tail. I'd ridden camels before and I could make mine stop and get to its knees, though it was much easier if Al Maraj's stopped and got to its knees first, but it was difficult to exercise any other kind of control.

We processed in single file up a dry river bed, the camels sure-footed in the rubble. I glanced back at the others, wrapped in gutras and sunglasses. We looked like bandits, and there was something lawless about being out here in the middle of nowhere, on the edge of the ancient burial mounds at Al Arish ... I stared out over the humped forms stretching towards the horizon, hundreds, perhaps thousands of them, left over from some barely-remembered Gilgamesh-era civilization. You could feel for a moment here that you were in touch with a different world, of trade in pearls, spices, copper, gold, tortoiseshell, cornelian, with ships plying the Gulf between Mesopotamia and the Indus valley and stopping off at the ancient bustling Hawari port. People had lived here since the start of human time, had fought and traded and loved and died. Had died in very large numbers, to judge from the burial mounds – which were empty now, plundered over centuries, so that Al Arish was desert again, only humpier. Nothing was left of all those people and the things they'd had with them, hoping to take to the afterlife: they had been baked away by the sun and whipped by the wind, so that anything that was left was secreted inside particles of sand.

The burial mounds aside, there was very little to distract you. A single thorn bush poking up optimistically here, a line of stones scattered down a ridge there. After a time – I've noticed this before in the desert – your mind tends to float, big thoughts to drift in. Whole religions have been known to arrive on occasion.

I was fortunately spared having a new religion revealed to me, though I did wonder what I was doing here. Less in a what-is-the-point-of-it-all existential way than in the sense of why was I in the desert with a couple of film stars and a number of people I'd only just met?

After we'd been travelling for about forty minutes, Al Maraj seemed to slow his camel so mine could catch up. I hoped he wasn't going to take advantage of the fact we all looked like Bedouin to start speaking Arabic again.

'It's a relief to get out of Qalhat,' he observed as I drew along-side. 'There's too much politics in Hawar at the moment.'

This was a bit like saying there was too much weather: I wasn't sure what I was meant to reply. But I wanted to make an effort, because he had earlier.

'Because of the emir's stroke?' I asked politely.

'Yes. How's Matthew?'

What? How was that relevant? It's very hard to make an effort with someone when they keep jumping subjects. Perhaps he'd decided I was too thick to have a discussion about politics – probably the question about the emir's stroke revealed some catastrophic level of ignorance – and he'd moved on to something he thought I could cope with, such as my own child.

All in all, it was very difficult to know where you were with him. One minute he was deliberately making fun of me in Arabic, the next he was blustering incoherently because I was on my way to bed with James; now he was presumably making some kind of effort to be pleasant.

'He's OK . . .' I answered cautiously.

'Things are tense here at the moment. Mohammed Alireza's causing a lot of trouble.' He'd gone all disapproving again. The pleasantness had just been to get me off my guard. Now he was warning me again that Matthew needed to be careful, even though he was so discreet that his own mother hadn't realized he was gay until a few weeks ago.

'Surely,' I said, 'if the Islamists are prepared to blow up

Hawari Muslims and Millie Franklin, they hardly needed a gay person to get agitated about. We're all symbols of whatever it is they hate – decadence or materialism or whatever. Matthew isn't any more at risk than I am, or you.'

'Even so . . .'

He trailed off: even so *what*? Definitely, he was homophobic. It was the only possible explanation. He didn't like the thought of Matt being gay but he knew that wasn't an admissible position for a sophisticated person, so he kept implying something dire could happen if Matt did anything about it. He wanted me to believe that if Matt didn't stop being gay *now*, something awful could happen.

'Just tell him not to be reckless,' Al Maraj urged as we reached the top of a jebel; below us in a hollow, a young man in a thobe was tending a fire. The camels picked their way down towards him – mine fell behind again – and then when we reached the bottom, collapsed in their lolloping fashion so we could all dismount. Everyone unwound the scarves from their faces, making a lot of noise about saddle soreness and about the scenery, which was spectacular now that the sun was setting and turning the rubbly landscape rose.

A whole lamb, the local feast dish, ghouzi, was roasting slowly on the fire. The boy who'd been looking after it strolled over to me and introduced himself as Hamad. 'Thank you,' Fiona said officiously, alarmed that anyone might assume I was in authority, 'someone will come and talk to you in a minute.'

'I was at nursery with Matt,' he told me, ignoring her. I shook his hand, trying to place him in the photograph I still had of Matt's nursery class. 'Hamad Al Khalifa,' he added, and then I did remember because Al Khalifa was the name of the Bahraini royal family, of which he was a member of a junior branch, and all the western and Indian mothers at nursery had laughed about marrying off one of their small daughters to Hamad.

'Perhaps you should get back to work?' Fiona suggested. Her voice conveyed contempt, as if it was typical that I'd know the staff; but then Al Maraj came over and said, 'Oh, great, I see you've met my nephew.' It turned out that Hamad was his elder sister's son; he was on his gap year, and had a place at medical school in London for next year.

'Nezar said he couldn't trust just anyone to do the ghouzi,' Hamad explained. 'He thought you'd do this all the time and have very high standards.'

'Me?'

'I was concerned that Annie would know, for example, that it's perfectly possible to get to this place in a four wheel drive,' Al Maraj said, putting his arm round his nephew. 'D'you really have to go? Won't you stay to eat?'

'Can't, it's a girl thing,' said Hamad, pulling a set of car keys from his pocket. He grinned and said he had a Land Rover parked behind the hill, opposite where we'd come down.

I went off to organize my bedroll in the spot that James had selected for us. Not that it really made any difference whether our brand-new, top-of-the-range, film-company-provided sleeping bags were together, because we'd be surrounded by the rest of the group, and out here noise carried for miles, even the slightest disturbance of stones.

'Has he changed much?' Jens the Danish architect asked, straightening up from arranging his sleeping bag on my other side and looking over to where James was standing by the fire, still deep in conversation with Rosie.

'Not really.'

Al Maraj called us over to eat. 'I've ignored all special diets and Hollywood fads unknown to the Bedouin,' he said as he sliced off juicy pieces of meat.

'So no eating only foods beginning with "p" or whatever the latest thin people's craze is,' I said cheerfully to James, as we helped ourselves. He smiled, but asked Fiona for some nutritional advice on the chickpea salad anyway. When we sat down he admitted his nutritionist had taken him off carbohydrate for five months.

'So Nezar, you still think you can get us all out of here before we're blown up?' Brian asked, once we were all settled round the fire.

'They should lock up that imam or whatever he is,' Rosie said. 'He was on the television earlier saying we're at war. Does that mean I'm at war with you, Nezar?'

'Depends whether you remember you owe me your last two jobs.'

'I can't understand why he's so popular,' Chrissie said.

'He gives people something to blame,' Al Maraj answered.

'Although blaming a load of twelfth-century knights does look a bit desperate,' I pointed out.

'Why do they need someone to blame anyway, with all their oil money?' James said, 'doesn't make sense.'

Al Maraj explained about the ruling family and the Swiss bank accounts and the uncertainty about how to compete internationally, to be modern, without abandoning Arab and Muslim identity.

'I still think they should do something about that bloke,' Rosie said.

'Yeah, well, they did lock up him up, but then three years ago they let him out again. And he's got a good story. A fight for the purity of Islam.'

Jens said: 'That's not exactly a political programme, is it?'

'No, but then the Americans are basing their entire foreign policy on a story about being involved in a vast project to end tyranny. And most of us base our lives on stories about love.' He looked at me. 'We're all a bit fond of illusions.'

'You don't mean that!' Fiona objected coquettishly, 'that love's an illusion?'

'Don't I?'

'No! You don't believe that at all.'

'How long does the average Californian marriage last?'

Fiona frowned.

'Six years,' he told her.

'So, what, you think arranged marriages are better?'

'Any rational person would have to conclude they were.'

'I notice *you* haven't agreed to one . . .'

'I think he may be winding us up,' I said.

'Perhaps love's not quite as dangerous as thinking God wants your nation to sort out the world,' Al Maraj said, 'but it's not far off.'

After dinner the camel handlers taught us a Bedouin game which involved chasing one another around the edge of a circle, similar to the nursery game I knew as duck duck goose. Later, Al Maraj produced a guitar that Hamad had left for him, and he played and we sang Simon and Garfunkel and Beatles songs, to which he and Dymphna knew all the words. I tried, and failed, to imagine them singing along to one another in the office.

It wasn't so bad. I'd have preferred to have James to myself, to be out here in the middle of nowhere with no one knowing what we were doing. And if we had to have other people around I might have chosen different characters, ones who didn't give the impression that they were policing us. But James was sitting beside me, holding my hand in the voluptuous darkness and the sky was teeming with stars.

Before we climbed into our separate sleeping bags, I got out my torch and suggested we go and sit at the foot of the jebel for ten minutes and look up at the sky. We padded across the shale and settled ourselves at the bottom of the hill, close together, pointing out the constellations we knew, noticing stars that were normally invisible, exclaiming at the milky way as it slid thickly across the sky.

'It's fantastic to be with you again,' he murmured, slipping his hand down the back of my waistband. 'Frustrating, but fantastic all the same.'

'Oh, look, a shooting star. Like you.' The star fell across the sky and faded.

'No, that's not me. Not really. I only want to be down here with you.'

'Oh yeah?'

'We understand each other, don't we?'

'I hope so.'

'I understood about your dad adjusting to Matt being gay, after all. I know why you find Chris so annoying but you still can't bear anyone criticizing him . . .'

He kissed me. And then – perhaps coincidentally, but I had my doubts – someone coughed in the campsite. From his minders' point of view, if that was what Al Maraj and Fiona were, this was a perfect date, because there was absolutely no chance of sex.

'Tell me about Fiona,' I whispered. 'Is she in love with Al Maraj? I thought it was you at first, because she so obviously didn't like me, but now I think maybe she doesn't like me on his behalf.'

He seemed genuinely puzzled. 'You think she doesn't like you?'

'She tends to give that impression.'

'Oh . . .' he said doubtfully. 'Well, she's worked for me for a couple of years. She's very good. Organizes my whole life. I don't know about her and Nezar. You think she fancies him?'

Is it a man thing, not to notice what's going on around you, or was James particularly thick?

'You spend all your time with them. I thought you might tell me.'

'Yeah, come to think of it, she is always going on about how wonderful he is. But then, he is . . . Anyway, she won't have much luck there.'

'Oh?'

'No. He's always working. And you heard him over dinner.'

That's what I mean, you see. No idea that not everything people say comes pure and unfiltered from the source, like spring water, that some things might be complicated by nuances, depths of flavour, calling for some discrimination. It was pretty clear to me that not only had Fiona been flirting with Al Maraj, he had also been flirting back.

I woke up at dawn with a stiff neck and James snoring softly in my right ear. I wriggled out of my sleeping bag, pushed on my trainers, and went round the back of the jebel to wash in the bowl of water that had been left out.

Fiona was already there. 'Morning,' she said, brighter than usual. 'Sleep OK?'

'Not badly,' I answered politely. I hadn't slept much at all.

'Enjoying catching up with James?'

'Mmmn.'

'He's an enthusiast, of course. Gets very caught up in things.'

'Uh-huh.'

What did she mean? She made James sound like some kind of innocently frolicking dolphin, and me as an entanglement in which he might unfortunately be caught.

'It makes it difficult, sometimes,' she confided, 'you know – dealing with him. To be honest, I thought at first this thing with you – but you're good for him. Sort of steadying . . . I can see why . . . Because he's hopeless, really. Not steady at all. And you're not quite what I thought you were, and perhaps you should . . . Anyway,' she dusted herself down, 'better get some tea.'

I blinked at the back of her, wondering what all that had been about. Completely incomprehensible. Was she trying to apologize for previous offhand behaviour? Or was it a warning? But if so, what about?

I went back to the camp, where Al Maraj and one of the Bedu were crouched over a fire in a hollow in the ground. 'Morning,' Nezar said cheerfully, 'we're just making Arabic bread. The Atkins lot won't like it. There's tea.'

'Charming as this is,' Fiona announced, joining us, 'I am glad I am not a Bedouin person.'

The Bedouin person looked up at her.

'You don't find you see things more clearly out here in the desert?' Al Maraj asked.

'Not specially. And I certainly don't want to *be* seen more clearly – at least not unless someone can provide me with a mirror.'

Al Maraj said, as Fiona had intended he should, that she looked lovely. Actually, he said politely that we both looked lovely. She stalked off again.

When everyone was up, those who were allowed ate the Arabic bread. There was labneh for those who were OK with dairy. The Bedu got the camels saddled up again while we were eating, and we trekked back by a different route. I noticed Fiona slid in behind Al Maraj this time and I also positioned myself better, tucking in behind James; but this route was narrower, mainly along a wadi, and we had to travel single file, so it didn't do either of us much good.

When we dismounted at Umm Hisin, Fiona reminded James he had a meeting with Todd at noon – perhaps in case he got any funny ideas about coming back with me. Ours was the last car back at the house; as we came up the drive Fiona was waiting, holding her mobile, and, as we opened the doors, she was already explaining that because of the bombings, the scenes that were due to be shot in Oman had been brought forward, which meant that James and Rosie would have to fly down to Muscat tonight.

So having engineered a date with virtually no touching, Al Maraj and Fiona had now organized for him to leave the country.

Obviously this wasn't about me. It was about international terrorism – or local terrorism, anyway – and several major corporations needing to get a film made. All the same, I felt his friends wouldn't mind at all that he was being whisked away, were probably delighted that we were being thwarted by the shooting schedule. I knew the film crew meant to have left Hawar by Ramadan. I felt sad, all of a sudden, and wistful: James and I were going to have so little time.

Nine

Cheryl had been out of the country on the day of the bombing, but as soon as she got back she jumped over the low picket fence dividing our properties, pushed through the foliage and came into my kitchen. 'Isn't it terrible?' she was already asking as the flyscreen clattered behind her, 'you just don't expect it here. I was even a bit worried about flying back from Sri Lanka – you really should go, Annie: the windsurfing's great. You need quite a strong core, but you can work on that – but Tel said that was silly and we weren't even flying HawarAir. You think they've got everyone in prison, don't you? They used to lock them up before they did anything like this. Still, Tel says they will have arrested half of Ghafir now. Taken the opportunity. Poor Millie Franklin . . .'

I'd been to visit Millie that morning; she'd come out of the high dependency unit the day before. Despite the stitches, she didn't look as bad as I'd expected and she was surprisingly cheerful, eager for news about James Hartley. I told her about his having invited me to camp in the desert with his colleagues: the outing had been so chaste that this hardly seemed to be giving anything away. I also told her he was now in Oman, but not that he'd been ringing me every day, whispered calls behind my bedroom door which left me staring up at the bedroom ceiling, incredulous that this was happening to me, here, now, when I'd almost given up.

'He must really like you, to have invited you out with all those film people,' she said, determined to be encouraged anyway. 'D'you think he's been in love with you all this time?'

'No!' I laughed. 'He's had loads of other girlfriends.'

'Precisely! He's never found one who's good enough to stick around. You wait!'

I smiled, knowing I only had to wait until this evening for James to tell me again that he'd never felt like this about anyone else, and that when he got back he'd prove it.

Katherine joined me in the corridor as I was leaving the hospital. 'Your friend Diane Bonneau called to say she's having some people round next week – is that right – for her birthday? And she said if any of us wanted a few hours out of the hospital ... Only I think it'd be good for Maddi. She seems very low. Would you mind taking her?'

I said that of course I'd be delighted, although I privately doubted that a thirtysomething's birthday party was really what she needed.

I called Will when I got home and told him Katherine thought Maddi was depressed.

'I speak to her all the time,' he said defensively. 'Katherine's just making a fuss. What, does she think I'm not helping?'

'No one's saying it's got anything to do with you. It's under-standable: Millie could have been killed.'

'There's a lot of pressure, working for an investment bank. I've only just started and now I'm involved in this big Saudi deal and all I do is work and sleep.'

'Will, it's fine,' I said gently. 'It's fine.'

James arrived back from Oman on Wednesday and invited me to meet him at the Al A'ali House as soon he'd finished his personal training session at six o'clock.

I arrived a few minutes early and the door was opened by the tall Indian.

'Who's that, Sandeep?' Fiona called out, and then poked her head out of the dining room, peering over the top of her glasses. 'Oh,' she said, when she saw me. 'Is James expecting you?'

'I hope so ...'

'He didn't mention it. Does Nezar know about this?'

'I have absolutely no idea.'

'I'll have tea, thanks, Sandeep. Annie?'

I protested that I didn't need tea and I was quite happy to wait in the garden but Fiona flapped her hand at me. 'Come through. You know, I was just thinking, if James read all the letters from women claiming to have known him before, he'd never get anything done.'

'But I did. Know him,' I said. I was obliged to follow her, but I loitered in front of a painting on the dining room wall. It was by a contemporary calligraphy artist, cobalt brushstrokes soaring into white space.

'Beautiful,' Fiona said briskly, nodding at it. 'Apparently it's called I Follow the Religion of Love.' She tidied some papers on the table. 'Which I believe is a quote from an Islamic poem by a medieval mystic.'

'Ibn Arabi?'

'Of course,' she straightened up from her work and looked over the top of her glasses again, 'James wouldn't have been able to tell you that.'

'No, well, I only know it because I've lived here twenty-five years.'

'That it was a quote from a poem, I mean. I'm not sure James has ever noticed the picture at all.'

I shrugged. He had other qualities.

'You know what Cary Grant once said?' Fiona carried on. 'He said he'd like to be Cary Grant, too.'

I couldn't really see where this was going, paintings and Cary Grant.

'It's the same with James. He's fed up with trying to live up to everyone's idea of James Hartley. And the thing is, he imagines you understand something about him that he doesn't even understand about himself.'

'And you don't think that's right?'

'Annie, there probably isn't anything to understand. He thinks he can be different with you, that you don't need things from him, because you knew him before . . .'

'I've always thought that when two people are attracted, it's more a sort of a chemical thing,' I said, still staring at the picture.

James himself arrived at that moment, slightly sweaty but irresistible in tennis whites – which was probably as well, because Fiona was needling me and I didn't trust myself not to say something offensive. There was no mileage for me in quarrelling with her. She was probably only being obstructive because she thought that's what Al Maraj wanted. Besides, being in Hawar and looking after James and making sure the film got made must have required the logistical capacity of a four-star general, and I could see that she didn't need me wandering about getting in the way and messing things up.

James had to sign some letters before he did anything else, according to Fiona, so I hung around for him down by the pool. Then we swam. He had to do a lot of what Americans call laps, because it was part of his fitness regime, and I couldn't keep up, so I made my way up and down the pool at a statelier pace a couple of times and waited for him to finish.

'Was Fiona giving you a hard time?' he asked with concern as we slopped back up the path to the house in our flip flops. 'You looked pissed off when I arrived.'

'No,' I lied, 'though I guess for her I'm an unnecessary complication.'

He pulled me towards him. 'You feel very necessary to me.'

Upstairs, with the windows open on to the garden and the muslin curtains blowing in the breeze, the sex had the same rhapsodic, masterclass quality as before. And, like the last time, I wondered if James was pretending to be James Hartley, even when he was saying all that stuff about how great I was and how he hadn't felt like this before.

'Annie, what are you doing for Christmas?' He leant up on his elbow on the scurfed-up sheets. 'No, don't answer. Why don't we spend it together in London?'

'What?'

'I could rent a flat.'

'What about Matt and Sam?'

'Them too, obviously. We could have some quality time. No schedule, no pressure. Just a couple of weeks, being normal.'

Normal? What was normal for James? Not the same as normal for me, that was for sure. And what about the whole secrecy thing? Surely someone would notice if he shacked up with me for a couple of weeks? Some of those people he claimed hung about on street corners all over the world, waiting for him with their long lenses.

I didn't say this, because I was too busy processing the information that he wanted to extend our relationship beyond his stay in Hawar. He'd told me more than once how *real* our affair felt, implying that it was of a different quality, more solid and dependable than the switchback flings he had with younger, more ambitious and temperamental women. But for that very reason, I had learnt to think of it as an interlude, an aberration. DCOL, I believe it's called. Doesn't Count On Location.

Up to this point, I'd been mildly sceptical about the idea that we were keeping our affair secret because it was too precious to expose. When he said being with me felt like coming home, I was pleased, but I was also careful to reason that it was an easy enough thing to say. I had some kind of hold over him, for sure: he seemed to think we had some kind of connection, that I understood something crucial about him that very few other people did. But I'd thought this was mainly sentimentality about the past on his part. I wasn't really suitable, and he would find reasons to move on. In the pool, for example, I'd asked him if he wanted to come to Diane's tomorrow, and he'd looked pained and said, 'Annie, I'd love to, but you know how it is . . .'

'Yeah: you want to see me, but you don't want to be seen with me.'

He shook his head, as though the secrecy was something that

had been imposed on him and he was battling hard against it. 'It's tough for me too.'

I'd turned away, disappointed. And that was how I'd imagined it would end: as something that was too complicated to explain to other people and too difficult to accommodate. I thought he'd take the opportunity of leaving Hawar, of the enforced separation, to bid me a regretful, sentimental but slightly relieved goodbye.

This, though, did not currently seem to be his plan. He wanted to try to keep things going. I can't say that my doubts all fell away, but there seemed no harm in hanging around to find out whether there was some way to knit our lives closer together. If he was prepared to put in this much effort – inviting me to London, getting a flat – it would have been churlish to tell him I was working on the basis that the relationship had no future. Especially since I very much wanted to believe it had.

I was encouraged, too, that he wanted the boys around; that seemed to imply he was after something more than an opportunistic shag for old times' sake. And they'd love being in London at Christmas and not having to stay with my dad. And we could see Maddi and Will.

So I promised I'd think about it, and began, cautiously, hesitantly, to think that the secrecy really might be a way of giving the relationship space.

The following day, a huge bunch of flowers moving under their own steam arrived at school. It was only when they were in my arms that I could see there had been a slender and not very tall Keralite underneath them.

'For Mrs Lester?' he announced, tipping them towards me: peonies and roses and stephanotis, spiked with greenery. 'You know her?'

'Yes, that's me.'

'Madam, someone like you very much,' he said.

In my office, I unpinned the card. 'Sorry about tonight,' it read, 'but think about London.'

'Those surely aren't for you?' Diane demanded, when she found me five minutes later trying to cram them into the school's only two vases: 'it's *my* birthday.'

She spotted the card on my desk and picked it up. 'What's London? That you have to think about it?'

'Nothing.'

'No!' her eyes widened, 'they're *not*?'

'Not what?'

'From *him*?'

'Who?'

'James Hartley! Are you *seeing* him? Did you invite him to my party?'

'No. Yes. It's complicated.'

'Oh, yeah? I saw the way he looked at you on Al-Hidd . . . Well, I'm not surprised.'

Anwar had parked his car across the entrance again and was heading for my office and I was almost glad to see him, because Diane promptly left for her classroom, not wanting to be lectured about Palestine. He looked disapprovingly at the overflowing vases, but presumably couldn't think of an Islamic reason not to have flowers in your office. If he'd known they were anything to do with the film, it would have been different, because in Anwar's world Hollywood was fatally polluted by the twin evils of sex and Zionism. (*Now Eden* was being financed mainly by Arabs, but this didn't seem to make any difference.)

'America is a country of hypocrites,' he announced, leaning against the filing cabinet. I didn't give him an opening: he just starts in like that.

'A whole country of them?' I don't know why I bother. Sarcasm is lost on him.

'Americans claim that they are good. And what is this goodness? They can afford stealth bombers, but not drugs for poor people who need them.'

'What, like Africans?' I asked innocently, because he once expressed amazement when a Nigerian girl won the school maths prize three years running. Then it occurred to me that he might not realize I was being sarcastic; he might think I agreed with him, and this might encourage him to say something vile. 'You mean anti-retrovirals?' I added, since he thought that Aids was a judgement from God against people who had sex, and drugs were too good for them.

'The Americans also do not take the Palestinian question seriously,' he went on, ignoring me. 'They think they can march into Iraq, regardless of the fact that they are making things worse in Palestine ... And the Al Majid are just as bad: when people here are angry, they say, "Be angry about Palestine! That is a much greater injustice! Nothing will go right in the region until the Palestinian question is solved!"'

Since Mohammed Alireza started posting his sermons, it had become quite difficult to follow Anwar. The range of things he likes to complain about has got much larger and in his mind they all seem to be related, even if no one else can see how.

In fact, he was right about the Al Majid, but I couldn't afford to agree out loud with anything he said, in case he assumed I was on his side about the rest of it. He drifted off eventually, and I finished my work and then went home to get ready for Diane's party.

'Look, we really don't have to go,' I told Maddi, when I collected her from her parents' house in Al-Liyah.

'You do, because she's your friend, and I do because it'll please my parents.'

'We won't stay long,' I promised. 'Have you spoken to Will today?'

'Briefly. He was on his way into a meeting.' He always seemed to be on his way into a meeting, or about to make an urgent call, or write something for some senior person who needed it now, this minute, half an hour ago. It was difficult to find a space in his ricocheting schedule, what with all the

Saudi deals and the jumping in taxis and talking to lawyers.

There were a couple of hundred people in the Bonneaus' not very big flat and I lost Maddi almost immediately. All the conversations seemed to be the same: the bombings and whether there'd be any more; the prime minister and the crown prince and which one of them was running the country; the war in Iraq and whether that would make things even more unstable; Tony Blair and did anyone have the faintest idea what he was doing. It was hard to see how any of it was going to cheer up a depressed person.

There was also quite a lot of teasing about my flowers, which in Diane's retelling had become an entire garden centre delivered to me at school from James Hartley. The incident, I thought, was typical of the gulf between his world and mine: he swore me to secrecy then sent an enormous and show-offy floral tribute, not realizing that in Hawar, flowers have to be flown in from Europe and cost a fortune and a bunch large enough to camouflage an entire person was bound to be a topic of conversation at parties for weeks.

I bumped into Dr Al Rayyan in the kitchen, looking suave in one of his immaculate grey suits, which I could never see without a pang of guilt because Sam once cut his face, close to his temple, on our back step when he was three years old and, when I rushed him round to the surgery, he'd bled profusely and I'd watched as several thousand pounds' worth of material had been stained by my son's excitably leaking vein. Yousef said now that he'd been talking to Maddi, and she seemed depressed. This worried me, because presumably he's trained to recognize depression. When he said it, it didn't sound metaphorical any more. It sounded serious, clinical. 'It's a bad business,' he frowned, then said: 'How's Matt?' He had of course witnessed the coming out.

'OK,' I answered cautiously, adding that on the whole, I'd been pleasantly surprised by people's reactions. 'A few have said clumsy things, but usually they've been inept rather than actively hostile. Funnily enough, the worst reaction I've had is from someone who lives in America.'

'Not your friend James Hartley, I hope?' Yousef said quizzically.

'No.' I looked at him sideways. 'His producer, Nezar Al Majid. That's quite weird, isn't it? I mean, they must have loads of gays in the movie industry.'

'Ah, Nezar,' Yousef seemed surprised. 'I know him a little.'

'Oh?'

'He helps with the Shaikha Maryam Centre.'

When I first arrived in Hawar, local people had what can only be described as a horrific attitude to the disabled. You quite often saw physically and mentally handicapped children tethered like goats to posts on waste ground in the dusty villages. But now we had the very beautiful Shaikha Maryam day centre, opened by Princess Diana. I knew that Yousef gave his time there for free.

'I wouldn't have had him down as being anti-gay,' Yousef said, frowning.

'No, well ... I suppose disability's a different thing. And of course it's easy enough to give money.'

Yousef looked at me oddly, but he didn't have a chance to say anything, because Maddi joined us then and asked if I could possibly take her home.

Now that James was back from Oman, he and I were seeing each other every night. Sometimes I arrived at the Al A'ali House in time to watch the end of his tennis game with the professional from the Sheraton; sometimes he was already with his personal trainer, Frank, who'd had one of the bedrooms fitted out with machines that looked like medieval instruments of torture, except in nice blond wood. James would be hanging upside down on a sort of stepladder, or lying down with his legs in stirrups on a kind of rack. Eventually, his muscles stretched and twanged, he'd be allowed out to join me in the pool.

Frank would then head back to the hotel and Sandeep would serve dinner, and James and I would lie around watching movies or just go to bed.

I felt I was floating along in a haze of sexed-up domesticity, lazy and precious. On Sunday morning I was in this blissed-out state, writing a letter about the year three trip to the emir's collection of historic Qurans when Will called from London.

'Have you seen the *Sunday Times*?'

'No.' The British papers arrived a day late. He knew that.

'There's a photograph. On page 17 . . .'

'Uh-huh?' I was still concentrating on my letter.

'Of Matt. Coming out of a gay club.'

That couldn't be right: there weren't any gay clubs in Hawar.

'The club's in London,' Will said testily.

'But Matt's here.'

'It's an old photograph. From the summer.'

'And it's in the paper?'

Even I, who found Matt hugely interesting, didn't think the fact he'd been to a gay club last summer was newsworthy.

'Yes, and he's arm-in-arm with Shaikh Rashid.'

'Shaikh Rashid the crown prince?'

'Yes, what other one is there? Under the word "GAY" in pink neon lights.'

'You're joking . . .'

'No, mum, I'm not . . . Why didn't he tell us? Didn't he *think*?'

'Perhaps it doesn't mean anything,' I hazarded, although I didn't really believe that.

'They're together, holding hands, practically. They've been to a gay club. I work for an Arab bank! Why doesn't he *ever* think about anyone else?'

'Hang on, Will . . .'

'Everyone will know. I have to work in Saudi Arabia . . .'

Will was so pompous sometimes. He'd never even been to Saudi Arabia.

'And you'll probably have to leave Hawar . . .'

'I don't see why.'

'Then you're stupid.'

'Will . . . !'

'Did *you* know Shaikh Rashid was gay? Of course not. No one did. It's practically treason.'

It was impossible to get him to calm down. He rang off, saying he was going to call Maddi and grumbling that I was a fool if I thought they'd let me stay here, knowing my son had been fucking the crown prince in a country where you couldn't even utter the word 'gay'. Will never normally uttered the word 'fuck', at least to me.

I stared at the Quran letter for a few minutes, trying to get the sentences to stop swimming, then pushed away the keyboard, got up and went into Sue's office.

'Something's happened, I'm afraid. I need to go out.'

She looked up. 'Anything I can do?'

'No . . . thanks.'

She said to take as long as I liked. I went out to the car, then drove across Qalhat in the clogged mid-morning traffic. I had to queue to get into the car park outside the Hyatt, then I walked, sometimes breaking into a run, through the gate to the souk and up the crowded narrow streets. I tried not to push into people, but they all seemed to be dawdling, women in abayas drifting in front of me in annoying groups. I passed dusty shops bursting with white goods and electronics, merchandise spilling out of the doors. I cut down an alley riotous with cheap clothes into the gold souk where necklaces drizzled down the windows, gaudy and fake-looking. I caught sight of Salman in Soft Hands tailors, and passed Sweety Sweets, which Matt used to say when he was small was the best possible name for a shop ever. Finally, out of breath and sweaty, I arrived at the offices of Palm Publishing at the northern end of the souk.

I pushed through the door into the scruffy 1970s building and asked the Keralite on the desk to ring up to Matt's extension.

He wasn't answering his phone.

'Could you try someone else? . . . Doug Reed?'

Doug was the only other person I knew at Palm Publishing. He'd been in Hawar almost as long as I had, although I didn't know him well. The last time I'd had any real dealings with him, he'd been the chief reporter on the *Hawar Daily News*, trying to write a story about Dave's accident. I probably hadn't been very helpful and it hadn't got anywhere. But he'd hired Matt. He might know where he was.

'The general manager?' asked the Keralite disapprovingly. 'What is your good name?'

He tried the number.

A few minutes later, the lift pinged and Doug came out, a bulky Englishman of the overfed, oversunned and overboozed type. He indicated that we should move over to the waiting area. It was hardly more private, just a couple of easy chairs arranged on either side of a coffee table displaying Palm Publishing's latest magazines, but it was at least out of earshot of reception.

'Is Matthew OK?' he asked in a low voice.

'Oh . . . He hasn't come in?'

'No, not this morning . . . We saw the piece. On the internet. Someone alerted me first thing.' He patted my shoulder awkwardly. 'Probably keeping his head down.'

'Yes.'

'Scoop right under our noses!' he added, trying to make light of it. 'Knew he was gay of course, but well . . . not about this.'

'No, I don't think anyone did.' I bit my lip. 'It might not be what it looks like, of course . . .'

'Hmmn.'

'Yes, well, anyway, sorry.' I picked up my bag. 'Umm, I'll tell him . . . thanks for your time. I'll tell him to come back.'

'I'm sure he's OK,' he said in way that was meant to be reassuring, except that he was too rumpled and askew and juicy, somehow, to inspire confidence. 'You tell him not to worry. Get back when he can. He's a good lad.'

I rang home but only got the answering machine. I tried his mobile for the umpteenth time, then stood in the shade of an overhanging balcony in the souk, beside bales of shiny material, and called Jodie.

I thought of Matt's smile, playful and lurking, as if he knew some secret joke he was considering sharing with you. He'd smiled like that even when he was a toddler, as though he was always spotting things that were irresistibly funny and had to struggle not to laugh.

It turned out he wasn't with Jodie. And she hadn't heard about the photograph, so I had to explain about that as I pushed my way back down through the souk towards the car.

'Oh God!' she gasped, 'I knew he was seeing someone, though he wouldn't talk about it. I assumed he must've been married . . . Oh, poor Matt!'

She didn't have any idea where he could be. I made her promise to make him get in touch if he called her, then got back in the car and headed towards the Jidda Road, telling myself that sooner or later he'd have to come home. I shouldn't panic. The fact he hadn't turned up for work didn't mean he was dead in an irrigation ditch following some hit-and-run accident on a back road, or that he'd been the victim of a fatal mugging in this country where no one was ever mugged. He hadn't been murdered in what police would later discover was an expat feud over drugs and gambling. These were shameful prejudices, routes of thought and feeling I didn't want to share.

I was almost home when the phone rang. I snatched it up from the seat beside me, but it was a number I didn't recognize.

'Annie? It is Adel Al Buraidi. We met at the Horwoods'?'

I'd sat next to him at dinner several weeks earlier. He was the latest in a long line of men to whom Antonia had introduced me, and one of the least suitable. He spoke English with a thick-tongued Gulf accent and worked as an investment manager for the Al Majid. I don't know what Antonia imagined we'd have in common. He told me he loved London, then went on to compare the relative merits of Claridges and the Savoy. I had never visited either, so after that we ran out of things to say.

'I am calling to offer help.'

Was this what happened? You got a phone call from someone you once sat next to at dinner, telling you to leave? And that was that? Twenty-five years of your life, over in a phone call from someone who liked Claridges?

'Oh?'

'I am sorry about this business with your son.'

Had they got Matthew already? What had they done with him? I had to stop panicking: I wasn't even listening properly. In a minute he'd say something important and I'd miss it.

'You may remember, I work for the Al Majid?'

'Yes.'

'I have tried to explain that you are a good family.'

I said nothing.

'I've assured them this can still be managed.'

'What does that mean? Where's Matt?'

'You don't know?'

'No! Do you?'

'No,' he admitted reluctantly.

'What about Shaikh Rashid?'

'I very much doubt he knows where your son is,' he said, as if the matter were way beneath the notice of a crown prince, adding, 'he has been in meetings all morning.'

I thought, I bet he has.

'I assume that when your son turns up, he will be thinking about leaving Hawar?'

'You'd have to ask him that,' I replied coldly, although I was encouraged that Al Buraidi thought Matt was alive. 'Is that supposed to be a threat?'

'In the eyes of many,' Al Buraidi went on blandly, 'the existence of that photograph already makes Shaikh Rashid unfit to rule. It is important he doesn't have anything more to do with Matthew. If Matthew understands that – which I'm sure he does

– he can stay a little while. Long enough to sort himself out. Say, to the end of January?'

It was a threat. 'And is that what Shaikh Rashid wants?'

'You think I would be having this conversation with you if not?' He laughed, although there was nothing funny. 'The crown prince isn't actually *gay*. No one wants this to end unpleasantly.'

'I'll have to find him first,' I said shakily, and rang off before I started crying.

We were all in service, I thought bitterly, as I waited at home all afternoon – me as much as the house maids and labourers in the corrugated sheds in the shanty towns on the edge of Qalhat. This was a feudal society. We all had our sponsors, and our sponsorship could be withdrawn. My life was comfortable, so I couldn't always see it, but I was here to serve someone's purposes and as soon as I stopped being useful, I could be got rid of. The locals made a big thing about it being part of their culture to look after old soldiers and retired retainers, to make sure people who had been faithful to them saw out their lives in comfort, and I'm sure as long as those people stayed loyal they did look after them with meticulous care. But if you were faithless, if you ceased to play by the family's rules, then their obligations ceased. You could be cast out. And not to be part of a family was the worst thing that could possibly befall you.

There was no future here for Matt, and perhaps not for me either. Perhaps not – it was easier to admit it now – for any of us expats. The oil was running out. Hawar was located on a geographical and political fault line, where ways of life crashed into one another like continents. Western, Arab, Islamic, Christian, atheist, traditional, modern, family, tribe, oil, money, designer clothes under black abayas, education, repression, dictatorship. It was hopeless. Values bumped up against one another and we only pretended that they could knit together. In reality, the place was unsustainable: it was like living in a confidence trick.

The phone rang, but it wasn't Matthew. It was Sam to say he

was at Faisal's. He didn't mention the photograph, so I didn't either. I assumed he hadn't heard yet. I didn't want him to think he had to come home and be with me.

I sat staring into space, willing Matt to come back from wherever he was, running over the conversation with the spooky Mr Al Buraidi, telling myself that if he believed Matt was alive and capable of making decisions about his future, then he probably was.

And they hadn't found him, so that was round one to Matthew. Although that wasn't a very good way of thinking about it, because it was obvious all the other rounds were going to be to them.

The afternoon wore on. Cars came and went through the compound. Children returned from school. Someone had a tennis lesson. The heat seeped out of the day. There were the sounds of distant splashing, the thwack of balls on the tennis court. Maria sashayed in, checked the house, and drifted out again. She looked at me sideways, but said nothing.

At five o'clock I called James to tell him I didn't think I'd be coming round.

'Couldn't you leave Matt a note to call you when he gets in?' he asked when I'd explained.

'But, James, he's disappeared! I can't just go off and have fun . . .'

'I'm sure he's fine. He's probably with a friend. Or gone to the beach.'

'Matt wouldn't go to the beach when he was supposed to be at work . . .'

'You're not going to achieve anything sitting there. You might as well sit with me.'

'I'd love to, really, but I won't be able to focus on anything till he turns up.'

'It's a bit irresponsible of him to disappear . . .'

'He must be distressed. He won't know what to do . . .'

'Are you sure the picture means what it seems to mean?'

'This Al Buraidi bloke thinks so.'

'Bloody paps . . .'

'You could always come round here?'

'He's not going to want me there when he eventually turns up,' he said, although I wasn't sure he was right about that. Of all the people we knew, James was the most likely to have useful advice about having your picture in the newspapers. 'Anyway, it's too complicated,' he added. 'Cars in the morning. Briefing with Fiona, that sort of thing.'

He was earning millions of dollars for this movie. When he dropped something, other people bent down to pick it up. He had, as far as I could work out, specialists to attend to all different parts of his body. How difficult was it to divert a car?

Matt eventually walked in out of the dusk at six-thirty, opening the front door and strolling in as casually as if he'd been at work, switching on a table lamp, heading for the kitchen. He was well into the room before he realized I was on the sofa.

'Why are you sitting in the dark?' he asked in surprise. 'I thought you weren't here.'

'Matt, where've you been?' I tried to keep my voice under control but it rose hysterically. 'You weren't at work.'

'Oh . . .'

'Your phone's been off. I've been frantic . . .'

'Sorry . . .'

'Matt, come and sit down.'

'Oh, right . . .' He slumped beside me. 'You know?'

'Yes. Did you think I wouldn't?'

'I thought the paper didn't arrive until tomorrow.'

'Will saw it.'

'And was he his usual tolerant and forgiving self?'

'There's no need to be like that. He was worried. How did *you* find out?'

'Rashid rang me, first thing. He warned me to switch my phone off and stay out of the way, so I went up to Saffar.'

'Oh, Matt . . . !'

'I know, I know – I should have rung you, but I never thought you'd find out so soon. I thought I had some time. Sorry, I didn't think. You can see, though, why I couldn't tell you who I was seeing?'

'Yes. Someone knew, though.'

'We were so careful . . . Apart from that time in London.' He shook his head. 'And I thought no one there would know who he was, or care.'

'How long have you been seeing him?'

'Two years.'

'Two *years*! *How*?'

'I met him at Shazia's stables. Initially. And then that became a way of seeing each other: we'd go riding and meet in the desert, near Wadi Ghul. Shazia didn't know. No one knew, except for this one bodyguard who helped.' He rubbed at his forehead, pressed his fingers into his temples. 'It's my fault: that's what I keep thinking. I suggested going to that club last summer. It can't have been a coincidence – that we were photographed, I mean. Someone must have been watching. Friends of the prime minister, or people in his pay.'

'He *is* gay, is he?'

'What?'

'Shaikh Rashid.'

'– You're asking me if someone I've been seeing for two years is gay?'

'Sorry, no. It's just that this bloke called . . .'

'What bloke?'

'His name's Adel Al Buraidi. He says he works for the Al Majid.'

'Ah,' Matt said bitterly. 'And what did he have to say for himself?'

'He seemed to think you should leave Hawar.'

'Immediately?'

'No, he's given you till January.'

'Or they kick you out, is that it? Is that why he rang you?'

'I think he just couldn't get hold of you. But that was the general idea.'

'That means they're going to get Rashid out of the country straight away.' . . .

'He said Shaikh Rashid isn't gay. He seemed to be implying you'd seduced him . . .'

'Yeah, right, like I'd do that. He's the crown prince, mum.' He put his head in his hands. 'Well, I'm only here because of Rashid,' he said bitterly. 'Hawar's not exactly a big gay scene.' He was trying to make a joke of it, but he was close to tears. That was when I realized that it hadn't been a lark, or a fling. Shaikh Rashid hadn't been a trick, or a fuck buddy. It had been serious, something for which they had taken risks. Now he was bereft.

'We were stupid. We thought we could keep it secret. We wanted to think that together we were capable of anything.'

'What will happen to him?'

'I don't know. He said he'd ring me this afternoon and he didn't so they've probably taken his phone. That's the only reason he wouldn't be able to get a message to me – because he'd be trying.'

'I'm sorry . . .'

He shook his head. 'Once the emir had his stroke . . . you could sort of see it coming. Whoever placed that picture knew what they were doing. They hung on to it until it could do Rashid maximum damage. It's so unfair! He's lovely, mum. If you met him – which I don't suppose you will, now – you'd see how funny and generous and intelligent he is . . .'

'He's the crown prince. Surely they can't push him around?'

'D'you think Hawar's ready for a gay emir?'

Something about this question set off an echo in my head. Reminded me of something I'd heard only a few days before, from someone else entirely.

'What?' Matt said, frowning.

'Nothing, I . . .'

I couldn't be sure, but I had a feeling Nezar Al Maraj had known. He'd also said something about the crown prince liking to ride at Wadi Ghul . . . And that probably meant other people had known too, whatever Matt thought – because Al Maraj didn't even live here most of the time.

I didn't want to think about this now. 'What about Sultan Qaboos?' I asked. 'He seems to manage OK.'

'He got married. And as far as anyone can work out he leads an entirely blameless life: gardening and horses and Omani good works. No photographs in the *Sunday Times*. Anyway, he came to power in a different place in different times . . .'

'It wasn't that long ago.'

'He was backed by the British, when that mattered, and there weren't all these Islamists.'

'But . . .'

'Mum, Hawar's on a knife edge. Mohammed Alireza has a huge following. Rashid says it's much worse than we think and the Iranians are probably funding him . . .'

'And Rashid being heterosexual is going to make a difference to any of that?'

'No, but being gay doesn't help. His advisers will do their best to persuade him the only hope for Hawar is to get married quickly and persuade everyone he's straight. Never speak to me again, and hope he can pull the country round behind him.'

'And he'll do that?'

'I expect so.' Matt sighed. He was only a boy, but love had barrelled into him with all its usual careless authority, and being young didn't stop you getting beaten up by it.

'Is it worth it? Sacrificing his happiness for Hawar?'

'It's what he was brought up to do: it's what he's for.' He shrugged. 'Perhaps it is. It might really matter.' Then he smiled and tried to make a joke of it: 'Giving me up? Course it's not.'

'Someone must've had that photograph since the summer . . .'

'Like I say, biding their time. Waiting for their moment.

Which is now, because the emir is almost certainly too ill ever to rule again ... And they've got Rashid exactly where they want him.'

'What will happen to him?'

'He always said they'd send him to a psychiatrist, although only because people like them don't throw you down the stairs. It's just another way of beating you up.'

'Poor Shaikh Rashid.'

'They don't care, really, whether he's gay or not. Well, some of them do. Some of them probably do think he's mad or sick or possessed by the devil. But mostly, it's political. The prime minister will be rubbing his hands: suddenly his radical nephew isn't dangerous at all, because if he ever tries to do anything, to get rid of corruption, to support human rights, to bring the Al Majid under the rule of law, they can bring up the thing with the Englishman. So un-Islamic. So decadent and western. So unlike the stern, manly Gulf Arabs. For the establishment, an emir with a past is really very useful. He might not be able to do anything significant ever.'

'So it's *not* worth it? If he can't change Hawar, what's the point?'

'I don't know.' He looked exhausted. 'Except this feels like a moment when this part of the world actually matters, when there might be more at stake than a tiny tribal shaikhdom.'

I could tell he was in pieces. Shredded. I moved closer and put my arm round him, but he was too big, too scratchy, too muscular for me to make it better. He was a big man, torn up by love, and there was nothing I could do.

Ten

If we'd lived anywhere except Hawar, the fallout would have been much worse. We'd have had photographers trampling through the marigolds and reporters lurking in the carport with their notebooks, avid for information about us, eager to turn our silence into meaning. As it was, the local media – the *Hawar Daily News* and the other Gulf papers, the television and radio stations – had nothing to say about Shaikh Rashid's visit to a gay club in London with his British boyfriend. The *Sunday Times* simply didn't arrive that week. Officially, it hadn't happened.

I could tell everyone was gossiping, though, from the way they looked at me and asked in specially concerned voices if I was all right. Only rarely did anyone directly refer to the photograph, which reinforced my sense that I'd let the side down, got involved in something unmentionable. We expats were here on sufferance; there were rules that you didn't transgress. This was way too shameful to speak of.

Cheryl was one of the few who did, perhaps because for her, the relationship with Shaikh Rashid seemed to be a mitigating circumstance, as if it was less bad to be gay with a hereditary monarch than with anyone else. She did complain, though, that the whole thing was now so public that she'd been forced to explain to Tel that they had a gay living next door. *That* hadn't been easy, she said reproachfully.

Matt, who knew everyone was talking about him in low voices at parties and in the supermarket, that the phone lines were humming, confessed he was dreading going back to work on Monday. 'I wasn't out to everyone,' he said. 'Not all the Hawaris. Sometimes it's just too much hassle – you know, the whole tedious double-take. Every time you tell someone it's the first time for them … And now they'll *all* know, including the sicko homophobes.'

I said something trite about his having done nothing wrong and owing it to himself to be positive and act normal.

'Normal is seeing Rashid.'

But the crown prince hadn't called. His phone now gave an unobtainable signal and Matt's emails to the secret address they'd been using bounced back. Every attempt to reach him disappeared into a vacuum, as if it had been soaked up by a huge indifference. There was more finality about it than if he'd died. The silence was resolute.

Will, on the other hand, had called from London to object again to what he called Matt's thoughtlessness. 'I don't know what's got into him lately,' Matt complained when he came off the phone. 'He's not making any sense. I mean, I know what's happened to Millie is hard for them all, and Maddi's not with him and stuff – but why is he hostile to *me*? Compared to me, he's got everything.'

Matt went to work on Monday looking pale, but said at the end of the day that it had gone better than he'd expected. Doug Reed had called him into his office and told him how good it had been to have him at Palm Publishing and assured him he had a job for as long as he wanted. Perhaps Doug had also spoken to the staff, because although one or two of the Hawaris and Pakistanis seemed to be avoiding Matt, no one actually said anything. I suspected his colleagues had become quite fond of him, even the ones who now had to disapprove.

Neither Matt nor I could quite understand why the Al Majid were prepared to let him stay till the end of January. Perhaps they thought it would be easier to keep an eye on him here. Perhaps it was something to do with their pride in their gentleness, their measured and transparent methods of exerting their great power. At any rate, I didn't have any more secret agent type calls from Adel Al Buraidi. What with the news blackout, the whole thing went superficially quiet, like a phoney war.

'You know,' James said one evening as we lay on the sofa, 'if you need help with this Matthew business, you should ask Nezar. He's in Paris right now, but you could always call him.'

That explained why I hadn't seen him. I'd been hoping to raise the subject of his vague and unhelpful warnings about Matthew. I murmured, 'Mmn, thanks,' and thought privately that if I needed help, I'd hope to get it from someone a bit more user-friendly.

'Amazing to think I originally turned down this part!' James murmured, winding a strand of my hair round his finger. The French windows were open on to the garden and there was a warm breeze. 'I only agreed because Nezar persuaded me ... And then when I realized you were here, I thought you'd probably be with someone else and I'd feel all the same old jealousy and regret. It's amazing I found you after all this time of thinking about you, missing you ... Odd, isn't it, that two people can have something that lasts and lasts? I could stay for ever.'

'You haven't tried it in summer,' I pointed out as he pulled me towards him.

The only slight drawback to these long, lazy evenings was James's fondness for talking about Thornton Heath: the crappy pub we used to go to on Friday nights, sitting in my bedroom listening to The Stranglers, walking down the High Street on Saturday. I said that while some of this had undoubtedly been OK (The Stranglers, mainly) the rest had been rubbish, and drab boring rubbish at that. But he laughed and said his memories of it were great, so it must have been me.

We started making plans for Christmas. He had to be in Los Angeles until the 16th, which was the day we were expecting Eid to start, but he could fly to London and we'd come over from Hawar – he insisted on paying, he knew I could afford it and would I just shut up about the money – and we could meet at the flat he was going to rent for us. There were various restaurants he wanted to take me to – he said airily that he'd be able to get reservations, even though some of them were booked up months in advance – and we could go shopping – there were lots of things he wanted to buy me – and we'd have great times at home together, like this.

I felt obliged to point out it wouldn't be exactly like this: the boys would be there, and he said, 'Yes, I know, with the boys.'

He seemed genuinely determined to make me happy, to find the best flat, to plan a series of treats. He liked the idea of introducing me to luxury, telling me that this was a pleasure for him, because I made him look at things freshly, could be counted on to be enthusiastic, wasn't jaded, like so many people. I didn't myself know a lot of people who'd be cynical about being flown first class to London to eat top food in otherwise inaccessible restaurants and sleep with James Hartley. Still, if he thought this was some kind of testament to my niceness, I wasn't going to disillusion him by explaining that in the real world it was nothing special.

He lay with his head on my lap one evening and told me how much he liked it that I took him seriously. 'You listen when I talk about work,' he said.

'Why wouldn't I?'

'You're not looking for information you can use against me.'

'You must have had some very funny relationships.'

'I have.'

I think he felt he could be honest with me. If he confessed to anxiety about the range of parts he might get, or insecurity about whether he could still open a movie, it didn't diminish him in my eyes, because I didn't care about the minute calibrations of fame that seemed to obsess him and his colleagues. I didn't have any purchase on them: all the people he talked about as rivals, as lesser or greater stars, were to me unimaginably huge.

'I may not be able to get action parts much longer,' he said gloomily. 'And the truth is, I'm not sure I can make the transition to something else.'

I assured him that he was a fantastic actor and incredibly good-looking, and pointed out that in any case, men seemed to be able to go on and on in movies, getting cast opposite women like Rosie.

On his last night in Hawar, I lay awake for a long time, concentrating on the feeling of my forehead against his back, the distance my arms reached round him, the place my toes touched his calf. His flesh was firm, under control, seemed unmarked by the past, undamaged by food, drink, mistakes, the normally bruising business of living. Earlier that night, he'd said I was beautiful, not in spite of having had three children, but because of it. This was perhaps the best compliment he could have paid me – that experience, disappointment and struggle had made me lovely. It was like being told that you have a kind of moral beauty, which has to be better than having great cheekbones.

In the morning we – he and his perfect body, me and my wonderful soul – scurfed up the sheets one last time, slowly, sadly, a little frantically, and then he was up and dressed and ready for the car that would take him out to the airport and the private jet to London for a couple of meetings before he flew on to LA. This is it, I thought, from the carved Hawari bed, watching him leave: no more lying on the white sofas with the French windows open, no more catching at me as I twisted away from him in the floodlit swimming pool, no more languorous evenings and long nights.

I waited until he'd left, then showered and dressed and went to school, where I listened above the clatter of the air conditioning for planes above Qalhat, tearing away into the sky.

Appropriately enough, Ramadan started the following day. The shops closed early, the streets were subdued. There were a few hours in the morning when things were more or less normal, but an air of lassitude settled over the emirate. Hawar has never been a place where people exactly rush, but, come Ramadan, inertia isn't just a fact of life, it's something to strive for actively. Or passively, I suppose. Hawar has adopted many American things, such as McDonalds and SUVs and big fridges, but an avid and show-offy dedication to productivity isn't one of them. During Ramadan, people are glad to have even more licence to hang back and procrastinate and generally take their time.

Anwar came in to school on the third day of Ramadan. He looked pointedly around my office, probably checking for water bottles sticking out of my bag or coffee cups hidden behind the reference books. Then he lounged in his favourite place against the filing cabinet and launched into a string of complaints about the iftar tents at the hotels, where people could break their fast at sunset and party on into the night, possibly even away from their families, in places where alcohol was available – which, he claimed, were irreligious and meant that the true meaning of fasting was getting lost.

Finally, he fixed me with a meaningful stare and said: 'People are talking about your son.'

Oh, I thought, here we go.

'In Islam, we believe in family values.'

'Yes, we do too.'

I've noticed homophobic people are very fond of claiming that homosexuals undermine the family. But they never say how. And that's because they don't. Gay men are for example famously nice to their mums.

'Homosexuality is a tumour on society,' Anwar continued sententiously. 'It must be cut out.'

I looked at him directly. 'Anwar, have you been asked to revoke my sponsorship? Because if you have, could you just get on with it?'

'No, not yet,' he admitted, but then continued: 'Homosexuality is a reversal of the natural order of things. It is a crime against women.'

I stared at him blankly, until it dawned on me what he was trying to say. Then I wanted to laugh. There are quite enough men around wanting to have sex with us without needing Matt to make up the numbers.

Perhaps there aren't that many with whom we want to have sex in return – the human race would have to be threatened with imminent extinction to interest me in Anwar, and even then obliteration of the species might well seem preferable – but that's a whole other issue.

'In your culture, you see, people are slaves to their lusts. Women are naked on advertising posters. They are nearly naked in the street. This creates chaos, and you have the sex crimes. And other crimes, for that matter. In our culture, women take responsibility for maintaining order.'

I'd had enough of this. 'In our culture we think men should make a bit of an effort too.'

You can see why you might want to wear an abaya if you had to deal a lot with men like Anwar.

'You misunderstand me,' he said smoothly. 'The homosexual removes himself from the good influence of women and so cannot be expected to have a decent manner of living.'

'If you mean Matt, he lives with me. He hasn't removed himself.'

'Your son's presence here reminds people of the sinful act. I won't say makes it acceptable, or that it starts to seem normal, because it could never do that – but it loses its gravity in the hearts and minds of the people.'

It's always other people who need to be protected from sex. Anwar could know about Matt and remain as pompous and self-righteous as ever, but apparently if other people so much as got to hear about him, whole ethical systems could collapse.

Sue came in from her office with some papers for filing and saw immediately what was happening. She ushered Anwar away on the pretext of needing his advice.

At the door he turned back. 'It is good that your son is leaving,' he said and then, with more effort, 'and good that you are staying. You have powerful friends.'

I wasn't sure who he meant. Al Buraidi? It seemed unlikely. Anwar probably assumed we had powerful friends because in his mind Matt had committed such a huge transgression that it was inconceivable that the authorities would let any of us stay.

Anwar had no power – I doubted he even had any real say over my sponsorship – so I knew I shouldn't let him rattle me. All the same, it was difficult not to feel vulnerable. It had never seemed to matter before, not having any say in the politics of Hawar, but I could see now that I'd been bought off with luxury housing and swimming pools and wearing-shorts-to-the-super-market. Like the shi'ite villagers who'd been rehoused in Hassan Town with flushing toilets, I was part of the price the Al Majid paid for their houses in Switzerland and Monaco and their secret bank accounts. You could drift along for years thinking it was a fair exchange, no harm done, because, after all, Hawar was only a little backwater of a backwater. But you only had to do something that didn't suit, didn't conform to their ideas of how you ought to behave, and then you discovered that there was politics here after all and you were tangled up in it even though you had no rights. Your irrelevance had always been part of the deal. You were a mercenary. And who cared about mercenaries? Richard Crossley-Tennant at the British embassy? Not really. Not half as much anyway as he cared about oil and arms deals and regional relationships.

An affair with the crown prince would have been awkward at any time. This, though, was a particular time, when the mostly benign dictatorships of the Gulf were suddenly exposed as never before, with Iran on one side and Saudi Arabia on the other, flexing their muscles, looking for regional dominance; when American troops were massing to the west and there was an idea going around that somewhere quite close to here the world could be saved. The whole geopolitical machine had turned its cumbersome workings in our direction, was aware of our existence and anxious about our vast resources and political precariousness.

To make matters worse, the Al Majid were meanwhile busily fending off unrest from below. Mohammed Alireza had marked the start of Ramadan with another one of his internet sermons, claiming Saudi Arabia was a puppet regime of the United States and urging all good Muslims to fight for democracy and sweep corrupt regimes from power.

I often felt during those weeks that I had no one to talk to. The boys communicated with me if and when it suited them, but they were often busy with other, more pressing things. Matt was unhappy and monosyllabic. Sam and Faisal claimed to be planning the first edition of their newspaper, although when they were at our house, this seemed mostly to involve listening to loud music. I hoped the readers of the *International* were prepared for a shift in news values in favour of previously unheard-of bands.

The expat urge to build a community, however tenuous, however approximate, no longer seemed quite to include me. I wasn't an outcast, exactly, but I'd come to the notice of the authorities; I was known to be trouble. When I was dealing with other people I often felt they were hanging on a little more tightly to that part of themselves that they kept in reserve, remembering that it was important not to need one another too much, not to become too interdependent, because living here was only a temporary arrangement, even if it happened to end up lasting decades.

James had listened to me when he was here – and it had been this, as much as the frequent and rewarding sex, that had been so exhilarating. There had been long parts of the day when I didn't have to be as tense and watchful, because James was there, and he was on my side. But his dyslexia meant he 'didn't do email' – so all his correspondence, including on the internet, including to and from me, went through Fiona. I explained about spell check but I think his fear of words was too deep-seated. He assured me I could still write to him, but I didn't like the idea of having to pass through his personal spam filter. I wouldn't put it past her to file me straight in trash. He hated reading nearly as much as writing, so it was likely that she'd have to relay my messages out loud. I couldn't imagine her doing it in anything but a sarcastic voice.

The only way to reach him was by phone, but it quickly became apparent that the telephone was as much of an obstacle as an aid to communication. When we'd been together, legs entwined on the sofa, sitting on the edge of the pool in the dark, I'd had no difficulty talking to James about what was bothering me – whether it was Anwar or Matt, Sam, Maddi, or something more distant like Mohammed Alireza's latest sermon. He listened, and he was sympathetic, and he made me feel better. He might not have a view about whether it was reasonable of Alireza to call for democracy in pursuit of the worldwide imamate, but if *I* cared, that was enough: he claimed he did too. Now we were at opposite ends of the day. I was busy with the morning when he was shattered after a day's shooting, and it was difficult to get the mood right.

Sam had reacted to the news about Matt and Shaikh Rashid with his usual spaciness.

'So, like, someone *outed* him?' he said slowly.

'Someone who doesn't want what he wants for Hawar, I suppose.'

'I bet it was the prime minister. What a shit.' Sam chewed on a piece of toast; he was on a flying visit to the kitchen to stoke up with food. 'Still, dunno why we're surprised.'

'What d'you mean?'

'S'what they're like, innit?'

'Who? Is this racist again? . . . because I'm not having it . . .'

'Can't I be just a tiny bit racist?'

'It's not funny. And we don't know it was Shaikh Jasim.'

'It's the way they do politics, though, innit – the Al Majid? Pulling strings. Getting people removed.'

'Shaikh Rashid was trying to change that.'

'Yeah, well, exactly. So it's only Alireza left now.'

'I'm not sure it's worth investing much hope in him.'

He dropped the crust in the bin. 'Gotta go.'

'Where?'

'Just out.'

'No, Sam, where?'

'Wiv Faisal.'

He imagined this was ghetto and would annoy me. Lots of things about him annoyed me, but not him feebly pretending to talk ghetto.

'You're not getting into trouble?'

'Does that mean drugs?'

'No,' I lied. 'But you never tell me anything.'

'Mohammed Alireza's really smart, you know. If you read what he says, it's clever.'

'Surely he's not why you keep making racist comments?'

In reality, though, I knew why that was. In his mind, Dave's death was the fault of some above-the-law Saudi prince. I'd got myself into a mess here. I needed to tell him the truth. Ever since his outburst at the Franklins' I'd been waking up in the night in a cold sweat, knowing the time had come to talk to him, that I couldn't dodge it any longer. I'd lie restlessly, shifting in the sheets, unable to get comfortable, while my mind circled and pecked unsatisfactorily at the question of how to raise the subject, what to say. But, in the mornings, one or other of us was always dashing off somewhere and, later in the day, he was with Faisal or we were exhausted, preoccupied, or in my case, lacking the required emotional energy. I still hadn't got round to it, and it was nagging at me, like an injury or an illness I was trying to ignore but that kept forcing itself on my attention. When he and Faisal returned this particular afternoon, for example, they'd found a new band called Trope, and they offered to play me some of their tunes and I was so pleased they were talking to me that I didn't want to spoil it. Too often with Sam I felt inadequate – like the duff second-string goalkeeper no one thinks will ever have to play and then he does and everyone can see why he was on the bench. So in the brief moments when it was going well, I wanted to enjoy it.

I thought long and hard about whether to tell Chris, Karen and my dad about the picture in the *Sunday Times*. They hadn't seen it, or Karen would have called. They read different Sunday papers and obviously it was hardly a proper story, so no one else took it up.

In the end I figured Matt hadn't done anything wrong and I should be honest. Otherwise the bigots would have gained a bit more ground.

'So he's been in the papers?' dad said excitedly. 'Is it a nice picture?'

He went to the library to look it up in their back copies section and reported back that it was a very nice picture. He didn't quite seem to have got the point.

He told me he'd called the lady whose name he'd been given by Gay Switchboard. She was called Maureen and she ran an organization for people who have gay family members – mostly parents, but they were welcoming of grandparents too. Apparently, she'd been making cakes when he rang and he'd had to hold on for a minute while she took them out of the oven. 'I mean, she had a gay son and she was doing that! So she must be doing well!'

Was this a jibe at me? Had I not made enough cakes since Matt came out? It was too hot for cakes in Hawar. I'd made quite a lot of salad. By the time I'd thought this far, I realized I was being ridiculous.

Anyway, she'd been really nice, this Maureen, he said, and she'd persuaded him to go to a meeting in South Croydon, and he'd had nothing on that day so he had, and all the people had been very friendly and some of them were much younger and really struggling with their homosexual relations.

'Relatives?' I suggested, 'homosexual relatives?'

'That's what I said.' They'd had a couple of speakers, he explained, from an organization that helps gay runaways and kids who have been thrown out by their parents. 'There's a lot of that goes on, apparently.'

'Yes.'

'And then they end up living on the streets. This boy came along, he told us his dad had told him he never wanted to see him again after he came out so he'd run away and lived rough in the West End and done things he didn't want to talk about – you can only imagine . . .'

'Yes.'

For a long time now, my father's life seemed to have been shrinking, until it was more or less contained by a corridor with the kettle at one end and *Countdown* on the telly at the other. He saw very few people: most of his old friends and acquaintances had moved away from the neighbourhood. My mum had been the sociable one, who'd known what was going on with the various families in the street, who'd hardly ever come home from the butcher's without some snippet of gossip. He would have liked to have conversations at the butcher's himself, but it had become a halal butcher's now and he bought his meat shrink-wrapped in Tesco's. He would have joined in if someone else had started talking in the queue for the checkout, but perhaps there was something too reserved about him, because they never did. He had no idea how you got going with people. So he saw fewer of his old acquaintances and the routines that had stopped him collapsing when my mum died, that had made him get dressed in the mornings and eat his food at the table rather than out of the saucepan, had hardened into habits of mind; the rituals had become an end in themselves. They gave him the illusion of control. He needed to hang on tightly to them, because the outside world – about which it was hard to have much perspective when you viewed it entirely from an armchair in front of *Countdown* – was forever threatening to throw him off course. I only had to make a stray remark about some man I'd sat next to at a dinner party and it became a doomed love affair, or to complain I was feeling tired for him to decide I had cancer.

It was quite encouraging that he was interested in something new, something beyond the question of how long it took to get through to the gas company or how odd it was that they were diverting all their calls to India and whether he was ultimately having to pay for the cost of the phone call. The plight of gay teenagers and what they might be forced into was definitely a more worthwhile preoccupation than my non-existent fatal diseases. It was also possible for him to talk about it in a tone that wasn't peevish. On the other hand, he was one of the most antisocial people in the world, so if Matt's sexuality had driven him to going to meetings, he must be finding it very painful.

The radio and television stations were still leading their bulletins with news of the telegrams that the crown prince, Shaikh Rashid bin Hassan al Majid, had sent to other crown princes: fraternal greetings on the occasion of foreign national days, best wishes for the success of forthcoming diplomatic encounters. The fact that his telegrams were still being listed ahead of the prime minister's presumably meant there hadn't been a family coup, but there were none of the usual pictures of him in the *Hawar Daily News*. In any normal week, you would have expected at least a couple – Shaikh Rashid attending a passing-out parade at the HDF barracks, Shaikh Rashid visiting the women's craft centres in Hassan Town. Matt thought he'd probably left the country.

'Did you talk about this before?' I asked him one night after dinner, when we were sitting on the veranda. 'About what might happen if you were discovered?'

'All the time. He thought he was like that gecko,' he gestured up to where the creature was hanging with its feet on the ceiling, basking translucently in the stored evening warmth of its upside-down world: 'he thought he could be different, turn things up the other way, persuade people to see them from his point of view.'

'What, you could get away with it?'

Matt shrugged. 'Being heir apparent can make you think you have a lot of power – growing up believing that your country is also your family business.'

'But you surely didn't think it could somehow survive people knowing?'

'Sometimes, he almost convinced me. I figured – well, he knows more about Hawari politics than I do, plus he's very charismatic, plus this society is probably a lot less rigid than we think it is.'

'Where do you think he is?'

'Who knows? Some place where they mess about with your hormones.'

Maddi had left, too. Millie was home from hospital now; I'd been to visit earlier that day. Her right cheek was stitched together in three different places, making her face look twisted and lopsided. It was shocking at first, not least because she'd been so beautiful, but Peter had spent all his free time since she was injured researching the best surgeons and they were due to fly to New York in the next couple of weeks for a consultation. Millie said if the plastic surgeon could fix it so that people didn't avert their eyes when they saw her, she'd be happy.

Katherine told me in the kitchen that they were trying not to get Millie's hopes up too much, but the surgeon was cautiously optimistic. 'Obviously she's not going to look quite like before. Fortunately she never took this modelling business very seriously: she always wanted to go to university. This man we're going to see, who's our first choice, thinks from the stuff he's had from her doctors at the HDF that he'll be able to get a good result. So we're all a lot more cheerful than we were. Except Maddi, of course. She still seems very low.'

'Perhaps she'll improve now she's back with Will.'

'Yes. He's very busy, though, isn't he? I hope he'll ease off a bit once she gets back. They think work's very important, don't they?' she added, as if it was a generational thing, rather than that my son was especially self-obsessed.

I was used to thinking of Will as my trouble-free child, the one who did all the right things, became head boy and cricket captain and protected his less brilliant, less sporty younger brother. It was difficult to get my head round his new incarnation as the sulky uncooperative one. I didn't like Katherine's imputation that he wasn't capable of making Maddi feel better, but I was worried she might be right.

As she carried the tea outside, Katherine said, 'Look, I haven't said anything before now – with all this going on – but I'm sorry about this business with Matthew.'

'Thanks. It's been quite hard for him. It was a serious relationship.'

'Will he have to leave?'

'Yes. In the new year.'

'He was always going to London, though?'

'Yes, in March. A couple of months won't make that much difference. The hard thing is the ending of the relationship, the way it happened.'

'Does he know what's happened to Shaikh Rashid?'

I sat down next to Millie, under the bougainvillea. 'He can't get hold of him. We think he's probably not here.'

'But meanwhile you're going to be in London for Christmas!' Millie said mischievously. 'Sorry, I think we're not supposed to know, but Maddi told me. I don't think she could resist.'

'It's fine. *I* don't mind you knowing. It's James who's anxious about it – although I'm not sure how he thinks we can continue to keep it quiet if we're staying together in London.'

'How exciting! Have you found a flat?'

'I suspect Fiona Eckhart actually found it, but yes. It's in Knightsbridge and it's enormous and has something called a wet room, which is sort of a supercharged bathroom, and something else called a multimedia suite. And a hot tub on the terrace. It has whole rooms I didn't know existed.'

'Is an outdoor hot tub going to be much use to you in December in London?' Katherine asked.

'That's what I said, but James told me it's exactly when you need one.'

'God, Annie,' Millie said, 'how glamorous! It all sounds pretty serious!'

'I don't know. I thought so, when he was here.'

'You did a good job of keeping it secret . . .'

'He was very insistent about it. I'm relieved you know: I haven't been happy about the secrecy, because it puts me in a false position. But I did promise not to tell – so if you could avoid saying anything? . . . It was easier when he was here, because I was so caught up with him I didn't have time for proper conversations anyway. Everything seemed so easy, and exciting. Now it's harder, not least because we're finding it quite hard to keep up the intensity over such a distance.'

'How often do you talk?'

'Every day, but it's my morning and his night and I'm distracted because I need to get Sam to school, and he's had a day on set and he's often quite hyped up. We often find it difficult to hit the right note.'

This morning we'd both started speaking at the same time. In the slightly ratty pause that ensued, it was clear to me that he wanted to offload whatever was bothering him, so I gave way. I couldn't help reflecting, though, that my son was embroiled in a sex scandal which could destabilize a whole country and our residence permits could be cancelled at any time, resulting in deportation, and my daughter-in-law was depressed, perhaps clinically, and war was about to break out up the coast, possibly unleashing hideous weapons . . . and James wanted me to be upset because Rosie was getting the laugh?

But this was a futile way of thinking. He was a celebrity, which meant that the tiniest things that happened to him were thought to be hugely important. That must be very unsettling to a person. He was doing well to maintain as much interest in the wider world as he did.

I suspected the technology had been invented to bring us together before we were evolved enough to deal with it. (All human beings, I mean; James and I weren't specially unevolved.) Globalization works for a lot of things, like finance and food and entertainment (or at least, it sort of does, apart from the downsides), but it's not much good for love affairs. You can't conduct a reliable relationship over thousands of miles and however many time zones, even with the use of a mobile phone. James was winding down when I was revving up, and after a couple of weeks of half-communicating, of umbrage seeping down the line, I was struggling to remember what it had been like when he'd been here.

Katherine sympathized, when I said some of this. 'I always used to ring Maddi at Oxford when she was about to go into a tutorial. Or that's what she said, anyway. I expect she was just doing something more interesting.'

'Once you get to London you'll forget all about the phone calls,' Millie assured me.

I thought that must be true. James had been so effusive in Hawar, so convinced that there was something precious, unique between us. It seemed impossible we could get together and not feel that again.

Eleven

The sunlight sliced through the intense December blue sky, bouncing off the oleanders and hibiscus and the fluttering leaves of the tangelo trees with their swollen, fat-skinned, bitter fruit. The compound pool was as blue as James's eyes, for which journalists have reached many times over the years for comparisons – cornflowers, blown glass, lagoons – but which were today perfectly recalled by the pool at Al Janabiyya compound. The vegetation shivered with light.

School had broken up for Eid and what we had to call the festive season in a rush of end-of-term concerts and class parties, plays and reports. Matt, Sam and I were flying to London the following morning; this was my last swim before I finished packing.

The previous evening I'd been looking again at the internet pictures Fiona had sent of the flat. 'It's huge: we'll spend half our time looking for each other,' I told James.

'No, we won't, because I'm going to lock you up. You can be my sex slave.'

I had been relieved to learn that Fiona wouldn't actually be moving in with us. She was renting a mews house round the corner and flying back to LA for a week over Christmas. James did want to bring his cook, despite having a long list of restaurants at which it was imperative we eat. He said she understood his dietary requirements; I replied, perhaps a bit tetchily, that I thought I could probably recognize a carbohydrate.

'But you might fry things.'

'I don't "fry things".'

'You won't notice she's there, I promise.'

He assured me I could cook Christmas lunch, if I was that bothered about it – which, yes, he could see I obviously was and that was fine.

The only drawback would be having to deal with Fiona when I first arrived, because James couldn't get into London until the following morning, but I hoped this wouldn't involve much more than getting the keys. I privately planned that if there were to be any future in this relationship, Fiona would have to become a bit less ubiquitous.

I decided to do one more lazy length. As I slowly breast-stroked towards the tennis court, Cheryl opened the gate and trotted up the steps to the poolside.

'Hiya!' she called out. 'Might actually get a bit of a tan today.' The air was clear of humidity, so that for once the sun wasn't diffused into a damp haze. 'How are you?'

'Fine,' I called back from the water.

'Good. It's great for your serotonin levels to be exercising. After all your troubles. How is Matthew?'

'Fine,' I lied.

She put her bag down. 'Such a shame he won't be able to have children.'

I hate talking while swimming, especially to someone who isn't even in the water, but I couldn't let this pass. 'Well, he might,' I said. 'All sorts of things are possible.'

'I don't suppose he minds – it's probably different for them – but it's sad for you.'

I gave up on my last length, and swam to the steps.

'I don't think it's any different,' I objected. 'For them, as you put it. He's brilliant with kids.'

'Hmmn,' she said, working out if the sunbed was facing the right way.

'And I'm not that bothered about perpetuating my genes. That's not why I had him.'

Cheryl spread a towel on a bed, unpeeled her sundress and settled down. She looked along the length of her honed body approvingly, wriggled her toes, pulled a water bottle from her bag and stowed it beneath the bed, then opened a magazine. It was one of those hectic celebrity things, artificial and gossipy, that make you feel slightly queasy if you look at them too long. Someone must have brought this one in from abroad because you couldn't buy them here, on account of all the cleavage and thigh.

Cheryl squinted at the magazine in the sunlight. She had a thing about being younger than she really was, which meant she didn't need reading glasses. I climbed out of the pool.

'Oh, look,' she called out, as I picked up my towel. 'There's an article here about James Hartley and Rosie thingy.'

I dried off, smiling at hoarded memories of a peach dawn, the lines of James's body, scrambled sheets.

'I told you. I did, though, didn't I? It always happens on film sets. Did I ever tell you about that time in the Hawari Players? . . . No, well, best not . . . Tel'd kill me . . .'

Even now I didn't register what she was saying. She turned the magazine round to face me, showing me the spread, and I wound the towel under my arms and came over. I still thought I was humouring her.

As I came closer I could see a double page, a photograph pasted skew-whiff across the centre fold: a man leaning back against a red Ferrari, a woman facing him, her face half-hidden.

I gasped. I couldn't help it. Something inside me went into spasm. They were kissing.

Minutes earlier, this very image had been sliding in and out of my head: the way James's head tipped when he moved in to kiss me. Me. Not her.

Cheryl flipped the magazine to face her. 'She's young enough to be his daughter. Honestly!'

I slumped on to the sunbed.

Cheryl tutted and peered at the small writing, turning the page at an angle. 'Here, you read it,' she said, thrusting it at me.

'Huh?' I was disintegrating.

'Don't get it wet, mind. At least three of my step class want to borrow it.'

I glanced down and the page swam in front of me.

'Really, what can she see in him?' Cheryl said irritably, applying sun screen to her legs. 'Publicity, I suppose. But look at her: she's gorgeous. No, aloud!'

'What?'

'Read it aloud!'

'I ... don't think I can.'

I'd already read it, taken in the glib, bouncy prose:

So, it seems all the rumours about James Hartley and Rosie Rossiter are true! The proof is here in these pictures, taken in Hollywood this week.

James and Rosie, his latest co-star, were completely wrapped up in one another as they shopped on Rodeo Drive.

The couple are back in LA after filming their latest project, *Now Eden*, in the small Persian Gulf state of Hawar, where they had a narrow escape when the film set was attacked by Al Qaeda suicide bombers. Six people were killed and friends of the couple say the tragedy helped bring the pair of them together.

'What they went through out there was pretty bad,' said one. 'They turned to each other for help through the trauma.'

I shook my head in disbelief. He'd spoken to me this morning. And yesterday, and the day before that. When had this photograph been taken?

I tried to think whether there had been any change in his attitude. He'd been a bit distant, maybe, but then he was on the other side of the world.

Did these magazines fake photographs? Could they have made this up?

'Are you all right, love?' Cheryl was looking at me with concern. 'Oh, no! It was such a long time ago ... Surely you didn't think ...?'

Keep your dignity, my mum used to say. Don't let people see how hurt you are. That was bloody stupid advice.

'James and Rosie finally tore themselves out of their passionate clinch,' the sickening prose breezed on, 'and went back to their shopping. Looks like things sizzled in the desert heat. And they're sizzling still.'

I dropped the magazine on to my lap. 'It wasn't even hot.'

'What? What does it say?'

'It says when they were here it was hot.'

'I mean about them.' Cheryl snatched up the magazine and peered again at the picture. 'I suppose she gets a lot of help to look like that: nutritionists, personal trainers, that kind of thing,' she said sadly.

'And that the bomb was Al Qaeda, when everyone knows they were shi'a. And that those two suffered trauma because of it.'

I stood up shakily, feeling like my body didn't belong to me any more. I had to get back to the house. Out of the reach of Cheryl's perplexed sympathy. Away from this poolside with its sunshine on the water and this luridly coloured magazine glittering in front of me.

'I have to make a phone call.'

I stood in the middle of the sitting-room floor dripping on to the carpet, phone to my ear, drumming my fingers on the back of the armchair. I couldn't think straight: my mind was whirling away across the ocean ... It would be five o'clock in the morning in Los Angeles.

James would probably have his phone off. Or he'd be expecting this call and there'd be some divert to Fiona, who'd probably set up this whole thing, because nothing happened without her ... She was probably the so-called friend. Yes, that was it: she and Al Maraj had probably organized this between them. They'd always disliked me.

Maybe he'd changed phones ... I knew he had a phone

specially for me. I was the only person who had the number. (I wondered now if Fiona had it, or Al Maraj.) Maybe he'd thrown it in the trash now. New relationship, new phone.

'Annie,' he groaned, 'darling, it's like night time . . . You OK?'

'No.'

I expected him to interrupt then, to offer some glaringly obvious, completely plausible when you thought about it explanation of why he'd been kissing Rosie on the street in Hollywood.

But he didn't say anything, just made a sleepy grunting sound.

'I know about you and Rosie.'

'Huh?'

I was trembling, my damp bikini chilling on my flesh in the brisk air conditioning.

'I've seen the picture, James.'

'What? . . . Shit!'

'Why are you surprised? It was in a magazine.'

'Christ, Annie, it's the middle of the night. I can't talk about this now.'

'But we're supposed to be going to London tomorrow. Or we were.'

'What? . . . Annie?'

I imagined him in a big bedroom with ocean views and pale wood floors on the other side of the world, tangled up in his million threads per centimetre linen sheets.

'You're having an affair with Rosie! You can't still expect me to be coming to London.'

'Oh, shit.'

'Is that all you can say?'

'Calm down. You're overreacting.'

'How? How can I possibly be? You tell me I'm beautiful and you love me and what we have is unique and then you fuck Rosie . . .'

'It is unique.' He was finally waking up. 'I do love you.'

'No, you don't. How can you possibly?'

'This is ... trivial. It doesn't make any difference to my feelings for you. Christ, Annie, I didn't ever say I wasn't going to sleep with anyone else for the rest of my life. It doesn't mean anything.'

'That is *so* pathetic.'

'But everyone does it.'

'No, they don't.'

'Annie, you have no idea what my life is like. I get women propositioning me all the time.'

'You said you hated all those actresses. You said they use you. And that Rosie would sleep with you but you wouldn't even know if she liked you!'

'Exactly. It's just sex, Annie. Meaningless. You have to understand: it doesn't make any difference to us. If you hadn't seen that picture you wouldn't have known. I didn't think you got those magazines there. They're rubbish.'

'Have you never heard of the internet?' When he didn't answer, I said: 'So you knew the picture had been taken, then? You knew it was around?'

'The thing with Rosie is nothing. It doesn't alter my feelings.'

'It alters mine.'

'Don't be silly. I love you, Annie.'

'Was it going on when you were here?'

'No, I've explained,' he said this wearily, as though I were the one being tiresome, 'it's a fling.'

'You know what's really galling? You insisted on keeping our relationship secret but you made sure you were photographed snogging Rosie in the street. She's not using you: you're using her. You hope people will think you're younger.'

'It was designed to get people talking about me and Rosie and the film, that's all,' he said irritably.

'The film's not out for months.'

'These days you have to start the publicity really early. It's quite an art. This was just part of it. You know, a stunt.'

I didn't believe him. He'd already admitted they were having an affair. 'The point is that I'm not good enough to be seen with you in public, but Rosie is.'

'How often do I have to tell you? This – being with you – is really important. Different from being with anyone else. I see it as being for ever.'

'Except when you're off having sex with starlets.'

'I'm a highly-sexed man, Annie. You're not here. Look, if it bothers you, I'll look into treatment. They can do quite a lot now for sex addiction. I know several people . . .' You could almost hear his brain calculating the PR value of sex addiction rehab.

'It's not about sex,' I said exasperatedly, 'or not entirely. It's about thoughtlessness. Complete inability to see things from my point of view. You didn't think about the effect of this picture on me. And I doubt any treatment would make a difference: the selfishness is too deeply ingrained.'

'I told you, I didn't ever think you'd see it.'

'That seems to have been a bit of a punt. What with you being globally famous and all . . . And what about other people? Didn't it occur to you that the reasonable conclusion might be that you were ashamed of me?'

'Look, some people don't think this is the right relationship for me, but I don't care . . .'

'Yes, you do. You think I'm wrong for your image.'

'Annie, let's talk about this when I get to London. I can explain it. Having sex with Rosie, with other women, doesn't alter how I feel about you. I don't have that understanding, any of that history with them.'

'I'm not coming to London. It's over.'

'We had a great time in Hawar, didn't we?'

'It was an illusion. I didn't realize I was seeing someone who thought I was just one of a whole series of sexual options.'

'You don't want to stay there, though, surely, for the rest of your life?'

'It's over,' I said, and put down the phone.

I stumbled round the armchair and fell into it, picking up the cushion and holding it to me for protection. He was as bad as those married men who played footsie with you at dinner parties, as desperate to prove he could still pull. How could he understand me so little as to think I'd settle for something so second rate? He must have a very inflated idea of himself.

My mobile was ringing again. It was James. I switched it off and, while I was about it, unplugged the land line. Then I went slowly into my bedroom, peeled off my bikini and ran the shower.

'You look terrible,' Sam said when I came out three quarters of an hour later, all cried out, at least for the time being.

'I've got bad news . . .'

'Not Matt?' he asked in alarm.

'No, no, nothing like that . . . It's London. We're not going. It's over. With James.'

'God, mum, what kind of timing is that?'

'Sorry, no choice.'

'What happened?'

'He's having an affair with Rosie.'

'The stick woman? Oh God, no . . . Really? How did you find out?'

I explained. 'He didn't seem to think there was anything wrong with it, either. He was incredulous that I might have thought he wouldn't sleep with anyone else. He seems to take the view that if you get a lot of offers, you're bound to accept some.'

''Course, some gay men manage it,' he said thoughtfully. 'Have relationships that aren't monogamous, I mean. Not Matthew, obviously. He's lovesick.'

'Yeah, well, it may be the future of pair bonding in advanced societies, but it's not going to work for me.'

'He didn't tell you? That he was intending to sleep with other women?'

'No: d'you think we'd have been wasting our time going to see him in London if he had? He was too busy telling me how wonderful I was.'

'Shit.'

Only yesterday, he'd talked about the future. Not just Christmas in London, but how we might arrange to see each other afterwards. How I could come to LA, and how his next movie was probably going to be shot in Tuscany, and we could meet there ... I should have realized that when he talked about wanting me to be his sex slave, he was describing his desires exactly: he'd have been happiest if he could have kept me in a cupboard.

'Why does he want another woman?' Sam asked. 'You'd be more than enough hassle for most people.'

'It was the same when we were young,' I said sadly. 'All him, him, him.'

'What, did you forget?'

'Yes. I suppose I did. All I could remember was that I hadn't quite trusted him. That would seem to be because he's not trustworthy.'

'He did like a lot you, though. You didn't imagine that.'

It was possible, I thought sourly, that he had felt as much as he's capable of feeling. Unfortunately, that wasn't all that much.

'He's a bit of a sad fuck, really, isn't he? We should go to the flat anyway. He owes us.'

'Sorry, Sam, but no.'

'So what's happening tomorrow?'

As soon as I thought I could manage the conversation, I called my dad.

'I'm really sorry, I know it's a lot for you and I wouldn't ask if I didn't really need to get away ...'

I was sick of Hawar. Sick of the emir and crown prince and prime minister gazing down at us from the wall of every public building, fraudulently smug in their mishlahs. If they'd had any real confidence they wouldn't have had to remind us who was in charge every time we turned our heads. They were forever neurotically asserting Hawari nationhood because for most of its history Hawar hadn't been a nation at all, only an unpromising tract of desert bounded by a couple of mountains, a wadi and the sea, occupied by tribes that were sometimes feuding, sometimes allied. Power had shifted and eddied for centuries before the British laid a grid over the land in an effort to make it more manageable, more amenable to an empire that had since faded. Perhaps now power was shifting once again. The Al Majid knew they had either to reform or to retreat into Saudi-style stasis – but reform threatened them, because of popular Islamist opposition, and not reforming threatened them too. It would be easy, if you were an organized and determined opposition, especially if you had no compunction about the methods you used, to bring the country to its knees. All you'd have to do would be to sabotage the desalination plant. Citizens had got used to having water in their taps, to bright green lawns and hedges of hibiscus and pomegranate all the way up the Seef road, to frangipane trees overhanging the gate to the souk on Bab Al Hawar filling the air with creamy perfume. Those things felt like a right now. But you only had to go ten miles into the desert to see how preposterous it was.

'So, is James coming with you, then?'

'No, that's the point. James and I have split up.'

And decadent, that was another thing about it. Hawar was decadent. Where there should have been debate, there was a vacuum – except that now, religion was swilling in to fill the empty space with apocalyptic terrors and prohibitions and the fatuous promise of a historic, preordained moment.

'He'll be coming round, though? Because I'll have to clean up.'

'No, dad. When I say it's over, I mean it's over.'

'For good?'

'Yes.'

'But he said it didn't mean anything . . . ?'

'Dad . . .'

'OK, OK, but you can understand me being a bit thrown, when you're arriving tomorrow!'

I called Will and then Karen to tell them that we would now be staying in Thornton Heath rather than Knightsbridge. I used Sam's phone because I kept getting a beeping noise on mine when I was talking to dad and I suspected it was James.

'I've only just got my head round your last photograph crisis,' Karen complained. 'What is it with you lot? And where are you going to stay, because you know what Chris is like about Matthew . . .'

I promised Karen we wouldn't be bothering her.

'No one ever thought it would last with James anyway,' she said.

'I feel so stupid,' I told Will, 'so shallow, like some sort of stupid fan, fooling herself into thinking she could have a relation-ship with a film star.'

'That's not fair. He wanted you to believe he was letting you in to something beyond all that.'

'Yeah, well, I don't think there is any beyond. How's Maddi?'

'Oh, you know . . . You don't need all that now . . .'

He was wrong, I thought as I finished my packing. Knowing I was involved in other people's lives was exactly what I needed. I might own some fairly ridiculous underwear, in the cir-cumstances – scraps of black lace and ribbon that I'd bought at the absurdly named Lovely Ladies designer lingerie shop in the Pearl Mall and which would now only be removed by me, which hadn't been the plan when they were purchased – but at least I wasn't emotionally adrift like *some* people. While I may be lacking in the lingerie-removing department, some people were lacking in the ability to relate to other human beings depart-ment. At least I could take refuge in the knowledge that I was meshed in a double helix of worry about my children, implicated in all their happiness and trouble, which is better than worrying that you might one day be minimally less famous; better than pathetically sleeping with young women to pretend you aren't getting older; better than having your whole identity rest on something that could slide away on a bad box office receipt.

I tried very hard not to think of all the things I'd been planning to do in London and now wouldn't do, the districts I'd hoped to get to know that would now forever be posh people's districts. (I didn't want to be one of the posh people – at least, I don't think so – but I didn't like the idea that some things were closed off to me. You can't reject things when you've got no experience of them, otherwise you end up like Anwar.)

I tried *very* hard not to think that this was it. That this had been my last chance, and now the boys would move on and I'd be on my own, always offered the worst room in the hotel, shown to the back table near the kitchen where they put the ugly old sad people, because I was a lone woman and no one wanted to look at me.

Matt found me sitting on the end of the bed by my open suitcase at eleven o'clock when he came in from having a drink with Jodie.

'Sam told me.' He sat down next to me. 'What a bastard.'

'Yeah, I'm sorry about the flat.'

'It's OK. Sounded a bit gross anyway.'

I squeezed his hand. 'Who wants a stupid multimedia suite?'

'Yeah, and water coming out of your walls?'

'Oh, well,' I stretched out my legs in front of me, pointing my newly painted toes, 'I was feeling guilty anyway. It seemed tactless to be happy when you were so upset about Rashid. At least now I won't have to worry about being inappropriately cheerful.'

'Yeah,' Matt said, 'we can look forward to a Christmas of unrelieved misery, with only Uncle Chris's homophobia to give us a bit of a laugh.'

Twelve

We flew into London to the sort of pointless, indeterminate weather in which England specializes at the turn of the year, on a day that couldn't make up its mind what to do with itself and dribbled away its few hours of daylight in a kind of irritable funk. The plane cleared the clouds at the last minute to reveal an overcrowded landscape of ring roads, retail sheds and light industrial units. By the time we left the airport in our hire car, the motorways were clogged with rush-hour traffic, steaming in the drizzle.

I felt worse than I had the day before. The shock had worn off and underneath there was the sharp pain of realization that I'd fallen for a person who, for all that he'd had his face on the side of buses on every continent, was hopelessly weak and trivial.

Travelling felt more than usually unreal: I couldn't see past the neon-lit interiors of Hawar International Airport to the point of it. Why were we still going to London? Why had we been going in the first place? How had I ever believed in any of it? I bought a lipstick in duty-free, in an attempt to assert myself against the cavernous artificiality of airport life, to have something that I owned, that was part of me. But it didn't work: I didn't feel any less like an alien. I walked automatically to the gates, got on the plane and had already started turning right towards economy before Sam tugged me into first class. I could have made some grandiose gesture with James's tickets – i.e. thrown them in the bin – but he'd never have known, it wouldn't have made me feel any better and the boys wouldn't have forgiven me. The first-class experience was wasted on me, though. Champagne was the last thing I felt like drinking, I wasn't hungry and, when you came down to it, you were still breathing recycled cabin air for three thousand miles before being herded and processed through passport control and baggage reclaim then released back into the world.

At this point, you can often feel as if you've got your life back. You've been in suspended animation, in a place where time is meaningless and space is empty, and then all of a sudden you're on the M25 and it's five o'clock. But I was still in a stricken blur when Karen called, on Matt's phone because I hadn't bothered to switch mine on after the flight. I thought James might well rate his seductiveness highly enough to think it was worth continuing to pester me.

'No, it's still over,' I heard Matt answering. 'No, it's OK, granddad doesn't mind.' There was a lot of talking at the other end, and then he said, 'Hmmn, OK, well, I'll tell her.' He rang off. 'She says she needs to talk to you because granddad's gone mad and been to another one of those gay meetings.'

'It's a famous sign of insanity,' said Sam from the back seat. His Walkman batteries had run out.

'She says you've got to make him move into a flat.'

'Somewhere with no gay people,' suggested Sam. 'Like Warlingham. They're not allowed in.'

We drove into Thornton Heath, down streets I'd known all my life but which were now alien. When I was growing up they'd been uniformly white and lower middle class, narrow-minded and resistant to difference. But now they'd become the confusing, slightly run-down outskirts of a world city. The shape of them was still there, like a skull beneath the skin, but the surface was completely different. Did the people who attend the Ghanapathy Temple walk along the road to shop at the Bismillah Grocery? Did they eat at the Hummingbird restaurant next door? (The Hummingbird advertised itself as the gateway to the Caribbean, which, to judge by the view through the grimy windows, seemed to be setting people up for quite a lot of disappointment.)

In the streets, men and women in all kinds of dress, much of it unsuited to the weather, seemed to slide past one another uneasily, looking as if they were keen to get somewhere less public and stressful, as if they hoped they were only in transit. As we drove over the bridge across the railway line, we saw a sign saying 'cash for crap', and Sam said: 'Why don't they just buy up the whole place?'

Dad had cooked a stew, which was perfuming the house with gravy. He took me upstairs to show me which bit of the wardrobe I should use.

'You shouldn't have given up your room,' I said.

'No, it's nice to have you here.' He spun the door handle round. 'You remember this doesn't work?'

'Dad, you could get locked in here!'

'I keep a screwdriver in the bedside table.' He paused. 'I was hoping James would fix it, actually. He used to be handy.'

'We'll get it done while I'm here.'

'Oh, well, it's OK, I'm getting on now. I'm used to it.' He changed the subject, because he didn't want me to fix it, he wanted me to have a man who'd fix it. 'So, no word from Matthew's friend, the shaikh?'

'No. Matt thinks he's probably abroad, having – being made to have – some kind of therapy.'

'Will that help?'

'I don't think it's a famous cure for homosexuality, no.'

'People get very upset about gays, of course. I told you about that boy I met?'

'At your meeting?'

'Terrible, what happened to him. We had a couple at the last one.'

'A couple of what?' I opened my suitcase and immediately saw two dresses I'd been planning to wear to the sort of restaurants at which a person like me would normally only be able to get a table with several months' notice.

'Gays. I got talking to them at the end. You wouldn't have known. Well, apart from the bright jumpers.'

'I don't suppose I'd have known anyway. I seem to have terrible gaydar: Matthew, the crown prince . . .'

'They were just like a normal couple. Had a mortgage and everything.'

'Yes, well, I suppose they would.'

'I expect Matt wanted to be normal too?'

'Yes. Difficult with a prince, though.'

'We don't seem to be very good at hanging on to people, do we?'

I looked up at him. 'Matt and Rashid were separated for no good reason. And if you mean James, he's not a person you'd want to hang on to.'

'It's a shame, though,' he said, spinning the door handle thoughtfully, then went downstairs to see to the potatoes. I sat on his candlewick bedspread and looked around. He hadn't decorated since my mum died and there was dirt in the corners of the skirting board, crusting around the edges of the faded wallpaper. I should have booked a hotel: neutral territory, somewhere that didn't have all these cross-currents of expectation, obligation, anxiety.

I disappointed him. I didn't have a husband. I'd brought up Matt to be gay. Will was too busy to come and see him. Sam didn't speak. I was going to spend the whole time we were here apologizing to him for us, and to the boys for having brought them to this old man's house with its smells of Bisto and Glade.

And then I felt mean, because he was my dad and their granddad, and it wasn't so hard, surely, to see things from his point of view for a week or two over Christmas.

Still, it wasn't what I'd promised them. It was small, over-heated rooms, steamy with their grandfather's anxiety: Were the boys going out? After dark? Did they know about all the gangs round here? Loitering between the house and the station, mooching about, looking for trouble? It wasn't safe. They should stay in.

Maybe that was why the boys were being so obnoxious at breakfast the following morning.

'Does this tea taste dusty?' Sam asked, which it did. Matt held up the tub of butter substitute as if it was a fascinating anthropological object, never previously seen by civilized peoples. He was perfectly familiar with butter substitute; he was just being brattish, making out that nothing so cheap and nasty had ever come within his ambit.

They ought to have been able to deal with this, I thought crossly. It wasn't as if I'd inflicted it on them deliberately. I didn't want to be here any more than they did: they could have made an effort. Although it *was* pretty annoying that the muesli tasted of polythene and all the flakes and fruits were indistinguishably limp.

I was quite relieved when they both announced that they'd decided to go into town. Sam was meeting Faisal, who was in London with his family for the Christmas holidays, and staying off the Edgware Road, as Sam said pointedly, near some shops.

I decided to drive to the supermarket. I knew my dad would think when I got back that I'd bought too much, too expensively, but would insist on trying to pay for it all the same. But at least I could prevent the boys having to eat food that had been stored in grubby Tupperware since the last time we'd been here.

While I was out, I switched on my phone again. There was a voicemail message from James insisting that I'd overreacted, that I didn't understand, that if we could only get together he could explain everything and make me see there was nothing wrong with our relationship. The way he said 'our relationship' made it sound like something technical and fixable, with defined and manageable limits. I erased this message and listened to a couple of others, from Maddi and Antonia, both saying they wanted to see me.

Maddi was at work when I called her back and she sounded more energetic than she had in Hawar. I don't think listlessness is allowed in management consultancy offices. Even so, I thought I detected a tinny, synthetic quality in her voice. She invited us all to dinner at the flat and she and I also arranged to have lunch near her office on Wednesday.

'Darling,' Antonia exclaimed when I got through to her, 'how thrilling that you're here too! We're staying in this new club place in Notting Hill, and we're having a few friends over on the Friday after Christmas, so naturally, I thought of you . . .'

I hesitated. The last time I'd been to dinner with the Horwoods, Antonia had sat me next to Adel Al Buraidi. I asked if he'd be coming this time.

'Oh, yes, he *is* rather good-looking! And he said he's been helping you . . .'

'Did he?'

'Over this difficult business with Matthew . . . Putting in a good word. Anyway, he can't, unfortunately, he's not in London. But I have got someone I'm absolutely dying for you to meet . . . Now, where are you again?'

'Near Croydon.'

'Really? I thought somewhere in town? Knightsbridge, I thought Di told me . . .'

'It fell through.'

'Oh . . . ? Croydon? That's a bit of a funny place. I don't know anyone who lives there . . .'

'No? I do.'

'Must be a bit lonely, all the same? Can you get to London from there?'

I assured her it was possible. I didn't particularly want to spend an evening with the Horwoods but I felt I ought to take every opportunity to get out of the house, where nothing seemed to have changed much since I was sixteen. James had got away, and spectacularly, but I was back in Thornton Heath in my dad's house, stuck. Going backwards, if anything. Sam told me recently that when the universe has expanded as far as it can it will ping backwards like an elastic band, hurling the stars and planets together in a sort of reverse big bang. The big crunch, I think it's called: anyway, my life was crunching – flying backwards to the same old house with the same old responsibilities, dependent on my dad, no different from when I'd been an adolescent. All that remained for me now was to become as helpless as a small child before finally attaining the status of primeval atom.

Karen arrived as I was unloading the shopping, explaining that she'd been out of the office looking at a property, and thought she'd pop in.

'I'm so sorry about James,' she said, following me up the path.

'Don't be. He's appalling. If he hadn't been famous I'd have noticed sooner.'

'You don't think he had a point?'

'What?' I was struggling with the key in the front door.

'You know, that you couldn't really expect him to behave like ordinary people?' She nodded at the lock. 'Your dad says that always sticks.'

I got the door open, put the bags down in the hall and went back for the rest of the shopping. 'I can't see that being photogenic and remembering a few lines entitles you to go round treating people as though they don't matter, no.'

'You should've got more out of it,' Karen followed me to the car. 'At least got him to buy you something.'

'I didn't think of it as a business opportunity.'

'No, well, I expect that's where you go wrong. Why you haven't been able to get a husband, despite being nice-looking and quite intelligent. You don't look out for yourself ... God, this street is awful,' she looked up and down it; 'you've got to persuade him to move.'

'You're the estate agent, Karen. If you can't, I don't see how I can.'

'How can he bear to live in a road where people park their cars in their front gardens?' We went inside. 'And this kitchen! It's not even hygienic. He wants something more modern.'

'He says it was good enough for mum, so it's good enough for him. Deep down, he doesn't think he deserves anything better. He might move if you could find him a hovel. Tea?'

'I thought you'd never ask.' She settled herself at the kitchen table, while I stowed the shopping and boiled the kettle. 'How's Matthew?'

'Miserable.'

'Yes, well, I suppose it was a bit sordid, having his picture taken under a big GAY sign.'

'Well, it was sordid of the paper to print the picture.'

'All this fuss and publicity hasn't changed his mind, then?'

'It's not a choice, Karen.'

'Yes, I did say that to Chris ... Still, it's a shame. Not what you'd want, is it? For your child?'

'That depends on the child.' How were you supposed to get through to people? 'It's part of him, like being so straight is part of Will, or not communicating is part of Sam.'

'It's going to make life harder for him, though, you've got to admit.'

'Only if people think it should.'

'Well, I know you like to have an answer for everything, Annie, but let's face it, it *is* harder, or he wouldn't be moping around right now.'

Will and Maddi were renting the upstairs half of a converted house in a terrace of brick cottages in Battersea, on a narrow street that would once have been inhabited by factory workers but was now occupied by graduates who drove Volkswagen Golf convertibles to the country at weekends.

'It's like being part of Team England,' Will had admitted ruefully when they'd found the flat through someone who'd been two years ahead of Maddi at school. A part of him liked that, in the same way I would have liked staying in Knights-bridge – something that might have been closed off to us, but wasn't – but I think a part of him also felt like an impostor.

At this time of year, all the neatly painted doors were

decorated with tasteful Christmas wreaths. 'And all the girls who live here wear the same clothes,' Will said when I remarked on this: 'cashmere, mainly: loads and loads of cashmere.'

'All the men wear the same clothes too,' Maddi pointed out. 'Suits,' she added, 'like you.'

'I still think we should be living somewhere a bit more edgy.'

She shrugged.

'It looks like they're camping,' Sam whispered to me when we left our coats in the bedroom, which, like the sitting room, was still full of unopened boxes and pictures stacked against the walls. Maddi asked us to excuse the mess, saying she'd spent so much time in Hawar since they moved in, she hadn't had time to get things straight. I was disappointed that Will hadn't used the time that she was away to organize the flat for her, so that she might have felt she was coming home rather than to some half moved into developer's painted shell.

One way and another, we weren't a particularly animated party. Matt was mostly morose at the moment, anyway, but tonight his mood wasn't helped by the fact he was tense with expectation that Will was going to say something tactless and dismissive about Rashid. I'd nearly exhausted my reserves of wryness about James. Maddi admitted her mind kept wandering to Millie and her parents, who were due to arrive in New York in a few hours. Sam would have preferred to be somewhere else. And, for quite a lot of the meal, Will was. As soon as Maddi put the bowl of Moroccan chicken stew and green salad on the table, his mobile rang and he excused himself to answer it in the bedroom. He stayed there for half an hour.

'Does he do this often?' I asked. Maddi smiled ruefully, without any attempt to make excuses for him.

Eventually, I got so irritated I left the table and made indignant faces at him round the bedroom door. He waved his hand, to show he was coming. A few minutes later, when he still hadn't appeared, I went back.

'What, so I'm supposed not to take calls from my boss?' He put his phone back in his jeans.

'It's not like we come round every week. Can't you say you're having dinner?'

'No, it doesn't work like that.'

'Look, I know they pay well ...'

'It's not about money,' he said irritably, 'you don't understand.'

'It's an Arab Bank. They must realize you have a family?'

'Are you two coming out so we can have pudding?' Sam called through, 'or is Will on the phone again?'

I knew Will thought I didn't understand the pressures of his graduate job, that I was applying the values of another time and place – when husbands finished work at five o'clock and came home for tea and didn't think about their jobs till next morning – but this was unfair. I could see exactly why he wanted work that preoccupied him. I just thought he ought to be able to manage it without being rude.

'Someone in Saudi asked me the other day if I was anything to do with you,' he said grumpily to Matt when he rejoined us. 'I told you this would happen.'

Matt raised his eyes to the ceiling. This was what he'd been waiting for. 'You could just say you're not,' he suggested; 'disown me.'

'Oh, I did. I pretended I didn't know what he was talking about and changed the subject. But he knew I was your brother all right.'

'I didn't fall in love with Rashid to hurt you.'

'You should've thought.'

Maddi started talking loudly over them about the Iraqi sanctions and how much opposition to them she'd noticed this time in Hawar – 'posters of starving children and collecting boxes outside the mosques'. Sam, who'd started reading the papers in his role as editor of the *International*, pointed out how incredible it was that the Americans had lost the moral argument with a mass murderer; and, for what was left of the evening, they squabbled about what the Al Majid should say and do about the sanctions, which I suppose was better than squabbling about each other.

A couple of days later, I met Maddi for lunch at a fashionable restaurant near her office, where the walls were roughly plastered, the floor was stone and the tables and chairs were made of deal. It was probably lovely in summer, but on a rainy day in mid-December, the atmosphere was chilly and damp.

Maddi was wearing expensive black trousers, a green silk shirt and a soft camel coat, but the first thing I noticed was that the flesh around her thumbnails was red raw and the skin was torn where she'd been picking her cuticles.

'Sorry Will was so useless at dinner,' she apologized, as soon as she sat down. 'He's in the middle of some deal and he's a bit stressed.'

'I wish he wasn't so angry with Matt,' I said gloomily. 'It's not as if his clients aren't all super-rich: they're probably quite sophisticated. I don't know what he's so worried about . . .'

'No.'

'He's got you, a great job, somewhere to live. Look . . . you don't think . . . ?' I hesitated – 'I know this'll sound stupid, but you don't think that there's something a bit homophobic about it?'

She looked up from the menu, startled.

'I know,' I said quickly, 'it doesn't really make sense. He's twenty-three and he's got a degree: he's not the kind of person you'd think would be bigoted. And he's always been very generous towards other people – but he overreacted at the wedding and he's been completely irrational about Shaikh Rashid. And he *is* religious – I wondered if maybe that has something to do with it?'

'I don't know. It doesn't seem likely. He hasn't been to church since we left Hawar.'

Neither of us wanted to discuss Will, because we couldn't seem to do it without criticizing him. And if things had been bad enough for us to form an alliance against him, that would have implied that I'd failed in his upbringing and that she'd decided to marry someone self-obsessed and inconsiderate. I changed the subject. 'How's your work?'

'OK,' she said cautiously. 'I could do with a bit of Will's commitment myself: I can't seem to take it as seriously as I should. I seem to get very impatient with the meetings, the hours discussing tiny little things, the office politics ... They let me have all that time off, so I feel I owe them, but I can't get excited about it. They're one of the top graduate employers, they reject hundreds of applicants a year, and I should feel lucky to be there. If I don't, their view is that there are plenty more where I came from. And they're right about that ... and I know Millie's going to be OK, and I shouldn't let the fact that she came so close to dying get to me, but there's a fault line in my life – or that's how it feels – before the bomb and after. And my job doesn't seem to matter as much as I'd expected.'

As I left the restaurant, City workers were reeling unpredictably through the afternoon gloom. A group of screechy girls in Santa hats scattered off the kerb in front of me, dodging a gang of young men shouting about how rat-arsed they were. Being rat-arsed seemed to be the main aim of the day, and it didn't matter much what happened after. Being run over by a bus would only prove you were really, really lashed. Snatches of tinny Christmas music filtered out of bars and boxes wrapped up to look like presents sat in the windows of the shops along Bishopsgate. I had a pang of homesickness for Hawar, where Christmas only lasts a day and a half and you don't have all this effortful, dismal jollity.

The train rattled ponderously through the south London suburbs. I trudged back to dad's in the drizzle, rain dripping off the bare trees on to the shiny pavements. Why had I ever thought that this was a good idea, that Christmas in London would be fun?

Sex, that's why. Sooner or later, someone would work out how to harvest the pheromones and turn them into a weapon.

There was no one at home. My dad had mentioned something earlier about going to the library and the boys had escaped into town. I made a cup of tea, skimmed through dad's *Daily Mail*, then started to make some mince pies.

I had to think of this trip as a punctuation mark, I decided as I weighed out flour and butter. It might not be much fun in itself, but by the time I got back to Hawar I'd be over James. The fuss about Shaikh Rashid would have died down. The next time a flaky film star attempted to seduce me, I'd know better.

The doorbell rang. I wiped my floury hands on my apron – I was in the middle of rolling out – went up the hall, opened the door and was astonished to see Nezar Al Maraj on the front step.

This was so much not what I expected that I nearly fell over. I couldn't have been more surprised if an orange tree had sprouted in dad's front garden, bright-fruited among the soggy ground cover and privet.

'I'm sorry to call round like this,' he said. 'Your phone's off.'

'Yes . . .'

'I don't want to interrupt . . .'

'It's OK, no one's in . . .' He looked at me expectantly. 'Er, well, I suppose . . . come in . . .'

He stepped into the hall, waited till I'd closed the front door then followed me down to the kitchen. I felt suddenly hot and bothered. The kitchen was airless. The gas cooker was pumping out its gas mark 8 heat for the pastry.

'You're cooking.'

'Mince pies.'

He hovered by the table.

'Sit down,' I offered, pointing to a stool. 'Tea?'

'Thanks.'

I turned away to fill the kettle. I couldn't think what to say.

But I didn't have to make it easy. He must have come for a reason.

'I'm sorry about James,' he said eventually.

'Are you?'

'Well, yes and no,' he admitted. He was honest, at any rate. 'I guess this isn't what you were planning,' he said, as I pulled at a stuck cupboard door. It jerked back suddenly, nearly throwing me off balance.

'There's nothing wrong with it,' I said huffily. 'I'd rather be here than force James to take time out from his other girlfriend.'

'Are you OK?'

'Oh, yeah, great.'

Why was he here? He'd got what he wanted. I put the teapot on the table. That was it, then. Tea made. Now what?

He stared at the teapot and then at me, but still didn't speak.

'Look,' I said wearily, 'I know you thought I was in the way . . .'

'No! That's not true.'

'But if you've come to gloat, you needn't. There's nothing you could possibly say to me that I haven't already thought.' He tried to interrupt, but I pressed on.

'I know I was bad for his image . . .'

'What?'

I hesitated. The kitchen seemed suddenly much too small – crammed with jars, scraps of paper for shopping lists, postcards, plants, an unused, dusty spice rack, a toaster shedding crumbs. The air was too thick to breathe. I started again: 'I know you thought my affair with James was a mistake, and it turns out you were right. But it wasn't a mistake because I look too old or fat in photographs. It was a mistake because James is spoilt and egocentric.'

'I agree,' he said. 'And you don't look old or fat.'

I stared at him. He wasn't handsome – certainly not in the way that James was. But against the formica worktops and lino-tiled floor, he seemed to suck the energy out of the atmosphere, to blaze like a geranium on a drab windowsill on a murky afternoon.

'I know you think I went after him,' I blundered on, 'but actually, he made all the running. I was quite cool, in fact, because I couldn't see how he could possibly be serious. I thought it would be a one-night stand. Then, you know, a fling. Unimportant.' He tried to interrupt again, but I wouldn't let him. 'He was the one who kept going on about the future, saying the relationship was so special and different and he wanted us to be together. *He* suggested we come to London – I wouldn't have dreamt of it – and he was the one who talked about what we were going to do afterwards. He kept making plans and he was the one who used the word "forever". And not just once, either. Not me: I wasn't pushing the pace.'

'I'm sorry, I did try to warn you, that evening in the desert.' He looked up at me. 'I was useless. And I asked Fiona to warn you, too. The thing is, I couldn't be sure of my motives. And, I thought, this once, James might think about someone other than himself.'

I poured the tea uncertainly. He wasn't really making any sense.

'I was in a state. And I didn't think you'd believe me if I told you what he's really like. I know how persuasive he can be when he puts his mind to it.'

I tried to imagine Nezar Al Maraj in a state. It seemed improbable. He hadn't looked in a state.

'Has he done this before, then?'

'Never in quite the same way – you were a special case, because of the past, and because – well, because you are. But James thinks the world was created for and around James Hartley. Other people are incidental. He can use them or dispose of them or whatever.' He sounded bitter. 'I hoped you might have already known that. He said you were the one who left him – I think that's been quite unusual for James – and I thought you might have remembered it. But if not, I thought I probably couldn't persuade you.' He toyed with his mug, pushing the handle from side to side. 'He does love you, you know, in his funny way. He appreciates how beautiful you are, and funny and wise . . .'

'Wise?' I said bleakly.

' – Unfortunately he hadn't worked out what being with you would entail.'

'No. Fitting in shagging the other women was always going to be a problem, I guess. But, look, it's over, OK? I'm out of the way. I'm not going to cause any more trouble.' It had suddenly occurred to me they might think I was going to kiss and tell, to sell my story to the newspapers.

'Annie,' he said suddenly, 'will you have dinner with me?'

I stared at him stupidly. 'There's no need.'

'Huh?'

'I'm not that sort of woman.'

'What sort?'

'You know. The sort who sells her story.'

He stared at me in confusion. 'Any time,' he said, as if that were the issue. 'Tonight, tomorrow, after Christmas . . .'

And now, slowly, dully, I began to understand why he might have come.

I stared at him. 'But you've . . .'

'No. Whatever you're going to say, no.'

'But you laughed at me the first time we met . . .'

'I didn't want to stop talking to you.'

'Oh . . . well, it certainly didn't feel like that. I thought you were ridiculing me for my Arabic. And the second time, if I remember rightly, you hardly said anything at all.'

'I could see how things were going with James. I didn't think I could compete. And I was miserable because I thought he wasn't good enough for you.'

'So you come round here when I've been dumped . . .'

'You dumped him, I think. He's been ringing me every half hour asking how he can get you back. I'm afraid I haven't given

237

him any very useful advice. I thought it might do him good to try to work it out for himself.'

'I'm not desperate, you know!'

'No,' he agreed gravely.

'And you're homophobic.'

'What?'

'You don't like Matthew being gay. You kept saying something awful would happen.'

'Annie, it has. Matt and Rashid may never see each other again, and Rashid's been damaged politically.'

'Well, then,' I faltered, 'you messed that up as well. All those vague, dire warnings . . . It was just confusing!'

'I know, I'm sorry, I didn't know how much to say.' This was awful. Embarrassing. I wished he'd just leave. 'You still haven't said.'

'Said what?'

'About dinner.'

Dinner? 'No,' I said quickly, 'no, no, no. It's too late. We haven't even been polite up till now. It's hopeless . . . you can't just come here and ask me out, after everything . . .'

'Look, I know it's probably too soon after James, but I wanted to see you and I couldn't help myself.'

I thought I heard a key turn in the front door and I didn't reply.

Al Maraj stood up. 'Well, James is obsessed with you too, in his pathetic way, so . . .'

Then he heard it too: the creak of the front door where it needed oiling, the sound of my dad wheezing slightly as he let himself in from the cold.

'Ann?' he called querulously down the hall.

'In here, dad,' I called uncertainly.

He shuffled into the kitchen, unwinding a scarf.

'You remember Nezar Al Maraj, dad?'

Al Maraj put out his hand and dad took it uncertainly.

'Aren't you James's friend?' he asked suspiciously.

'I'm the producer of his latest film.'

'Well, you can tell him from me that he's behaved appallingly. Upsetting Annie. You can tell him if that's what being rich and famous does for you, you can keep it.'

'Dad . . .'

'Well, it's true. What he's done to you is terrible. He's not the person we used to know.'

'Actually, dad, he is,' I said wearily.

'I was just leaving,' said Al Maraj, easing himself out from behind the kitchen table, where he somehow seemed to have got stuck.

'You're not the one who doesn't like gay people?' dad asked suspiciously.

'No,' Al Maraj said, 'I'm not. Annie, sorry to have disturbed you . . . no, it's fine, really, I can see myself out.'

'What was he doing here, then?' dad asked, before Al Maraj had even got to the front door. 'He didn't finish his tea.'

'He was just passing.'

'Passing? On his way to where?' He picked up the teapot and weighed it in his hands, to see if there was another cup in there. 'Oh good, you're making mince pies.'

I looked down at the pastry, which was yellowing and sweaty, crusting around the edges. Despairingly, I gathered it up in a fat ball and threw it in the bin.

Thirteen

A late, low-slung shaft of sunlight was slanting across the wallpaper in the lounge. I slumped into an armchair and stared at the dust motes dancing in its light, a blizzard of them, so thick that it was surprising that they didn't clog up your nostrils and stick in your throat. They whirled pointlessly about, fragments of people and things. It seemed astonishing that they were there all the time, that human beings could coexist with so much debris.

I kept trying to think of it as a joke – you wait fifteen years for a man to come along, etc. – but my heart wasn't really in it.

Al Maraj? Thinking I was attractive from the beginning? I couldn't have been that obtuse, surely?

I really wanted to go on believing he was an opportunist, that he was just saying that stuff, that he thought I was desperate and would sleep with anyone. But I could see that that didn't altogether make sense, because he wasn't anyone. He was highly presentable and quite the most interesting person I'd met in ages, and he was perfectly capable of getting an attractive girlfriend, without having to confuse women in steamy kitchens in order to entrap them on the rebound.

Then I felt cross with him for not making more effort in Hawar if he'd thought I was attractive all along. Did he seriously think I was going to fall for someone who appeared to be permanently in a bad mood?

Eventually, I admitted to myself that even if he'd been making quite a lot of effort I probably wouldn't have noticed, because I'd been so ditzy, so dazzled by James's condescending to pay me some attention. My intuition about people, about which I'd always rather prided myself, had taken itself off on an extended break. This made me feel foolish, so I concentrated on remembering the things about Al Maraj that had previously dismayed me: how much he scowled when I was with James, how he'd failed to warn me that my son was having sex with the crown prince. It was all very well for him to claim now that he'd been trying to alert me, but if you wish to inform a person they are dating a sociopath and that their son is on the point of destabilizing a small nation, it is advisable to do something other than glare.

I tried to suppress the other feeling his visit had left me, a sort of light-headedness, like you get with flu.

With the boys, I did my best to turn it into a joke. Who's the least likely person you can think of to ask me out? (They didn't guess: that's how unlikely he was.)

They soon got fed up with that. Sam had only met him once anyway, and said he couldn't be arsed to get excited about another man I wasn't sleeping with.

Matt pointed out that he was rich, which I told him was irrelevant given that a) I was perfectly capable of earning my own living and b) I had always thought he was horrible and while I was prepared to concede that this could be an over-statement, he was undoubtedly inept.

Will was too preoccupied to bother about my non-relationship with Al Maraj. Previously, whenever I'd tried to open a conversation about Maddi's depression he'd been dismissive, implying I was wittering on like a woman who didn't understand graduate jobs. He didn't have time for a depressed wife. But now, in the kitchen before lunch on Christmas Day, he was more open, which made me think things must be quite bad. It was one thing to admit they had troubles to his friends, another to confess them to me.

'She's got no energy or enthusiasm,' he complained. 'You watch over lunch: she'll just slip out of conversations into her private thoughts. She never used to do that. She'd've thought it was bad manners.'

'Perhaps it'll pass. It can't be easy, her first Christmas away from her family.'

'She's twenty-three.' He didn't say 'and she's with me', which was what we were both thinking and which should have been enough.

'Even if the Franklins had been in Hawar,' he pointed out – they were in New York – 'she could hardly have taken any *more* time off work.'

I think Maddi was genuinely making an effort to join in over lunch, but she often fell silent and gazed absently into the middle distance. Her hands were even worse than they had been earlier in the week, the skin around her nails peeling and raw. I couldn't think that Christmas in this small, stuffy house was helping much, with everyone feeling disappointed they weren't in Knightsbridge with a film star, and my dad in a state of high anxiety.

'Aren't you doing too much food?' he'd asked as I prepared Brussels sprouts.

'I'm not sure there's any such thing as too much for the boys.'

'I won't want too big a meal, though.'

'No, well, you can have whatever you like.' I threw the last sprout into the colander and smiled at him. 'It's Christmas.'

'I don't want to be overfaced . . .'

'No one's going to make you eat.'

'You won't want to be wasting food, though. Throwing it away.'

'If there are any leftover vegetables, I'll make soup,' I promised through gritted teeth.

'All I'm saying is don't go to any trouble for me. I can have whatever's left over.'

His efforts to prove how undemanding he was could be very demanding. In the end, with a bit of encouragement, he ate a perfectly normal size dinner. Afterwards, I persuaded him to sit down with me in the skirling light of the coal-effect fire in the lounge and stop fussing over the boys while they washed up. He continued to fret that they might be dropping the best plates or putting away all the cooking utensils where he'd never find them again, but at least in here with me he wasn't telling them that. When at last he exhausted the potential for disaster of the washing up, he turned his attention to what might happen when Chris and Karen and Andrea arrived to play games. (Someone could knock over the tree and tread baubles into the carpet.)

In the event, though, the day passed off without major mishaps. The food was good, the wine that Will and Maddi had brought was delicious and probably horribly expensive and the vegetables turned out to have been prepared in more or less the right quantity. In the afternoon, Andrea arrived with her parents and the karaoke machine she'd been given for Christmas, and we were still up at one o'clock singing the greatest hits of Robbie Williams and Britney Spears. Chris, who had a good voice, was so keen to keep giving his 'Angels' that he refrained from getting completely pissed, and was less rude than he might have been. He didn't say anything overtly homophobic. Maddi didn't burst into tears; in fact, she brightened up quite a lot after she'd spoken to her family and sang 'Hit Me Baby One More Time' several times with Andrea, complete with choreography. Even Matt didn't look too mournful and, in fact, was livelier and funnier than he had been for weeks and only mentioned Shaikh Rashid where he fitted naturally into the conversation. Dad made an obvious effort not to worry out loud more than once every hour. And I tried not to think about Nezar Al Maraj. So I guess everything went according to plan, except that it was unquestionably Plan B.

It was past ten o'clock when I stumbled into the kitchen on Boxing Day. Dad had had an exceptionally late night for him and the boys never got up before ten if they could help it, so I was the first downstairs.

Or so I thought. The kettle was already boiling by the time I noticed the envelope on the kitchen table. It said 'Mum' on the front in Matt's handwriting. I picked it up and tore it open. I knew already it wasn't a good letter. Otherwise it wouldn't have appeared on the kitchen table first thing on Boxing Day morning when the person who'd written it should have been in bed.

Whatever it said – and I kind of knew what it said – was going to ruin this torpid, slightly hungover morning.

> *Dear Mum,*
>
> *Don't panic. Seriously. I've gone abroad for a few days. I'm really sorry I couldn't warn you, but I know you'll understand.*
>
> *I realize it's tricky, but if there's any way you can avoid telling people I've left the country – even granddad, Will and Sam if possible – that would be brilliant. Maya's family has a house in Yorkshire: maybe you could say I'm there? (I know you're crap at lying, but just this once.)*
>
> *I promise I'll explain the whole thing later. I love you and I'm taking care, honest.*
>
> *Matt xx*

I read the note, then read it again. Then I stuffed it in my dressing gown pocket and walked up and down the kitchen three times. Then I sat down. Then I stood up.

What did he mean, don't panic? He was going somewhere so secret and dangerous he didn't trust me to know about it. He'd disappeared out of his bed on Christmas night leaving me with some rubbish cover story saying he knew that I'd understand.

Well, no, I didn't. I understood some things – that he'd gone to see someone he wasn't supposed to meet, who was presumably surrounded by bodyguards. But not why he thought that was in any way a good idea.

Matt and Rashid couldn't have found each other and certainly couldn't have exchanged enough information to make this possible without other people knowing. Whoever was policing Rashid would be monitoring all his phone calls and emails. And they would be particularly on the lookout for Matthew, who, not being a spy or an international terrorist, didn't have the faintest idea how to cover his tracks – who, if anything, was rather flamboyant and garrulous.

I switched on the kettle again. He'd be in the air by now. And the next thing I knew, he'd be found knifed in some Beirut backstreet, or floating down the Nile . . .

How could he have done this? How could he have taken such a stupid risk, without thinking of me, or all the people who loved him? Didn't he appreciate how dangerous it was? That the people who took an interest in the future of Shaikh Rashid did so because they were protecting what was left of the oil revenues and because they were desperate to maintain a status quo that allowed Saudi Arabia to go on quietly subsidizing the Hawari economy? For which you had to assume they'd do almost anything?

It was so utterly out of character. Matt was the last person you'd think of as taking clandestine flights to foreign countries for illicit meetings. He'd never shown the slightest desire to needle history, to nudge it along a bit. All he really wanted was to be left alone to live like a normal person. A normal person who liked grooming products and scented candles, admittedly, but definitely not a person who fled from the house before dawn on secret missions.

When dad wandered down half an hour later, I was still sitting in the kitchen, staring into space. He had a headache – he'd had two glasses of wine, a couple of snowballs and he'd gone to bed extremely late. Sam had stayed up after everyone else, watching some movie and probably finishing off the vodka, and when he eventually got up he had a hangover too. Neither of them questioned my frankly risible story that Matt had taken himself off to Yorkshire at first light on Boxing Day morning without telling anyone he was going. If Matt had really been planning a trip north, we'd have had discussions for days beforehand about what clothes he ought to take and whether it was possible to spend several days in Yorkshire in winter without getting wet.

We'd have had descriptions of Maya's parents' house – which, knowing Matt, would have been big and built in the reign of Queen Anne. I wasn't even sure that trains ran on Boxing Day, but they didn't question that either.

I spent the day clearing up. We ate leftover turkey, mashed potatoes and pickles, all of which tasted to me of nothing. Sam played CDs, fiddled about with his new iPod and watched old movies with his grandfather. It was all very disquieting. Subdued, but alarming at the same time.

Finally, at eight o'clock, I had a text: 'Arrived safely. All well, Inbox now full! Stop worrying. Really, no need. I love you.'

I immediately rang back, but he'd already switched off his phone. I loosed off a text to join all the others I'd sent through the day . . . Call me . . . Where are you? . . . This is not fair, etc., but if his inbox was full perhaps he didn't even get it. At any rate, I didn't get a reply.

I lay awake most of the night, half-expecting to have to get up and go downstairs to the hall to answer dad's phone, to speak to the British embassy in Syria or Jordan. When I finally drifted off to sleep, I had a nightmare about a gun going off in a back alley in Libya. (I don't know why Libya. I know nothing about Libya so it's unfair on Libyans that in my dream they were all liars, insisting the gun had gone off by accident.) The purgatorial atmosphere of this dream hung around me all through the next day.

I was so tired I could barely function. Sam went up to town to see Faisal. Dad went back out into the garden and worried that he'd seen an unseasonal squirrel and that he was certain it was getting his bulbs. I nearly snapped at him that it was ridiculous to worry about squirrels when Matt was missing, until I remembered he thought Matt was in Yorkshire.

Even if I'd told him that Matt had flown half way round the world to meet a prince with whom he was in love, I'm still not sure he'd have believed me, because the whole thing had the irresponsible, creatively-slipshod quality of a dream.

By this time, I hadn't heard from Matt for more than twenty-four hours. He'd said in his note (which I kept re-reading, hoping that I might have missed some vital clue) that he was only going to be away for a few days. He hadn't hinted that he wouldn't be coming back to Hawar with us on Saturday, for example. But I'd now sent him fifteen texts without getting any response and he could have been anywhere, doing anything.

I kept thinking I should have been able to stop him doing something so reckless. As I wandered aimlessly around the house, unable to settle, it seemed to me I'd made a mess of everything. This was galling: I'd always prided myself on having quite a good touch emotionally, but it now seemed less of a touch than a wild jab. I'd got James all wrong, and Al Maraj, and Will wasn't happy, whatever he might say, and I had no idea what was going on with Sam. I hadn't paid him enough attention over the last few months, what with the wedding and Matt and James Hartley, even though he was the one who was changing fastest, so that I sometimes felt everything he said or did was capable of surprising me. At sixteen, he was a person still in search of a personality: one minute talking like someone from South Central LA, the next holding forth about politics; now a bit racist, now thoughtful; now mature, now like a child. If he was looking for something to fix on, to build his identity around, then I probably needed to give him more help.

'You seen this?' he asked me through a mouthful of toast on Friday morning, looking up from dad's paper. 'Says here that the Ministry of Information in Hawar has closed the Al Jazeera bureau.'

'Why?'

'It's not clear.'

I looked over his shoulder. The story was a few sentences at the bottom of a column headed 'News in Brief'. One of these sentences was entirely taken up with explaining that James Hartley had been filming in Qalhat a few weeks ago, where he'd 'been the target of a terrorist bomb'. This seemed to be the main reason to be interested in the place. Hawar almost never made appearances in the British press and this story was probably only running now because nothing else was happening between Christmas and New Year. Although the piece was so short, it managed to convey the impression that closing down Al Jazeera offices was a generally good thing and the Ministry of Information had been sensible.

'Someone from Hassan Town probably rang some phone-in programme to complain about the ruling family,' Sam said gloomily. 'The same thing happened before in Kuwait, and I think the Palestinian Authority closed their bureau a while ago. Al Jazeera could soon be the first Arab TV station without offices in any Arab country. Honestly, how can Matt've got involved with those people?' He meant the Al Majid. 'If they don't like something they just close their eyes and ears to it. And then think they can do the same to everyone else.'

'I think, to be fair, that's the sort of thing Shaikh Rashid wants to change.'

'Yeah, well, he's not making much progress, is he? Why has he given up Matt if they're still shutting down the only place people can go to express an opinion?'

'I guess it'll take time,' I said, uncomfortably conscious that Shaikh Rashid's attention was probably somewhere else right now.

'They won't give up their power,' Sam said, turning the pages of the newspaper. 'They want it all. Freedom to go off to Monte Carlo and drink and gamble and have sex for them, nothing for anyone else. It's like when dad died . . .'

I paused, lifting my hands out of the washing-up bowl. 'What d'you mean?' I asked carefully.

'I *mean*,' he answered pityingly, 'they didn't find the other driver, because he was a rich Arab. Never mind that he'd killed someone. He was allowed to escape back to Saudi or go hide in his fuck-off mansion.'

'No. That's not right.'

'What?'

'That's not what happened.'

'Huh?'

'He was drunk. I'm sorry. Dad.'

'What d'you mean?' He was glaring at me, but I could tell he was afraid.

'I should have said.'

'Why didn't you? *Drunk*? How come we didn't know?'

'When you were younger,' I faltered, 'I wanted you to have an idea of him that was – I don't know – good. I wanted him to be someone you could admire.'

'So what happened?'

'He'd drunk about three-quarters of a bottle of brandy before he got in the car.'

'The accident was *his* fault?'

'The blood results were off the graph,' I said wearily, sitting down on the stool opposite him. 'His car crossed the central reservation on the Arad Road and hit a pick-up truck. He spun round and went into the side wall of Jashanmal's Furniture warehouse. The other driver was very lucky.'

'You know who he was? The other driver?'

'Yes, although he panicked and drove away: that part was true. He could see dad was an expat and he was old enough to remember when the British had been in charge. The police picked him up as soon as he took his truck in for repair, because he didn't have an accident report. I met him.'

'Why didn't you *tell* us?' Sam's eyes were hot. 'Or did you? Am I the only one who didn't know?'

I shook my head. 'I didn't say because I wanted you to believe in him.'

'But if it was an *accident* ... Oh God,' he looked at me, realizing, 'it wasn't a one-off, was it?'

'No.'

'What, he drank all the time?'

I nodded.

'And you think you've *helped* by not saying?'

'I don't know. Probably not.' I swallowed. 'The driver of the pick-up truck was in his sixties. He lived in Hassan Town. He asked to meet me. He kept on apologizing for not reporting the accident, but we knew that dad had died immediately; it wouldn't have made any difference. The police gave him a hard time, but nobody really wanted to make a fuss. It wasn't actually his fault and – well, you were right about the conspiracy of silence in a way, but it wasn't to protect a rich Arab, so much as to protect us.'

'Yeah, and their precious emirate . . . *Why* did he drink?'

He obviously thought that that was my fault.

'I don't know. He felt that the world was against him.'

'Was it?'

'No.' Although it's difficult for the world to be on your side if you are an alcoholic. 'Of course not. He was . . . somewhere else when he was drinking. Somewhere that felt better.'

'We weren't enough for him?'

'No. Sam, surely you can see why it was difficult for me to talk about it when you were small?'

He looked at me in a way that was both despising and pitying.

'Did other people know he was an alcoholic?'

'No. They knew he liked a drink, obviously. Until near the end, he covered it up pretty well, but in the last few weeks things had started to slip, almost as if he was giving up, giving in to it. He'd made a couple of mistakes at work. And a few weeks beforehand he'd shouted at a woman in the street for running over his foot with her pushchair. The night he died he hit someone in a bar.'

'Do other people know how he died? Like, I don't know, Faisal's parents, or the Franklins?'

'No. It looked at first sight like a hit-and-run accident, and that's how it stayed.'

'How convenient. Did he hit you?'

'No.'

At least that was true. He hadn't hated me. But I hadn't been able to help him in the way that would have made a difference. I hadn't been able to make him stop.

'I wish you'd said.'

'I'm sorry, Sam.'

'Are we like him?'

'Yes and no.' Sometimes a ghost of Dave stole across the boys' features. But in the ways that really mattered they weren't like him, not least because I was so determined they shouldn't be. Sam, for instance, floundering around for a way to be an adult: if I had anything to do with it, that was going to involve facing up to what he felt.

Friday was the evening I was supposed to have dinner in Notting Hill with Antonia and David. It was the last thing I wanted to do, but I didn't see how I could back out without concocting a lot of complicated lies, which would have been more effort than actually going. It would also have meant disappointing dad and Sam, who approved of my going out, thinking that it was a sign that I was getting over James. They had no sense of how little thought I'd given to James in recent days.

I drove into town and followed Antonia's directions to the Pembridge Club, which turned out to be two large, stucco-fronted houses in Notting Hill knocked together and furnished to appeal to the resident abroad market, blandly but with touches of the exotic – a Chinese carpet here, a Korean rice chest over there, a sofa scattered with cushions covered in Indian silk. Antonia and David would have felt at home here, among the sort of trophies that expats carry away from their postings in exchange for bits of their lives left abroad.

Antonia showed me into a chintzy room, softly lit by table lamps, where a waiter was serving pre-dinner drinks. It was warm and comfortable; you'd never have guessed it was raining outside and that a greasy film had settled over the city.

'*Do* come and meet Johnny,' she urged, taking me by the arm. 'You're *so* going to like him.' She lowered her voice. 'He's a bit obsessed by how much money his ex-wife managed to get off him, but if you can ignore that, he's lovely.'

Unfortunately, I didn't manage to ignore Johnny's obsession with his ex-wife, which wasn't surprising as it was his only topic of conversation. We were placed next to each other at dinner, during which he explained to me that you need to squirrel your money away well before your wife leaves you: it's no good trying to move it once she's run off with someone else and filed for divorce. The key thing is to build up your secret offshore accounts in good time. Fortunately, he'd had advice from friends, and he'd thought ahead and done it, or he'd have been fleeced even more, and she'd have had an even bigger house in Chelsea to share with her personal trainer.

It was OK sitting next to him, though, because I just had to say 'Oh, really?' whenever he paused for breath and then I could go back to worrying about Matthew.

The other guests were two couples called Miles and Juicy, and Adam and Harriet – or it may have been Miles and Harriet and Adam and Juicy. I called her Lucy for the first half-hour because I'd never met a person called Juicy before, and also because it's an adjective. And, in fact, whichever one of Adam or Miles was her husband did sometimes call her Fruit.

'So what happened to South Ken or Knightsbridge or whatever it was, darling?' Antonia asked, when we got to the salmon. 'Seems a bit of a come-down ... Oh, but that reminds me, you'll never guess who I bumped into in Harvey Nicks yesterday? I'll give you a clue: someone from the film!'

'Nezar Al Maraj?' I said without thinking.

'No, but close! And it's funny you should say that, because she asked if you'd seen him. I mean, as if I'd know! The other one, Fiona thingy ... Eckhart? We met her on Al-Hidd, with James Hartley, d'you remember?'

'Ah, yes.'

'What happened with you and James Hartley?' David asked. 'There was a rumour going round that he kept sending you flowers . . .'

'Well, he did once,' I said vaguely.

'What d'you mean, what happened?' Antonia tutted at her husband. 'What on earth *could* have happened? He's a film star, darling . . . Anyway, she remembered me. She was quite chatty and, really, I don't know why she told me, because I could know anyone – and in fact I *do* know a lot of people – but apparently, James Hartley *met* someone recently, some scheming woman who very nearly got her claws into him, Fiona said, and she's had to clear up the mess. There was some flat he nearly bought her or something.'

Rented, I wanted to say. He rented it.

'That's why she was here. I asked her along tonight, but she couldn't make it.'

That, at least, was a relief. I'd have had to leave.

'Who was this mysterious woman?' Adam asked. 'Isn't he with that Rosie Thingy from *The Undetected*?'

'To be honest, she was a bit cagey. But she did say she's hoping to come back to Hawar: she's made lots of friends among the shaikhas, through the producer's sister. Al Maraj, is he called? Are they together?'

'What?' I realized she was asking me. 'I don't think so.'

'Oh, are you sure? I rather got the impression they were. Why would she think *you'd* seen him?'

'I don't know,' I replied honestly.

'You don't even like him, do you? That's what I told her: "I'm sure Annie said she couldn't stand him."'

On the way home, I had a text from Matt: 'All well. Can't get back for flight on Saturday. Arriving Hawar soon. All love.'

I called straight back, but I wasn't surprised to find the phone had again already been switched off. How on earth was I supposed to pretend to dad and Sam that Matt couldn't make it from

Yorkshire to Heathrow for the flight home? I don't think I have a particular talent for untruths, even though Sam now regarded me as a pathological liar. Having finally come clean to him about Dave's death, I didn't want to start lying about another thing. He was still scowling at me disappointedly every time we passed on the stairs and avoiding meals with me almost entirely, spending every available hour at Faisal's flat and frequently sleeping over.

It seemed that Matt was expecting an awful lot of cooperation from me, considering – although in truth, neither dad nor Sam seemed in the least bit curious about Matt's supposed trip to Yorkshire. In their different ways, they were both too busy being self-absorbed. Sam was hardly at home and my father was, as I pointed out to him, so upset by the fact we were leaving that he was unable to take any pleasure in the rest of our stay.

'There's going to be a war,' he pointed out unnecessarily on Friday, when I was on my way upstairs to pack.

'The embassy will get us out if we need to leave,' I promised briskly, although I didn't believe it. If there were weapons of mass destruction heading in our direction, Richard Crossley-Tennant wasn't going to have time for much except a few panicked phone calls.

'I don't know why you want to go back there, after everything that's happened.'

'It's where we live.'

'You don't even speak the language.'

'No, well, it's very complicated. They mix up all the singulars and plurals, for a start. Instead of saying "the shoes are big", you have to say, "the shoes, she is big".'

'And if they're making Matt leave, I don't know why you'd want to stay . . .'

'Dad, I have to earn a living.'

'I don't understand why you haven't found someone. It's not as if you're unattractive. Even James Hartley went out with you.'

We hadn't gone out; we stayed in. The only place James Hartley would have wanted to go out with me was Kabul, where I could have worn a burkha. 'Dad,' I said wearily, 'we've been through this before.'

'It's not as if you don't meet people. What about that bloke who was here the other day?'

'Which bloke?'

'The Arab.'

'Nezar Al Maraj? You can't pair me off with random men I only vaguely know . . . Look, I've talked to you about this before. I only want to live with someone if I can't bear not living with them. Otherwise, it'd be worse than living alone. It wouldn't solve anything. You know that.'

'How likely are you to find someone you feel like that about?' Dad asked irritably. 'Especially in Hawar.'

Fourteen

I concocted a story about Maya's family flying back to Hawar via Cairo and offering to take Matt with them. It would be tricky when he arrived back with nothing to say about the pyramids, but he'd have to deal with that. I wished afterwards I'd said they were coming back via Rome, because Matt had actually been there, but Cairo was the place that came into my head. I thought that Matt probably really was in the Middle East and at the time it seemed better to stick to the truth as far as possible.

'What, so he's not going back with you?' Karen asked disapprovingly, somehow conveying the idea I was an inadequate mother who couldn't keep her children close by her, or under control at all.

I was angry with Matt for not saying goodbye to his grandfather, especially after dad had made such efforts with his sexuality. But dad himself was indulgent and said he was looking forward to having Matt to stay again soon. 'Perhaps he could come to our relatives' group?' he suggested, 'and talk about the situation for gays in the Middle East?'

As we set off for the airport, Sam finally registered how unlikely it was that Matt would have given up the chance of a first-class flight back to Hawar, so I confessed that not only was he not with Maya, but also that I had no idea where he was.

'You've been lying to me *again*?'

'He asked me to keep it a secret.'

'So you did? Without thinking of me?'

'I wanted to protect him. I never thought we'd get to this point, going back without him.'

When we landed in Hawar, I half-expected the immigration officer to tear up my green landing card and throw it back at me.

I couldn't believe the ruling family and their henchmen didn't know that Matt had disobeyed the very clear instructions to stay away from Shaikh Rashid; nor, since that was the case, that they'd let us in. But we were waved through with the usual indifferent hauteur.

The front-page story in the *Hawar Daily News* on the day we arrived was that the United States had deployed its first full combat division to the Gulf since 1991. President Bush had also made a speech warning Saddam Hussein that unless he changed his ways, he was heading for war. As Sam pointed out, he didn't say which ways, and it was unfair not to be a bit more specific.

Given that Saddam had already let in the weapons inspectors, war now seemed inevitable. There was a feeling of helplessness among people in Hawar, of matters having been taken out of our hands. Jodie came round the following day, looking for Matt, and said her dad was hardly ever getting home these days: 'I think it's get the hajj over and . . .' she shrugged.

'Seems odd that they're so scrupulous about Ramadan and the hajj,' I said, 'as if war could be conducted with rules, like croquet.'

'But you can't have it so that anything goes,' she objected – 'atrocities and stuff.'

I shrugged. Once you were killing people, it didn't seem that big a leap to kill them horribly.

Jodie had come up to the compound because she knew Matt was due back but she hadn't been able to get hold of him on his mobile. I was forced to tell her I had no idea where he was. There was no point in pursuing the Maya story with her because she and Maya had been shopping together in the souk that morning.

She stared at me. She knew there was only thing Matt could be doing in such secrecy. 'Bloody hell, good for Matt! Who'd have thought?'

I swore her to secrecy and hoped Matt would come back soon, because I couldn't see how we could possibly keep on lying. He must be due back at work; I was going into the British Primary tomorrow and the International School term was starting in a couple of days, although Sam was already well ahead of the game. The day after we got back, he triumphantly announced that following a month-long campaign of persuasion (about which, needless to say, he'd told me absolutely nothing) Mohammed Alireza had finally agreed to be interviewed for the *International*.

'Is that wise?' I asked in alarm.

'What d'you mean?'

'Well, it's not the sort of thing you usually cover, surely?'

'Probably not.'

'What does Mr Koppel say?'

'It's not his magazine. It's for students.'

'Sam, please be careful.'

'Are you saying Mohammed Alireza should be censored?'

'Of course not,' I answered irritably. 'But he seems perfectly capable of getting his message across without your help. We don't need any more trouble, that's all.'

'What, so you think we should censor ourselves, then? To protect the Al Majid?'

There was no way I was going to win if Sam turned this into an argument about free speech. 'If you want to finish your IB . . .'

'If I'm editing a magazine,' Sam retorted pompously, 'I think I should do the best job possible, and cover the subjects people are interested in.'

Matt walked in the following morning as I was getting ready for work, looking as if he'd just been round the corner. I was drying my hair and didn't hear him open the front door and come through the house. He knocked on my bedroom door, then poked his head round, smiling a bit blearily. I caught sight of him, squealed and dropped the hairdryer on the floor.

'Matt!' I rushed at him. 'Thank God you're back!'

'Hey, mum.'

'Where have you *been*? I've been so worried.'

'I told you I'd be OK.'

'You didn't say you were going to be gone this long . . .'

'Any chance of a cup of tea?' He disentangled himself from my frantic hug and I let go reluctantly and followed him into the kitchen. The blood was flowing back to my brain after the initial faintness and, though I had a thousand questions for him, unfortunately the one that came out was, 'Are you mad?' The second was hardly any better: 'What were you *thinking*?'

'I'm back, aren't I?'

'Where were you?'

'Cairo.'

'No!' I laughed; he looked puzzled. 'That's where I told everyone . . . oh, it doesn't matter. How did you know where to go? How on earth did you organize it?'

'I didn't. Nezar did.'

'*Nezar*?'

'I thought you knew . . . He organized the whole thing.'

'How would *I* know? I knew nothing, Matt. Nobody told me where you were or what you were doing. I've been worried sick . . .'

'Oh. Sorry. I told you it'd be OK, though.'

'What's it got to do with Al Maraj, anyway? You hardly know him!'

'I dunno . . . *You* know him.'

'Barely.'

Matt looked confused. 'Oh, well, he organized the plane and flew out with me and everything.'

'You went on a private plane?'

'Yeah, with these big armchairs and a sofa . . .'

I didn't want to know about the soft furnishings. 'And, what, Al Maraj came with you?'

'He took me to the house where Rashid was staying.'

'Why on earth did he do that?'

Matt shrugged. 'I thought it was something to do with you . . .'

259

'No. And it was very wrong of him to give you that impression. It would have been a lot better if one of you had told me what was going on. It was one thing for me to tell granddad and Sam you were in Yorkshire, but lying about why you weren't coming back to Hawar was really difficult. It was very unfair.'

'But you did see him just before Christmas, right . . . ?'

'Yes, but that was . . .' I blushed. 'We didn't discuss you. So,' I asked suspiciously, 'what's in it for him? Has he done some kind of deal with the Al Majid?'

'Well, there was some kind of deal, must have been, to let me see Rashid,' Matt answered reasonably. 'He's virtually a prisoner. If he wants to be crown prince, he has to do what they say. They made it pretty clear that this was the last time I'd be allowed to see him.'

'So Al Maraj is working for the ruling family?'

'No.' Matt shook his head. 'He found some way to persuade them – I don't know what, but the only people he was working for were me and Rashid.'

I stared at him, trying to make sense of it. 'So, how was it?'

'We had four days. Not whole days, but I was allowed to see him four times. We talked and talked, and we were on our own, and it was fine.' He smiled. 'And in the end, he told me the best thing would be to find a boyfriend who doesn't come with the responsibility of a small country.'

'Oh. I'm sorry.'

'No . . . it's OK.'

'And that's his decision? They're not coercing him?'

'Well, they are, obviously, because he'd rather be with me. But they haven't driven him mad, if that's what you mean. He's seeing a psychiatrist and an endocrine specialist but he's still the same. He was quite funny about the treatment, which mainly seems to consist of giving them sperm samples. He's had to provide about twenty so far. They give him pictures of women, though. I suppose they think they'd be encouraging it if they gave him boys . . .'

'And what do they want him to do?'

'If he agrees to get married and acts like a good husband, he thinks they'll leave him alone.'

'Seems rather hard on whoever gets chosen as the wife.'

'Yes,' Matt looked away. I think he didn't approve; certainly, he didn't want to talk about it.

'And what about you? Was it worth going all that way?' It sounded as though he'd gone only to be told it was definitely over.

'Yes,' he said decidedly. 'It was painful, but it was also wonderful, and it would have been much, much worse not seeing him. I know now that he'll always be thinking of me a bit.'

'I'm sorry, Matt.'

'Perhaps he feels guilty. He says he doesn't: he's always quoting this thing about how in Islam judgement belongs to God – but the religious establishment is so hostile to gays, and there are a lot of things about being a Muslim that he really values.' He frowned. 'Are you ever going to pour that tea?'

'Is it the right decision, though? For him?'

He shrugged. 'He says when the Americans invade the whole region'll be in a mess and there'll be a job to do in Hawar because people are sick of the repression but they're even more afraid of the religious fanatics. But Nezar doesn't think it's worth it.'

I wished he wouldn't keep referring to him so matily.

'What, Al Maraj thinks he should give up politics? For you?' I said. It seemed unlikely.

'We were talking about these doctors Rashid's been seeing and Nezar said specialists couldn't restore lost opportunities to an old person who's missed out on erotic experience.'

'Right.' I felt suddenly hot.

'He thinks Rashid's closing down that whole side of his life, and it's wrong.'

'Maybe things will change?' I said hopefully '– maybe the Gulf won't be homophobic for ever.'

'Yeah, except they seem to be changing in the wrong direction. It's getting even more difficult to be gay in Hawar.'

'Did Al Maraj come back with you? Only we ought to thank him . . .'

'I did thank him, mum. What d'you take me for? He said since I was coming back here, he wanted to make sure it all went smoothly, so he came too. He seemed to think it was better I didn't take a scheduled flight. But he's gone to Paris now.'

'He *must* have had an ulterior motive . . .'

'Yeah,' Matt said, amused. 'I think he did, mum. He's very cross with you.'

'Oh?'

'For not being over James.'

'But I am!'

'He thinks you're still obsessed with him.'

'That's nonsense! How dare he? You know that's not true. Didn't you *tell* him?'

'Mum, I had a lot on my mind. Anyway, how am I supposed to know what's going on with you? It's way too complicated.'

People get things wrong all the time. It's not surprising when you think about it. The politicians deciding whether to invade Iraq, for instance, might have had more information about Saddam and WMD than the rest of us, but in the end George Bush couldn't feel like an Iraqi, however many intelligence reports he read. He'd be basing his decision about whether to start a war mainly on instinct and intuition. It seemed rather a big intuition, that it was a good idea to invade a country, but I felt in those weeks that I was scarcely in a position to criticize because I'd lost so much confidence in my own judgement. Before now, I'd flattered myself that this was rather sound, and that this was because I was good at seeing other people's points of view and the various different sides of a question. I even thought this might be something to do with being a mother, because it's what so much of motherhood is about. Yet when it came to James, I'd been dazzled and blind-sided, thrown off balance by factors that a more sensible, wiser person would have ignored, such as how flattering it was. I could also appreciate now that I might have made some rather serious mistakes about Al Maraj, having been distracted first by James and then my own prejudices. Unfortunately, knowing all of that didn't get me very far because Al Maraj wasn't here and I had no idea where he was, and he seemed to think I was still obsessed with James. Added to which, Fiona Eckhart had probably reported back that I went round telling everyone I couldn't stand him. There were a lot of things I would have liked to say to him, to ask and explain, but when last heard of, he'd been heading for Paris – which meant, frustratingly, that I had no choice but to get on with my life, with going back to school and all the usual start of term mayhem: new pupils to settle in, muddles with the music timetable, meetings to organize with parents and visits to set up with the Ministry of Education.

At least Matt seemed a lot happier since his visit to Shaikh Rashid. He only had a few weeks left at Palm Publishing, and he'd started to talk about what he planned to do afterwards. Life seemed finally to have regained some of its old, regular, uneventful rhythms. The January weather was beautiful: a breeze filtered through the palm trees and brought up goose bumps on your arms in the early morning, in spite of faultless blue skies and warm sunshine. Everything was etched more sharply in the clear winter air: the hibiscus flowers looked brighter, the bougainvillea more purple, the sea azure instead of its faded summer yellow-grey. When I'd first arrived in Qalhat, I wouldn't have thought it was possible for the emirate to be anything other than the drab dead colour of dust, but now it looked completely different: we had architecturally striking buildings, new hotels with lagoons and flamingos, a golf course and a university. And pavements everywhere – proper ones with kerbs and trees, not like before, when roads petered out at the edges into ditches or were simply the unmade gaps between buildings.

When I'd first arrived, there had been no point in having leather shoes, because you couldn't go out without wrecking them. To get to one of the concrete and glass skyscrapers in the diplomatic area, for example, you'd have had to cross dusty open spaces where plastic bags drifted about, catching on the rubble. Now the entire district was manicured, with hedges and palm trees and fewer and fewer patches of stony ground each year. Where all the houses had once been the colour of dust, of the desert, and had had a kind of desiccated uniformity about them, as if it was too much effort to keep the sand out, the thousands of new homes built in the last twenty years were faced in gleaming marble, or, like the whole of Hassan Town, whitewashed and shining in the relentless sunshine. The smarter ones had swimming pools, bouncing bright blue light off their white walls, and most had gardens, because a garden here was almost as big a status symbol as a Ferrari, so that now the emirate was patched with vivid green.

The atmosphere had changed, too. Hawaris never used to talk about politics. Or rather, they talked about politics all the time, just not to us. Now people expressed their opinions much more freely. It's amazing what a difference it makes when you don't think you might be taken to an offshore prison and forgotten. All the same, putting things down in writing remained a serious matter. The Ministry of Information monitored the newspapers and, every few years, the editor of the *Hawar Daily News* was deported for a month for allowing into the paper something 'insulting to the Hawari people', which meant one or two of the important ones. What had happened to the Al Jazeera reporters wasn't surprising or unusual.

'D'you really have to do this Alireza interview?' I asked Sam over breakfast a week into term.

'He's the most important opposition leader in Hawar. It's amazing that he's given an interview to a high school magazine!'

'No one else will take the risk of doing it. They don't want to be deported.'

'They won't deport me. I'm a kid.'

'Sam, they'd *love* an excuse to deport us that didn't involve revealing that the crown prince had had a homosexual affair.'

'Well, sorry, but it's a really big story.'

'Look,' I said seriously, 'I'm asking you, please don't write anything that will get us into trouble. I can't stop you doing it, and I don't want to. But I don't want to be given forty-eight hours to leave, either.'

Our house in England was rented out. There was no work anywhere nearby anyway. How would I get a suitable job at short notice, even in London? Sam was well into his IB and there weren't many schools in England that offered the same courses. Those that did all seemed to be private, and I couldn't afford them. I reminded him he'd claimed he nearly had a nervous breakdown staying at dad's for a couple of weeks. How would he survive months?

He and Faisal set off for their interview with a long list of questions and a tape recorder and came back talking about how charming the internet cleric had been, serving them tea and talking for as long as they wanted, and how much charitable work he was doing. 'You know he's set up all these women's discussion groups?' Sam asked.

'Would they be to advance the cause of feminism, then?'

'You're so hostile! This is what happens, you see: you've fallen for all the propaganda about Islamic fundamentalism. Actually, Alireza said Hawar is a great place for women to work.'

'OK, OK . . .'

'The people in power here *want* you to be frightened, because then western governments will prop up their regime. They used to encourage people to have the same fears about communism.'

'Are you going to put that in your article?'

'I dunno yet.'

'Look, Sam, the Al Majid aren't all bad. The emir's advisory council has four women on it and a Jew.'

'So?'

'Well, not one single woman was elected to parliament, though plenty of them were standing. Your Alireza may be as enlightened as you say, but a lot of his constituency are extremely backward looking.'

'Whatever, I'm not sure I can leave the Al Majid out of it. That would be like – you know – colluding. In oppression.'

'So, what, you're going to criticize them and in the process single-handedly overthrow the government?'

But then something happened that drove all thoughts of Alireza and Sam's school newspaper out of my head. I was at home in the kitchen after school on a Tuesday afternoon when I heard the front door open and someone come into the house. The handle squeaked, the door shushed across the carpet, then I heard it softly click shut. At first, I thought it must be Cheryl, because Matt was still at work and Sam had already phoned from Faisal's and Maria only ever came through the back door. But Cheryl would have called out or come into the kitchen. And this person walked into the sitting room and stopped.

All I could hear was the wheezy gush of the air conditioning. And silence. Whoever was there was standing still and listening, and I was suddenly afraid. I thought of Ghafir up the road, of how quickly things could change, how places that had been peaceful could pull apart in fear – Yugoslavia, Rwanda, Sudan. People found reasons to resent and hate their neighbours – religious or ethnic – to blame them for feeling out of control, to believe that the only solution is to get rid of them, whatever it takes.

I walked slowly, softly, on bare feet, into the sitting room.

It wasn't a machete-wielding mob from Ghafir.

It was Will.

'What on earth are you doing here?' I asked, my voice snagging with relief and annoyance.

'I'm on my way to Saudi,' he said, not looking at me. He seemed fascinated by a patch of wall above the telephone and he was staring at it as if he couldn't tear his eyes away.

'Why didn't you ring?'

'I . . .' he faltered. 'I've got something to tell you.' He was pale, I saw, and there was something stiff about him. Then his shoulders slumped and he began to cry.

He was ill. I went over to him, but he drew back, flinching.

'I . . . Something terrible . . .'

'What?'

No, someone else was ill! 'Maddi?' I gripped his arm and pushed him towards the sofa. It wasn't difficult; once I had hold of him there was no resistance. He slumped down and I sat beside him. 'Tell me!'

'It's not her fault,' he whispered. 'I shouldn't have got married.'

'What?' She was having an affair? And it wasn't her fault because of the way he'd been working? Or was he telling me she was clinically depressed? But we half knew this – so what, had she – surely not – tried to kill herself? . . . all these thoughts slid through my head and I didn't fundamentally believe any of them. I just didn't want to hear that he shouldn't have got married.

'I shouldn't have got married,' he repeated, 'because I love someone else.' And that was it. He'd said it. There was no putting it off any more, and everything fell away, even though I couldn't see how you could get from where we'd been to here in a matter of seconds.

'I'm sorry.' He slumped forward, speaking through his hands. 'I love someone else.' He swallowed. 'Andrew.'

'*Andrew?*'

'Yes.'

'Since when? How come? What, are *you* gay, too?'

He didn't answer.

'And Sam?'

'What?' He looked up, bewildered. 'What's it got to do with Sam?'

'No, no . . .' I was in free fall. 'So . . . why *did* you get married?'

267

He shook his head miserably, as if he couldn't even begin to talk about that.

'Does Maddi know?'

He nodded.

'Did she know before you married?'

'Please, mum . . .'

I don't know why he was like that about it. It wasn't any more absurd than anything else.

'And Andrew?'

'Well, obviously *he* knows . . .'

'It's not obvious at all, Will! You got married five months ago. And you're saying now that you've been having a relationship with Andrew?'

'No. Had. Before.'

'So, what, you decided to take a break to get married?'

'Mum . . .'

'Well, I'm sorry, but what did you expect? You only got married in September. You planned it for a year. And now you turn up here and say you're in love with the vicar?'

'I know. Hang on a minute . . .' He got up and went into the kitchen, to get the tissues. He stayed out there for a while and when he came back his whole face looked as though whatever had been holding it together was coming apart, as if something – stitches, muscles, nerves – was dissolving.

'So, when did you – realize this – about Andrew?' I asked, as if this were something you could discuss, rather than something to which the only rational response was to throw things and weep.

He sat down beside me, blowing his nose.

'Soon after we met. When I came back from Oxford last summer.'

'You were already engaged to Maddi?'

He nodded.

'And you didn't think of calling it off?'

'I love Maddi. It's just . . . it's different with Andrew.'

'Right. I see,' I lied. 'So you had a relationship? While you were engaged?'

'I know it's appalling.'

Appalling was an understatement. It was incomprehensible. Stupid. Cruel. Appalling didn't even *begin* to describe it. 'And had you never found men attractive before?'

His handsome face was all blotchy, like a six-year-old's. 'I didn't think of myself as gay. That's not *me* – I mean, I'm not like Matt, flamboyant and ... screechy. I'm sporty and *so* straight.'

'Except you're not.'

'Being gay just – I don't know, didn't seem to be on the list of options.'

It was 2003. He had a degree in history. He had not grown up among crazed religious fundamentalists.

'How did Maddi find out?'

'I had a picture of him in a drawer.'

Apart from anything else, it was so insulting. Poor Maddi. No one deserved this, least of all her. I'd seen a lot of Maddi lately. I hadn't consciously formed this thought until now and would have rejected it at any other moment, but quite a lot of the time recently I had preferred her to Will.

'*You* must have seen that things weren't right ...' he said, as if it were somehow my responsibility to have seen it coming.

'I thought you were working too hard ...'

He nodded briefly, knowing it was unbearable.

'Did you come out here to tell me?'

'I was coming to Saudi tomorrow anyway. But I thought I'd better talk to you. Maddi and I can't go on.'

'And Andrew? Are you going to talk to him?'

'I might, later, but that's not really the point. Of us splitting up. He wants to ... he has a vocation ...'

So he was in love with someone who didn't want to be with him. It was like Matt all over again, although you could just about see with Shaikh Rashid that Hawar's need might be greater. You'd have thought, though, that God might be able to manage on his own.

'Please don't judge him,' Will said.

'He *married* you to Maddi.'

'He thought I'd moved on . . .'

Moved on, I thought disgustedly. Psychobabbling vicars. 'He knew that *he* was gay, presumably?'

'He thinks he can manage it. Keep it under control.'

'Does sleeping with passing bridegrooms count as keeping it under control?'

'No, of course not. He thinks he can live according to the teachings of the Church. I don't think you should mock him.'

'Funny teachings, that cause such mayhem.'

'Yes, well, I was going to ask if I could stay here tonight, but I don't have to.'

'Will,' I touched his arm. 'You don't need to ask. Of course you can stay. I'm sorry . . .'

'No, it's OK.' He put his head in his hands. 'I know it's awful for you.'

'What about the Franklins?'

'Maddi wants to tell them.'

'But she hasn't yet?'

'No. She's thinking how to do it.'

'Right,' I said, 'well, I hope she can think of a good way.'

Fifteen

I sat staring into space while the air conditioning switched and clicked, purred and whooshed, the soundtrack to our lives. Will and I had sat in this room when Dave died, talking and talking. He'd sat here crying when all his friends went to boarding school and he'd had to stay behind. It was the place where, time and time again, I'd talked to him and he'd talked to me, and I'd treated him as a confidant which I could see now was a terrible mistake because I hadn't given him space to be foolish and troublesome, to try on attitudes and make mistakes. And when he needed to be a kid, to admit he'd messed up and needed to start again, he didn't know how.

I'd treated him as an adult, except when it came to sex, which I hadn't talked about enough. That was a legacy of my childhood, when sex had been unmentionable, and if you didn't talk about it you could act as if you didn't have any embarrassing fluids or desires that would make people cringe if you said them out loud. I hadn't been as reticent, as fearful as my own parents: I don't think I'd let the boys think their bodies were always threatening to catch them out or let them down. But I'm not sure I'd been able to shake off the inherited terror of speaking about sex entirely. And Will had a subtle, noticing intelligence. If anyone was going to pick up on my embarrassment, it would be him.

I'd considered the possibility that Sam might be gay. I'd given that quite a lot of thought. But the idea that Will might be had never once entered my head. He was married.

Of course, the fact Will was gay didn't mean Sam *wasn't* (it seemed, if anything, to make it more likely) – but whether I had two or three of them, you had to wonder how it had come about. Even if you viewed gay sons as a really good thing, you had to ask what was it about your genes or your childrearing techniques that had brought you to this statistically curious position?

Will went off to change into his swimming trunks. He'd come straight to the compound from the airport and wanted some exercise. He tried to smile encouragingly at me as he crossed the sitting room on his way to the pool and I – still in the same frozen position in which he'd left me – tried to smile encouragingly back.

I was furious with him. But I couldn't separate that out from being furious with myself.

He came in from his swim after forty minutes. I knew he would have been powering purposefully from one end of the pool to the other the whole time. No slobbing about in the shallows kicking his legs and turning his face up to the sun for Will. I'm not sure the exercise had done him that much good: he was moving gingerly, as if bruised, as if disturbing even the air around him might hurt.

When he came out of the shower, he told me diffidently that he'd decided he was going to see Andrew after all. In his cotton twill trousers and light blue polo shirt, he looked the part of the off-duty banker: preppy, keen, clean. It was weird how badly he wanted to fit in. He'd hardly done a rebellious thing in his life. Evidently he'd been saving up all the little rebellions for a really big blowout.

As soon as he'd gone, I called Maddi, knowing that if I didn't do it straight away, while I was still in a daze, I might lose my nerve.

She was at work, and told me to wait while she went outside. I heard the ping of a lift and the clatter of her heels on an echoey surface, then the snarl and rumble of traffic as she pushed out of the air-conditioned building on to the street.

'He's told you, then,' she said flatly.

I could hear buses swishing through puddles. I wondered if she was having to stand in the rain.

'I'm sorry. I'm really, really sorry. I don't know what to say.'

'Don't, Annie. Don't cry. I should have realized.'

'No, I . . .'

'He fooled everyone. Including himself.'

'But it's the twenty-first century! And he has a gay brother. Why didn't they talk to each other? I can't have made it easy enough . . .'

'It's not your fault, Annie.'

'How *could* Andrew have stood there at the wedding and said all that stuff? If anyone knows any just impediment?'

'It explains why they couldn't take the rehearsal seriously. All those stupid jokes. They were nearly hysterical. Not surprisingly. Has he seen him yet?'

'No.' I didn't want to tell her he was on his way over there now.

'You know, even after he told me, he still seemed to think we could make a go of it,' she said disbelievingly. 'And then when I explained we couldn't, it was as if the clouds had cleared, as if he'd been waiting for someone to give him permission.'

My son needed *permission* to be himself. How was this not my fault? If he'd had therapy, he would have had to characterize me as some monstrous blockage, a tumour stopping up his emotions. On the other hand, therapy might have decided him not to get married, in which case it would have been worth being characterized as a cancer.

'I don't know how I fell for it for so long,' Maddi was saying sadly. 'It's not like I didn't know him. I've known him all my life. I thought I did, anyway.'

'He does love you.'

'Yeah, yeah, like a sister or something. Don't.'

'No, I . . . he does. I do, too.'

'Thanks. It's just a pity I'm surplus to requirements.'

'Maddi . . .'

'What am I supposed to say, Annie?' she snapped. 'My whole life has come crashing down. My marriage is a joke. *I'm* a joke. I'm sick of it. And whatever I say, it won't make any difference. Everything's shit.'

Sam called at exactly the same moment that Matt came in from work. 'OK if I stay over at Faisal's?' he asked.

'No.'

'Why not?'

'I need you back.'

'What for?'

'Will's here.'

'So?'

'I'd like you to come home, that's all.'

'But if Will's there, you surely don't need me?'

'Sam, I am going to ask you something and I want you to answer honestly: Are you gay?'

'Mum, you asked me this before. And the answer's still no.'

'Post-gay?'

'Not this again! Look, I didn't know what the fuck it was before, and I still don't.'

'Sam, that's not necessary!'

'Nor is this. I've got a girlfriend, OK? She's called Holly.'

'Oh.'

'D'you want to know if we've had sex?'

'No.'

'Exactly. Now can I stay at Faisal's? We're finishing off the newspaper.'

'I suppose. Just this once.'

I put down the phone and turned to Matt, who was looking perplexed. '*Will's* here?' he repeated. 'Were we expecting that? And what was all that stuff about Sam being gay? He's got a girlfriend, you know. They have sex in his room when you're at work.'

'Thanks,' I muttered, sniffing.

274

'What's the matter?'

'It's bad news: Will and Maddi are splitting up.'

'Oh, mum, don't cry!'

'No, I'm not. He's in love with Andrew.'

'Andrew? What, Andrew the *vicar*?'

'You didn't know?'

'Bloody hell! Of course not. You think I'd have been able to keep that to myself?'

'No, well, it's a pity, because it would've helped if you'd talked to each other.'

'And is Andrew in love with Will?'

'Apparently not.'

Matt looked baffled, which you would.

'They had a relationship. In the summer,' I said wearily, blowing my nose. 'Then Will apparently decided to stop being gay and get married. Now he's changed his mind again. Andrew never wanted to be gay and still doesn't.'

'I did wonder about Andrew. I thought it was all repressed, though.'

'Apparently not.'

'Does Maddi know?'

I told him what Will had told me, and that I'd spoken to Maddi.

'How did we miss that?' Matt asked. 'I mean, if Will is, *anyone* could be. There could be loads more of us, all over the place.'

'Yes, well, your granddad thinks it's something to do with plastic bags.' I looked at him seriously. 'I think he may need your help.'

'Mine?' He was used to being the second-in-command, the slave, the minion or junior pirate, and he was bemused by the idea of having to take the lead, and perhaps a little bit pleased. It must have been quite annoying having Will diligently excelling up ahead of him his whole life.

'He hasn't had much practice at getting things wrong,' I said.

'And now he's made a catastrophic mess of the most important thing of all.'

'But I'm what he didn't want to be . . .'

'Yeah, and what he is.'

In the kitchen, Maria said quietly, 'Will, madam? He is OK?'

He still wasn't back from Andrew's. But she knew he'd been here, and, in her osmotic way, she probably knew that he was not in fact OK. But I couldn't bring myself to tell her the truth, to say that he was leaving Maddi and in love with Andrew. She would eventually find out, certainly about Maddi and probably about Andrew. Her life was tied to his by a million moments of love and duty. She'd held him when he was a day old, his tiny pale pink body in her dark arms. She'd padded round the house with him on sturdy bare feet when he was whimpering with tiredness and at once his breathing had been easier. But I couldn't do it. She was a Catholic and I had no idea about her attitude to homosexuality. It was almost inconceivable that she didn't know about Matt's relationship with the crown prince, but she'd said nothing. Perhaps she didn't want to confront it. If she had to acknowledge it, perhaps she would have to disapprove. Perhaps she'd even have to leave.

Neither of us would have wanted that, so I hadn't told her Matt was gay and now I didn't tell her Will was gay. It was a betrayal – of them, of myself, of her devotion – but I was frightened for all of us.

Will called from Andrew's to say they were talking and he wouldn't be back until later, so we should go ahead and have supper.

'Is that encouraging?' I asked Matt.

'I dunno, mum; I don't really want to go there.'

We ate at the kitchen table, or rather Matt ate while I pushed my food round my plate. He did his best to distract me by describing a spa that one of Shaikh Jasim's companies was building in the desert and that he'd visited for the magazine this morning. I half-listened to his description of the hydrotherapy circuit, the buckets and the seven different types of shower, trying to keep my mind away from Will and Andrew, or Maddi, miles away in London, hating her job, her marriage over, everything shit.

Matt insisted on opening a bottle of wine and sitting and drinking it with me until he went to bed at eleven o'clock. I said I'd sit up for a while: I was hoping to see Will, if he came back, which I was also hoping he wouldn't. In fact, he arrived about forty minutes later. He didn't look good. He was an odd, greyish colour: distempered, dried-out, like salt cod.

'How was it?'

'He was surprised. He thought it would be OK with Maddi.'

'Did he?' Another one with the emotional sense of a slug. 'So, he thought repressing the part of yourself most likely to give your life meaning would make you happy?'

'Mum . . .'

'I'm sorry, Will, but how you could think . . .'

'Anyway, he's praying.' Will got a glass of water from the cooler in the kitchen and headed for his old room.

'What about?'

'What it means.'

'I see,' I said, though I didn't.

Will got up early the following morning, had a shower and ate some labneh and honey standing up in the kitchen. When I tried to talk to him, he pretended to be preoccupied about where he'd put his tickets and how long it would take him to get out to the airport. Maria came in and he had a brief conversation with her, throughout which he pretended he was still with Maddi, that she was less depressed now, and that they were settling in nicely to their flat. I thought if I were Maria, I would never forgive him.

His taxi arrived and I stood at the front door with my mug of tea waving him off, feeling more forlorn than I had on his first day of school or when he went to university. As he left, he turned to me and said: 'Please don't tell anyone. Not yet. I don't want the Franklins to find out except from Maddi. And I don't want people to know about Andrew. Tell Matt, too? Promise?'

'You're being very considerate of Andrew. Under the circumstances.'

'I love Andrew,' he said, turning away.

'So he's waiting for God to speak?' Matt asked, when he got up and I told him Andrew was praying, and we couldn't say anything about him and Will. 'He hasn't been that reliable in the past, has he?'

'Andrew?'

'God. Like, he could've stopped the wedding. Sent a thunderbolt or something. He's not been very keen on gays, either, come to that.'

I had no idea what Andrew's prayers were supposed to achieve. If they were a way of communing with his conscience, it seemed to me the process could take ages.

Matt went off to work and I drove into school, feeling groggy from having slept so badly. I was parking my car outside the British Primary when my mobile rang.

'Annie, can I see you?' The voice belonged to pretty much the last person I wanted to hear from.

'Andrew, I can't help you.'

'I know you're angry . . .'

'Actually, that doesn't begin to describe it.'

'But I have to talk. And you're the only person who knows.'

Oh, great. He didn't want to talk to me because I was wise or full of insights or anything. I was the only one available.

'Are you free at lunchtime?'

'I suppose so,' I said ungraciously, wondering how many more humiliations my children were going to heap on me. We agreed to meet at Indochine, a noodle restaurant near the Gulf Hotel, at two o'clock. I finished parking the car and shut the windows, thinking if God wasn't capable of sorting out Andrew's head, I didn't see how I could. I wasn't interested in the theological pinhead dancing that had let him go ahead with the wedding, or made it OK to be having sex with one of his parishioners in the first place. It was wrong, all of it, nothing could excuse it, and I felt I would have been happy never to see him again.

An hour later, I was struggling with the peripatetic music teachers' timetable, and specifically, whether moving the year five violins to Friday would clash with anyone's saxophone lesson, when someone came into the office. At first I kept my head down, but then some ambiguity in the atmosphere made me look up.

When I realized it wasn't a parent or a teacher, but Nezar Al Maraj, I was so flustered I dropped my pencil.

'Look, I'm sorry,' I said in a rush, straightening up, my face flushed from bending down, and from having Al Maraj in my office. 'I was probably rude to you in London. And I've been stupid. You were very kind to Matthew and I don't want you to think . . .'

He smiled, in a way that changed my breathing: in breath, OK, out breath, all over the place. Then he said: 'I want to take you to lunch. But I'm leaving again this evening, so it'll have to be today.'

'Oh, no! I can't!'

He looked confused. He hadn't expected to be turned down. Not again. Not on a Wednesday lunchtime in January.

I considered for a moment saying yes and then ringing Andrew and telling him that after all, today was impossible, that something more important had come up. I couldn't do it, though. In the end, lunch with Al Maraj wasn't more important than Will's happiness, or even than Andrew's wanting to speak to me because his whole life had been undermined in the last twenty-four hours and he had no one else.

'Oh. Right. OK,' Al Maraj said. He didn't quite know where to put himself. He half-turned to go.

'No, it's that . . . I have to meet Andrew . . .'

'The chaplain?' He frowned. 'You can't put him off?'

'No . . .' I gazed at him speechlessly, as if by looking really hard I could get across to him the whole story: that Will was in love with Andrew (despite being recently married, and to a person of another gender – married, indeed, in a ceremony conducted by Andrew) and that I had to find out whether Andrew loved Will, if there was any chance . . . But of course, it was too unbelievable for someone to work out simply from a look. And too farcical. Somehow I didn't think that farce was Al Maraj's natural milieu. If I *had* managed to convey the truth through intense expressions, he'd have thought our family was madder and more irresponsible and out of control than he already did . . . But in any case, I'd promised Will that I wouldn't tell anyone yet.

Al Maraj had done so much for us, and now he must have thought I couldn't be bothered to postpone lunch with Andrew, even though Andrew was here all the time and he wasn't. Worse still, I hadn't even tried to come up with a convincing excuse, because if I really had been having lunch with Andrew, *obviously* I could have cancelled.

I hadn't wanted to have dinner with him, and now I didn't even want to have lunch, and it was pretty clear what I thought of him, even after everything he'd done . . . He was at the door, leaving.

'Some other time?' I suggested desperately.

He was tempted to sweep out, I could tell, but he hesitated and came back. He took out a business card and scribbled a number on the back. 'That's my mobile,' he said shortly. 'Call me.' He handed it over and finally smiled. 'Any time.'

And then he was gone and I was left holding his card. I wanted to call out after him, to ask why we couldn't make a date now, or when he'd be here next, but it was already too late. I seemed to find it hard not to be rude to him, even when I didn't want to be. Presumably there's a limit to what even people who find you quite attractive will put up with. Especially a person like Al Maraj, who has a lot of dignity.

I wouldn't have thought I could have felt any more antagonistic to Andrew than I already did. But now I was disappointed as well as furious. I set off for lunch in a mood of steaming despair.

He was already waiting at a corner table when I arrived at Indochine, looking handsome but washed out, his big body baggy, lumbering. He got up as I came over and perhaps would have kissed me, but I sat down straight away, as if I hadn't noticed.

'I'm sorry,' he said quietly.

I nodded and picked up the menu, as if I wasn't interested in what he had to say. I knew I wasn't being very helpful, but the whole thing was excruciating.

'Have you spoken to Maddi?' he asked with concern.

I said incredulously, 'You're not pretending now to care about Maddi?'

'I know how it looks, but that's not how it was ...'

I don't think he'd slept: his eyes were bloodshot and redrimmed. 'Oh, what, so it was a good idea before? The sort of thing a vicar should be doing?'

'Will was fine till he met me.' Andrew rubbed at a dark speck on the paper tablecloth. 'He'd been happy, until ... If we hadn't met ... I thought if I got out of the way ... I wanted to let them get back to normal.'

'And how exactly were they supposed to do that? What would normal be for someone who's been having gay sex with the vicar?'

To Andrew's credit, he didn't rise to my flippancy. 'He does love Maddi, you know,' he said quietly.

'So much he had an affair with you while you were planning the wedding!'

For Christ's sake, what did they teach them at theological college? Had he missed out the module on basic ethics?

'Anyway,' I said wearily, 'all that's in the past. They've split up now.'

Andrew still needed to talk about what had gone on before. 'He didn't think of himself as gay . . .'

'So what? If you'd been a woman, it would have been the same' – though if he'd been a woman he might have had more sense – 'the point is, he wanted someone else at a time when he shouldn't have been able to think about anyone except Maddi.'

'I thought if I could just get out of the way . . .'

I'd never heard anything so egocentric, and I live with teenagers. 'You were thinking about yourself. You wanted to make some big renunciation.'

'Excuse me, madam, have you decided?' The waiter was hovering, waiting to take our order.

'What? Oh . . .' Despite having been holding the menu since I arrived, I had no idea what was on it. I looked down vaguely, ordered the first thing I could read, and handed back the card in its plastic folder. Andrew did the same.

'They'd been happy before . . .'

I ran out of patience. 'You're gay and you can't face it.'

'The Church tests me. I know you don't have much time for religion . . .'

'It's got nothing to do with what I think. The point is, the Church hasn't exactly helped you, or Will, or Maddi.'

'The Church has the idea that – well, that homosexuality leads people away from marriage,' Andrew said stiffly, 'that the marriageable population, if you like, includes many people who may, at some time, have same-sex inclinations . . .'

'And your job is to get as many of them married off as possible? What for? D'you get some kind of bonus for delivering your quota? What is it, a form of crowd control?'

I was being unhelpful. Sarcasm wasn't going to make it better. Andrew was unhappy and didn't know where to turn and all I could do was be horrible.

The noodles arrived, glutinous and sloppy.

'You know what I think?' I went on, 'you're so neurotic about homosexuality that you're incapable of thinking. If Will had been seeing another woman, you'd have known what to say. But because it was a man – never mind even that it was you for a moment – you panicked.' He tried to interrupt, but I held up my hand. 'He loves you, Andrew ... I know you're going to say he loves Maddi too, and maybe he does, but he loves you with the sort of passion that can see you through, that makes the bad things hurt less and the good things better.'

He stared at me. I thought he was going to cry.

'If you don't love Will, you should tell him so clearly. If you do – well, that's good, isn't it? You could be a family. I thought you were supposed to approve of that?'

'You haven't seen my family.'

That was true: I knew very little about him. Once or twice when he'd been at our house he'd mentioned parents and an older sister, but I didn't have a clear picture of where he came from, beyond the fact that it was in Kent. I knew he'd been to a minor public school and Cambridge. So either he'd been reticent or I hadn't been curious enough. Certainly, something about his position had seemed to deflect personal inquiries. He was the chaplain, and that was enough. I knew less about his family, I now realized, than I did about Shaikh Rashid's, whose antecedents were celebrated at every turn and whose free ways with congratulatory telegrams were constantly reminding us about his illustrious connections.

So I softened a bit and asked him what he meant by that, and he told me that his father was a solicitor and his mother ran their large Victorian house and was active in the local Conservative Association and they didn't know he was gay. 'They wouldn't be able to cope. My father thinks multiculturalism has gone too far, not that there is any in Tenterden. He wouldn't actually know what it looked like if he saw it ...' He shook his head. 'And it's the same with being gay. They wouldn't understand how it was possible. They'd be terribly distressed.'

'So you've lied to everyone, all this time?'

'It wasn't that hard. It didn't even feel like lying. I didn't look gay or act gay: at my boarding school I played rugby for the first XV: front row. It was easy enough for me to hide it. And it seemed to me that the message I was getting from all directions was that that's what I should do. A cross I had to bear.' He smiled ironically at the image: he'd genuinely believed he was behaving in a way that was Christian, saintly even.

'And you haven't told anyone in the Church?'

'One or two, once I was ordained, but they advised me to keep quiet. Even the gay ones. It's how the Church copes.'

'It isn't coping.'

'Perhaps not,' he acknowledged. 'But it still seems worth working at it from the inside . . .'

'How? You're not visible! No one even knows you're gay.'

Andrew hadn't told his parents he was gay, or his school, or his superiors in the Church. He'd spent his whole life pretending to be something he wasn't, so it was hardly surprising he hadn't been able to help Will. He seemed to think marriage was like some giant institutional condom, a prophylactic against desire. He'd been preoccupied with his position (which wasn't even that impressive: how many people really care about the Anglican chaplain to a shifting expatriate population in one of the smaller Gulf states?) and as a result, he'd been prepared to mess up not only his own life, but Will's and Maddi's as well.

Despite all this, I was, very reluctantly, starting to feel sorry for him. He knew he'd made a terrible mistake, and he was confused, and lonely, and afraid. Will loved him in a way he'd never loved Maddi, which made me inclined to give him the benefit of the doubt. Sometimes you have no choice but to back your children. And, in his defence, Andrew had been hopelessly shackled by his upbringing. He'd been raised with an assumption that what worked once for people like him would work for ever, that the insular, assured world of public school, Oxbridge and the Church could be a guarantee of a sense of superiority, of easiness as one moved among others who had not benefited from their excellence. Andrew had found himself instead in a world that was physically shrunken but in most other ways expanded, of multiple possibilities, competing moralities, alternative ways of asserting yourself, of acquiring status, in which no one cared much about those other things any more.

It was impossible for me not to have some sympathy about this, because I was acutely aware that if I'd had a different background myself, I might have made better decisions. If I'd had more, or better, education, or confidence, I might not have married so young; it might never have crossed my mind that I needed rescuing by a photocopier salesman who liked a few drinks. If I hadn't left school at sixteen and gone to work in insurance, if my mother hadn't died and my father and brother hadn't wanted me to replace her, I might have trusted myself to turn into the competent, smart, not-badly-read person who knows quite a lot about indie music that I've since become and I might not have married without much faith in myself, without a sense of who I was and might become. But you can only have the background you do.

'I know what you think of me,' Andrew said at last, 'and you're entitled to. But I'd held it all together for so long, I thought I could go on. I was brought up in that stiff upper lip tradition of not noticing things you don't want to acknowledge. Will proved too much for me.'

I nodded. Neither of us had eaten anything. I got out my credit card but he insisted on paying, and I could see that this mattered to him, so I let him. I felt sad now, rather than angry, but I wasn't sure there was anything more to say. He still had to decide if he wanted to be himself or the person everyone thought he was. I still thought it could go either way.

I thought I'd probably have to wait for Will to get back from Saudi Arabia to find out whether there was any future for them. I couldn't influence anything; I could only wait out the days and worry. I feared for Will if Andrew decided that, after all, being a priest and feeling respectable was more important to him. Will didn't seem especially interested in being gay as an idea; I couldn't see him trying to meet people in bars or clubs. For him, the gay thing seemed subordinate to the Andrew thing.

I hoped very hard, in a way that probably wasn't so different from what he'd have called praying, that Andrew would make the right decision, the one that would be good for all of us. Give him time, I thought, and some benign influence (i.e. Will) and he'd probably be OK. He was capable of turning into someone passionate and principled.

Talking of which, I'd put Al Maraj's card in my purse, in one of the flaps designed for credit cards, which meant I saw it at least a couple of times a day. I'd also added his number to my mobile phone, although I had not, yet, got round to ringing it. I kept putting it off. Perhaps, I thought hopefully, there would come a time in the not too distant future when my life wouldn't be in a state of permanent upheaval and I could make the call in reasonable confidence of getting through the conversation without being interrupted by calamity.

Sam had finished editing the newspaper. I persuaded him to let me read the interview with Alireza before it went to press and was relieved to see that he'd muted the internet mullah's criticisms of the Al Majid. He said grudgingly that since his readership was mainly expat, he'd focused instead on what Alireza had to say about the west. 'Saddam may be wrong but it is not America who should correct him,' that sort of thing.

The paper came out on Wednesday evening. Sam claimed the people who'd had time to look at it at school had commented favourably on the way he and Faisal had managed to spice up the usual stuff about students and teachers with a few articles of broader interest. According to him, his history of the Islamic world teacher had said: 'It's, like, offering a whole different International School perspective.' Since she was a Hawari who wore an abaya in the classroom, it was unlikely she sounded this stoned, but her response had obviously been positive. Sam and

Faisal celebrated with some beers in the Al Shargawis' garden out at Jidda. When I went to pick him up, a slim girl with long blonde hair wearing white shorts and a halter-necked top was leaving the house and getting into her mother's Jeep. She looked as though she belonged in an American teen soap.

'That's Holly,' Sam said.

'She looks nice. You should invite her round. When I'm there, I mean.'

'Yeah. Our house is a bit gay, though, isn't it?'

'Sam!'

'Jokes!' he said. 'God!'

In other words, I thought the newspaper crisis was all over. Then early the following afternoon I was filing some papers I'd been putting off since the start of term when my phone rang.

'Mrs Lester?'

'Yes?'

'Bob Koppel, from the International School.'

There are times when a call from the school principal is almost guaranteed to be bad news. An hour before the weekend starts is one of them. I was so alarmed to receive a call from Mr Koppel that I dropped a whole folder of pupils' dietary requirement forms on the floor.

'Is everything all right?' I asked, bending down to gather them up.

'Not *really*.' Mr Koppel was from Tennessee and enunciated every syllable of his rather formal sentences; his students claimed it took him three times longer than normal people to say anything. 'Some officers from the Ministry of the Interior have been here at the school this afternoon.' I was picking up the forms, but I froze. 'I'm afraid that they have taken Sam in for questioning.' When I didn't say anything, he added, 'I'm sorry, Mrs Lester.'

'*Why?*'

'Have you seen the newspaper he produced with Faisal Al Shargawi?'

I sat back on my heels. 'No, but I read the interview with

Mohammed Alireza and it was OK, I thought, considering, and he said the English teacher – Ms Templeton, is it? – had approved it.'

'Yes, it's not the interview. Ms Templeton did vet the interview, in her role as overseer of the school newspaper. We don't usually insist on seeing the newspaper copy before it's printed, you understand, because it's never been an issue before. But we had heard rumours about their . . . ambitions for this interview and Ms Templeton was nervous about it – we all were – but she said that in her opinion it was acceptable. At least once they had been persuaded to make some changes. No, it was the cartoon, which, unfortunately, she didn't see.'

'Cartoon?' I said blankly.

'Maybe they put it in at the last minute and forgot to show it to anyone. Maybe they thought, since it was a drawing, that they didn't need to.'

'A drawing of what?' I asked suspiciously.

'The prime minister. Of course, Sam is a very good caricaturist. He has drawn several likenesses of me that I wish I hadn't ever seen. So there's no mistaking it.'

'Oh *no!*' How could Sam have been so stupid? 'What is the prime minister doing in this cartoon?'

'He's speaking to an angry crowd of Hawaris. With a few of our more recognizable students mixed in. And he's shouting "No to USA". But written across his back is "Yes to USA".'

That was it, then. We had no chance. I might as well go home and pack.

'What exactly have they got to question Sam about?' I asked. How many avenues of inquiry did a piece of weak satire present?

'Well, the other thing, I'm afraid, is that underneath the drawing Sam and Faisal urge our student body to demonstrate on February the fifteenth, when I believe there are anti-war demonstrations planned in some other countries. They suggested meeting by the Qalhat Gate and marching through the souk. As you know, since the bombs last year, the authorities have been very sensitive about public demonstrations of any kind.'

'And no one saw this cartoon before it was published?' I asked, although I believe he'd already told me that. Perhaps I was trying to shift the blame.

'The paper came out late yesterday afternoon. And no, no one spotted it beforehand. Or indeed, until today.'

'Surely, though, you can just tell the students not to demonstrate?' Didn't he have *any* authority over these kids?

'Yes, yes, we can be firm about that. I don't think, to be frank, that the police are that bothered about the threat of a demonstration. Not by a bunch of foreign students anyway. I think the cartoon is much more of a problem. All the officers have told me is that they were taking Sam to the police fort. The central one,' he added, as if this information might help.

'Have they arrested Faisal as well?'

'I'm not sure that they would claim to have *arrested* Sam, exactly. Helping with inquiries was their formulation, I believe,' Mr Koppel drawled. 'But no. They seemed to think after questioning them here that Sam was primarily responsible. Is there anyone who might help you?'

'You mean, like the British ambassador?'

Mr Koppel coughed. 'No, I was referring to . . . Matthew's . . . He has – well, connections – with the ruling family, I believe?'

The idea that Matthew's connections might be helpful was funny.

'Are you all right, Mrs Lester?'

'Yes,' I said exhaustedly. All I'd asked of my children was that they behave with a degree of decorum, stay out of trouble long enough to get Sam through school. It hadn't been so much to ask, surely? – don't sleep with the crown prince, don't publish cartoons of the prime minister showing he's a hypocrite. 'Did they say how long they were going to keep him there?'

'No, they didn't . . . A mother's pleas can be effective in this sort of situation, I believe.' I think this was his way of saying he hadn't got the faintest idea how to get Sam out of police custody and didn't even want to try, because the school was already in enough trouble. 'The officer in charge of the case is an Assistant Superintendent Abdulrahman.'

'Right,' I said. 'Right, I see.'

The police fort was a long, two-storey, whitewashed building in a compound by the Hafeet Roundabout, on Abu Dhabi Highway. It was surrounded by crenellated walls and punctuated by towers; you approached under a double arch and entered a large compound which housed the headquarters of the police, public security and the traffic and licensing directorate.

'I have to see Assistant Superintendent Abdulrahman,' I told the guards under the arches when I walked in at about five o'clock that afternoon.

'Do you have an appointment?'

'Not exactly, but I think he'll see me.' I had no idea whether he would or not. 'My name's Mrs Lester. It's about my son, Sam.'

The guard looked sceptical and made a phone call. This did not elicit a reply one way or another. 'They will ring back,' he said dismissively. 'Please wait.'

Sometimes Hawar drives me mad. Everyone's so bloody polite.

I waited, and waited, and waited. I wasn't the only person standing in the guard room: several other people were also hoping to be informed whether they could enter the compound. They all looked a bit scruffy and desperate.

After about ten minutes of tapping my foot and sighing irritably through my teeth and generally making noises to remind them I was not a person to be left hanging around and that I had better things to do than wait all day, I went back to the desk and asked if they could call again.

'The office said someone would call back,' the guard said in a bored voice.

'It's important. Please could you try again?'

The guard picked up the phone and dialled. 'Engaged.'

Ten minutes later, I asked him to try once more. This time, as he put down the phone, he said someone would come and get me.

It took her fifteen minutes to arrive. She was a female officer in uniform and a headscarf and she didn't seem to speak very good English. She handed me a guest pass, which I attached to my handbag, and led me across the compound to the building on the other side. I had my bag checked, went through a security turnstile and followed her up to the first floor, where I was shown into an anteroom with chairs arranged around the walls and a coffee table in the middle.

And there I waited again. The room had two doors, one through which we'd come, and another, into an office. I knew this because every so often the headscarf woman, or another police officer, or a civilian in a thobe, would pass me in the anteroom and go inside. Each time, I caught a glimpse of a large uniformed man behind a desk. Whenever the door opened, I would half get up from my seat and move about hopefully to show I was there. If he noticed, he ignored me.

They were doing this deliberately. Making a point. It wasn't as if it had never happened to me before. The Hawaris like to take things at their own pace. In any meeting, it is important to pass the time of day, to inquire after the family and everyone's health. The human aspects of an encounter are more important than the technical ones, such as a start and finish time. How can you do business if you don't understand the person you're dealing with and their current state of mind?

As the minutes passed and I became more and more anxious about Sam, and more and more despairing about the future, I wanted to stand on the chair and shout through that it didn't matter about anyone's cousin's wedding or the expansion of the family business: could someone just see me NOW? If they were trying to ground me down it was working: I felt humiliated.

My phone rang. I started guiltily, thinking I should have switched it off. Perhaps Superintendent Abdulrahman would think I wasn't that keen to see him if I could sit here chatting on the phone. I should be focusing all my energy on willing him to put me at the front of the queue, on beaming thoughts through his half-open door to impress him with the urgency of my suit. I was about to reject the call and switch off the phone, when I saw that it was from Nezar Al Maraj. I changed my mind.

'OK,' he said. 'This time really is the last. I'm back in Hawar, which I didn't expect . . .'

'Oh, thank God!'

'Well,' he said, 'that's a better reception than last time.'

'Something awful's happened . . .'

'Something else? What now?' And he didn't even know about Will.

'It's Sam this time.' I told him about the cartoon. 'I'm at the police fort. I think they'll have to deport us this time.'

'Have you seen this Superintendent Abdulrahman?'

'He's actually only an assistant superintendent. And no, I'm still waiting.'

'Well, hang on, I'm coming over. Just don't agree to anything, OK?'

He rang off. I was putting my phone back in my bag when the female officer appeared again and told me the assistant superintendent would see me.

I went through and he stood up behind his desk. He was in his forties, heavily built for a policeman. His expression was friendly and he shook hands with me.

'*Salaam aleikum.*'

'*Waleikum as salaam.*'

We sat down and he smiled gravely at me.

'How long have you lived in Hawar?'

'Twenty-five years.' Which is obviously long enough to know how unwise it is to let family members draw insulting cartoons of the prime minister.

'Your son was born here?' he continued pleasantly.

'All three sons.'

A man in a thobe came in with a coffee pot and two tiny bowls.

'You like our Arabic coffee?'

'Very much.'

I took the cup, knocked back the cardamom flavoured liquid and held it out for a refill, drank this slightly more slowly, then shook it to show I'd finished.

'So, three sons!' said the superintendent, when this ritual was over. 'That must be a cause of great happiness.'

I wondered how much he knew about Matthew.

'Yes.'

'I also have three sons.' He told me about them. One was at Hawar university. The other two were in high school. 'But they can also be difficult sometimes,' he sighed.

'Yes.'

'Your son Sam, for instance. Even though he has done this foolish thing with the drawing, and he has incited his fellow students to demonstrate, he doesn't seem very sorry.'

'Ah. Perhaps if I could see him?'

'We don't really demonstrate here in Hawar,' he added blandly, which was untrue. There had been several demonstrations in recent years, and some of them had been more like riots. 'We don't find we have the need.'

'I'm sure the demonstration can be stopped very easily. It was just a couple of kids suggesting a protest to their friends. It's not anything organized.'

'Interesting, that it came in the same issue of the newspaper as an interview with Mohammed Alireza, who is a well-known agitator.'

'I don't think I understand?'

'Your son promotes the cause of Alireza; perhaps he is acting on his behalf?'

So that was their line. 'Definitely not. Sam doesn't need

anyone to put ideas into his head.' After I'd said it, this didn't seem such a clever remark. I was trying to ingratiate myself, parent to parent, but Abdulrahman was probably hearing that Sam was a revolutionary with a head full of seditious thoughts.

'Well, you know him best. But as I say, he doesn't seem to realize the gravity of what he's done.'

'Perhaps if I could speak to him . . .' I tried again.

'He keeps justifying himself, rather than accepting he has injured the Hawari people. You, I am sure, wouldn't like it if I insulted your queen?'

'No,' I agreed politely, though frankly he could have said what he liked about the Queen if he let Sam go.

'You see my problem, Mrs Lester? We can't be sure that Sam isn't mixed up in some kind of organized subversion.'

He was acting on the orders of the prime minister. He couldn't really think Sam was anything except an overenthusiastic sixteen-year-old who was against the war. Most Hawaris were against the war, too. He was playing with me and he'd been delegated to do it, so eventually they could pretend they had a reason to ask us to leave.

'I'm sure if I could see him,' I persisted, 'I could persuade him to tell you whatever you need to know.'

'We need to know the truth, Mrs Lester,' he replied severely. 'Not what you think we want to hear. You will be aware that there is a war against terror. We have to be careful.'

'You're not suggesting Sam's a terrorist! It was a cartoon! It was meant to be a joke.'

'No one in Hawar finds it particularly funny. In fact, your son doesn't find it funny. He keeps explaining it, justifying it. You will know already that young people all over the world are getting caught up in dangerous shadowy organizations. When we have suspicions, we have to think of our security. We have to take action.'

'I can promise you Sam isn't a terrorist. And he's not involved with Mohammed Alireza.'

Alireza wasn't a terrorist either and I felt bad for implying that he was. He was a perfectly respectable opposition leader who happened to have a political creed that was based on Islamic principles. And he was shi'a, so all this stuff about 'dangerous shadowy organizations', which was presumably meant to frighten me with images of Al Qaeda, was nonsense, because they were sunni. So now I was colluding in spreading inflammatory Al Qaeda innuendo.

'I am very sorry, but we will have to keep him in for questioning a little longer. Then we will make a decision. But you must understand, in our country, he has already committed a serious offence. And our security is under threat, as you know. We had two bombs here last year. The terrorists came from a village very close to you. If there is any suspicion . . .'

'That's crazy! You're not suggesting now that Sam's involved with those guys at Ghafir?'

The superintendent looked displeased. I was getting too heated. It was unseemly.

'I suggest you go home and wait. If you leave your number with the sergeant, we can call you when we have any news.'

'Can I see him first?'

'I am afraid not at the moment.'

'How long are you entitled to keep him?'

'In this country we are not allowed to detain suspects for more than three days without charge, except where there is suspicion of terrorism, when it is three weeks.'

I looked at him disbelievingly. I was tempted to ask him to release Sam and promise that we'd be on the next plane out and never come back, but I thought of Al Maraj and kept quiet.

'I am sorry your son has caused you so much trouble,' he said as I stood up to leave, 'but thank you for coming in.'

Sixteen

I walked slowly across the parade ground of the Interior Ministry compound, leaving Sam behind. What was it like for him in there? Would he be in an office, like the assistant superintendent's, or in a cell? With other people, or alone? Were they interrogating him? Had they given him something to eat? He was always starving after school, and it made him irritable. No wonder he wasn't cooperating. Would they keep him overnight? Were they allowed to do that, given that he was a juvenile? Why hadn't I pointed that out when Abdulrahman had gone all legalistic on me? Then I thought they were probably allowed to do what they wanted.

I headed out through the arches and onto the highway, where the rush-hour traffic whipped past, the sun cannoning off metal and windscreens. I walked down the side street where I'd parked the car, past small detached houses built in the early years of the oil boom, with metal-framed windows and concrete block walls, rendered and painted the dirty-sand colour of Hawari dust. It was a beautiful day: the air fresh, faint smells of coffee and cardamom in the air, a butterfly in a pomegranate tree in someone's front garden. I thought how fond I was of all this. It had got into my blood, this scruffy town with its big, anxious ambitions. I belonged here as much as I belonged anywhere, even though that might not be recognized by the locals, legally or in any other way. I would miss it when I left.

A car screeched up the street and stopped beside me.

'How did it go?' Al Maraj asked, getting out.

'Terribly. As you see, I don't have Sam – he's still in there – and they didn't tell me anything. Except that he was being difficult.'

'Did you see him?'

'No, I tried but they wouldn't let me.'

'Where are you going now?'

'Home, I suppose. My car's over there.' I frowned. 'How did you find me?'

'I'm a fixer.'

I smiled, in spite of everything.

'Don't go home,' Nezar said. 'Come and wait at my house. It's nearer the police fort and you won't be on your own because Dymphna's there. You can get Matt to come round too.'

I protested, but he was insistent. I didn't have much energy left for arguing and I longed for once to rely on someone else. So I got in the car and Nezar drove through the city to the Al Dhafra district behind the souk, twisting down backstreets where men sat on benches drinking tea and children wandered barefoot through the dust. Finally he pulled up alongside a high wall, where a carved wooden door was set into gypsum-covered stone. He unlocked it and led me into the courtyard of an old Hawari house, with a central wing in front flanked by long arms at either side, creating a paved courtyard, in the centre of which a fountain splashed lazily into a bowl tiled in vivid Persian blue. The upper storey was overhanging, creating shaded walkways on the three built-up sides. There was a frangipane tree in the eastern corner, and a windtower in the west. It was stunning.

Dymphna came hurrying out of the open doorway ahead of us. 'Annie,' she said, smiling warmly, taking my hands between hers. She looked anxiously at Al Maraj. 'Everything OK?'

'Hmmn,' he answered non-committally. 'Can you organize some tea?' He turned to me. 'I need to go and see someone.'

'D'you think you can help?' I asked stupidly, because he wasn't going for fun.

'I don't know,' he said seriously. I clamped my lips together and nodded. I'd have preferred to go with him, but I knew it wouldn't be helpful, so I didn't ask.

He turned and left and I watched him go. Then Dymphna led

the way into the majlis, which was sparely furnished with several white sofas and an enormous Persian carpet on the flagstone floor. 'Is there anything you need, Annie?' she smiled. 'Anyone you want to call?'

I told her there was, but that it was fine, I had my mobile, and she disappeared to get tea and fresh lime juice. I sank on to one of the sofas and rang Matt. 'Sam's been arrested,' I said when I got through.

'I thought you said the interview was OK in the end?'

I explained about the cartoon.

'Shit, how did he think he could get away with that? Doesn't he understand *anything*?'

'I wasn't paying him enough attention,' I said miserably. He'd had this whole other life, and I'd been so caught up with stupid James Hartley that I hadn't bothered to find out what it was. What did I think he and Faisal had been doing? Geography coursework? Building spaceships out of matches?

'Mum, it's not your fault. Where are you?'

'At Nezar's house on Khalidiyah Street.'

'Oh, that's *his* house.' He'd noticed it, even if I hadn't. 'I'll come now.'

Dymphna brought sweetened Arabic tea in little glass cups, and sparkling water with fresh lime juice and little biscuits.

'If anyone can help, Nezar can,' she said, perching on the arm of the sofa opposite.

'I feel embarrassed about how much he's done for us. And I've been so useless. I must have seemed very ungrateful and hostile.'

'Ah, yes,' she laughed, 'James told us you thought he was some kind of gofer on the film.' I blushed at the mention of James and sipped my lime juice, staring at the stone flagged floor. 'Nezar didn't mind,' she added. 'He still kept going on about you. Really!' She laughed at my expression. 'How lovely you were, and funny, how much he admired you.'

I stared at her. I was so far from admirable it was difficult to know where to begin. Sam: he'd do. The whole point of being sixteen is to get into trouble. But I'd shunted him away, parked him off in a corner of my brain, thought because he wasn't making much noise I could ignore him.

If Nezar could admire me after all the mistakes I'd made, he must be besotted with lust. This didn't seem to me a great basis for a relationship, because what happened if the lust/madness wore off and he started to see me clearly? On the other hand, *not* being besotted with lust wasn't a great basis for a relationship either.

Matthew arrived, and I went out into the courtyard to meet him.

'Any news?'

'No. Nezar's gone off to talk to someone. I don't know who, but he didn't seem very confident, and if the prime minister's made up his mind . . .' We paced the courtyard together. 'I took my eye off Sam,' I said sadly. 'I thought he and Faisal were making websites for bands.'

'They were. And it's not your fault. Has Faisal been arrested?'

'No, it's us they were after. I hate this place.'

'Hawar? No, you don't.'

'Who comes here? People who are more interested in making money than anything else, and who don't care what it takes.' I sat down on the edge of the fountain. 'I don't know why I stayed after dad died. I've made mistake after mistake.'

'That's rubbish.'

'No. Look how wrong I was about Nezar. I resented him because he disapproved of me seeing James, but he was absolutely right, because James was selfish and trivial . . .'

'He didn't like you seeing James because he fancied you himself.'

'And I thought he was homophobic when actually he was worrying about your relationship with Shaikh Rashid . . .'

'Mum, not everything is your fault. Are we going to sit on this fountain till they get back?' I'd been wrong about him, too, thinking he was a sweet gangly innocent who needed protecting

– a bit gay, as the children in the British Primary playground were always being told not to say – when, in the ways that mattered, his sexuality had made him tougher.

Dymphna came out to offer us pastries, fruit and nuts, but I couldn't eat anything. She offered to show us round the house and Matt accepted, but only on condition that I went too. So we trailed up staircases and through the various rooms and I can't say I noticed much, but Matt exclaimed enough for both of us. Eventually, we came out on to the roof of the east wing, in front of a long narrow swimming pool hidden from the prevailing winds by a barasti screen. The three of us stood looking over the parapet. The sun was low in the sky, kicking off the panelled glass sides of the Hawar Telecoms building, falling in bright wedges on the low flat roofs. The aerials, solar panels and satellite dishes of Qalhat were spread out in front of us. In the distance, beyond the towers of the diplomatic area, you could glimpse the sea.

Dymphna was explaining that the house had been restored by a firm of French architects who specialized in sustainable buildings and traditional building techniques and that it could be cooled for all but the hottest three months in the old ways, by wind and water.

'It's very good of Nezar to help like this,' Matt said, at the bottom of the spiral staircase. The pair of them were getting on like best friends.

She grinned. 'Oh, I think he'd do anything for Annie.'

'Well, he should stop after this,' I said.

'I don't know,' Matt said. 'Maybe we could get him to sort out Will and Andrew. Go for the treble.'

I frowned at him, but Dymphna was too polite to ask what he meant. I hadn't even started to think about what it would mean for Will if our family were deported. Would they ban him from coming into the country as well? It would make his job impossible. It was a relief he wasn't here, or he'd have been shouting at us again, and this time he'd have a point.

'Of course, it's OK for me,' Matt said as we sat on the edge of the fountain, 'I'm leaving anyway. But where will you go?'

I shrugged. Sam and I seemed to face an empty future, a void in which we'd have to start everything from scratch. Nothing would be familiar, obvious, easy. I couldn't get the tenants out of the cottage and, even if I could, Sam wouldn't want to live in the middle of Devon ... oh God, I'd been through all this already, it was pointless. Thinking about the future didn't make it any less of a blank, any easier for me to orientate myself. Even if Nezar found me funny and admirable and all those things Dymphna said, I didn't see how I could have a relationship with him if I was homeless and jobless and desperate. It was bad enough that he'd helped us so much already. I didn't want a relationship to which I brought only trouble and dependency; it wouldn't work.

Over the walls, the evening sounds of the souk swelled, subsided and finally petered out. Shopkeepers carried their bales of fabric off the streets, hauled their sacks of spices into their shops, took their trays of garish toys inside. I heard the rattle of metal screens pulled down over shopfronts, the closing and locking of doors, the coughing engines of pick-up trucks, the crunch of tyres over debris. People shouted goodnight to one another and drifted away, until the only sound left in the courtyard was the rustling of the acacia tree hanging over the wall. The sky thickened to black; stars prickled all over. A sliver of moon appeared over the tree, shining on its desiccated bark, its twigs, its whispering leaves.

Dymphna saw I was shivering, and brought me a shawl from the house. I couldn't help noticing that she kept looking at her watch, as if she couldn't believe how long Al Maraj had been. It was getting late. Did Sam know we were still trying to get him out? How would he cope with a night in a cell? And what would that mean: who would he be with? My images of prison were gleaned mainly from films and newspaper reports: beatings, bullying, abuse. And that was just the other prisoners. There had always been grim rumours about the prisons in Hawar, that there was no air conditioning, that the conditions were filthy. Some of those stories dated back to before the Al Majid cared what Amnesty International was saying about their human rights record, which wasn't the case any more, but the truth was I had absolutely no idea what it would be like in a cell in the bowels of the Ministry of the Interior.

Eventually, at around nine o'clock, a car stopped in the street outside. A key scraped in the lock and the carved wooden door opened. Sam stumbled through. He was dishevelled and dirty.

'Sorry,' he muttered as I hugged him.

I looked past him and met Al Maraj's eyes and was powerless, suddenly, against a tidal slosh of desire. And even though I'd felt something similar for James, that had always seemed slightly unhinged, as if I were indulging some kind of romantic parallel universe fantasy, an affair that could only exist under very specific conditions (as it turned out, in the grounds of the Al A'ali House). The whole period with James had felt, even at the time, like a made-up game with a pretend friend, something infantile about it. This was different. It already seemed to exist beyond time and place: I would be stuck with it, wherever I went. It did not seem like a delusion and it wasn't childish. It made perfect sense, because I was already certain that Al Maraj was capable of revealing to me the best of myself.

That was what I thought. All I managed to say was 'Thank you.' Then I turned to Sam: 'Are you OK? Did they treat you properly?'

'I'm fine, basically. They didn't do anything, just asked me a few questions then left me in a cell.'

I pushed him away and looked at him. 'What were you thinking? You knew they were only looking for an excuse!'

'It seemed important.'

'To do what? Overthrow the monarchy? Stop the war?'

'To tell the truth.'

I looked helplessly at Nezar but he was pretending to be interested in something in the fountain.

'You think they're hypocritical, so we have to be too?' Sam said; clearly, he hadn't been that shattered by his experience. I could see why the police had found him annoying. If he'd said this sort of thing to them, it was amazing Nezar had managed to get him out.

Al Maraj interrupted. 'This is an interesting discussion, but perhaps now might be a good time simply to enjoy being with each other?' Sam and I both looked at him. He smiled. 'Don't you want to go home?'

He offered his driver to take us back, then collect my car from Hafeet and deliver it back to the compound. I protested that I didn't want to cause him any more trouble, he'd already done far too much for us, but he overruled my objections and a handsome Pakistani driver had already appeared.

'Was it difficult to get him out?' I asked Nezar quietly, as we walked towards the gate.

'Extremely. I'm afraid I had to make rather a large commitment on your behalf.'

'So we do have to leave?'

'No, but you might think this is even tougher. Look, I'll come and talk to you about it tomorrow.'

He kissed me briefly on the lips and touched me on the back and I looked up at him and thought nothing was going to be the same, ever again.

No one said much in the car. Once we got home, Sam went off to have a shower and I made some pasta while Matt rinsed the salad. When Sam slid back into the kitchen he was wearing an old dressing gown that was too short in the sleeves, his hair sticking damply to his forehead. It didn't seem very long ago that he used to appear like this every evening, in pyjamas and dressing gown, straight from the bath, bouncing on the sofa, wanting a bedtime story and his *Thomas the Tank Engine* video.

'Where did they hold you?'

'In a cell. In a block behind the Ministry.'

He said the conditions hadn't been too bad. The cell had been air-conditioned and he hadn't had to share it with any violent rapists or murderers, or anyone, in fact. The main problem had been boredom, because after the first half an hour they'd left him alone. Despite what the assistant superintendent had implied to me, there had been no big interrogation. 'They asked a few questions when I first arrived, but what was there to say? I pointed out – which they already knew – that the Al Majid haven't closed the US base and that they'll give the Americans all the assistance they want for the invasion, so it's ridiculous to pretend in public that they're against the war. I mean, either you're against it and don't let the planes land, or you're in favour of it and you do. I don't really think anyone can argue with that. So then they left me alone.' They'd given him food, although he claimed it had been inedible – 'a sort of dhal, I think,' he said – which probably meant it really had been unpleasant, because Sam will eat anything.

'Look, you may be right about the Al Majid,' I said, sitting down opposite him.

'I *am* right.'

'OK, you're right about the Al Majid, but, even so, what did you think you were doing putting that cartoon in at the last minute, when it's been clear for weeks that we were on borrowed time here?'

'I didn't think I should necessarily put our family before the people of Iraq,' he said pompously.

'Yeah, and what did you think a cartoon in a school newspaper could achieve, exactly?'

'Well, like I said, I could point out the truth.' When I raised my eyes to the ceiling, he added, 'A lot of people think those street protests last year in Arab countries made the Americans think twice about the invasion.'

304

'Sam, the Americans and the British are going to war with Iraq whatever you and I do.'

'I still think we should stand up for what we believe in.'

He had far too much adolescent self-righteousness and he was very annoying, but in a way, it was quite difficult not to feel a little bit proud of him.

The timer pinged for the pasta and I got up to turn it off. 'It's very lucky that we know Al Maraj, that's all I can say.'

'Mmn.' I think there was a part of him that was sorry he wasn't being deported for his radical politics.

'D'you know what he did? Who did he see? How did he get you out?'

'I dunno. I didn't even know he was there till they released me.'

It must have been someone very important. Sam would have been arrested on the orders of the minister of information, who would almost certainly have been acting for the prime minister. So what had Nezar had to promise that was tougher than leaving? If they were planning to humiliate us, would we be able to comply? Would we want to? Perhaps Nezar had concluded we had so little dignity left, we were beyond humiliation. Well, I would just have to insist that wasn't true.

I washed my hair the following morning, which I don't always on a Friday, and put on a bit of mascara. Not too much, though. I didn't want to look as though I'd gone to some enormous effort, as if I couldn't think about anything else but Nezar coming round or anything.

Then I tried to have a normal day. I went out and bought croissants from the French bakery for the boys. I made the mistake of leaving these out on the kitchen table, so that when Cheryl dropped by without invitation half way through the morning she assumed they were leftovers, and immediately sat down and starting nibbling one as she leafed through the *Hawar Daily News*. In fact, the boys were still in bed, but I was loading the dishwasher when she arrived and didn't notice what she was doing and it would have seemed rude to ask her to stop eating their breakfast once she was already half way through it.

'Tel says they won't find any weapons of mass destruction now,' she announced, looking up from an article about American troop reinforcements that she'd spotted while picking at croissant crumbs on the newspaper, 'so the war *must* be about oil.'

'I suppose ...' I agreed vaguely, although it was hard to see how Iraq could withdraw its oil, given that it didn't have anything else.

Then the doorbell rang and I went to answer it. Al Maraj was outside, and I couldn't help smiling. I only had to think of him and I smiled – so actually seeing him, actually having him bend down and kiss me, I felt as though I might smile for ever.

I'd have to get rid of Cheryl, though. Given that I had to prove to him that we did have some dignity left and couldn't be made to do humiliating things just because the prime minister wanted, it was quite important he shouldn't meet Cheryl. I was just debating how I could get her out of the house before I got Nezar in and she was able to say something crass and embarrassing, when a Jeep came trundling over the speed bumps and pulled up outside our house. I recognized it as Andrew's; he jumped down from the driver's seat, followed in quick succession from the other side by Will and Maddi. They all waved at me self-consciously, and came up the path.

'This is a surprise!' I said, in a tone that may have sounded less than thrilled.

'Ha! Yes!' they all said.

I hugged Maddi, catching a whiff of her grassy perfume, which made me feel sad. 'How come you're in Hawar?'

'I handed in my notice. And I was still on probation, so they let me go.'

Nezar shook hands with everyone and said genially: 'I guess we haven't seen each other since the wedding?'

Maddi flushed. Will and Andrew looked at the ground.

'Anyway, come in,' I said brightly.

Then we were all in the sitting room. I looked around and said loudly: 'Well, this is nice!'

Nice? What was I talking about? It was hideous. And then, just as I was about to offer everyone a drink, which was part of my plan to go into the kitchen and get rid of Cheryl, she came out into the sitting room to join us.

'God, Maddi!' she exclaimed in her broad New Zealand accent, 'we didn't expect you back again so soon. Nothing wrong? It's not Millie?'

'No, nothing like that.'

I introduced Cheryl to Nezar. 'But she's about to go to her step class,' I said.

In fact, though, she seemed in no hurry to get away. 'Goodness me, Annie,' she exclaimed, 'where've you been hiding this one?' She turned the full force of her smile on Nezar. 'How come we've never met before?'

'I'm not often here.'

'Where d'you get all these good-looking men, Annie? She knows James Hartley, you know,' she told Nezar.

'Yes.'

'Nezar's the producer of James's film,' I said wearily.

'Oh, I *see*. Well, if I'd known he was a friend of yours, I'd have been in here more often.'

'Surely, that would hardly be possible?' murmured Will.

Nezar's presence seemed to have gone to Cheryl's head. 'So, Maddi, what brings you here, then?' she asked roguishly. 'Can't keep away from your gorgeous new hubby?' Maddi smiled weakly. 'I thought you lot got all that out of your systems before you married these days!'

'Right,' said Will. 'OK. Enough.'

Cheryl frowned at him. I looked from Will to Maddi to Andrew, and then back again. Nezar looked at me. Will and Andrew looked, shiftily, at the floor.

'Oh, for God's sake,' Maddi said eventually. 'Look, if you're not going to say, I am.' She turned to me. 'Annie, they wanted you to be the first to know. They're going to live together.'

It was suddenly all too much. 'Oh, Maddi . . .'

'No, really, it's the right thing. And it's about time.'

Cheryl made a screechy sound. She looked round the room, working out which two Maddi meant and struggling to believe that it could be them. 'Hang on a minute, am I getting this right? *Those two* are going to live together?'

'Apparently,' I said.

'Has this been going on long?' Nezar asked, confused.

'I'm afraid so.' I could see he was baffled. I wondered if this was the final straw, if he was deciding finally that he couldn't have any more to do with us. The ruling family, the Church of England: it appeared there was no institution too mighty for us to take on. We were embarrassing on a national scale.

'What, are *they* gay as well?' Cheryl demanded.

'So it would seem.'

'But we only just went to the wedding!'

'I know,' Maddi said, 'I'm very sorry about that.'

Cheryl turned to Andrew. 'Aren't you here under false pretences?'

'I hope not. Though I've talked to the bishop' – this was to me – 'and he thinks I should leave.'

'I'm sorry.'

'Don't be. You were right, what you said. And there are other things I can do.'

'What, you're leaving Hawar?' Cheryl demanded. 'Or the Church?'

'Both.'

'You're leaving because of *him*?'

'There's no need to say it like that,' Will said.

'Actually, because of me,' Maddi said. 'They'd never have got their act together if I hadn't shouted at them. It turns out that even men who don't need women need women.'

Cheryl looked from one to the other. 'So you and Will are

splitting up?' she said to Maddi, shaking her head in disbelief. Then she looked at her watch. 'God, is that the time? I'm supposed to be at step class in ten minutes. I got completely distracted . . .' And she tripped off.

'There you are,' Maddi said, 'you won't have to tell anyone. It'll be all over the emirate in half an hour.'

'Right,' I said, looking around, 'coffee, anyone?'

Nezar followed me into the kitchen.

'I'm sorry about this,' I said sheepishly.

'No, don't. It wouldn't be you without some major drama.'

'Don't imagine it's like this all the time. Mostly it's very dull.'

'I find that hard to believe.'

'Anyway, we managed to sort this one out entirely without your help.' He kissed me, which was very nice, but I drew back and said: 'Look, you'd better tell me now. It's worrying me. What've we got to do?'

'Later,' he said, 'here's Maddi.'

'Can I come in?' She reached into the cupboard for some cups. 'It's OK, you know,' she told me, when Nezar had gone back into the sitting room to talk to Will and Andrew. 'You're allowed to be pleased. It's the right thing.'

'Maybe, but . . .'

'You know it is. And this is why I've been depressed. Because of Millie, too, of course, but the real problem was that I obviously couldn't make Will happy. For a long while neither of us could bear it. We couldn't talk about it because we couldn't even think about it. In a way, it was a relief when I realized about Andrew.'

'Did you really shout at them?'

'As soon as I got off the plane, I took a taxi to Andrew's, because I was so furious with him, but it turned out Will was already there. It's OK,' she grinned at my expression, 'they were only talking. And they seemed to have reached the right conclusion. Or nearly. The shouting may have helped a bit.'

'Maddi, I'm so sorry . . .'

'Stop apologizing.' She looked out into the sitting room. 'Honestly, I don't know why those two look like they're about to have root canal work. They've got a boyfriend.' She picked up the tray of coffee. 'Let's go and rescue them.'

No one wanted to linger over the coffee. Maddi was dreading talking to her parents, but she knew she'd have to do it straight away now, before they heard via Cheryl. Will was anxious about what the Franklins might say or do: they'd always been so fond of him, so approving of what he'd made of himself, and he'd hardly have been human if he hadn't enjoyed that. Now their approval was about to be changed into fury. Andrew was the one with the car, so it was agreed he'd drive them all back into Qalhat and that he and Will would wait at the chaplaincy while Maddi went to her parents. 'And then if you need us, you can call,' Andrew told her. No one bothered to point out to him that he was the last person the Franklins would want to see.

So they left, all looking slightly bilious, and Nezar and I were alone, or nearly. 'I should warn you that Matt and Sam are here,' I said as he started kissing me again.

'What, still in bed?' He wasn't used to teenagers.

'I know, I'd have got them up by now if all this . . .'

'It's quite a good idea, though,' he said.

In my room, with its windows over the garden, I felt as if everything was opening up, as if a whole new way of looking at things was beginning. Afterwards, I cried. I'm not sure why. Relief, probably.

He turned to me. 'Look, I'm afraid I haven't been entirely honest with you.'

'What?' He had a wife. Something like that. She was locked in an attic.

I looked at him fearfully. 'Is this the commitment, the thing we've got to do?' In the heat of the moment, the exhilaration of leaving everything behind and losing myself somewhere perfect and new, I'd forgotten all about it.

'It turned out that the only way of getting Sam out was to tell them that you and I were getting married.'

'Oh,' I said slowly, 'that was a bit presumptuous of you.'

'It was all I could think of. But you can break it off. I'll be the one who looks stupid. You'll be fine now.'

'How am I supposed to break it off when you haven't even asked me?'

So he did, and I said that if all those police officers were expecting it, it didn't seem right to disappoint them.

While Nezar was having a shower, I made some lunch.

'Who's in your bathroom?' Sam demanded. He was finishing the croissants, which he insisted weren't going to spoil his lunch, which was ridiculous but I couldn't be bothered to argue. When I told him, he said: 'Is it going to last? Because I quite like him. Better than that last one. At least he comes round to our house.'

I didn't tell him yet quite how lasting it was going to be. I told him about Will and Andrew instead.

'And how d'you feel about that?' he asked, sticking his finger in some hummus I'd put on the table and sucking it. 'I thought Andrew really annoyed you.'

I explained that if Andrew was prepared to give up everything for Will, I felt I should do my best to overlook the things I'd previously found difficult about him. I knew what an effort it must have cost him to have abandoned not only his career but his whole carefully constructed sense of himself, so it seemed only right for me to try a bit too. Besides, none of the things that had made me despair of him applied any more: he'd given up his tired ideas of respectability, he loved Will, and he was prepared to tell everyone so.

A couple of hours later, Will, Andrew and Maddi came back from town, visibly relieved and a bit hysterical. Maddi's interview with her parents had not gone well, though Millie had stuck up for her: Peter and Katherine had been disbelieving at first, then confused and furious. The greater part of the time had been taken up with furious. There had been a lot of crying.

'I got out alive, that's about the best that can be said for it,' Maddi said. 'It would probably be a good idea for Will and Andrew to stay out of my dad's way for a while.'

I shook my head sadly, thinking of the months Katherine had spent on the wedding.

'Anyway,' Maddi said, carrying a bowl of tahini and a plate piled with pitta bread on to the veranda, 'I pointed out that they only have one gay son-in-law, whereas you have two gay sons.'

'Did that help?'

'Well, yes and no. They still don't want to see any of you ever again.'

Katherine had apparently claimed that Will had only married Maddi as a cover for his relationship with Andrew. She'd also said – although this wasn't quite logical – that he'd done it deliberately to humiliate their family.

'She'll come round,' Maddi promised, as we sat down on the veranda to bread, salad, tahini and what was left of the hummus.

I thought privately that the coming round could take some time. I looked around at my children, at Maddi, and Nezar, and couldn't help remembering that other Friday when we'd sat here, organizing the wedding and getting excited about James Hartley. It seemed years ago rather than a few months. Now there would be another wedding to organize, though there would be rather less fuss and slavish sticking to convention with this one. I hadn't said anything about it to the boys yet; as I told Nezar, I thought it made sense to save up the news for a quieter day, one when we hadn't already had a couple of major dramas. This was Will and Andrew's moment – and, oddly, Maddi's too – and I was happy enough to leave the limelight to them. I was, though, extremely glad that this was now and that was then.

Not that I didn't have worries. Two of my sons would have to negotiate life as gay men, for a start. Will and Andrew were already making plans to live together in London, where it was obvious they'd be as conventional a couple as it's possible to be, just in a gay way. Andrew had been in touch with a friend of his who was starting a drugs project in the East End; Will intended to carry on working at his Arab investment company, visiting Saudi and working for his Gulf-based clients as long as he could. He said he didn't see why his sexuality should make a difference, which was admirable, and ethically correct in my view, but possibly a bit optimistic.

Matt would go to university in the autumn as he'd always planned – and though he would have been appalled by the idea right now, eventually, no doubt, he'd start seeing someone new. He claimed, though, that he'd had enough of relationships for the time being, and I thought it could well be a while before he was able to feel about anyone the way he'd felt about Rashid. I worried he might struggle to look at the world with quite the same freshness as he used to; that there might be more suspicion and reticence, a sore and scarred part of himself held in reserve. While that may have been a necessary loss, it was still a loss.

My third child, meanwhile, still didn't have the faintest idea what kind of person he wanted to be – which seemed to be partly my fault, because his expat childhood had accustomed him to being neither one thing nor the other, not fully at home here in Hawar, nor in what was technically supposed to be his own country. Identity for him was still a dressing-up box of options – which gave him a sense of opportunity, but it would have been astonishing if it didn't also leave him with a sense of vertigo.

Most alarmingly of all, there was a war coming and we had no idea how long it would last or what it would mean for Iraq or the Gulf. The belief that in its aftermath democracy would roll down the shores, knocking down the dictatorships like dominoes, seemed daft to anyone who knew the region. Whether war would exacerbate tensions between sunni and shi'a, Saudi Arabia and Iran, the Muslim world and the west – well, those were much more open questions. And if there were to be some clash of civilizations like people kept insisting there would be (and so many seemed to be hoping) Nezar and I would have to accept that we could never be quite sure which side we were on. But that was fine. We'd be OK about that. Pleased, if anything.

So the future couldn't be guaranteed – but for me, for now, it was enough to know that I'd be living with Nezar, that I'd be able to spend time in Hawar but also in London or New York, to come and go. When I thought ahead to what being with him would be like, that was the sort of image that came to mind – a constant coming and going, a long conversation, an absorbing exchange that promised we'd never get stuck with habits of thought that stopped us thinking. And this top-level summit or symposium of ours wouldn't involve merely words, but also things we couldn't articulate or even fully understand – feelings, sensations, beliefs and intuitions; things that, like dust motes spinning in sunlight, are invisible to most people most of the time, but there anyway, inevitable, essential and lovely.